This book is a work of fiction. The characters, incidents, and dialog are products of the author's imagination, and any resemblance to actual events or persons, living or dead, is coincidental.

Published by Tickety Boo Press Ltd

www.ticketyboopress.co.uk

Edited by Teresa Edgerton and Gary Compton

Cover Art by Gary Compton

Book Design by Big River Press Ltd

Uncommon Purpose

by

P J Strebor

Book One

Hope Island Chronicles

Published by Tickety Boo Press Ltd

ACKNOWLEDGEMENTS

No one makes this journey alone. I know, I've tried it solo and it didn't work out too well.

Many thanks to Teresa Edgerton who was the first professional to discover my lack of brilliance. We didn't always agree but when she's right, she's right. Thanks TE.

My appreciation to J Scott-Marryat as well. He is a great editor and critiquer. A man of rare insight and common sense.

Also grateful thanks to my friends at SFF Chronicles who were always there with encouragement and advice. Their support helped me through the tough times. You guys rock.

And finally, to Gary Compton at Tickety Boo Press for a marvelous cover and the editorial team who helped put the final spit and polish on my story.

CHAPTER 1

It is better to die on your feet than live on your knees.

Emiliano Zapata. Mexican reformer & revolutionary *(1879 - 1919)*

Time: 3rd January, 305 ASC. (Athenian Standard Calendar)
Position: Francorum Sector. League space. Tunguska Fault.
Status: Independent freighter *Bellinda*, en route to planet Iberia.

Nathan Telford's heart beat furiously as the cold grip of fear tightened around him. On his screen he tracked the incoming barrage, his eyes widening as his dread intensified. Bellinda's few remaining defensive pulsar turrets fired at the unstoppable wave of destruction but managed to stop only two of them. He averted his eyes from the screen as the rest of the torpedoes ploughed into Bellinda's dying shields. Nathan's small hands gripped the edge of the workstation as the old freighter shuddered under the impact of nuclear detonations.

Nathan blinked to clear his vision and stared at the screen. Several spouts of mist showed where the shields had failed and air escaped from fissures in the hull. Parts of her armor cladding had terrible gaping wounds exposing her vulnerable skin. Many of her bow and chase DPTs were smashed and useless.

"Stop it, stop it," he implored. "Please God, just let us go."

In answer to his pleas, the enemy ships fired another salvo of torpedoes. He winced, drawing back from the screen. "Stop it," he screamed.

Bellinda lurched violently under the assault. His sweaty hands lost grip on the workstation and he was thrown to the deck.

***

"I don't suppose they've closed to pulsar range?" Celia Telford asked.

"Negative Captain," Mary said from the tactical station. "They're sitting well outside of our defense envelope. They don't want to destroy us."

At the first officer's console, Lucas snorted. Of course the Imperial Navy ships did not want to destroy *Bellinda*. She represented a great prize for the Pruessens. Her cargo of high tech appliances would fetch a pretty penny for the E boat crews. Not to mention capturing a serviceable freighter along with her entire crew. Yes, the bastards must be salivating over that prospect.

"They're launching fighters," Mary said. "Six of them, Cobra class."

"Weapons Officer, are we ready to bake?"

"Aye, skipper," Salome said, "all pulsars are fully charged and the energy buffers are cloaked behind our new force field."

"Excellent. Stand by."

"The Francs are supposed to have a heavy cruiser and two destroyers in orbit to protect the Iberian system," a bitter voice snarled from the Nav Station. "Typical, bloody unreliable Francs."

"Save it for later, David," Lucas snapped, even though the same thought had struck him.

Lucas tracked the fighters as they streaked in, line abreast, oblivious to any danger. The two remaining stern turrets went first, quickly followed by one guarding the bow.

"Captain," Mary said, "they're coming about for another pass."

"Very well."

The turn completed, the Cobras charged into *Bellinda's* waiting guns.

"Weapons Officer, stand by ... aaaand, fire!"

Twin beams of blue-green fire struck out from *Bellinda's* bow. Two fighters exploded in a brief flurry of fire.

"Yeah, get em," Lucas hissed and slapped his flat palm against his console.

Bellinda fired again and again. As they passed her, Salome engaged the stern pulsars, destroying another and damaging one more.

As the remaining fighters limped home a cheer went up from the crew.

Lucas sighed.

His mother often talked about Telford's luck. Her words echoed in his mind as the ship shook under a fresh volley of torpedo strikes. "Telford's luck is rarely ambivalent." On a scale between good and bad luck, stumbling onto a squadron of Imperial Navy E boats certainly qualified in the latter category. They had handled their share of headhunter attacks in the past but E boats were another, more dire proposition. Lucas feared that the family's luck had finally run out. They were caught too far from the nearest hyper ingression point to escape into hyperspace. To attempt to match harmonics this far inside the system would be a death warrant for everyone aboard.

More torpedoes fell against *Bellinda's* weakened shields.

"Captain, our shields are down," Amy reported from the Damage Control Station. "Shield blisters twenty-eight through fifty-two have been destroyed. All chase DPTs are gone. Stern pulsars gone. Grav maneuvering plating down to twenty-three percent. We have an imminent hull breach running along sections port twenty-eight through to thirty-five."

"Seal off those sections," the captain said. "If you can."

"That's it," Lucas whispered.

Mary glanced from her readouts and into her husband's eyes. A short despairing gesture. Lucas nodded.

The captain's shoulders sagged under the weight of her next decision. They had held out for as long as humanly possible in the forlorn hope that the Francs would come to their rescue. That faint possibility was now all but gone. The captain's next decision would be mortally significant.

Lucas felt ice run through his gut at the very thought of making such a decision. In his mother's hands lay an impossible choice. Surrender her ship to spare her family and crew or refuse to capitulate to a life of slavery and blow the reactor.

"We're being hailed, captain."

The captain pulled herself upright and straightened her shoulders.

"Put it through, Jack." Her voice barely rose above a whisper.

On his linked console, the face of a middle-aged Pruessen Naval officer appeared. The officer's unblinking blue eyes were a perfect match to the hard, unyielding line of his jaw.

"I am Captain Hartman of the Imperial Naval vessel E516."

Lucas noted his stern, uncompromising tone. *Not the sort to bluff.*

"I order you to come about and prepare to be boarded. You are now a prize of the Pruessen Empire."

"Captain Celia Telford of the Athenian Independent Trading vessel Bellinda. Captain Hartman, can you guarantee the safety of my family if I comply with your order?"

The Pruessen's chin rose minutely. "We are regular navy, captain, not headhunters. I can guarantee you safe passage into Pruessen space free from interference by... that element. After that, your fate is in the hands of the good Lord."

Slavery. The very word conjured the most vile of images to any free-thinking Athenian.

The captain looked about the bridge gauging the feel of her senior officers, her crew, and her family. Lucas noted the fear that stood clearly on their faces, but also the determination not to yield. Yet, would they consider death to be a preferable option to slavery? And not only their deaths, but that of their families. Lucas hoped that he would never have to make such an agonizingly crucial decision. Let alone on behalf of a family and crew of eighty-nine men, women and children. Three generations of Telfords gone in a white flash. Who could make such a decision?

The main hatch opened and Nathan stepped onto the bridge. He strode quickly to the tactical station and strapped into the jump seat beside his mother.

Lucas stared at Mary, who shrugged. This was no ordinary seven-year-old. Nathan knew perfectly well what was going on. Lucas would bet a month's pay that Nathan had been following the battle from the moment he had ordered him not to do so. In the same breath he wanted to shout at his son to return to their quarters, and to hug him to his chest one last time.

Nathan stared at each of his parents and then his sister. He spoke to his mother but Lucas could not hear the words. *He's where he should be. With his family.*

"Captain Telford," Hartman said, "I need your answer."

Celia Telford faced the enemy, the shadow returning to her eyes.

"I accept your conditions, Captain Hartman. We are coming about now and will open our main boat bay for your marines once we have reached zero accel.

"Did you hear that, Helm?"

"Aye-aye, captain," Rebecca replied.

Hartman's face relaxed moderately.

"Captain, may I be excused for a few minutes to inform my crew?"

"Of course, Captain Telford."

"Thank you," Celia said, around an exhausted sigh. Yet, as the image disappeared from Lucas' screen, their captain reemerged. "Jack, put me through to the chief engineer."

It took only a moment for the chief engineer to respond.

"Aye, captain?"

"John, we are expecting guests shortly. Are you ready?"

"Just waiting for you to give the word." John Telford sounded remarkably calm, considering the implacable circumstances.

"Good, stay on line. With any luck one of their ships will get cocky and come into range. At least I hope so." She grinned wolf-like at the surrounding family and crew. "It would be nice to take at least one of the bastards with us."

"We are at zero accel, captain."

"Very well, Becky, stay icy."

Rebecca nodded, her eyes remaining fixed to her readouts. She, like many of the crew, was ex-Athenian navy.

"Boat bay doors are fully open," Lucas said. "Are you going to wait until the marines are onboard?"

"I'll play it by ear."

"Why don't we close the gap to the leading ship?" Nathan asked his mother.

Mary brushed the strand of hair from over Nathan's right eyebrow. Lucas forced a smile. All too often the seven-year-old acted like an obstinate middle-aged man. Yet it could not be denied that his acceptance of the current circumstances and his determination to never compromise were true Telford characteristics. Lucas could tell that Nathan fought the crushing fear even knowing the end was near. He knew what family obligation demanded of him.

"It's up to the captain," Mary said.

Lucas thought it was a pretty good idea.

"E516 calling, captain," Jack reported.

"Put them through." The Pruessen's image steadied on her screen, his forehead furrowed. "Yes, Captain Hartman?"

"Captain Telford our scans show that you have one active pulsar remaining on your ship. Disengage it immediately."

"My apologies, captain," Celia said. "I assumed with the shellacking you gave us that all of our weapons were gone. I will attend to it immediately." She drew her hand across her throat and the image disappeared. A tired smile crossed her face as she turned to her first officer. "Nice try son, but you better close it down."

Lucas returned the gesture and nodded once.

"Jack, pipe me through the ship please."

"Open channel, captain."

"Good evening family. Well, it would seem that the old Bellinda has finally run aground. We have been in tight fixes before and talked of this possibility on many occasions and so, now the time has come. Take a few minutes with your loved ones to say goodbye, make peace with the universe and remember that death is only a new awakening."

Within a minute the hatch snapped open and family members from the Telfords and their crew rushed into one another's arms. Some sobbed uncontrollably while others attempted to soothe their distress with platitudes. The clock ticked down toward the end.

It took only minutes for the imperial landing boat to cover the distance from the *E516* to the enormous number one freight boat bay. The crafty E boat skippers were taking no chances and kept well out of blast range.

"Rebecca, prepare to go to maximum thrust. E516 is nearest so we will try ramming her. If you can get us close enough I will hit the self-destruct. "

"I'll do my best nana," Rebecca said as she began making calculations.

"Captain to family and crew. Stand by. The time is near. John, are you ready?" Lucas felt his skin prickle as the seconds ticked over. "Chief Engineer, respond."

"I can't let you do this." The voice quavered with such fear that for a moment no one recognized it.

"Jasper? Is that you?" Celia asked.

"I don't want to die Granma."

"Jasper put the chief engineer on."

"I won't let you kill me." Jasper Telford's pathetic whining ended as the channel went dead. Seconds later the chief engineer's voice came on the line.

"Celia, that gutless piece of shit has sabotaged the self-destruct. He's locked himself in the core room, I can't get to it. We can’t self-destruct."

An odd feeling swept over Lucas. His relief collided with a tragic sense of loss. He suspected that the rest of the crew battled with such contradictory emotions. Would they ever see Beachport again?

A cold chill settled on his skin as the sound of armored feet vibrated through the deck plates.

***

With a full company of Imperial Marines stationed onboard *Bellinda,* the crew had little choice but to accept their fate in the stoic tradition of their forebears. Imperial Naval engineers oversaw their every action thereby closing off any attempt to sabotage the vessel.

The same engineers had done a remarkably good job in replacing *Bellinda's* destroyed shield blisters. With haste and typical Pruessen efficiency the entire repair process had taken less than half a day. Attempting to ingress into hyperspace without shields would be inadvisable. The destructive forces within hyperspace were a death warrant for unshielded ships. Without waiting for a test run, the Pruessens led *Bellinda* to the local ingress point and escorted her into hyperspace.

Hope lingered within the minds and hearts of the crew during that all too brief journey. As long as they remained within League space they could hope for a miracle. If the Francorum navy could find their backsides with both hands a possibility of rescue lingered.

As *Bellinda* crossed into hyperspace that fleeting hope evaporated, along with the spirit of all onboard. No one would be coming to their rescue. Not into hyperspace and certainly not across the northern frontier and into the Quarantine Zone. Lucas saw the despair on the faces of every crewmember on the bridge. He was not immune to the intense sense of loss.

It had been fourteen years since the disastrous end of the second Franco-Pruessen war. Fourteen years since the Coalition League Navy had driven the invaders back across the Northern Frontier.

The Pruessens, beleaguered, outgunned and facing certain defeat fought bravely as the time to surrender counted down. President Schmidt, leader of the Pruessen Republic, had earned a reputation for ruthlessness and unpredictability, but no one, on either side of the border, could have imagined that he would release a pathogen as a last resort to avoid the total annexation of Pruessen. Germ warfare had long since been abolished by every civilized society and so the very thought of someone using such an insidious weapon did not occur to the brightest of leaders. Until the day it appeared on the planet Derwent.

The plague that was supposed to be Pruessen's salvation got loose from its cage and turned on its masters. For in a turn of ironic justice President Schmidt had released the plague without first developing an antidote. With a dormant incubation period of forty-two days, the plague stampeded through Pruessen space with staggering speed.

The populations of entire star systems perished as the infrastructure of Pruessen imploded. President Schmidt fell to a, more or less, bloodless coup and the reign of Emperor Thaddeus began. Amidst the horror of an out-of-control plague and with the arrogance that Athens had come to expect from her northern cousins, the Pruessen Empire came into being.

The League's decision to quarantine the area north of the frontier came as an inevitable conclusion to this tragic tale. With half a million casualties from the brief war, the Coalition League Navy had accomplished their mission. Pruessen's ability to wage war ended.

So, an uneasy peace became the norm for many years. Then the headhunters began to venture into league space, raiding soft targets for whatever booty they could plunder. Although no better than pirates, Pruessen tolerated them as a means to an end. Each year their forces grew and the technical sophistication of their ships increased. Some CLN admirals were rumored to have bet a year's wages on them being supplied and maintained by the Pruessen military. Commerce raids like the one that had nabbed *Bellinda* were far more rare but still no less dangerous.

For three days, *Bellinda* journeyed through hyperspace and with each passing day a dark cloud of depression settled over her crew. The feeling of hopelessness deepened as they egressed into normal space and settled into orbit around the planet Kulak. They sat there for a full day before things took a turn for the worse.

Lucas Telford tried to push aside the ugly images that kept creeping into his thoughts. It only caused his heart to sink and his blood to boil. This situation should not have occurred, but once again the Francorum Navy's reputation for unreliability held true. *Bellinda's* crew would now pay the price for another example of Francorum's complacent attitude to her League responsibilities.

Captives from Iberia brought onboard had said that the Francorum warships had left three days before the raid. The Pruessens somehow discovered this and struck into the system without serious resistance. They stripped it of everything of value including forty-two hundred of its population. Since the decimation of the North during the Plague war, the thriving slave trade had made the unfortunate detainees one of the most valuable commodities in the North. Especially if in their heads they carried the much sought-after high tech training that the north had lost since the collapse of their civilization.

With their holds packed with high tech bootie and Iberians, the Pruessens were preparing to depart the system. Following the system hyper beacon, *Bellinda* had egressed blind from hyperspace and into the waiting arms of the Pruessen squadron. In another hour the enemy squadron would have been gone. The difference between freedom and slavery. An hour.

For now the question lingered in the air like a sword: what would happen to them? He had a few unpleasant suspicions but pushed them to one side. Captain Hartman had promised them safe passage as long as they cooperated. The Pruessen Marines who had come aboard had been coldly efficient but reasonable. Under the strictest orders from the captain, the Athenians offered no resistance to their presence aboard. Could not if they wanted to. Every station had at least two marines observing. They were large, well armed and encased in unpowered body armor. With the Athenian's weapons confiscated there seemed little chance of overwhelming such a force. A brilliant escape plan would be useful about now.

The entire crew stood in the enormous number one cargo boat bay with a small contingent of marines guarding them. The gathering represented the Telford bloodline of twenty-two, plus wives, husbands and crewmembers. Although not of the bloodline, the crew had been part of *Bellinda's* compliment for so long they were as good as family. It was the way of the Independent traders to carry their entire family aboard. From the day they left family behind on Saint Joan, before fleeing south after the first war, the same mantra had governed their actions. Live as a family or die as a family, but never leave family behind.

After the first hour of waiting the crew began to shuffle their feet as children whined and the older folk took their rest on the hard deck plates. A nervous anticipation hung in the air, reflected in shifting eyes, brief, urgent discussions and a rising sense of apprehension.

Lucas walked slowly to where his mother stood speaking with Captain Hartman. A dozen pairs of well-trained eyes tracked him as he did so.

"Excuse me, captain," Lucas said, "may I have a word?"

She excused herself from the Pruessen captain and followed her son as he gestured for them to step out of earshot.

Lucas shot a quick look at Hartman whose hard features remained static. He could not be certain, but the Pruessen's eyes could have surrendered the slightest hint of regret. What had the old girl been up to? "Captain?"

Celia smiled as if nothing in particular had happened recently. "Rogert has just given me the heads-up on what to expect."

"Oh, has Rogert?" Lucas said. "Anything you'd care to share with your first officer?"

"Certainly son," Celia said. "We are to be turned over to the Human Resources Section."

Lucas' brow knitted. "A HR department?"

She snorted. "You know how the Pruessens are with euphemisms. No, sadly this is a cat of a different color." She took a deep breath. "The HRS is the most feared entity within the empire. A malignancy with the power to appoint any person, Pruessen or other, into any role they see fit.

Break the rules, even slightly; show a trace of disloyalty, commit the tiniest infraction and the HRS will fall on you like a house. According to Rogert their absolute power is feared absolutely by absolutely every human soul within Pruessen."

Lucas shuddered at the thought of such indiscriminant power being placed into the hands of mere humans.

"I warned you about Jasper -"

"Jasper's gone," she snapped. "Probably on the auction block by now, so get over it. This is where things get tricky, so the two of us have to be on our best game. Remember, nothing comes before the interests of the family. Right!"

"Right."

Mother and son locked eyes for a long moment.

"What's next?"

"Yeah," Celia said, "like I said, this gets tricky." She rubbed her chin, never a good sign. "The *gentleman* we're about to meet is the adjutant of the Kulak's Internee Labor Camps. He put down the last uprising of slaves in the empire eighteen years ago, here on Kulak. Since then his power base has grown, significantly. He was awarded a gold eagle baton in recognition of his service. From the emperor himself." She shook her head. "According to Rogert he's an unpredictable psychopath with a God complex."

A chill ran down Lucas' spine.

"A character with too much power and too much time on his hands." Quietly she added, "A megalomaniac who kills for the pleasure of it."

Lucas shook his head. "So, what do we do? I assume that you have something up your sleeve."

"We will bide our time, son," the captain whispered. "When they think they have us sufficiently whipped, then and only then, will we strike."

"That's your master plan?" Lucas couldn't help shaking his head at the old girl.

"Yes." No humor in that remark. "But for the time being we have to take it on the chin. With any luck they'll keep us together."

Lucas considered that for a moment. The Pruessen Empire depended on their slave population. Even more so since the end of the war. A slave sat at the bottom of any social ladder. Yet at the same time they were a valuable commodity. However, slave owners could be unpredictable.

Yesterday the Iberian captives left the ship. The poor devils would be down on Kulak by now, awaiting their turn at the auction block.

His eyes scanned the eighty-eight crewmembers who filled out a small section of the huge number one boat bay. Their heads still held high, their faces cast with determination.

Jasper had been removed from the ship, under heavy guard, before the crew could get to him. Lucas hoped he was on the auction block awaiting his turn. He liked to imagine a fat, elderly Pruessen businessman taking a fancy to him. That, and a thousand other horrors would never make up for his cowardly betrayal.

His eyes came to rest on his family. His wife stood close to their children, Rebecca by her mother's side with Nathan wedged between them.

The sound of clicking heels on deck plates broke the mood. Lucas straightened his back as a small group of HRS goons marched into the boat bay. They stood out from the Pruessen naval personnel, their brown, high-collared tunics and knee-length black boots sending a strikingly clear message. WE are the masters. The smallest of the men, blond and overweight, stood for some time running his narrow eyes over the family. Lucas noted his pearl-handled sidearm. Not a standard pulsar pistol but something far older. As the Pruessen examined the latest consignment of 'stock' he tapped the gold eagle head baton into his left palm. Having made his assessment of the cargo he tucked the baton under his left arm and held his hand out to his assistant. The large, ugly guard slapped the clipboard into his waiting hand. It took no further investigation to know who this man was. His nametag, pinned with exact precision over his left breast pocket, contained one name: Manson. He ran a cursory eye over the group one more time then read from his clipboard.

"The following slaves will report to landing boat 1 for immediate disposition."

"Excuse me, Major Manson." Celia Telford took one step toward the HRS officer. Six raised Pulsar rifles greeted her. Manson looked up from the clipboard, his eyebrows arched dangerously. The captain held up her hands at the ridiculous show of force. "May I have a word with you, major?"

Manson glared at her with a combined sense of outrage and amusement. "And you are?"

"Celia Telford, master of this vessel."

Manson motioned for his overeager bodyguards to lower their

weapons and gestured for the Athenians to approach him. Lucas felt the stone weight in his gut twist. Like all people possessing the ring of absolute power, Manson did not seem like the type to see reason. The Athenians stopped three paces from the HRS officer and stood to attention.

"What can I do for you, Captain Telford?"

"Major it's about the distribution of my crew," Celia began. "I fully understand that our status has taken a significant downturn, but if this vessel is to continue to operate for our new, ah, owners, in an efficient manner, then I will need my crew kept in place. I assume that the HRS plans to use this vessel and her crew."

"Of course, Captain Telford," Manson said. "We have great need for your ship and its trained crew. However, I have examined your crew manifest and find a large number of personnel who are not essential to the efficient running of this vessel."

"Might I have an example?"

Manson smiled. A cruel, dangerous smile. He turned to a smirking henchman who stood at his right shoulder, and shook his head.

"Why certainly, captain." Manson consulted his clipboard. "Doctor Joan Makowitz Telford. We provide full healthcare facilities for our slaves. An onboard doctor is not required." He looked up as if the conversation were over.

"Who else major?"

"All personnel who have been deemed unnecessary to the efficient running of this vessel. That is all that you need to know." His amusement disappeared in an instant.

"May I show you something, major?"

His expression showed irritation and curiosity. He replied with a curt nod.

"This crew is an integrated package. Three generations working together to maintain the vessel. Remove one component and the whole becomes less effective. We have cadet programs to train the next generation of crew members. The crew operates more efficiently than normal crews because we are a complete family unit. The elderly of our family look after the children and as each progressive generation comes to age they are trained to take over from the rest of us." Celia stopped before her immediate family. "Here is a perfect example of what I mean. My daughter-in-law is second officer and will follow my son when my time comes to retire. My granddaughter will follow her, and my grandson will follow her. And so on."

"And what is your function aboard this ship, my dear?"

"Helm officer, major." Rebecca Telford, just out of flight school, stood a half-head taller than the Pruessen. She blanched as Manson ran his eyes over her body.

"I see," he said and turned to Celia. "You've had your say Captain Telford and for some unfathomable reason I listened. Now join your crew." He turned a cold glare to her. "And captain, don't ever interrupt me again."

He returned to his position, retrieved his clipboard and continued where he had left off. Forty-five of *Bellinda's* family and crew were sent down to Kulak. Only the briefest of farewells was permitted them. Shared tears, an occasional hug, a few fleeting words and they were gone.

After the wrenching ordeal, the remainder of the crew were ordered back to their stations. For an hour Lucas and Celia considered their options.

"We must endure," she said. "Endure the impossible and wait them out."

Lucas' anger burned away any rational reply. He could tell that his mother felt the same stunning loss as he. Forty-five loved ones lost forever.

The bridge hatch had opened and six of Manson's guards stomped onto the bridge.

"All slaves will stand to attention," the head guard shouted. "You scum will not dare to look at any Pruessen. Eyes to the deck, slaves."

They complied. Endure, his mother had said.

"All clear, major."

Manson did a circuit of the bridge his hand resting on the butt of his ancient weapon. He finally stopped, standing behind Rebecca.

"Turn around."

Rebecca, keeping her eyes averted, complied.

Manson held out his hand. "Come with me."

Rebecca shuddered but did not move.

"I said, come, with, me."

Rebecca shook her head.

Manson's outstretched hand dropped to his sidearm. He drew it and turned to Celia.

"Captain Telford, look at me." She followed his order.

The gun jerked in his hand and the projectile hit Celia Telford in the chest, throwing her backwards. Lucas caught his mother as she fell and cradled her in his arms as they slumped to the deck. Clamping his hand over her torn tunic did nothing to stem the gushing blood that flowed onto the deck. His tears mixed with her blood as his mother died in his arms.

He felt the warm barrel press against his head. He was numb with shock and grief.

"No," Rebecca screamed. "Don't kill my father." Her voice quavered with fear. "I will comply with you, major."

"Very well, my dear."

He turned to face the Damage Control Station. "You," he said to Amy Covington Telford, "look at me."

Oh God, no.

Manson raised the gun and fired.

Lucas turned in time to see Amy fall, blood running from her ruined head.

"The next one of you, *things*, who looks at me, will die."

Manson took Rebecca from the bridge. Tears shone in her eyes. With his mother's body attended to he and Mary returned to their quarters. They held one another close as tears flowed. Time appeared to stand still until his comm. beeped.

"Yes," he managed to say.

"Lucas, you've got to come quick. The guards are dragging the women away."

"Fuckers," Lucas hissed.

He told Mary of the most recent atrocity as he headed for the hatch. It snapped open and a rifle butt struck him a blinding blow to the forehead. He fell to the deck, his head swimming. Boots slammed into him from every side.

His body broken and unresponsive he could only listen as his wife screamed and fought until multiple blows rendered her unconscious. When the ordeal finally ended the brutes left, laughing. Mary wiped her tears and began, without a single word, to treat his wounds.

Later she tried to shower away the shame. Her whimpering reached Lucas' ears.

Once finished with their foul business against the women, the guards beat every male crewmember. Manson had successfully marked his territory.

Nathan, all of seven years old, limped into their quarters, bruised and bleeding. His right eye was swollen shut. Mary tended to his wounds. Like her he said nothing, taking the stinging pain while his lips compressed with hatred.

Later, she sat by Lucas. Her words, spoken in a whisper carried more bile than he could ever remember hearing from her sweet lips. “I’m a God-fearing woman, as you know, my love. However, after today I think the good Lord would forgive us if we kill every last one of these fucking animals.” It had been the first time in twenty-three years of marriage that he had heard her cuss.

CHAPTER 2

O divine art of subtlety and secrecy! Through you we learn to be invisible, through you inaudible; and hence hold the enemy's fate in our hands.
Sun Tzu, *The Art of War*, c. 500 BC.

Time: 22nd February, 309 ASC.
Position: Pruessen Empire. Kulak system.
Status: Freighter *Bellinda*, en route to Kulak four.

Four years as slaves and it came down to the actions of this single day. Time, it was all about time.

The mood on the bridge had become somber in the last two hours. The air seemed warmer, tainted with a stagnant dryness that parched the back of the throat. Lucas Telford's logic told him that his imagination must be playing tricks on him even though the sensation felt palpable.

A nagging pulse hammered at the back of his head. He had little doubt that all of *Bellinda's* thirty-nine remaining family and crewmembers would be experiencing similar feelings of apprehension. Depending upon how chance played out, they would either regain their lost freedom or die in the attempt.

Lucas sat in the captain's chair unmoving, except for the fingers of his right hand that strummed lightly against the armrest. It remained as the only outer manifestation of a deeper anguish. Four years as a slave of the Empire had forced him to develop a superficial mask to cover his emotions.

His anguish remained deep within him, hidden from all. If he had miscalculated even slightly, family and friends would suffer the dreadful consequences, and the fault would be his alone. Their painstaking examination of every possible consideration could not guarantee a successful outcome. Yet the entire crew had unanimously agreed that taking this desperate chance would be far preferable to spending one more minute under the oppressive heel of the Empire.

Following the beacon out from Kulak prime *Bellinda* entered hyperspace and travelled for fifty-one minutes before egression back into N space. She deliberately dropped well short of the egression beacon for Kulak four. For the last twenty minutes the ship had been crawling toward her destination at half speed. It would be just a matter of time before this state of affairs would raise the attention of their captors. The success of the bold escape plan pivoted on the predictability of such a reaction.

With typical Pruessen efficiency the bridge and other key areas were under surveillance by their captors. Shortly after egression back to N space, components from her hyper generator had been removed and transferred to the escort ship *Kania*. The standard security protocols that the Pruessens employed were highly effective and predictable.

No last-minute instructions could be issued, no reassuring encouragement would be permitted to betray their hidden intent. Everything had to appear like the unfolding of another uneventful day in the lives of a ship of slaves. The bridge crew sat at their stations, unmoving, focused, determined.

Lucas desperately wanted to spare Nathan the coming nightmare but knew that he could not risk even the most inoffensive change to the normal routine of the ship. No matter how slight the variations, the chronically mistrustful Colonel Manson could see it as suspicious. Twenty-two years as the adjutant of the euphemistically called Internee Labor Camps had him seeing plots in his dreams.

Nathan sat in his usual place, the jump seat beside his mother, engrossed in his studies, observing the conventional running of the ship, and rarely uttering a sound. The ship currently had six cadet crewmembers with Nathan the youngest of the Telford clan to take up such a position.

During their four years of imprisonment, *Bellinda's* crew had travelled from one side of the restored Empire to the other. They had been in the thick of battle, re-supplying the Pruessen push into the Pilbara and Bentport systems. They had carried cargo and troops, food and medical supplies and every fashion of dangerous goods not considered fit for Pruessen Merchantmen. *Bellinda's* forays into warzones on resupply missions paled next to the dread generated by their infrequent visits to Kulak. Life as a slave of the Empire was harsh but a return to Kulak meant a return to a regime of such indiscriminant cruelty as to make their lives elsewhere within the Empire seem relatively pleasant. For a people who prized their freedom as highly as they did, the past four years had been an exercise in zealous restraint carried out within an existence akin to a living nightmare.

Everyone of *Bellinda's* people were forever changed by that first shocking day in Kulak. The exercise to break them came close to achieving its aim. Some of the crew were traumatized and all of them had changed. Their rage focused them onto a single goal. Escape.

Two years later they returned to Kulak. Their naivety had been brutally torn from every one of them. Manson renewed his status with more of the same pointless cruelty. He did not need to prove his point. He simply did it, because he could. Two more crew died for no other reason than to fulfill Manson's sadistic insanity.

They took it all. They endured. Now after four years of kowtowing to their masters, today would see them free or dead.

It did not follow the normal trend to have an eleven-year-old cadet serving on the bridge, even for something as mundane as shipboard orientation. However, Nathan had proved to be unlike the other children aboard the ship. And with the number of crew lost to them everyone was expected to lift their weight.

The other children, though older than he, were puzzled at how quickly he understood the lessons that they struggled with. The older students welcomed his presence in their study groups until he proved to be smarter than they. Then the ugly green monster made its presence known. Lucas and Mary Telford both agreed that he could learn more on his own, under their supervision, than he could within the restrictions of the formal shipboard education system. He had been a cadet observer on *Bellinda's* bridge for the last two years. Nathan asked few questions during his time on duty, concentrating on the lessons scrolling across his computer screen.

Nathan glanced up from the touch screen and the lesson he had been reading, as if sensing his father's eyes upon him. He had the deep, soulful gray eyes of Lucas' side of the family, with the obscure blue flecks lingering in the background. Lucas allowed a small smile to touch the side of his mouth and dispatched a wink. Nathan returned his smile with that peculiar lopsided smirk that briefly creased the right side of his face. Today a devilish glint hid behind his eyes and a touch of malice distorted his mouth. Lucas felt unfazed by his son's reaction. Nathan knew his obligation to the family as well as any of them.

Lucas forced his fingers to cease their strumming as he heard the interlocking bridge hatch slide open behind him.

"Attention on the bridge," Mary Telford ordered.

Every crewmember leapt from their duty stations and snapped to attention. In accordance with Pruessen doctrine their eyes were cast to the deck.

Four guards entered, their eyes alert, pulsar rifles at their shoulders. They fanned out into a semicircle covering the hatch.

With wide-swinging arcs of their rifles they scanned the bridge for danger. A ludicrous show of force against powerless slaves.

Unlike the squad of bored garrison guards who normally accompanied *Bellinda* on her intersystem voyages, these guards were professionals. The colonel's personal bodyguard stood thirty strong, were highly trained, physically hard, well armed. The crew survived their mistreatment at the hands of the guards only because of their status as a valuable commodity. The guards' strict orders forbade them from killing any of the crew. Beat them half to death, degrade them, torture them, but never kill them.

Manson did not see himself as a lesser being to whom such petty constraints applied. Looking directly at the colonel meant death.

The head guard, Mendlesolm, finally satisfied himself that the seven defenseless slaves presented no danger.

"All clear, colonel."

With his eyes averted to the deck, Lucas could only see the sparkling black boots and immaculately pressed trousers of the person who stepped onto the bridge. The black boots walked casually forward until they were under his lowered gaze. He stood without movement or sound for what seemed like many minutes. The two men had played this game many times before and Lucas resisted the urge to swallow the bile that threatened to choke him. The crew had found out the hard way just how much Colonel Manson enjoyed his games.

"Captain Telford," the colonel said, "how good it is to see you again." As always, his voice sounded unusually high for someone of his build yet still held the same inference of knife-edged menace. The gleaming boots walked to where Rebecca stood frozen by the helm station. "And how pleasant it is to see you again my dear." Lucas could only see her hands clench into fists, the knuckles jutting out white and bony. Manson turned on his heel and in two strides came level with Lucas.

"Now, enough of the pleasantries. Captain Telford perhaps you would be so good to tell me what sort of game you are playing?"

A shudder ran down Lucas' spine. For a terrifying moment he thought that Manson had discovered the plan. Then he remembered that it had been he who had *invited* the colonel to visit the bridge. He forced his pulse rate down and made certain that his voice did not betray him.

"Colonel Manson, sir," he said in low respectful tones, "I do not understand, sir."

"Still you play these games with me Telford. After all these years and everything that we have shared you still think that you are my equal. You are a piece of property captain, not an individual, not a person, but a thing." Manson tapped the baton into the palm of his left hand directly into Lucas' line of sight. "Why are we taking so long getting to Kulak four, Telford? We should be there by now but my people tell me that the ship is running only at half speed."

"Colonel Manson sir, we..."

Lucas doubled over as the baton slammed into his stomach. He leaned on his knees and pushed himself to a standing position.

"Did I give you permission to speak, slave?"

Lucas gritted his teeth and said nothing.

"Good, we understand one another at last." Manson's voice held a note of triumph. "Now tell me why this bucket is moving so slowly."

"Colonel Manson sir, my senior engineer informs me that he has a problem with the number three engine and that the number two is running erratically. As I informed your office on many occasions this ship is badly in need of a major engineering overhaul."

The baton came under his chin lifting his head upward. Lucas averted his eyes downward and to the side to avoid committing the cardinal sin.

"I don't care for your excuses Telford," the colonel growled. "I will not be late for my arrival at Kulak four because you Athenian wretches are playing games with me. It seems that you need yet another lesson." He gestured to Mendlesolm who stepped up to the helm station and grabbed Rebecca roughly by the arm.

David made the mistake of touching the guard. The butt of the rifle struck him in the stomach and he fell to the deck. Mendlesolm dragged an unresisting Rebecca to the back of the bridge.

"Colonel Manson sir," Lucas pleaded, "this isn't necessary."

The gold head of the baton cut a broad line across his left cheek forcing him to grab the arm of the captain's chair to remain standing.

"One more time Telford," Manson hissed into his face, "and this vessel will be looking for *another* new captain." He smiled at Rebecca before turning back to Lucas. "Now captain, you were saying?"

Lucas had no doubt that the colonel would interpret his labored breathing as fear. He surreptitiously examined the guards. They were relaxed, entertained by their colonel's performance. They were armed and confident, having witnessed such cruel, cowardly displays many times before. In their minds they truly believed that four years of slavery had beaten the fight out of the Athenians. They had actually slung their rifles over their shoulders.

"Colonel Manson sir, if I may talk to my crew I am sure that I can motivate them to greater efforts."

"If you cannot motivate them I am certain that I will find a way to do so." Manson smirked. "You have my permission, captain."

Lucas backed away from the colonel with his head averted until he bumped into the right armrest of the command chair.

"Jack pipe me through the ship, please."

The comm. officer nodded once.

Lucas took a deep breath and pressed the comm. stud.

"This is the captain speaking." He paused ever so slightly before continuing. "England expects that every man will do his duty."

"What?" Manson said. "What is that?"

Lucas raised his head to look directly into the colonel's eyes. His anger boiled to the surface. Manson's eyes widened in astonishment.

"It's a quote, from Nelson, you fucker."

The next few seconds were a blur of frenzied brutality.

Manson, sensing the obvious danger, reached for his sidearm.

The bodyguards tensed and reached for their pulsar rifles.

Lucas produced a knife from his left sleeve. It had many brothers and sisters, manufactured covertly in the ship's workshop. A narrow sliver of polished Decadone, short, sharp and made from an alloy that did not register on sensor scans. Lucas lunged at Manson, awaiting the expected agony of an energy blast tearing through his back.

At the same instant the main hatch slid aside. Four of *Bellinda's* largest crewmembers charged onto the bridge. In their hands were solid metal bars and sharp gleaming slivers.

Distracted by the attack on their colonel, the unexpected onslaught caught them napping. Garrison guards would have presented little problem. But these were an elite force.

The attackers closed with the bodyguards fast. Too fast to give them any chance to raise their weapons. The two guards closest to the hatch went down quickly: the first felled by a mighty blow that crushed his skull, the second to multiple stab wounds to the throat.

David jumped from the navigation station and charged at Manson. The colonel saw him coming and tagged him with his heavy baton. David staggered to the deck.

The third and fourth guards had precious seconds to react. Number three backed away and managed to raise his weapon up to his hip. As his finger closed on the trigger, Jackson – rising from the comm. station behind him – drove the knife into his throat. The guard jerked violently as he died, and his weapon discharged. Miraculously it missed hitting anyone directly, but the ricochet caught one of the attacking Athenian's in the thigh.

Colonel Manson got his hand around the butt of his pistol before Lucas closed the distance between them. He head-butted the colonel with stunning force then seized the weapon with one hand, trapping it in its holster. In the same fluid movement he shifted his stance and swung around behind him. As the sharp, cold alloy of his knife touched the colonel's throat, all resistance ceased.

Now, only Mendlesolm remained as a threat. The guard proved to be quick on his feet and remarkably agile in his thinking. In the tradition of all cowardly bullies, he backed away from the melee, dragging Rebecca with him. He came up against the unoccupied Damage Control console. His huge left hand held Rebecca by the back of her neck, while the right gripped his pulsar rifle. The barrel of the weapon pressed against the back of Rebecca's head.

Lucas stared into the guard's eyes, cold fury and hatred burning. He pushed the knife far enough upward to cause a trickle of blood to run down the colonel's taught neck.

All movement on the bridge stopped as if in a frozen image. The three Athenian attackers poised to grab the fallen weapons. Jackson standing stock still, the bloody knife in his hand. Lucas and Manson unmoving except for their heaving chests. Mendlesolm, cold eyed, determined never to allow the slave to win. Rebecca, inhumanly calm, her eyes sparkling with fury.

The seconds ticked by as the stalemate began. Rebecca decided to break it.

"Shoot him!" she screamed.

Nobody moved.

Rebecca struggled frantically against Mendlesolm's iron grip, to no avail.

"Someone shoot this fucker!"

Unlike Manson, who had completely surrendered to his fate, Rebecca fought back. In the one moment Lucas felt an intense pride in his daughter and a terror that chilled him to his depths.

They were at an impasse that could only end in tragedy.

Lucas caught a brief glint of movement from under the Damage Control console. A sharp jerky movement, of silver. It struck upwards once, twice, three times. Mendlesolm's mouth opened, distorted, his eyes narrowed in shocked agony. Finally a high-pitched scream tore from the guard's throat.

Sensing his grip slip from her neck, Rebecca swung about, catching the weapon as it slid from his hands. She raised the rifle over her head to smash the butt into his face. The head guard fell to the deck, his initial screams dulled to a pathetic whimper. Curled in a half-fetal position he clutched his blood-splattered groin. If he had not proved on so many occasions to be a monster, he may have been a figure deserving of some pity.

Everyone stared at the sight in stunned amazement.

Nathan had crawled from under the console's tiny crawlspace. He stood up clasping a bloody knife in hand. His eyes were sparkling with blue fire, his smile cruel, and his intense satisfaction perverse.

Rebecca turned and snapped the rifle up to her shoulder, aiming at the center of Manson's chest.

Lucas nodded sharply to his daughter who returned the gesture. He released his grip on the colonel and stepped aside.

Manson staggered against the navigation console, his hands at his throat gasping for air. Lucas could see that the sudden realization of his changed circumstances distorted his once-confident face. Now, only wide-eyed terror remained and he made sure to keep his hands well clear of his sidearm.

Rebecca Telford had a special reason for seeing him suffer.

"I surrender," he said, holding his hands up. "Under the charter for the treatment of prisoners by the League of Allied Worlds, I claim the rights and privileges of an officer of my rank."

The surrounding Athenians gaped at him in utter disbelief. Lucas relieved him of his sidearm and took the baton for good measure. The crew stood in place, their faces shrouded in hatred. As the seconds ticked by only the sounds of Mendlesolm's whimpering broke the hate-filled silence.

Manson's head swung from one side of the bridge to the other, finding only a wall of loathing, lips curled back showing set teeth, narrowed, hate-filled eyes, all weapons aimed at him. His gaze fell on Rebecca Telford whose hands gripped the rifle with white-knuckled intensity.

"If you surrender to me now, I will spare your lives." The rampart of cold eyes remained unchanged. "You will never escape this system. Our ships will hunt you down."

Lucas looked along the barrel of the rifle and into the eyes of his daughter. Of all the crew she had suffered most at the hands of this creature. She deserved this moment. He knew in his heart that she would put her obligation to the family before all else. Manson's mouth hung open, his chest heaving. "I was only doing my duty."

Rebecca closed her eyes for a moment then lowered the rifle to rest across her left arm. Manson sagged with relief until he saw the glint of unadulterated hatred in her eyes. A shudder passed through the colonel.

Lucas had never been more proud of his daughter. The temptation to obliterate Manson from existence must have been insufferable. However, the sad, simple truth remained. If they were to escape their prison, they needed Manson alive.

The colonel straightened his brown tunic, raised his chin and wiped away tears.

Lucas tapped the gold head of the baton into the palm of his left hand. Manson's puzzlement at the gesture pleased him.

"I will accede to any of your demands," Manson said, "if you give me your word that you will not harm me in any way. I know that you Athenians always keep your word."

Lucas nodded slowly. The gold head of the baton slammed into the colonel's solar plexus. He fell to his knees, a deep gasping groan his only comment.

A growl of satisfaction rang from the walls. Lucas sobered and looked down at the creature before him.

"As captain of the Bellinda and patriarch of the Telford family, I give you my pledge that no Athenian aboard this vessel will harm you. If you cooperate with us fully. Do you agree to give us your full cooperation?"

Racked with pain and still gasping for air Manson could only nod.

A low snarl, resounded from the crew.

Lucas held up a hand.

"The day is not yet won." The wall of faces hardened into a singular resolve. "We are still in enemy space and a long way from home. Everyone back to your stations." He gestured for Henry to take the colonel over to the vacant DC station. Tapping the comm. stud on the arm of his chair, he spoke into the recessed mike. "Bridge - Engineering. John what's your status?"

A few silent, nervous seconds passed before John Telford replied.

"Captain, we are in need of a cleaning detail down here," the elderly engineer said. "There is Pruessen blood all over the place."

A subdued chuckle sounded from the crew and even Lucas allowed himself a short smile.

"Did they give you any trouble?"

"Didn't know what hit them. But captain, there are a few of them still unaccounted for. I've sent a few of my people after them but, well...it's a big ship, right?"

"Call your people back and post your guards. I don't want those bastards getting anywhere near the vital systems. How long to bring the generator on line?"

"We've just started, but we will need the best part of half a day to fit the components and more time for fine tuning."

"Very well John, but anything you can do to shave time off that would be good."

"I'll do my best captain."

"I'm sure that you will. Bridge out."

He turned to the crewmembers who had overpowered the guards. "How's Harry?"

Harry Walder Telford had his torn thigh tied up in a tourniquet. "I'm fine, skipper." His drawn, pallid complexion said differently.

"Put him on the couch in the day cabin then get back here. I have a job for you."

As they picked Harry up Lucas turned back to the bridge. "Rebecca, reduce speed to one quarter."

"Yes captain," she replied.

He walked over to the first officer's station where Mary busied herself by cleaning the blood from Nathan's hands and clothing.

His expression hardened into the sort of unyielding mask that captains were supposed to have. Yet he felt an undeniable pride in his son. "Nathan, we shall need to talk later."

Lucas suppressed the urge to smile when Nathan, eleven going on thirty-one, raised his eyebrows curiously as if to say 'who me?' He had probably saved his sister's life, but he had disobeyed orders in the process. Again.

"Mary, I would like you to take the attack squad and organize search parties for the missing guards. Use some of our passengers if you have to, but I want those bastards found."

"Certainly captain." She seemed overly pleased with the task of bringing down the last of Manson's bodyguards. "Who do you want manning my station?" Her eyes shifted surreptitiously to Nathan.

Nathan may have disobeyed orders, but he had also showed

incredible courage and a mature initiative beyond his years. He had taken the disadvantage of his diminutive size and turned it into a plus. No one else on the bridge could have squeezed into the crawlspace under the Damage Control console.

"Nathan, you have been observing bridge operations for some time now. What do you do if anything out of the ordinary shows up on the external sensor feeds?"

"Report immediately to the captain," he snapped back. "If the captain is unavailable the next-senior bridge officer should be informed."

"Do you think you can cover the station while the first officer and I are away?"

"Yes, captain."

"Carry on."

"Aye-aye, sir."

Lucas turned away before the smile darted from the corner of his mouth. The sight of Manson sitting at the DCS darkened his mood. With enduring pain he recalled the day that Manson had 'retired' Amy Telford.

"Very well people time to get back to work. We aren't out of this yet."

Henry Telford guarded the colonel with an expression that said he would be extremely pleased if the Pruessen tried anything.

"I expect that we will be getting a call from Kania at any time now.” He turned his attention to the colonel. “This is where you keep your side of the bargain."

Lucas felt his gut twist as Manson's foul smile returned.

CHAPTER 3

The knowledge that the Athenian ship could not escape created a condition of complacency among her captors. Over the years the guard compliment on the ship had shrunk to a token force of less than a platoon of indolent camp guards. Although the garrison guards regularly rotated through duty on *Bellinda*, they all consider their assignment to the freighter as a great way of catching up on their sleep. Without such a flaccid attitude, *Bellinda's* interned Athenians could never have accomplished so much.

The task of restoring the hyper generator had been accomplished piece by precious piece, at enormous personal peril, right under the noses of the guards. They had either manufactured, stolen or purloined, through the underground black market, the parts they needed to rebuild their generator. Each individual component had been fitted into place on the gutted remains of the hyper generator, then checked and rechecked with painstaking care. If the part passed the test it was hidden away in one of a myriad of secret alcoves throughout the ship. Nathan and the other children were virtually invisible to the guards so they made the obvious choice as conspirators. Soon the pressure got to the older children and only Nathan showed the courage and tenacity to stand toe to toe with a guard and keep his nerve. All the time, concealed on his person, a small piece of technology that if discovered, would be fatal for him and many of the crew. The individual pieces of the hyper generator remained like hidden treasure waiting for the day when they would finally be fitted together to restore the generator to full use.

Kulak's close proximity to the southern frontier contributed significantly to their hopeful escape bid. Putting all other matters aside, Kulak contained something unique, something very special and something for which the crew would risk all. It bound them together with a fervent purpose akin to a holy quest.

"Captain, team six reports that the last of the security guards have been accounted for." Mary Telford took her hand away from the comm. earpiece and sat back in the first officer's chair sporting a satisfied smile. "Our people found the bastards hiding on deck nineteen near the reclamation bins."

"Along with the rest of the shit," David chimed in from the Navigation Station.

A grin cut the captain's face, finding a host of mirrored reactions throughout the bridge. It had taken far too long to track down the missing guards.

Years of abuse under the guards' unchecked brutality had resulted in a cumulative attitude. When Mary said that the guards had been 'accounted for' everyone recognized the comment as a less than subtle euphemism.

"Excuse me captain?" Mary asked.

Lucas straightened in his chair. "I said it's about bloody time." He realized that he had begun slurring his words. During the past eight hours he had divided his time between organizing search parties, assisting with the reconstruction of the generator, and arranging to have the Kulak slaves removed from the now foul-smelling holds and redistributed throughout the ship. There had been no time for sleep. A condition shared by all of *Bellinda's* crewmembers.

The comm. panel beeped once at his elbow. "Captain."

"Skipper, we have all the components fitted and have run the initial tests."

"Well done, John."

"Thank you, captain, but now we need to go fully active if we are to align the harmonics."

"And when you do that Kania will detect it."

"That could prove to be a bit of a problem."

Lucas snorted. "I'll see what I can do about it. Captain out."

He swung around to face Jackson Telford at the communications alcove. Predicting his captain's next order he pulled a sour face. "I don't want to hear it Jack," he said, shaking his head. "Just get the colonel up here."

"Captain we are thirty minutes from insertion into orbit of Kulak four."

"Very well," Lucas said.

They had run out of time. Once within the orbit of Kulak four any chance of escape would be gone.

Lucas tapped the comm. stud. "Janine, how are things going down there?"

The ship's cargo officer sounded exhausted. "The charges are set, the jettison thrusters are in place and the magnetic constrictors are at full capacity."

"Very well. Let's hope that your services are not required."

"I will have my fingers and toes crossed."

Lucas heard the bridge hatch rumble aside and signed off. He drew in a slow breath to calm his rising ire then stood and turned to face the newcomer.

Manson had recovered most of his confidence since the earlier encounter and stood between the two Athenian guards as he would if they were members of his personal guard. The smugness of the creature made his blood boil. Something caught the colonel's attention off to Lucas' right and shortly thereafter the smirk ran from his face.

Nathan sat in the jump chair next to his mother with his knife in hand. He brushed it across his palm back and forth while retaining venomous eye contact with the colonel.

Lucas suppressed a smile. "Colonel Manson."

The swine jerked his gaze away from Nathan and turned to Lucas. "How may I be of assistance to you, captain?"

"One performance only is required then you can spend the rest of the voyage in your quarters."

"And when we reach Athenian space, you will honor your pledge?"

Lucas swallowed bile. "I said I would, didn't I."

Manson nodded and pointed to the Damage Control console.

Lucas nodded curtly. So much depended on the one man aboard ship who Lucas most wanted dead. But he could not overlook the fact that he had given his pledge to this creature.

Now the game began.

CHAPTER 4

Time: 22nd February, 309 ASC.
Position: Kulak system. Pruessen Empire. The Tunguska Fault.
Status: Pruessen Naval attack boat *Kania,* on escort duty.

With everything in order Captain Janzen left the bridge, walked into his ready room and fell onto the couch. He rubbed his face vigorously. Intersystem escorts were such a doddle. Half a day out, half a day back. The same routine, ad infinitum. After two years of the constant monotony he was more than ready for a change.

As a full grade lieutenant in the Imperial Navy, he had jumped at the opportunity for his own command. *Kania* might not represent much of a ship but in the larger scheme of things, the prestige of any command position on his record could only be good for his long-term career prospects. He also had to admit that the title of captain felt pretty damn good. However, nothing ever happened in this back end of imperial space.

Janzen sometimes wondered why the Empire bothered to have a naval presence in Kulak. No League ship would ever violate their quarantine protocols by coming north of the frontier and the once-feared slave uprising had been squashed over twenty years ago. Twenty-two years under the HRS whip had cowered and beaten what remained of the population. Not just beaten physically and mentally, but to the point where their very spirit had been thrashed from them.

"Captain," his XO reported, "the slave ship has slowed again. We are matching speed with her."

"Very well." With the colonel aboard *Bellinda*, Janzen was loathe to contact him on a matter he probably had under control. He sniffed. *Besides, the guy was a fucking nut job.*

Janzen wondered about his future. Perhaps if he put in for a transfer he could cash in on his experience in Kulak. More through boredom than fatigue he drifted into a light sleep. He jumped as the alert condition alarm sounded.

"Captain to the bridge, captain to the bridge."

Janzen wiped sleep from his eyes and sprinted onto the bridge.

"XO, what's happening?"

"Bellinda reports a massive power surge in the reactor. They say they are in danger of a catastrophic core breach."

"Are we still docked with her?"

"Yes, sir."

"Helm, undock and give me some distance from Bellinda," Janzen said. "Comm, put me through to her."

"Aye captain."

On the visual display the captain of the slave ship appeared. Sweat dripped from his face. Through a thin smoky haze Janzen could just make out a crewman slumped over his console, blood running from his face. Telford coughed.

"Captain Telford," Janzen said, "report your condition."

The slave captain appeared disorientated and panicky. He coughed again.

"Sir, we have a major reactor overload. Conduits rupturing all over the ship. Reactor approaching critical. What are your orders sir?"

His XO whispered, "If she blows this close to the orbital space dock..."

Janzen nodded. *It will damage the OSD, perhaps too badly to be repaired. And it will destroy* Kania.

"Captain Telford, you will immediately come about. Take your ship out of the shipping lanes at full speed."

"But sir," he pleaded, "what about my crew?"

I don't give a shit about a bunch of slaves.

"Telford, do as you've been ordered," Janzen shouted. The slave's face took on an expression of shock and fear. Janzen softened his tone. "Telford, it's possible if you bleed off energy to your engines it will balance your reactor."

The slave's face showed a glimmer of hope. "Yes sir, my chief engineer thinks so too. He says we will need to maintain a full-power acceleration for four hours to stand any chance of closing down the reactor."

A slight spark of concern ran down Janzen's spine. He ignored it.

"Cutting in here, captain."

"Of course, Colonel Manson." A shiver ran down Janzen's back.

"My guards and I will keep things on track over here. And we will take as long as we need to take to solve this problem. I'm not going to waste any more of my time on this rust bucket than I have to. We'll be back when we're back. Acknowledge, Captain Janzen."

Although flustered Janzen managed to choke out, "Aye, colonel."

Janzen straightened his back as the screen blinked off.

"She's turning about and accelerating to full power," Behrens said.

Captain Janzen slumped into his chair beside his XO. *Well, you wanted a little excitement didn't you?*

"Captain," Behrens said, "permission to speak, ah ... candidly."

Janzen nodded.

"Sir, I agree that getting the slave ship away from orbit, and us, is sound. But sir I have concerns."

"Lieutenant you've been posted here for... how long now?"

"Two months sir."

"Yes, two months. I've been here two years and I know the minds of these people well enough to tell you that there is no problem. Slaves are broken and the Athenians aboard Bellinda are no different from any other slaves I've seen. And consider this." He held his hand and ticked off his points on his fingers. "When she was captured we removed all of her weapons, her long range communications and navigation." He tapped his second finger. "We have thirty of the colonel's personal guard stationed aboard her should the need arise. It never has." Third finger. "Finally, we have components from her hyper generator onboard. She's not going anywhere."

"I guess you're right sir," Behrens said. "It's just that I, well, sir, I ..."

"Spit it out man," Janzen snapped.

"Well sir, it just doesn't *feel* right."

Janzen laughed and slapped the youngster on the shoulder. "Relax lieutenant. If she's not back in," he paused remembering Manson's words, "a reasonable time we'll go and get her."

"Aye, sir."

CHAPTER 5

Time: 22nd February, 309 ASC.
Position: Kulak system. Pruessen Empire.
Status: Freighter *Bellinda*, heading out of system.

Lucas Telford examined *Bellinda's* disheveled bridge. Smoke lay thick in the air, the sharp tang making his nose twitch. *Time, it's all a matter of time.*

"Captain," Mary said, "we've cleared Kania's sensor envelope."

Lucas glanced at the first officer's station. Mary and Nathan stared back. Lucas smiled with more confidence than he felt. Nathan nodded, his mouth stretched into a determined line. *Spending his formative years in slavery has aged my boy. An eleven-year-old shouldn't have a man's blood on his hands.*

"Very well Mary, bring the extractors back up." Like any good first officer, his wife had anticipated his order. As he looked to the communications alcove the smoke began to thin. The body remained slumped over the console, blood drying where if fell.

"Okay Jack, time to come back to life."

Jack Telford raised his head. "Hey, what about my performance?"

"You play an excellent corpse."

"May I return to my quarters now?" Manson's outstanding arrogance came from playing God for so long. Yet he had met his part of the bargain. Now Lucas would meet his obligations to the four from his family, and crewmembers who had died at this sadist's hand. Including his mother.

"Certainly colonel. However I've assigned you new quarters."

"New quarters?" Manson stiffened, sensing danger. "You gave me your word Telford."

"And I keep my word." Lucas' smile creased into an ugly sneer. "No member of this crew will harm you." He glanced at Manson's guards. "Escort the colonel to his new quarters ... on deck fifteen."

All decks below sixteen were full of Kulak slaves. Manson knew it.

"No, no, you can't do this. You promised, damn you Telford you promised." His voice rose high and scratchy.

"You're right you sick freak, I did give you my word, and I honor it now. Guards, make certain that neither of you harm the colonel en route."

Manson struggled against the two large Athenians to no avail. "Telford you promised, you promised!" Manson's screams died away as the bridge hatch snapped shut.

Lucas fell into the captain's chair and took a deep breath.

"Jack, put me through to engineering."

"Channel open, skipper."

"John, what's happening down there?"

"Same as the last time you called me, Lucas," his uncle growled. "We're fitting the components as quickly as possible but you're asking me to do ten hours work in four so don't push it."

Lucas opened his mouth to reply.

"And before you ask," John continued, "we'll get them fitted in time. Then we have to calibrate the harmonics for ingression to hyperspace. And when we do that ..."

"Yeah, I know. Let's hope Kania isn't in range at the time. That would make things ... difficult."

John snorted. "Lucas, I've made no guarantees to you. This jury-rigged contraption might not even work."

"Have a little faith, John."

"After what we've been through I'm all out of faith. But you'll always get my best."

"I know I will. Bridge out."

The hours ticked by. From Lucas' point of view the hours rushed by. *Time, it's all about time.* He drummed his fingers against the side of his chair. *Time.*

If time favored their old freighter and her crew, they would reach the hyper ingression point without hindrance and escape their miserable imprisonment. If time worked in their enemy's favor and *Kania* caught onto their deception, everyone aboard *Bellinda* would die. Minutes were nothing, really, until your life depended on them. Easing himself from the captain's chair he stretched and stood between the helm and navigation stations.

"Rebecca?" he asked his daughter.

"Once we reached maximum accel I put her on coast mode to allow for the continuum resistance. We're going as fast as is possible in null space."

"David?"

"At current speed we will reach the hyper ingression point in thirty-eight minutes, skipper."

"Very well."

Thirty-eight minutes might as well be thirty-eight days, if Kania *is on her way to kill us.*

The family had bet all of their chips on this one bold and dangerous ploy to escape slavery. How ironic that they were slaves to the slow-ticking clock.

"Mary, any changes?"

"Scans are clear." She licked her dry lips. "For the time being."

"Elapsed time?"

"Four point nine hours since we left Kania in orbit. And three point seven hours since we cleared her sensor envelope."

"Did she continue to ping us on the way out?"

"Yes, right to their limit."

Lucas fell into his chair. He struggled to maintain a calm visage as his pulse throbbed in his ears.

"I don't think Kania's captain believed us, father," Nathan said.

The tension in Lucas' face softened. "You think not?"

Nathan shook his head.

"Perhaps. But we're committed now."

In the following silence, Lucas could hear the seconds as they ticked down. He hated the long silences. Their slave masters had forced them into silence. The five hundred slaves in *Bellinda's* lower holds were silent too. Twenty-two years under the absolute control of a brutal regime had crushed their spirit, turning them into something less than human beings. Lucas and what remained of his family and crew had endured violence, rape and death but at least some of them were together and their lot, though harsh, was mild compared to those poor wretches. *When we get home I'll tell of every hideous act I've witnessed and endured in the north. There will be public outrage. With a little luck it will lead to war with Pruessen and this time there will be no turning back until that perverted society is brought crumbling down. We'll see how high and mighty they are after ...*

"Contact!" Mary's voice shattered the silence. "Captain, I have a contact, coming in fast from astern." The blood drained from her face. "It's Kania."

A collective groan filled the bridge.

"Mary, Alert Condition one, button us up. Helm, stand by for evasive maneuvers. How long, Mary?"

"She will be in extreme weapons range in fifty seconds. She is on full tactical alert and her sensors are active."

Lucas sensed the spike in tension from the surrounding

crewmembers. *By now they will have read our hyper emissions. They know we can escape and they'll destroy us before allowing that.*

"Very well people, we knew this was a possibility from the outset." He kept the uncertainty from his tone. "Stand to your stations and do your duty."

Lucas checked the external feeds on his console. His screen crystallized into a live feed of the patrol ship that came to kill them. Sleek and fast, *Kania's* twin pulsar energy beams would rip *Bellinda* to pieces well before she made it to the hyper ingression point.

"Janine, stand by." Lucas said. "I will keep this channel open."

"Aye, captain." Janine's voice acknowledged from the cargo control center.

Silver orbs of deadly energy spewed from *Kania's* bow. The ship trembled. "Pulse beams, high and to port," Mary said. "She's coming in at maximum acceleration and will be in optimal firing position in twelve seconds."

"Very well."

Bellinda's great size meant she could absorb a lot of enemy fire. But one decent shot through her belly and into the engineering section would breach the reactor chamber and finish them all.

"Remember Rebecca, guard our stern and port side."

"Aye, sir." Her fingers flew across the helm panel, pitching the ungainly vessel about in a frantic attempt to throw off the patrol ship's aim and protect her stern quarter. Rebecca was good but two hundred thousand tonnes of freighter could not outmaneuver a fast attack ship.

Bellinda shook. "Pulsar beams. Direct hits on upper hull. Topside shields reduced by twelve percent," Mary reported. "She's in range for focused beam attack."

The ship shuddered as sustained beams ripped along her hull.

"Direct hit, focused pulse beams. We are open to space. Lower midships. Attempting to seal off."

A great plume of frozen air trailed behind the ship, along with detritus from the tattered hull. And hundreds of bodies. The Kulak slaves. Some were broken pieces of humanity, mercifully killed outright. Some of the bodies flailed their arms and legs in their death throes.

Someone cried out while others stared mutely at the carnage. Occasionally an anguished groan.

"Merciful God almighty," Mary whispered.

The stench of fried conduits mixed with sweat. Lucas rubbed moisture from his upper lip as the ship lurched.

"Hit to starboard upper. Sealing off."

The enemy warship maneuvered into firing position for the freighter's stern lower quarter.

"She has passed optimal and is closing," Mary said.

"Watch her," Lucas warned.

"I see her." Rebecca's hands were a blur across the helm controls. She could not outmaneuver the smaller vessel but she could outguess it.

A handful of heartbeats before *Kania* fired, Rebecca hit the bow thrusters for two seconds. The bow rose and the stern dropped.

The focused beams missed their intended target, the engine nacelles, and ripped into the boat bay hatches. Massive decompression blew out the hatches together with the untethered landing boats.

Bellinda heaved violently to port, pinning crew to their chairs.

"She's passed us," Mary said. "Switching to forward scanners."

The screen split in two. The great rent at the back of deck one gaped open like a jagged mouth, still trailing a gossamer venting of air.

“She’s coming about for another pass.”

Kania turned with remarkable agility and streaked toward them. *They wouldn’t try that, if* Bellinda *was still armed.* She kept coming but did not fire as wildly as before. As the silent seconds ticked by they waited for the coming storm.

“Rebecca!” Lucas yelled. “They’re going for our port side.”

“Damn.” Rebecca fought the sluggish freighter around but the old girl maneuvered like a cripple by comparison with the enemy warship. Almost on top of their ship, *Kania’s* beams struck, raking the starboard bow. The attacker rotated through her axis and took a snap shot at an oblique upward angle.

A single focused beam pierced the shields, tore through the hull and ripped through the bridge. The ship bucked and people screamed. A chunk of shrapnel the size of a fist smashed into the base of the ops console. The blast had torn through the deck, ripping a gaping hole in the overhead as it exited. The communications alcove had taken the full force of the blast. Now, only shattered consoles and the bloody remains of Jackson Telford remained. Bile stung Lucas’ throat and he forced it back. Crewmembers waded into the gory wreckage and set breach patches. Within seconds the smoky air cleared.

"Kania's coming around for another pass," Mary cried. "She's going for our reactor again. Coming in at flank speed."

Lucas' lips moved silently as *Kania* completed her turn. The enemy acted without caution, confident they had nothing to fear from an unarmed freighter.

"Enough of this," Lucas said quietly. "Rebecca, initiate rollover, now!"

The ship rolled over bringing the undamaged port side to face the onrushing warship. Rebecca sat motionless, her fingers poised over the attitude controls.

"Five degrees over," Lucas ordered."Janine, blow them all, now."

The explosive charges attached to each of the eight massive cargo hatches detonated in sequence. Six hundred and forty tonnes of ejected hatches flew directly into the attacker's path.

"We probably won't hit her, but if we can make her take pause it might be worth the effort." Lucas was thinking aloud again.

Kania took a snap shot as she avoided *Bellinda's* hatches, and the freighter trembled again. Had they given her a scare? Perhaps his tactics would tempt her young captain into acting rashly.

"Stand by, Janine. Rebecca, five degrees over. Janine, fire!"

Each cargo container sat on tracks and had been fitted with light thrusters. Each weighed fifty-two tonnes, empty. Each was loaded to the brim with mining equipment.

Three containers burst from the hold spinning like great oscillating cubes.

"Five degrees over. Fire!"

Each five-degree rotation covered a section of *Kania's* attack path. In quick succession, thirty spinning cubes covered forty degrees of space ahead of the patrol ship's flight path. Again, no one expected anything more than a few seconds of confusion.

Continuously on station for three years, and with no enemy to fight, *Kania's* crew had turned to fat. That remained one of *Bellinda's* few tangible advantages. She hurtled toward them at breakneck speed, impairing her ability to maneuver.

Kania wound her way through the staggered formation of containers, firing hurried shots as she closed. On and on she came, an unstoppable dealer in death.

Then something happened. *Kania's* helm officer must have panicked when cargo containers began filling his forward quarter. He maneuvered around all but one of them.

One of the containers struck the patrol ship on the starboard side, stern quarter. The sudden release of so much kinetic energy might not be enough to kill her, but it had to hurt her.

"Hit!" Mary yelled. "We *actually* hit her."

A great cheer burst from everyone on the bridge. The cheer dwindled and smiles faded as they waited. *Kania* veered to starboard, venting a stream of frozen vapor.

"Her shields are overloaded," Mary said. "She is venting radiation from her starboard engine, and her hull is breached along a thirty meter section of her starboard engineering section. Power is down. I suspect her reactor has scrammed." Mary sat back and wiped sweat from her lips. "I can't believe it, but she's dead in space."

"In other words," Lucas said, "she's fucked."

Mary giggled like a teenager. Nathan threw his head back and laughed without restraint, drawing the family in. Lucas sobered and held up his hand. He swallowed the last chuckle and cleared his throat.

"Mary," Lucas asked, "how badly are we hurt?"

"We've been in better shape, but most of the main systems are still functioning. We need to replace the critical shield blisters and set up force fields around the breached sections. If everyone pitches in we'll have her ready for transition in half a day." Mary smiled. "Even if Kania got off a distress signal, this far out it will take days to mount an appropriate military response."

"Very well," Lucas said. "This crew's first and only priority is to repair our damaged shields, and patch the old girl back together enough to ensure hull integrity. That completed, we will ingress to hyperspace and finally be gone from this wretched place."

"The good Lord be praised for our deliverance," Mary intoned.

"Amen," the family repeated.

Lucas caught Nathan rolling his eyes and fought down a smile. *Yeah, like me he's wondering where the good Lord has been for the last four years.*

CHAPTER 6

That which does not kill us makes us stronger. Friedrich Nietzsche.

Time: 12th April, 311 ASC.
Position: Approaching planet Delos. Athenian controlled space.
Status: Athenian Navy Monitor *Impudent* on combat interdiction patrol (CIP).

Captain Bradman looked at the D-O. "Are we in visual range yet?"

"Aye," Lieutenant Bettina McMurphy replied.

"Good."

Once the image had stabilized, the planet of Delos came clearly into focus. From an outside perspective it took on the appearance of an elegant green world with thick swirls of white clouds rolling serenely across its surface. Beneath its soft exterior dwelt a savage jungle environment that had resisted the Athenian Republic's best efforts to tame it for three hundred years. For one observing the world for the first time it gave no hint to its heartbreaking past.

Delos stood as a pungently clear reminder to every member of the League of Allied Worlds as to the necessity of establishing and maintaining the strict, twenty-year-old quarantine regulations. Despite the constant patrols by warships of the Coalition League Navy, idiots who had somehow been granted Master's certificates still chose to run the blockade.

One 'Line Runner' had tested their luck by venturing into the QZ and been stupid enough to get infected. To add to their monumental blunder they chose to land on Delos before the plague took them. This proved to be a tragic turn of events for the fifty-seven hundred colonists who were once again trying to make a home for themselves on the ferocious planet. By the time the colonists recognized the truth, the 'Runners' were dying and the colonists were infected. Since that terrible time Delos had been a quarantined world and one that even the stupidest of fortune seekers avoided. Another testament to unbridled greed.

Headhunters, on the other hand, were capable of anything.

"Contact on the surface, captain."

Only McMurphy knew Bradman well enough to detect his inner tenseness.

"I have a ship on the surface, captain." The tactical officer spoke without looking up, his eyes remaining locked onto his readouts. "Minimal power emissions. The core appears to be cold. Registration and configuration comply with Athenian standards." He paused for several seconds to consider his summation. "The closest approximation I could make would be that she is a Turgo class freighter."

"Helm, take us into a geosynchronous orbit above the site."

As the Helm Officer confirmed his orders Bradman gave his Operations Officer a curious look. McMurphy shook her head, confirming what the captain already suspected. There had been no reports of a missing or overdue Athenian-registered vessel in months. Most certainly not in this area.

"Can you get a name?"

"No captain," the T/O said, "but I have a registration number. Transferring to the operations officer."

McMurphy examined the records. The information scrolled across her screen but it made no sense. Then it hit her.

“Damn. She's an independent, captain. Details in a moment."

Bradman stifled a curse. He knew that all Independent Traders were crewed by families. When one such vessel was lost, on most occasions it meant the annihilation of an entire bloodline.

McMurphy continue to examine her readings until she saw it. She gasped.

Bradman narrowed his eyes.

"She's the Bellinda, sir."

“The Bellinda? Hmm.”

"She was reported missing, presumed lost. Six years ago whilst en route to Iberia."

It had been in all the net news broadcasts at the time.

"The last inspection of this planet was three years ago. Correct?"

"Yes, captain."

Bradman looked at her as if they had just discovered their own Flying Dutchman.

"What's her condition?" he asked the T/O.

"She's heavily damaged captain. I suppose that's to be expected though. Freighters aren’t designed for planetary insertion."

So, the mystery deepened. An Athenian freighter, missing for six years, suddenly reappearing like a ghost ship on the planet’s surface.

"She's been down there a while captain," the T/O continued. "From the oxidization on the hull I would estimate somewhere between twenty-two and twenty-six months."

Bradman lowered his voice. "What do think, Betty?"

As the boat's Operations Officer, McMurphy was expected to have all of the answers all of the time. However this one had her stumped and it must have shown on her face.

"I suppose we could send a couple of cans down to the surface and try to recover her logs." She felt doubtful that the captain would approve such provocative action. Bradman confirmed her opinion with a tight, dark smirk.

"Captain?"

Bradman's attention swung back to the Tactical Station.

"Lieutenant?"

The T/O cleared his throat. "Captain, I am detecting a life sign on the planet's surface."

The unique nature of the plague insinuated itself into the ecosystem of any planet it came in contact with, but had the singular characteristic of being fatal only to human beings. As such there were probably billions of life forms on the planet. It took a moment longer for Bradman to understand the full import of what his tactical officer had said.

"Human?" The incredulity in his voice surprised McMurphy.

"Aye, captain."

"You've double checked?"

"Triple checked, sir. And I've just run a diagnostic on the software. It's in perfect working order."

McMurphy did not need to look around the bridge to know that every eye had just risen from their stations.

"I detect no other vessels on the surface or in orbit captain. Therefore it would be logical to assume that the ... life sign was aboard the freighter when she crashed."

Bradman paused for a moment. "Are you suggesting, lieutenant, that someone has survived on a plague planet for two years?"

The T/O's back straightened. "At the moment captain, I am working with very limited input. However, until I obtain data to the contrary, the only rational explanation I can conclude is that there is a human being alive on the planet Delos, and that said human has probably been down there since Bellinda crashed on that world. Sir."

Rational? Rational! This had to be some kind of mistake. No one, but no one survived on a plague planet for longer than forty-two days. Yet in this instance two plus two did not add up to what it should be. Alive, for two years.

"How many life signs," he asked.

"The readings are fuzzy captain due to the inversion layer but I am reasonably certain that there is only one."

"Do you have a location?"

"Again captain it is hard to pin down. Hmm, I would estimate that the subject is within one to two clicks of the crash site."

"Captain?"

Bradman managed a weak smile. "D-O, I'm open to suggestions."

With an effort she returned her captain's gesture.

"Only one recommendation. We need to send a shore party down there to investigate."

"Are you volunteering?"

McMurphy shrugged, more in the negative than the positive.

"I don't blame you. This is a job for the eggheads at Mylor to figure out. There is no way in hell that I'm going to order one of my people to go strolling around on a plague planet. That is well and bloody truly above the call of duty."

"I suppose we could send down a couple of cans," McMurphy suggested. "Of course they would be of limited use without supervision."

"You want me to ask for volunteers?" the captain said, with a sardonic grin.

The sound of a cleared throat caused him to swing his chair around until his gaze fell onto the Auxiliary Operations Officer.

"I'll go sir," Ensign Ellen Gabreski said.

Although only on her second patrol, the ensign had so far exhibited all of the requisite qualities of a recent academy graduate. She still had stars in her eyes and words like duty, honor and Republic ringing in her ears. She wanted adventure, she wanted to make a name for herself, she wanted - one day in the distant future - to sit in the captain's chair. McMurphy remembered Bradman being the same way when he was her age. Still, volunteering to go wandering around on a plague world showed a whole lot of moxie.

"If you go down there, ensign, it will mean forty-five days in the tank, when you get back."

"I'm aware of the quarantine regulations, sir. But if someone has survived on a plague planet for two years..." She let the suggestion hang in the air between them for a long moment. "Wouldn't you say it's worth the risk to find out, sir?"

A possible antidote for the plague. Yes, McMurphy thought, she not only had guts but also made an extremely good point.

"Very well Ensign you have a go. Full quarantine procedures and no unnecessary chances. Understood!"

"Aye captain." The faintest hint of a smile touched her lips.

CHAPTER 7

Time: 12th April, 311 (ASC).
Position: Planet Delos. Athenian controlled space. Tunguska Fault.

The nightmare returned. Images overlapped, tumbling faster and faster. Horror. Pain. Violation. *Kania* tearing at *Bellinda*. Delos.

Nathan lurched upright in bed, his breath catching. He peeled the light sheet from his clammy skin. A shudder ran down his body. He groaned and licked his dry lips. Swinging his legs over the edge of the bunk, he supported his head in trembling hands.

"Damn you," he shouted. "Leave me alone." The returning echo was his only response. Nathan laughed and shook his head. "That's right, Telford, damn a deity you don't believe in. Brilliant."

Wiping sleep from his eyes Nathan sauntered into the adjacent ship's galley, poking around for leftovers. A piece of lizard jerky tested his teeth but he got it down. "Time to hunt, Telford, unless you want to eat this shit again today."

I wonder if I've gone a little batty in the last two years? He shrugged. "Only if I start answering my own questions."

His old flight suit had seen better days but with no alternative, he slipped the threadbare garment on and slung his pack and weapons webbing across his shoulder. Nathan strolled along the ship's central corridor pausing to stare through the space left by the blown-out hatch and into the vacant quarters. The room had not changed in the last two years but he could not bear to sleep in his family's old quarters.

Nathan arrived at the first barred hatch. He undogged it and slid ten levels down the service ladder until he reached the lowest deck. Sun streamed into the dim corridor after he opened the hatch. He tentatively scanned the landscape. Seeing no danger, he stepped over the coaming and stood for a few moments allowing his eyes to adjust to the early morning glare. Through the broad hull-breach he took in the clear blue sky.

The deck plates remained solidly unmoving as he walked through the superstructure until he stood outside the hull. The surrounding jungle greeted him as it did every day. A thick, green façade within which death awaited the unwary in a thousand ugly ways. The hot spot between his shoulder blades that always warned of danger remained quiet. *Without you I wouldn't have lasted two years on this world. Thank you, Prep.*

At the south-end of the crash site, water cascaded from a hidden aquifer. Leaving his weapons and pack hanging from a branch, he stepped under the waterfall. At this time of the morning the bitterly cold water stung his skin through his clothing. Having washed away a troubled night's sleep he stepped from under the flow and wiped his face. Within minutes the steadily climbing sun would dry his clothes until his sweat soaked them again. Nathan secured his weapons and hung the pack from his left shoulder.

He followed the overgrown four-kilometer depression that marked *Bellinda's* crash path. He stopped, as he did every day, at the large rock-encased mound. He hacked at the ever-encroaching vegetation with his machete. Standing back to admire his handy work he noticed for the first time that a flower grew here and there. A lump grew in his throat and he swallowed it.

Nathan left the graveyard and followed an animal track into the jungle. He found the small watering hole he had discovered a month ago. Keeping his movements to a minimum he waited noiselessly, as a good hunter did.

Another few minutes rewarded his stealthy patience. The marsupial he sought was small but mighty tasty. *Come on, you timid little shit.* At the short rise leading to the water it stopped. Its sharp ears flattened, the keen nose quivered. Nathan nocked an arrow onto his bowstring, salivating in anticipation. Assured of its safety the little animal skittered forward. A few meters from the water-hole it stopped, trembled with fear and scurried into the safety of the undergrowth before he could raise his bow. "Damn," he hissed. Then he heard it.

Nathan recognized the high engine whine, muffled by distance but growing steadily. A chill ran down his sweaty back.

Breaking from cover he sprinted toward the growing sound. There was only one safe place they could land. If he got there in time he could occupy the high ground and set his ambush. Nathan burst from the undergrowth into the clearing and skidded to a halt as a hot knot of coal burned between his shoulders. Prep was warning him. Experience had taught him what this threat represented. A pair of chameleon leopards crouched nearby. They were not visible to the naked eye but he could sense their presence, one to his right, one to his left. *I don't have time for this.*

"I'm just passing through, old one," he yelled. Nathan's raised voice tested the big cat's concentration. They could remain stealthy for short periods, usually when startled or preparing to attack.

Homing in on the first movement of long grass, he plucked pebbles from a pouch and threw them at the invisible beast. One pebble struck the cat and he materialized through a shimmering haze. A big male, three hundred kilos of looming death. "Take it easy, old cat." The female would be poised to attack from the opposite direction. Nathan nocked an arrow and aimed along the shaft at the small clump of depressed grass. When the female leopard materialized the male roared his warning.

"Go on old cat, get going." Over his shoulder the big male emitted a final snarl as it padded away. He had come to know this couple over the years. They had avoided confrontation as long as they all respected one another's territory. The female snarled as she slinked away.

He ran on. Ten minutes later he reached *Bellinda*. While he caught his breath the steadily growing whine from the invader's landing boat reached a deafening pitch. The craft landed on the flat outcrop two hundred meters from *Bellinda's* busted hull. He dried his sweaty fingers on a section of his pants not soaked in sweat.

A lone figure emerged from the landing boat and inspected the enormous broken ship. He wore a v-suit overlaid with light-weight, black armor. The black helmet reminded Nathan of something from years ago.

The suited figure examined the surrounding jungle before scanning the vista of the ship's crash path. If he did not start paying attention to this perilous environment he would be dead before Nathan could put an arrow into him. *Or perhaps I should just nick him? Let him find out what it's like to die of the Derwent Plague.* This would have the added benefit of torturing him with the knowledge that he had only forty-two days to live before the plague started to eat him alive.

"But what if he's not a Pruessen?" Nathan whispered.

Suit-man strolled along the crash path as if he were going for a walk through a city park. Not far from the funeral mound he stopped before the great fallen tree trunk. Nathan could not see his face through the tinted visor. The range was a little long but Nathan nocked an arrow and checked the wind. He aimed at the soft opening at the back of the enemy's neck. Something about the damn black helmet told him to hold the shot, so he sheathed the arrow and dashed down the hill.

Nathan's back flared a warning. From the edge of the clearing an enormous green shape disturbed the undergrowth. The snake made a beeline for suit-man. He continued sprinting down the embankment as the enormous snake slithered into position to attack the stranger. Finally, the dimwit noticed the threat and spun around as the snake coiled to strike. Suit-man grappled for his sidearm, took a panicked backward step, tripped over an exposed root and staggered heavily to the ground.

Suit-man pushed against his heels until the fallen tree blocked his way. Hampered by his thick, cumbersome gloves he continued to grope for his sidearm. The snake's fangs extended, each the length of a man's hand, loaded with a toxin that killed with slow excruciating pain. It struck, the fangs glanced off suit-man's forearm armor. *That had to hurt.* Again, suit-man tried for his pistol and the snake's fangs skimmed off the armor. Its black slit-eyes followed the line of the armor. The armored sections like the chest, head, arms and legs were protected. However, the soft gaps between the armor were vulnerable. Nathan shook his head. *Smart snake; big ugly smart snake. It'll kill suit-man now.*

The viper extended itself to three meters in height, its body straining tautly to strike.

Nathan drew back the bowstring, aimed and fired. The long wooden shaft ripped through the back of the viper's head, exiting through its right eye. White brain matter hung in stringy lumps from the tip of the arrow. The serpent swayed back and forth before collapsing to the ground, twitching spasmodically in its death throes.

Why did I do that? Something about the black helmet. I still can't remember...

Nathan shook his head dismissively. *If I've made a mistake I'll correct it now.* Striding down the hill he jumped onto the fallen tree trunk. Suit-man remained frozen on the ground.

Walking around the prone figure he stood before suit-man. The stranger began to rise but paused when Nathan tensed.

Go on, reach for your sidearm.

Suit-man rested on his knees, making certain to keep his hands clear of this sidearm. His helmet turned to face Nathan for tense seconds. Nathan followed his slow movements as he adjusted his helmet's controls. The sudden loss of opacity made suit 'man' squint.

Shock constricted Nathan's throat and he cleared it noisily.

"You're a girl," he blurted.

"Last time I checked," she said, sporting a sly grin. Her voice, coming through the helmet speaker, sounded comfortable, friendly.

"Pruessens don't carry girls on their ships," Nathan said.

"Not since the end of the war they haven't."

Nathan felt no threat from her.

"I'm Ensign Ellen Gabreski," she said, offering her hand. "Monitor Corps. We were patrolling the area and discovered your ship."

Nathan was too stunned to speak.

"My friends call me Gabby," she added.

Nathan recalled the picture of his father beside his fighter, the black helmet under his arm. *Monitor Corps. Of course, that's why I didn't fire.*

Taking the offered hand he said, "Nathan Telford, of the Bellinda." Nathan glanced at the broken freighter.

Gabby stood and brushed grass and dirt from her suit. She noticed his interest and turned slowly around. "I'm wearing a v-suit to protect me from infection."

"From the plague," Nathan confirmed.

Nathan's head tracked to the nearby funeral mound.

Gabby frowned.

Live as one or die as one.

"How old are you?"

Nathan squinted in concentration. "Thirteen ... and a half. By the Athenian Standard Calendar."

"You've survived on a plague planet for two years?" Her astonished tone said much. "On your own? How did you do that?"

He shrugged and stepped toward the viper. After pulling the arrow from its head he cleaned it in the sandy soil before slipping it into his quiver. Gabby kept her distance from the dead reptile.

"Southern Delosian Horned Viper," he announced. His smile fled. "Before the plague, they killed three of my family." *They were the lucky ones.*

"But through it all you survived. That's amazing."

Yeah, me and Prep. A winning combination.

"Will you tell me what happened, Nathan?"

Nathan winced then cleared his throat. He needed to tell someone. He brushed over some points. Iberia. Four years of slavery. Escape. "We spent two weeks changing course to avoid the Pruessen patrols before transiting into Athenian space. But the ship had been badly damaged, the boat bay destroyed, sensors and navigation damaged, many dead and injured. Our food supply ran out days before and the water reclaimator couldn't keep up with our demands.

"As we entered the Delosian system we sent out urgent distress calls on our jury-rigged short wave bands, but received no replies. The hyper generator had blown during system transition. We didn't have the parts to repair it so we weren't going anywhere. We could remain aboard and starve to death or attempt a landing." Nathan's throat constricted with the recollection. He swallowed deeply and took a shuddering breath.

"My father said Rebecca, she was my older sister, was the best natural pilot he'd ever seen – she got us down in one piece. Most of us survived the landing and we settled in. Everything went well for a while. We had been out of touch for four years. We didn't know Delos had been contaminated by the plague. Forty-two days after surviving the landing my family started getting sick." Nathan cleared his husky throat and blinked rapidly. "My family all died ... but I didn't. Don't know why *they* died and I didn't." A knot formed in his stomach at the memory.

He saw tears in Gabby's eyes. She reached toward him but he instinctively drew away from her.

"I don't like to be touched."

"All right, Nathan. Sorry."

Nathan brushed sweaty hair from his brow.

"What's that?" Gabby pointed to the bump at the corner of his right eyebrow.

Nathan smiled grimly. "Pruessen's don't care to be looked at. Our doctor had been removed from the ship so the broken bone never mended properly."

"I see."

No you don't.

"Well Nathan, when I get you back to Impudent I'll have the doc take care of that for you."

He glared at her.

Her eyebrows arched and she quickly added, "Or not."

"I need it to remind me."

"Remind you of what?"

"My family obligation."

"I see," she said again.

Nathan felt his temper rise. *No you don't, Gabby. No you don't. You grow up fast when you're a slave. Suffer through subservience to the Pruessen Empire then, then, you'll understand.*

"Nathan, before something else tries to kill us, how about we get out of here? I can have you aboard Impudent within the hour."

He nodded. While Gabby walked away to check in with her boat, Nathan stood before the funeral mound. His heart raced.

"I am leaving you now, my family," he whispered. "I will join

Monitor Corps. One day I will return to you - after I have killed every last Pruessen."

CHAPTER 8

Time: 27th May, 311 (ASC)
Position: Orbiting the ANS Bio-Deterrent Research facility.
Planetoid Mylor. Arcadian System. Northern Quadrant.
Status: Monitor *Impudent*, awaiting transfer of personnel to BDR facility

Nathan's first experience with his painful intuitive gift came to him at the beginning of his third month on the planet Delos. He had been alone for three weeks and he carried within his heart a dark, hollow place filled with pain. The loss of his family had nearly crushed his spirit but he determined that he could be of little use to their memory if he died. So he went through the motions necessary to survive and in a short time became quiet proficient with the bow that his father had fashioned for him. The Pulsar rifle would undoubtedly be a more effective weapon than his bow, but his unfamiliarity with the weighty firearm had encouraged him to stick with what he knew the best.

As part of his survival regime he hunted for food every day. On one occasion, as he strolled along a worn animal track enjoying the mild spring weather, he wandered into unfamiliar territory. The jungle fell away in an instant, the lush vegetation giving way to an open area of startlingly barren landscape. The winter rains cascaded down from the mountains into this basin area, washing away all traces of the jungle before it. The kaleidoscope of multicolored vegetation vanished before the orange-walled arroyo as though a new world had magically appeared within the one he knew.

He walked on, fascinated by the layered, rainbow effect that stared back at him from the steep walls. As he ventured deeper into the gully, the initial feeling of trepidation increased. He put the feeling down to the unexpected nature of his new environment, until the spot on his upper spine, directly between his shoulder blades, began to ache. It started with a twinge, like a mild electric jab, but as he continued into the arroyo it began to burn with ever-increasing intensity. He ignored it, putting the feeling down to a probable pinched nerve. However, along with the pain between his shoulder blades came a feeling of extreme uneasiness that permeated the rest of his senses. He found the combination of the two elements difficult to ignore. He tensed, surveyed the area and drew an arrow onto his bowstring. He could see no discernible danger yet the feeling of impending doom felt so palpable that he began backing out of the gully, watchful to any change around him.

At the lip of the arroyo he stood and surveyed the area with a critical eye. The gully seemed quiet and peaceful, nothing moved and no sign of danger reared its head. The restless turmoil had vanished from his mind and his backache had disappeared.

"Nitwit," he mumbled to himself and turned to leave.

The air suddenly split by the sound of a great crack like the splintering of a mighty tree. Nathan spun around in time to see the east face of the gully collapse and tumble in a great avalanche of fractured earth and stone onto the floor of the arroyo. Time and natural forces of weather and erosion had undermined the wall, and its time had finally come.

He stood transfixed to the sight of destruction for several minutes before returning to the ship. It took days for him to come to terms with the phenomenon and to appreciate that he owed his life to the gift. In the next two years the same premonition pain (Prep, as he came to call the bizarre phenomenon) had been responsible for saving his life on more than one occasion. Delos had proved time and again to be an extremely unforgiving place and he had little doubt that without Prep he may not have survived his time there.

Although he had no idea how the Prep manifested itself, he determined that he would never again question his odd premonitions of danger. It remained as the greatest mystery of his young life. However, having been treated as a freak by people because of his intelligence, he knew enough not to share knowledge of the Prep with anyone else. Fate had granted him a second chance at life and above all else, he determined not to play the part of outsider again.

The Prep had proved to be a friend and ally, but was, like an embarrassing malady, one he resolved to keep to himself.

***

Nathan gazed at the planetoid Mylor that swam in the center of his screen.

Since arriving in orbit, the screaming pain in his back warned him that danger lurked within that dark, foreboding place.

According to his brief research, Mylor orbited the system as close to the system aphelion as anybody could be, without actually leaving the system all together. He began to long for the warm, opened-skied world that he had so recently escaped from.

Nathan looked away from the planetoid but the feeling of impending doom remained as strong as ever. He felt powerless to do anything about his situation. A small part of him regretted his natural curiosity that had impelled him to investigate the tiny world that would soon become his new prison. Not for the first time since coming aboard *Impudent* had his inquisitive nature led him into trouble.

Ten days ago, thirty-three days into their journey, he managed to tweak the computer into giving him access to the outside scanners. Nathan had a vague suspicion that he should not be overriding the security lock outs, but could not help himself. What possible harm could it do? He waited until Gabby had put her head down for a nap before commencing his task. His first indication that his indiscretion had been discovered came with a rumble.

"Ensign Gabreski, wake up," Captain Bradman bellowed.

Gabby sprung from her rack as though hit with a bucket of icy water. Nathan turned off the feed and jumped out of his chair. The captain stood on the other side of the transparent observation panel, his furious expression threatening to melt the four-centimeter-thick composite window.

"Yes, captain," Gabby said, blinking away the sleep from her eyes.

"What's going on?"

"Sir?" Poor Gabby looked totally flummoxed.

Bradman glanced lazily at Nathan before returning his attention to Gabby. "You are supposed to be supervising the boy, ensign." Gabby glanced down at Nathan for a moment then her shoulders slumped.

"Sorry sir," she said. "What has he done now?"

"Your young charge has tied into the external scanners," he rumbled. "Did you tell him he could do that?"

"No sir."

"Why did you show him how to tie into the scanners, ensign?"

"I didn't, sir."

He turned his glaring attention back to Nathan who made the mistake of thinking that the same boyish smile that charmed the rest of the crew would work on the captain. Bradman's mouth tightened, his glare intensifying until Nathan's face fell.

"Are you telling me, ensign, that this boy got past our security lock outs by himself?"

Gabby looked as though she might be sick at any moment.

"Gabby didn't know about it, captain," Nathan said. "I just wanted to observe the transition back from hyperspace. I didn't think it would do any harm." He swallowed deeply but to his credit maintained eye contact with Bradman. Gabby winced with each word as though nails were being driven into her toes.

"Ensign Gabreski, I would be obliged if you would keep a closer eye on the boy in future."

"Aye, skipper," she said, straightening her stance as well as she could within the tight confines.

"And as for you young Mister Telford, from here on, if you wish to engage in extracurricular activities whilst aboard my boat, you will ask permission. No more hacking into our systems. Is that clear?"

Nathan snapped to attention. "Aye-aye, skipper."

Just for a moment the hard line of the captain's mouth softened. He nodded once to Nathan, gave Gabby a curious look, then turned to leave.

"Captain Bradman?"

"Yes?"

"Sir, I request permission to observe the next transition."

This time the captain's granite features began to melt in what appeared to be a most uncustomary way. His mouth warped as he struggled to suppress a smile. He glanced at Gabby, his head shaking slowly. Kneeling down brought him eye to eye with Nathan.

"Do you give me your pledge that you will keep out of restricted areas of the boat's data base?"

"Aye, skipper," he said. "Unless I receive permission."

"Very well. I give you permission to observe the transition." Bradman left the observation room with haste.

Nathan got to observe the boat's transition from normal space to hyperspace. He felt light and awed by the experience and not surprisingly attacked the boat's library in search of everything he could find on the subject.

Having given the captain his word, he patiently observed the rules. His acceptance of the situation prompted the skipper to grant him unrestricted access to the outside scanners.

He removed the ugly picture of Mylor from the screen and tied into the stern scanners. *Tsunami* maintained her close vigil, dead astern. Would one Monitor Corps boat really fire on another? Because of him?

What of Mylor? If his aching back could be believed, and it could, Nathan dreaded his forthcoming transfer to that dark rock.

CHAPTER 9

Time: 28th November, 311 (ASC).
Position: ANS Bio-Deterrent Research facility. Planetoid Mylor. Arcadian System. Status: Research ongoing.

Within the confines of the large, well-appointed office, Lt Cmdr Spotiswood sat across from the professor, his hands clenched firmly in his lap.

"You have seen the test results?" Professor Knightsbridge asked.

He nodded sharply.

"Can you explain results like that? We have given him every test in the book, then made up some to see where it would lead and we are still in the dark."

"Very well, I will ask again," Spotiswood said. "Is he a product of genetic engineering?"

Did the Pruessen's experiment on him during his years of enslavement?

"I do not know," the professor said, showing his impatience. "If he is the result of GE then it is at a level of sophistication well beyond our ability to understand. What I have been able to establish, however, is that there is a dormant strain in his genetic structure. It could remain dormant forever or prove to have no useful application. Or it could become active, today, tomorrow, next week, next year. There is no way of knowing."

"So, what do you propose to do?"

"Do?" the professor said. "We keep him here and do more tests and more tests until we figure out what makes him tick."

Spotiswood folded his hands in front of him and stared at the professor. "Or Kill him." A raised hand was all it took to stop Knightsbridge's reply. "You've done every test you can think of and you have nothing."

"I resent –"

"I haven't finished, Professor. Do you think I don't know what goes on in this facility? Why did you cut off his heating and serve only cold food?" Knightsbridge shifted in his chair. "Well?"

"He refused to cooperate with us," he finally said with a shrug. "Some discipline was required. He was interfering with the work."

Spotiswood sat back in his chair and stared at the Professor, who refused to meet his eyes.

“I am relieving you of all responsibilities regarding this project, forthwith."

"You cannot do that. He is unique. He could be –"

"He could be dead if I leave him in your hands for much longer. And Professor," Spotiswood said coldly, "don't ever tell me what I can and cannot do. The boy is an asset of the ANSIO Special Projects Division. We only let you borrow him to find out about the plague, which you have failed to do.”

"Very well, Commander Spotiswood,” he said stiffly, “let it be on your head then." He stood, turned on his heel and marched from the room.

Spotiswood let the tension out in a sigh. He’d come so close to lashing out. As an absolute certainty he would never allow Knightsbridge anywhere near the boy again. He shook his head, thinking of what the lad had been through.

Nathan had stopped answering their questions three months ago, in protest against his treatment. The professor had retaliated against him as he would against a new strain of infection. Still the lad refused to buckle under to the abuse and increased his active resistance to every attempt to test him. He fought his one-sided war with no chance of relief, within an environment not of his choosing, against odds he had no chance of winning against. It had cost the young fellow dearly, but although he had not won the battle he had not lost the war either. *He has guts, that’s for sure.*

Spotiswood slapped both hands against his knees, stood and strode from the office, walking briskly to the containment area.

As he stepped into the room the chill struck at him. The boy lay on the bunk like a mannequin with the stuffing knocked out of it. His forearm lay across his eyes and under the light blanket his chest barely moved.

Spotiswood grabbed a nearby chair and sat beside the single bunk. The boy did not move except for a single shiver.

His difficult time on Mylor had drastically changed the robust, brown-skinned youngster he had last seen four months ago. He looked terrible. Pale and sickly, he had lost considerable weight.

"Nathan, sit up please," Spotiswood said. "I need to speak with you."

***

After what felt like a lifetime, the man returned. He wore the uniform of an Athenian Naval Service Intelligence Organization officer, and carried the rank of lieutenant commander. Nathan had not seen him in such a long time, but remembered the eyes, sharp and dark like a Delosian hawk.

"Nathan, sit up please. I need to speak to you."

Nathan pushed himself up by sliding his back along the wall beside his bunk. The commander's eyes were a little less hawk-like than he remembered. He struggled to keep his eyes open.

"I am going to take you away from this place. Would you like that?"

Nathan's mind struggled to properly comprehend the words. So he gave what he hoped was a positive shrug.

"I'll take that as a yes. I can place you almost anywhere. Do you have a preference?"

He dragged his eyes up to meet the intelligence officer. "Warm. And doctor free."

"I'll see what I can do."

Nathan thought he saw something like a fleeting smile. Then the hawk returned.

"But you need to do something in return. Nathan, look at me." With a start Nathan realized he had begun to fade out. "This is very, very important. As you may know your physiological tests show absolutely no contagion to the plague and no discernible reason for your natural immunity. You are simply a one in a billion chance who lucked out. What? You need to speak up, Nathan."

"I said, all for nothing."

The commander nodded slowly before continuing. "Yes. But the point is, you are the only person to have survived exposure to the plague. Do you know what that means?"

"I'm really lucky?"

"You're an intelligent young man so I shan't mince words. You must not, under any circumstances, tell anyone about Delos. There are people who will stop at nothing to get their hands on someone who has a proven immunity to the plague. Nothing!" Spotiswood paused but kept his eyes locked onto Nathan. "If you tell anyone about this, there are people who will go to any lengths to get to you. They will kill anyone who stands in their way. And when they acquire you they will do things to you that will make the last four months seem like a party. Do you understand what I've said?"

He understood all right and he also sensed Hawkeye had chosen to leave something unsaid. For now, he only wanted to escape from this hellish place.

"I understand." He pulled the blanket around him. "All right, I give my pledge never to mention anything about myself to anyone. Can I go now?"

"Go where? You're an orphan. I can see to it that you are farmed out to foster care if you like, or I could offer you an alternative."

"Alternative?"

"You could work for me. You will get the very best training and although it will be hard, I believe you are sufficiently motivated to pass the tests. This is covert work requiring total dedication to the task. It will also be an opportunity for you to honor your family obligation."

"What would I be expected to do?"

"We can talk about the details later. You have a unique gift that could be very valuable to my organization, and in return for your service you will, on the odd occasion, get to kill some Pruessens. Interested?"

Killing Pruessens sounded like a very good way to spend the rest of his life. The temptation lasted only a moment. Nathan had given his father his pledge and that pledge would always have priority over his personal desires. He would never forget his father's words: *Nathan, if the worst should happen and you find yourself alone, seek out Caleb Penkovsky, on Kastoria. He's the best man I know. He can be trusted.*

"I would like to send a communication," Nathan said. "Is that possible?"

***

Spotiswood had given the boy two days to rebuild his strength and savor the richness of life. Nathan lay by the pool soaking up Arcadia's late spring sunshine. The commander stepped onto the patio and took a seat beside him. Nathan lay on his back, his eyes closed, his face relaxed.

"Good morning, Nathan."

He opened his eyes.

"Any word yet?" he asked.

"I told you not to expect a reply for at least a week. At this distance it may take longer." His communication to Kastoria was not what Spotiswood had hoped for.

Nathan examined him skeptically when he handed him the reader pad.

"What's this?"

"You need to read and thoroughly memorize every word."

Nathan's eyes dropped to the pad and he began reading.

Occasionally he would glance at Spotiswood with hatred. After ten minutes he tossed it back.

"All right, I've read it."

"Good. In about a week you will be interviewed by the news nets. They will ask you a great many questions and you will answer to the best of your ability." He held up the pad. "Using this information only."

Nathan snatched the pad back and scrolled through it.

"Bellinda was attacked by some unknown element, possibly northern pirates. My knowledge of the next six years is vague due to my injury. I was examined by doctors on the rehabilitation planetoid of Mylor," he stared at Spotiswood with hatred and disgust in equal measure, "who told me the blow to my head, probably caused during the attack, and my general trauma had caused amnesia. I recall being cast into slavery along with my immediate and extended family but to the best of my recollection this was done without the knowledge of the Pruessen government." He shook his head. "I recall us escaping and fleeing south. A ship, possibly a pirate, attacked Bellinda. I recall nothing after that until I awoke onboard an Athenian warship. Bellinda had been destroyed, my family lost and I alone survived in the rescue pod I was found in." He stared at Spotiswood, bewildered. "Why?" He looked as if he would vomit at any moment.

"Your father was right. If word of your experiences in the north was to emerge it would cause public outcry. It could lead to war with Pruessen."

"Good!"

"Athens will do anything to avoid war in the Quarantine Zone. That's the political reality, so get used to it."

"It's all a lie."

"Yes it is."

"I won't do it."

"You *will* do it, Nathan, or you'll spend the rest of your life on Mylor." *Oh, look at the fear on his face. That's got his attention.* "You'll grow old and never see the sky again. Never see a Pruessen, let alone kill one. And if Professor Knightsbridge had his way you won't last six months." Spotiswood gave him a moment to digest the horror story. He would not hesitate to honor his threat. There was more at stake than the concerns of a teenage boy.

"Do as you're told and you can live out your life in peace. Or war, if you prefer. What you do with your life is of no concern to me.

If you want to honor your pledge to your father you will do as I demand."

"You're a real prick, commander."

"Yes I am. Do you agree?"

Nathan lowered his head and nodded.

"I'll be keeping my eye on you. Make one slip, divulge one secret, and I'll know about it. I'll have you back on Mylor so fast it will make your head spin. Understood?"

Again he nodded.

Four days later the reply to Nathan's communication arrived.

CHAPTER 10

Date: 18th December, 311 (ASC)
Position: Penkovsky homestead, Mullally Province, Planet Kastoria, Athenian Colonial Space.
Status: Rehabilitation.

Caleb Penkovsky stood by the front door as the air-car touched down on the raised pad. For the first time in many a year he had butterflies in his stomach. *Nervous at my age? Well, why not? I'm about to become a father again.*

Bernice and the boy embarked from the craft and walked to the homestead entrance.

"Hello, wife." He hugged Bernie to him briefly. They would catch up later.

"Caleb," Bernie said, "this is Nathan."

"After all of those communications, it's good to finally meet you in person."

"Hello," Nathan said, his voice small, guarded.

He looked more nervous than Caleb felt. No, more than that. He was scared to death.

My God, what did those Pruessen bastards do to him?

"Welcome to Chez Penkovsky," Caleb said, guiding him through the front door. He felt Nathan squirm as he rested his hand gently on his shoulder. "I understand you're a big reader."

Nathan only nodded as he was ushered into the large, comfortable main room. His eyes took in the soft furnishings, thick colorful rugs underfoot, colors assailing his senses from every direction. He looked as if he'd never seen a room like this before.

"I like to read."

"Well then you're in luck," Caleb said. "I have a permanent link to the Orbital Space Dock, so you can access the net directly from Athens itself. With a week's delay, of course." He paused for a moment but when no response came he tried again. "We also have a cinema in town. It's an open-air set up, not as fancy as what they have within the Republic, but we get by."

Nathan's forehead creased.

"We were planning on going into town tomorrow night to take in the latest offering. Would you like that?"

"What should I call you?"

The sudden change of direction caught Caleb off guard, but he adjusted quickly. "Oh, you can call me handsome, smart, sophisticated, but don't call after hours." He grinned and Nathan returned the gesture with a tight smile. *Well, that's a start.*

"Since you're part of the family now you can call me Caleb"

"Caleb, I have never seen a vid, ah, movie before, but –"

Caleb's son jumped into the conversation without invitation. "Where did you come from? The core of the sun?"

"Lewis, behave yourself," Bernice snapped.

Lewis lounged indolently on the couch. Caleb could tell at a glance that the evil green monster had taken possession of his eldest child.

"Nathan, this is our son, Lewis," Bernie said.

Nathan offered his hand to Lewis and received a short, token response.

"Nice to meet you, Lewy," Nathan said.

"Don't call me that," the boy growled. "My name is Lewis, not Lewy, not Lew, Lewis. Got it, runt."

"Mind your manners, Lewis," Caleb warned. "Nathan is a member of this family and you will treat him with due respect, or I will be displeased. Got it?"

"Yes, father." Before turning away he shot Nathan a narrow-eyed look.

"Nathan, this is Lucilla," Bernice said.

Caleb considered Lucilla to favor her mother's side of the family as much as Lewis favored his father's.

"Hello Lucilla."

"Call me Lucy," she said, making a face at Lewis.

"Sure thing, Lucy." A short-lived smile.

Dinner moved along at a civilized pace with Lewis too sullen to make further nasty comments. Lucy badgered Nathan with questions until Bernice told her to mind her own business. Still, she was eleven years old. "Nathan?"

"Yes, Lucy."

"When you were a prisoner of the Pruessens, were you scared?"

"Lucilla Penkovsky!" her mother warned.

Caleb could barely believe it when a smile darted briefly onto Nathan's face. "It's all right, Bernie," he said, still struggling with his words. He sat for some moments apparently thinking things over.

"I don't remember much of it Lucy," he tapped the bump above his eyebrow, “but yes it was a difficult time." He passed his eyes over the Penkovskys, finally resting them on Caleb. "I'm very glad to be here."

Caleb nodded minutely.

After dinner, Lucy hugged Nathan and gave him a kiss on the cheek before dashing off to bed. Nathan blushed at her uninhibited show of affection.

A short time later Caleb showed him to his room and said goodnight. He stood by the door for only a few minutes before the sound of Nathan sleeping came to him.

***

The scream tore Nathan from a troubled sleep. He sprang upright in bed, bringing his knife to hand from under his pillow.

"What the frig was that?"

"Ricardo," Lucy said. As if it should be common knowledge to everyone she added, "Ricardo Rooster, Nathan."

Being scared to death by a farmyard animal embarrassed him no end. Now Lucy took an interest in his knife.

"Family heirloom," he said, by way of explanation.

"You sleep with it?"

He smiled while trying to think of how to explain to her exactly why he slept with a knife.

"It keeps away the boogie men."

"You said a bad word."

"Oh. Sorry."

"That's all right," she said bouncing to her feet. "Breakfast in ten minutes."

Nathan fell back onto his pillow and rubbed his face. *Right now Telford, no more acting like an idiot. These are good people, show a little respect.* With those thoughts firmly in mind he washed, changed into clean clothes and joined the family for breakfast. As he took a seat at the table he got the distinct impression that he and Caleb were underdressed. Lucy wore a frilly yellow dress, Lewis a simple but well-tailored suit and Bernice a smart pants suit, beneath her apron. She placed the stack of food before him.

"I hope you like pancakes," she said.

"So do I." He had only a vague memory of pancakes, but after the first delicious mouthful he remembered how much he missed them. His last taste had been nearly seven years ago.

Having attended to her family, Bernie sat down. As she ate she glanced at his casual clothing.

"If you look in your closet you will find a new suit."

"Thank you."

"If you hurry you will have time to change before church."

"Church?"

"Hello," Lewis cut in, "it's Sunday, you know."

"Thanks for that, Lew," Nathan said, ignoring Lewis' disagreeable reaction and keeping his eyes on Bernie.

"So, do you like the pancakes?" Bernie asked.

"Great." He tried his first tactic. "Is this church far away?"

"Taylor's Bend is only twenty kilometers away."

"Oh," Nathan said.

"Is something wrong, Nathan?" Bernie asked.

"I'm still pretty tired from the trip, Bernie," he said.

From the corner of his eye he saw Caleb pause with a fork halfway to his mouth. Bernie looked up, and after swallowing said, "I see."

Nathan sighed. *She does see.* "My family believed in that...religious...stuff. Right to the end they believed. I don't and I never will."

"Oh, for goodness sake. All you had to say was you don't want to go to church, Nathan," Bernie said. She looked at her husband who had his tongue tucked into a cheek. "You can stay here and burn with the other non-believer if that's what you want."

"What do you say Nathan," Caleb said. "Want to burn with a fellow heathen?"

"Sure."

"It could sting a bit from what I've heard."

"You get that," Nathan said, returning to the pancakes.

***

After breakfast Caleb showed Nathan around, introducing him to his chores and giving him a feel for the place. He showed him the harvesting machinery shed, the outbuildings and the comm. shack. Nathan seemed more interested in the sensor network than anything else but listened attentively to all he had to say. It pleased Caleb the way he took to his chores without complaint.

***

Caleb bumped into him in the kitchen and joined him for a cool drink.

"All done?"

"Yes."

"Good," he said. "How did you sleep last night?"

"Fine."

Caleb had checked on him during the night and knew he was lying.

"Feel like taking a walk?"

By the time they reached the ridge that marked the northern perimeter of the plantation, their clothes were sweat soaked. Nathan raised his face to the sun soaking up the warmth as if he had never felt its touch.

From two and a half kilometers away the high, sand-colored compound walls stood like a stark rectangle around the parched white bud of the main homestead building. Spiraling forks of coffee trees radiated out from the rectangle like broad, green spokes from a hub.

Moving to one of the nearby coffee trees, Caleb scooped a hand full of moist, black soil into his hand and sniffed it. Nathan followed his move without direction, wrinkling his nose at the slightly acidic scent.

"This is the reason my forebears settled on Kastoria," Caleb said. "This soil will grow anything, but combined with the generous rainfall, equatorial humidity and elevation that are unique to this region of Kastoria, it allows us to produce the finest coffee in any of the worlds of the Republic. It's difficult to imagine more perfect conditions for our type of crop."

He pointed to the northern escarpment. "Too high, up there." He pointed down to the low plains. "Too dry down there. But this is just right. That is why the niche markets in the capital pay top dollar for our product. And if they don't want the good stuff then they can drink that synthetic swill like everyone else."

Nathan nodded then focused his attention to the far end of the valley. Caleb handed him his spyglass.

"That's our nearest neighbors," he said. "The Okuma homestead. They have a daughter about your age. I think you'll like her."

Nathan spent time examining the entire valley before handing the spyglass back. Caleb held it for a few seconds before making his decision. "I understand you have a birthday coming up soon."

Nathan nodded. In a few weeks he would turn fourteen.

"Well then, you can consider this an early birthday present." He handed the spyglass back to Nathan. "Happy birthday."

Nathan's mouth opened but no sound came out. He shifted uncomfortably, his eyes downcast and mumbled a thank you.

"You'll find a few features on this that are not standard on commercial brands. I've had that since my days in the Marine Service, so I hope you'll take care of it."

“I will.” Nathan worked out most of the refinements and asked questions until he understood it all.

"Caleb," Nathan began slowly, "my father said you could be trusted."

"Your father always had remarkably good taste."

"You served together during the Cimmerian war."

Caleb nodded.

"What was it like?" Nathan asked.

"What was it like being a slave of the Empire?"

Nathan stood perfectly still for some time before answering. "You had to be there to understand it." Then the point struck home. "I see."

"Well here's something else to understand. You have not earned the right to ask me that question. Anyone who hasn't served in the military and come under fire doesn't rate an explanation."

"I’ll remember that.” He looked down and scuffed his foot in the soil. “I was just trying to understand the man my father was in those days."

"Lucas Telford was the finest man I have ever known. On the day I heard Bellinda had been lost, I wept, as I had not done since I was your age." He brushed the dirt from his hands. "I will tell you this much. We bled together. And during that time we gave one another a pledge. If one of us were to fall the other would take care of his family. Your father considered the possibility that you might be left alone if the worse that could happen, did happen. And so you are here because of my pledge."

"And mine."

Nathan's eyes wandered along the neatly furrowed lines of coffee trees to where the rain forest brushed up against the firebreak.

"I don't want you straying too far from the homestead Nathan," Caleb said. "There are a lot of dangerous animals outside the perimeter."

A short smirk darted onto Nathan’s face.

"I mean it, Nathan," Caleb snapped.

"All right, Caleb." Whatever he had experienced over the last seven years, the dangers of the rain forest held no fears for him.

"Will you show me the rain forest?"

Caleb nodded, forced down his frustration, and took hold of his rifle that hung from a shoulder strap. Nathan had been eyeing the firearm since they left the homestead.

“Do you know what this is?” he asked, brandishing the rifle.

“I’ve seen an image somewhere, but no.”

“This, young man, is a seven point six, two millimeter caliber, bolt action, repeating rifle. It fires a lead projectile powered by exploding gas."

"It's really old, isn't it?"

Caleb nodded.

"Where did you get it?"

"Abner Lawrence introduced me to it some years ago. He's an old friend of mine, a former marine. You'll like him. Anyway, Abner has a friend who makes them to order. Mainly for collectors and the like but occasionally for people who simply like its brutal simplicity. If you want to see how it works you can join us next time we go hunting. If that appeals to you."

"It does."

Crossing the dusty hundred-meter-wide firebreak, they followed the track under the canopy of the rain forest. Caleb stopped to give his eyes time to adjust to the relative gloom. Nathan stood with his head cocked to one side, sniffing the fresh moist odors, listening intently to the silence that accompanied their entry into the overhang. He looked like someone who had just returned home after a long absence.

Caleb shifted the hunting rifle in his hands, alert for any sound or movement, and followed as Nathan ventured deeper into the vegetation.

They continued along the track for nearly half an hour, exchanging only brief comments. After stopping to examine several types of dry wood, Nathan found a piece that conjured a smile. Caleb looked on as he propped one end into the firm soil and bent the other end toward him.

Nathan was obviously satisfied with his unusual find. "Caleb, do you have any woodworking tools in your workshop?"

CHAPTER 11

Time: 10th February, 312 ASC.
Position: Taylor's Bend, Mullally Province. Planet Kastoria.
Status: Settling in.

Moe Okuma's family had been neighbors with the Penkovskys for as long as she could remember. Of course, to her that had only been fourteen years, but the feeling of fond permanency comforted her. Within an environment like the isolated provinces of Kastoria, your nearest neighbors, even if they lived twenty kilometers away, could mean the difference between life and death. The Okumas and the Penkovskys were close not just as neighbors or allies, but like an extended family. Life in the provinces differed significantly from that of those who dwelt within the safety of the larger towns and cities. People of the land tended to have a more unwavering affinity with one another.

The newest addition to the Penkovsky homestead sat, as he usually did at this time of the day, under the huge plocker tree that grew at the north end of the Taylor's Bend High School. The droopy green tree spread its branches across the small knoll that overlooked the curve in the Arbicore River on which the township of Taylor's Bend snuggled.

Lunchtime at the school usually involved the speedy consumption of food, followed by as much fun as could be squeezed into the remaining time. Apparently, Nathan Telford's idea of fun consisted of isolating himself from the rest of the students to sit under the tree reading. Alone.

Moe had met him twice prior to the commencement of the new school year, once at her parent's place and once at the Penkovsky homestead. Visits between the neighboring families were all too rare and everyone looked forward to such occasions, making a celebration of each get together.

After dinner at the Penkovsky's, Caleb showed a selection from his vid collection, an event that she always looked forward to. Try as she might to avoid doing so, the antics of Laurel and Hardy always made her giggle like a girl, which embarrassed her no end. She found herself falling into uncontrollable fits of laughter whenever the larger one addressed the long skinny one with such condescension. The words, 'Well Stanley, here's another fine mess you've gotten us into,' caused her to shriek in a shamefully girlish way. She loved her visits to the Penkovskys.

The two times she had met Nathan he had displayed an extremely closed-mouthed attitude. When he did speak he did not seem shy, but kept his comments to a minimum. He seemed unusually nervous around her, yet showed no such reticent around Lucy. Then again, boys had always been a mystery to her. She tried to talk to him but he seemed unwilling to make up the other half of the conversation. Moe began to wonder if there was something about her that he did not like.

By the end of the first week at school, Moe came to understand that his wary attitude had not been directed exclusively at her. He appeared to be incapable of communicating with the other students and his guarded attitude kept him in a state of perpetual uneasiness around them.

A few of the local girls had said “Hi Nathan,” then giggled at his awkwardness. Some of the boys had tried speaking to him as well. His reply wasn’t unfriendly, just typically brief.

Moe surmised that being new to the school, and to the province, he probably felt like an outsider. He knew no one but his newly acquired family, with whom he still struggled to get past an arm’s-length relationship. Then there was the trifling matter of *Bellinda* and six years of Pruessen slavery to consider.

In class, Nathan never asked questions or for that matter ever volunteered to answer them. If he was called upon to answer a question he would do so, and usually his answer would be correct. On the odd occasions when he gave a wrong answer, Moe suspected that he did so deliberately. Why he would do such a thing baffled her.

Although taciturn, he seemed friendly enough, but any attempt to continue a conversation with him took on all the difficulties of home dentistry. Yet, she had never met a boy quite like him. Moe feared that she could be suffering from the terrifying effects of her first crush. He, on the other hand, probably didn't know she existed, even though they sat next to one another in class.

Moe burned to understand this strange, bright boy, and so had decided that today would be as good a time as any to start. She steeled herself as she marched up to the tree under which he sat.

"Hi," she said.

Nathan looked up from his pad and smiled gently. "Hello, Moe."

At their first meeting her mother introduced her by using her given names, Mary Anne. Moe detested that her parents had chosen to lumber her with such a girlie name. It had taken only a short time for her to rid him of that nasty habit. After that initial time, he never called her anything but Moe. Just as well if he wanted to stay healthy. Yet, it turned out to be another beginning that went nowhere.

"Hi," she repeated, feeling a little foolish. "Ah, what are you reading?" He handed her the computer pad and she tapped up the title of the novel. "The Odyssey? I've never read Homer, what's it about?"

"It's about a man who gets lost on his way home," Nathan said. "He has to endure many battles and overcome great opposition, but when he finally arrives back at his home he kills everyone who has dishonored his family." His eyes stared off-world for a moment. "He believed in honoring his family obligation."

"Charming," Moe said, handing the pad back to him. She franticly groped for something to fill the silence between them. "Not exactly Laurel and Hardy."

"Who?"

Fighting against her growing frustration and imminent meltdown, Moe pushed on. "I think it would all be Greek to me anyway." Her smile faded. He just sat there, evidently unsure whether to laugh or cry. Still he had nothing to say.

He made her feel like an idiot rather than the naturally likeable person she cared to think of herself as. His attitude infuriated her to the point where her infamous temper took over.

"That's a joke you know?" she snapped. "Don't you have a sense of humor? Or is it that you're too good to mix with the rest of us."

His eyebrows came together above his nose. He rubbed the bump that marred the perfect line of his right eyebrow. Several times he glanced at her, sizing up whether or not he should continue. His beautiful gray eyes took on a shade of pained confusion. He drew in a deep breath.

"I've been out of touch with things for a while. You know?"

He held her gaze for a moment before looking away. Shame forced her to do the same. When he actually decided to say something he certainly made it count. In that poignant moment of realization she felt as though a wild boar had gored her in the stomach.

Moe wanted to ask him a thousand questions so that she could, in some small way, begin to understand the kind of existence he had led that brought him to this place in life. However, Bernice and

Caleb had been unequivocal on that subject. Moe had been told to treat the subject of his past with the greatest delicacy. Old wounds, she had been told, should not be reopened.

She knew about *Bellinda* of course, and could only imagine in her worst nightmares how terrible it must have been for him. Yet for the first time it struck her as more than a speculative exercise. He carried the nightmare with him every waking day. She could not imagine what it would be like to lose your entire family. However, she suspected that something else lurked in his past, some terrible story of loss and suffering. Something had happened to him, leaving him in his current condition. Confused, solitary and cautious.

They sat for a time without exchanging a word and in that silent place of their own making grew the beginning of a unique understanding between them.

"It must have been bad, ah, in the north."

He nodded thoughtfully then caught himself. "I don't remember much."

"Well you don't need to worry. I'll protect you." She smiled and was rewarded by a return gesture.

"Thank you very much, Moe. I'll sleep easy knowing you're growling at the foot of my bed."

Moe laughed and another miracle happened. He did too.

They exchanged other fleeting comments throughout the rest of the da but within that reticent context the first tenuous strands of friendship were born.

Moe learned that his closed-mouthed attitude did not fully reflect his true intent. He simply chose to speak only when he had something to say. Considering the amount of rubbish Moe heard from people, she could not argue with his approach. He did not feel the need to fill the silent times between his words with inane chatter. Once she got used to the unaccustomed silence it actually felt pretty comfortable.

By the end of the school day she had decided that Moe Okuma and Nathan Telford were going to become genuine friends. Even if it killed him.

After class, she followed him out the front gate to where the waiting air-cars gathered in herds to chauffeur the students to their homes. Lucy ran up to Nathan and gave him a long hug. He brushed a curly brown tassel from her eyes.

"Did you have a good day, Lucy?"

"It was all right, I guess. How about you."

Around a soft smile he said, “Better than yesterday.”

“You’re funny sometimes.”

“Funny ha-ha or funny odd.”

“Both.” She giggled.

Nathan snorted and tussled her curly hair. They may as well have been siblings. What a change.

Moe stood back while they went through the big brother, little sister ritual. As he took her hand and began to walk toward the parking area, Moe took her chance.

"Nathan," she called.

He swung around with an awkward jerky movement then smiled openly. "Hello Moe." They had come to an understanding of sorts during the day and it showed in his moderately relaxed manner. "Is this where you beat me up after school?"

"What? No. Of course not."

His mouth formed a wry curved line. Moe rolled her eyes.

"Can I have a word with you?" she asked.

He nodded.

"You're pretty good at history and I'm struggling with that assignment on political turmoil in the early twenty-first century. So I was hoping you might help me out with it."

"I don't see a problem with that," he said. "When did you have in mind?"

"Now." She saw the uncertainty in his eyes. "And after we finish, my brother will fly you home."

He considered the proposal for a moment then nodded.

"Good," she said breaking into a grin. "And because nothing is for nothing, if you help me with history, I'll teach you how to have fun."

"An historic event in itself," he said returning her grin.

He turned around and leaned down. "Lucy, I'm going over to the Okumas. Tell your mother that I will be in by dinner time. All right?"

"Will you help me with my homework when you get home?"

"You bet."

"What will I tell mother if she asks what you're doing?"

"Tell her that I'm...having fun."

CHAPTER 12

Time: 22nd June, 312 ASC.
Position: Penkovsky Homestead, Mullally Province. Planet Kastoria.
Status: Hunting for clarity.

Moe stepped from the landing pad as her brother took the craft up and back home. She shifted her light pack on her shoulder and strode to where Caleb and Abner stood by the front verandah.

"Mornin' Moe," Caleb said.

"Mornin'. And to you too Abner."

"Yeah," Abner said.

Abner Lawrence, Calebs best friend, a born marine, a man not to be trifled with. But not a big talker.

Nathan stepped onto the porch. Bernie snatched a speck from the shoulder of his shirt.

"Nathan, dear, you be careful today. For me, all right."

Bernie should know better. That sort of open affection only embarrassed him.

"Yeah, all right." He let her give him a peck on the cheek then joined the others.

He forced a tight smile and nodded.

"What's that?" Abner asked, staring at Nathan's weapon of choice.

"That my old friend," Caleb said, "is a bow."

Abner shook his head.

"He bagged two hares with it, just last week. Nearly four kilos each."

"We're not hunting bunnies." He cast another disapproving eye onto Nathan's weapon.

Caleb carried one of the projectile weapons, Moe a standard pulsar rifle.

"All right you two, listen up," Caleb said. "This is Abner's show. He has the contract to remove the rogue, so he calls the shots. You do what he says when he says. Got it?"

"Yep," said in chorus.

Caleb nodded to his friend.

"Let's go. You two, stay close."

Moe looked at Nathan and rolled her eyes. A shrug of the shoulder was his response.

He's been in the province for six months. I've had four of those to humanize him but he's still not a big talker. Oh well, baby steps.

A hard twenty-minute slog brought them to the firebreak between the plantation and the tree line.

"Our beastie was last seen heading in this direction through the rain forest," Caleb said. "So we'll head on in and look for signs."

Abner nodded.

"Like buffalo shit," Moe ventured.

"Scat," Abner corrected.

"Pay close attention to Abner," Caleb said around a growing smile. "He's an expert when it comes to shit."

As the three of them laughed Abner shook his head. Just the trace of a shortly formed smile darted onto his face. They moved under the forest canopy, the relative coolness drying the sweat on bodies. They headed roughly north. After an hour Abner found scat. Moe pulled a face when he dug his hand into it. He sniffed his finger.

"About two hours old."

Out of the corner of her eye Moe caught Nathan tense. He nocked an arrow onto his bowstring, turned, aimed at Abner and fired.

The arrow passed dangerously close to Abner's ear before striking the snake in the head. The reptile squirmed, uncoiled from the branch and dropped from the tree onto Abner's shoulder. He cried out, and jumped about brushing the snake away.

"Fucking snakes. I hate fucking snakes." He shuddered.

Abner was beyond a doubt the toughest individual Moe had ever met. His display of emotion shocked her.

Everyone stared at him. He composed himself. "I don't like snakes, that's all."

Caleb stood up from examining the dead reptile. "Take a look."

Abner eyed the snake, his lip curling. "Shit. Tree viper."

"Well?" Caleb motioned his friend to Nathan.

"Ah, thanks kid."

Nathan held up his bow and raised his eyebrows.

Moe laughed and this time even Abner joined in.

How did Nathan spot the snake? More questions for my list.

"You know my friend," Caleb said, "in some societies if someone saves your life you have to be their slave."

"Funny." Abner did not seem amused.

They continued to track the beast for the better part of the day, finding a track here, some scat there. Leaving the forest behind they stepped onto the baked lower plains. And there it was. The Kastorian plains buffalo that had been causing havoc to plantations for weeks. He'd gotten a taste for the sweet green leaves on the vines and would return again.

"Lord, he's a big bugger," Caleb said. "Look at the spread on those horns. Got to weigh in at three tonnes."

"Closer to four," Abner said.

An after-effect of the ancient war fought within Tunguska, the animal populations on many planets grew monstrously large. Including the introduced species.

The buffalo's territorial dominance was threatened by the newcomers. His head went down, he kicked at the loose soil with a hoof and bellowed a loud warning.

Abner cocked his rifle, stepped forward and stopped.

"Come here, youngster."

Nathan stood beside him.

"You think you can hit him with your bow?"

"Hard to miss," Nathan said.

"Yeah, but you have to hit him in a soft part. These critters are as tough as battle armor."

Another bellow made Moe jump.

"I'll try," Nathan said, and nocked an arrow.

One last bellow and the buffalo charged. Nathan waited with his bow arm down waiting for the range to close. And waited.

Shit.

Finally he raised the bow, paused for only a second and loosed the arrow. It dug into the cheek under the left eye. The beast kept coming.

Abner aimed and fired. The buffalo's head snapped back as the bullet struck him between the eyes. The 12.5-caliber shell had a two hundred grain charge behind it. He collapsed to the ground sending up a cloud of dust.

Nathan walked over to the fallen beast and laid his hand respectfully on his head. He retrieved his arrow, cleaned the blood off in the soil and returned it to his quiver.

Abner showed the same respect then stood and placed his hand on Nathan's shoulder.

"Nice try. Keep practicing."

A compliment from Abner came as often as a solar eclipse. Nathan's fleeting smile said he knew as much.

Abner pulled his enormous hunting knife and knelt down beside the fallen beast.

He looked up at Nathan. "Do you want an ear?"

"What?"

"An ear. As a memento."

"Ah, no thanks." Nathan eyed Abner's weapon. "Will you let me fire it?"

Abner chambered a round and handed the rifle over. Nathan pointed the barrel to the ground and felt the weight. Not too much for a skinny fourteen-year-old. He brought it to his shoulder and aimed down the sights. He did that three times, getting a feel for it.

"Safety?"

Abner snorted. "Off."

Nathan turned to face a large rock that stood a good hundred meters away. He raised the weapon.

"Anchor yourself or the recoil will drop you on your arse. Here, dig the butt into your shoulder."

He showed Nathan how to position his feet, angle his body to absorb the brutal recoil. Satisfied he stepped back.

Nathan raised the weapon, sighted and fired. The shot went slightly wide of the rock. He muttered something Moe suspected was rude.

Handing the gun back he said, "Thanks, Abner."

"You are welcome, Nathan."

He rejoined Moe. "How's the shoulder."

"Still there."

"It's got quite the kick, hasn't it?"

"Hmm."

One thing she knew for certain about her new friend. He did not like losing.

She would continue his education and bring him out of himself no matter how much he resisted her efforts. What more would she learn about him in the future?

CHAPTER 13

Time: 6th January, 314 ASC.
Position: Port Cranbourne. Planet Kastoria.
Status: Moving on.

The city of Port Cranbourne stood at the mouth of the Zamesta River, on the shores of the muddy waters of the Bay of Sorrows. The capital of Kastoria, it was the commercial and administrative hub of the system. It contained the largest concentration of people on the planet, boasting a permanent population of just over a million people. Essentially Kastoria had developed into a world of widely dispersed farming communities with the bulk of the population spread thinly across its two main continents. As such, Port Cranbourne also had the distinction of being the only place on the southern continent with the facilities to educate students to a senior high school level. From all points on the continent's geographical map junior high school graduates flooded into the port to complete their education.

For Moe the day began as any other day in the eighteen months since moving south. Up just before dawn to join Nathan for the first of his exercise workouts. A leisurely ten click run from the dorms down to the bay and back. Nathan always pushed her to go faster so she pushed back. It worked well for both of them.

"I never thought I'd say it," she said, having caught her second wind, "but I actually miss Taylor's Bend."

"I know what you mean," Nathan said. "I miss my family."

"What?"

"Wadda ya mean, what?"

"That's the first time you've called the Penkovskys your family."

"No, I do it all the time."

"Buffalo shit."

He chuckled and managed to shrug while maintaining his pace.

Another breakthrough but not the first Moe had seen come over her friend in the last year and a half.

"Hey, remember our first day at school here?"

He smiled. "Yeah."

"I was scared to death."

"Not me."

"Once again, my friend, buffalo shit."

"Hmm, first time away from home had all of the kids a little rattled."

"Yeah, some of them had a really hard time fitting in."

"Hmm."

Yeah, he's not going to bite.

Even for Moe, entering this new world of adolescent politics held traps and terrors to freeze the heart. She observed in silent awe and heartbreaking admiration as Nathan struggled to overcome his natural reserve.

She had witnessed his remarkable growth over that time from a wary, reticent boy into a confident, mature young man. He had taken his lumps and pushed through, driven by an inner demon that refused to be cowered.

"I'm taking in the new exhibit at the museum after last class," Nathan said. "You want to come?"

"Ha. Soak up the rich diversity and fresh ideas of the city?"

"It's only an exhibition, Moe. You should open your mind to new experiences."

"You know what I told you, last time you said that."

"Ah, yeah. And if I recall, I told you that it was physically impossible."

They both chuckled. As the dorm came into view Nathan took off at a sprint.

For Moe and Nathan the pace of life at Cranbourne quickened with their growing maturity, the full, rich sweetness of life filling them with wondrous aspirations for the future.

***

Olivia Marshall spent her first day at Julia Bryant Senior High School in a self-absorbed state of misery. How could her parents have done this to her? All of her friends were on Athens along with her well-planned hopes for the future. Then out of the blue her father had been assigned to this primitive back world to replace the retiring Governor. Of all the damnable bad luck that could befall a girl. Olivia tried to comfort herself with probably the oldest dirge known to the human race.

Why me?

The Anastasia Kimbrough Academy for Young Ladies had been her home since her tenth year. The Academy accepted only the children of privilege from families of note, holding them to its nurturing bosom whilst studiously preparing them for a bright future within the highest echelons of Republican society.

Now, thanks to her parents, her well-planned future lay in ruins.

Bad enough for her to be marooned on this world far from civilization and friends, but to be put in with the general school population. Intolerable. The Kastorians frightened her, their dry, brash behavior setting her nerves on edge. They knew nothing of political correctness or polite reserve.

Olivia entered the classroom with her head held high, in the manner of a true Republican. She held her broad-brimmed hat in both hands to stop them from shaking. The swish of her long stylish dress against the floor made a few of the girls pay attention. Her heart raced as she struggled to maintain her poise.

Her introduction to the nightmare began with the teacher. She could not imagine how this colonial had been granted a teaching certificate. A thin young woman with long, dark brown hair, stood before the class. She turned and smiled as Olivia stepped into the room.

"You must be Olivia," she said. Olivia maintained her poise and offered her credentials that contained her transfer records from the Anastasia Kimbrough Academy for Young Ladies. The teacher glanced at them. "Good old AKA." She seemed unusually amused with Olivia's stunned reaction, but moved on rapidly. "I'm Elenora Duprea," she said. Not Miss Duprea, mind you, but Elenora. Then she touched her on the shoulder to turn her around to face the class. This would be an unforgivable faux pas within the better circles of Athenian society. .

"Ladies and gentlemen," she said, "we have someone new joining our class today. This is Olivia Marshall who has just arrived from the Republic."

The range of expressions varied immensely amongst the thirty-odd students. Some smiled with irritating indulgence, some grimaced, one leered and two of them sitting side by side at the back of the class exchanged knowing looks. That annoyed her more than anything else. These barbarians dared to think they knew something about her. Such presumption would earn them a good thrashing back home.

"I would like everyone to make her feel welcome," Elenora continued. "Most of you are aware of what it's like to arrive at this school as strangers. So please, show Olivia the same courtesy that you were shown when you first came here."

"My first day here a group of seniors gave me a wedgy in the middle of the quadrangle," one of the boys said. The class broke into open laughter, including the teacher. Unbelievable.

"Well I certainly hope you will treat Olivia with a little more respect than that," the teacher said, and again touched her on the shoulder. "Take a seat, Olivia."

She looked around the classroom and saw three empty seats. "Where?" she asked feeling as if she wanted to find somewhere dark to hide.

"Anywhere you like."

Incredible. Back at the Academy everyone had their place set out. 'A place for everyone and everyone in their place'. Olivia looked at the available seating and her eyes widened in horror. A particularly large boy, the one with the leer apparently stuck to his chubby face, patted his broad thigh and beckoned her on. Could he mean? No, surely not. Her startled expression only fed the insanity. The entire class roared with laughter as she stood frozen with disbelief.

"Jonathan!" the teacher warned. "Olivia, sit there," she said, pointing to the spare seat at the back of the room.

Olivia scurried to the seat, next to the girl with the lopsided smile, keeping her eyes averted from the rest of the class. The lesson commenced and for the next two hours she kept her head down, until the period ended and the bell sounded for recess. She stayed in place as the students filed out like the disorderly rabble that they were. When the cacophony ceased, she raised her eyes to find two of the colonials standing before her. The same two, both with amused expressions on their faces.

"Welcome to Kastoria." Moderately shorter than the boy and of slight but robust build, her lethargic colonial accent failed to cover the toughness that lurked behind her open smile. Her almond-shaped eyes had a twinkle in them that made the light hazel color shine with mischief from her chocolate-tanned face. "I'm Moe Okuma, and this troublemaker," she hooked a thumb over her shoulder at the boy, is Nathan Telford."

Olivia stared at the strange duo, caught in a paralysis of indecision. She did not wish to encourage any of these people, for she could not be sure if they intended to do her harm. She just wanted to run home and beg her mother to let her flee back to Athens, back to safety.

The girl, Moe, glanced over her shoulder and snorted softly at the ridiculously wry expression that greeted her. The boy had obviously been involved in some type of nefarious activity in recent times. His left arm hung in a loose, old-fashioned sling, bandaged to the fingers. His face bore abrasions and bruises, and a soft bandage covered a spot on the back of his head. Still, he did have a certain ...

"Perhaps you need to speak slowly," the boy drawled. "Republicans aren't all that bright."

"I understand you, colonial," she spat through set teeth. Olivia immediately regretted her outburst, noticing for the first time that the room contained only the three of them. No sounds came from the outside corridor. "If you dare to touch me I will have my father punish you in the most severe manner imaginable. He is the new Governor, you know," she added with menace. She assumed that fact alone should be sufficient to put these colonials in their place.

A quizzical expression covered Moe's face that was both curious and sadly amused at the same time. The boy, Nathan, began to chuckle. His eyes never left hers even though his head shook slowly. Olivia's blood boiled.

"Don't laugh at me you ... you ..."

"Colonial barbarian?" Nathan offered. That started the other one laughing.

Both of them laughing at her now. Her chest began to heave with fury at this unbearable outrage. "Don't laugh at me!" Her scream sounded oddly petulant, which surprised her.

"Then stop acting like an obnoxious core borer," Moe said. "If you weren't such a twit, and gave us a chance to talk, you'd have found out that we were only going to offer to show you around. You know, like where the cafeteria is, for example." She stared at Olivia with a mixture of contempt and pity."You know, we don't actually eat people out here in the colonies. Do we Nathan?" she asked without turning around.

"Not recently," he said, showing the same look of pity.

Pity! Now on top of everything else these colonials were showing her pity. Her anger had grown to a level where she dared not speak.

Moe stepped back from her table and looked at her friend. "It would seem that our welcoming committee of two is not appreciated." She shook her head again and turned to leave. "Let's go Nathan." He stood in place, his soft gaze locked onto her.

"I'll be along in a minute." His voice held no trace of bitterness or anger. Moe grunted disagreeably and left her alone with him.

Olivia should have been terrified of him, a rough colonial oaf covered in bandages. She could detect nothing in the way of malice in his beautiful gray eyes. On the contrary, his quiet manner had a decidedly calming effect on her.

He sat down on the table in front of her and put his feet on the chair, resting his forearms on his knees. "First day at a new school can be rough," he said. "I was not quiet fourteen when I first arrived on Kastoria, and I was pretty nervous about the whole thing." A shadow passed over his eyes. "Unlike you, I didn't have my family with me, which made it doubly nerve racking. But I adjusted to life here, and so can you. Kastorians are as fine a people as you will find anywhere. They are generally a warm and friendly people ready to give any newcomer a fair go. All we ask in return is a modicum of good manners."

He had been doing remarkably well up till that point. "Are you suggesting that I lack good manners?" Olivia said narrowing her eyes.

"Two people just tried to help you fit in around here and you spat on us for our efforts. You don't know anything about us and vice versa, but we have an old tradition out here in the colonies, that when someone offers you the hand of friendship you don't slap it away. On Kastoria that sort of behavior is generally considered to be ill- mannered."

He stood and strolled from the class room without another word, leaving her stunned and ambivalent.

What just happened? Had a colonial lectured her on good manners?

Although Olivia wanted, more than anything, to flee from this place to the safety of her home, she forced herself to remain and complete the rest of the school day. She spoke to no one and no one spoke to her. During the lunch break she sought refuge in the library and locked herself into a computer booth. Many of the students stared at her as she marched with stiff formality through the corridors, transiting between classes.

As the relentless day crawled on Olivia began to wonder if she had, in fact, been rude to Nathan and his friend. She detested bad manners and could not believe that she had been guilty of such a crime. Throughout the afternoon she heard nothing that the teachers said. Her mind reran the incident with the two colonials over and over. Had she been so scared of the unknown that she acted poorly?

It turned out to be the longest day of her life and when the final bell rang she ran from the classroom and fled down the stairs till she found herself alone in the front quadrangle where she sought out a shady alcove and wept. Her outburst lasted only a minute and she regained her control as the sound of stampeding feet grew.

***

Moe and Nathan walked casually down the front steps of the school and onto the quadrangle. The quad had for years been the traditional after-school meeting place for cliques of teenagers to discuss the day's events. Since recess, Nathan had slipped into one of his more reticent moods. Moe had a suspicion as to what might be on his mind and chose to confront the issue in her usual subtle way.

"So, did you have a nice talk with your little Athenian girlfriend?"

He shot her an amusingly dangerous look but said nothing.

He had never appreciated her attempts to make him out to be the great lothario of the school. He did not chase girls and appeared to be continually surprised - and at times a little embarrassed - by the attention paid to him by the mature Kastorian teenage girls.

Moe slapped him playfully on his good shoulder. "What's up, Nate?" Again, he just shook his head in that way that meant that he wasn't in the mood to discuss it.

Moe knew that he must be in a degree of discomfort after his hunting accident. Even with a broken arm, cracked ribs and lacerations from head to toe, Nathan had never been the sort of person to consult a doctor for pain relief. It appeared that something else prayed on his mind other than his injuries. Then, without warning, the gentleness returned to his eyes.

Olivia Marshal waited at the bottom of the steps leading from the quadrangle, her head held high in the tradition of an upper class Athenian. Her expression betrayed by the slight drooping of her shoulders. As they approached, she stepped in front of them. Placing her right hand over her heart, she bowed slightly from the waist in the traditional Athenian greeting. The quadrangle had never seen such a display and all sound and movement faded away.

Nathan returned the gesture and that must have really smarted with his ribs in their condition. Moe didn't know he could do that.

"I beseech you Burgess Telford, a word with you if I might," she said and then as an afterthought noticed Moe. "And you too, of course, Burgess Okuma." Moe resisted the urge to attempt the bow and held back the laugh that threatened to have Nathan at her throat.

His focus remained locked onto Olivia with an intensity that Moe had never seen from him with any other girl. She supposed that Olivia may be a snotty nosed, upper-class Republican cow, but with those wide, light brown eyes set into a fine-boned alabaster face, some people might consider her attractive. On the other hand, her pompous Athenian accent made Moe's skin crawl. Nathan didn't seem to notice.

"Earlier today," she began, brushing a mass of fine chestnut hair from her face, "when you approached me, it is possible that I may have misinterpreted your intentions." Her eyes dropped for just an instant then returned to Nathan. "I abhor poor manners and if I have judged you harshly, and displayed such bad manners, I wish to offer my sincerest apologies."

A comfortable smile settled onto Nathan's face as their eyes locked onto one another. Although both of them were included in her apology, Moe suspected that she no longer existed within the same universe as these two. She cleared her throat breaking the spell. Nathan blinked awkwardly before returning to the world of the living.

"I bet that must have taken a lot for you say."

Olivia shrugged.

"Apology accepted."

"That goes for me too," Moe added, rolling her eyes skyward.

"Thank you, Burgess Okuma," Olivia said, sparing her the briefest moment of eye contact.

"Olivia," Moe said. "You're in the colonies now so you might as well get used to how things are from the start. Isn't that right Nathan. Nathan?"

"Ah, yes," he said. "Moe has a point. Unless you're planning on leaving sometime today?"

"No, I am stuck on this...world, until graduation."

"How tragic for you," Moe said, maintaining a straight face.

He shot Moe a quick nasty look that Olivia missed.

"I guess you'll just have to make the best of things," Nathan suggested.

"Yes, I expect you are correct," she said. They continued to stare at one another silently until she finally groped for something to say. "Burgess Tel..." he held up a single finger. "Nathan, may I ask what happened to you?" she asked running her eyes over his damaged body.

"Hunting accident."

She nodded without speaking, so Moe took the opportunity.

"Yes, Nathan is one of the best hunters in the province." She kept her voice light although the guilt still stung her. If she hadn't broken cover too soon and spooked the buck, Nathan would not have been caught out of position. "Until that big buck got the better of him."

"Buck?"

"It's sort of a deer," Nathan said.

"A deer?" For the first time that day, she smiled without reserve. Naturally, her teeth were two perfect, straight white rows. "A *deer* did all that to you?" She held a hand to her mouth to contain a soundless giggle.

Nathan shrugged his good shoulder.

"The mighty hunter was bushwhacked by a three hundred kilogram stag," Moe said. "He was quite frisky, even for this time of the year."

She granted Moe the privilege of looking at her while she spoke but then turned a questioning eye on Nathan.

"Mating season." Moe had never seen such a lewd expression on her friend's face.

Olivia blushed, coyly. "Oh, I see."

The area around them had thinned out since their arrival, with students going about their after-school activities. However, a lone figure, who had been lurking at the periphery of their conversation, stepped forward.

"Burgess Marshall." The voice held a ridiculously deep note coming from a sixteen-year-old. Olivia started, then struggled to suppress a shudder as she recognized the owner of the voice.

"Burgess Sizemore," Jonathan said in introduction. He attempted to emulate the bow that Nathan had made look so easy but couldn't quite pull it off.

From the look on her face, Olivia recognized him as the one who had enticed her to sit on his knee during class. A blind man could tell that he should really have left it at that. As with many overly large young men, he considered that his physicality would be the salient factor in any attempted courtship. Considering his lack of success with the local girls, he should have given up by now, but stubbornly continued to believe himself to be in the same league with Nathan.

More in an attempt to court favor with Olivia than any other reason, he acknowledged her companions. "Okmunga, Tenfold," he said shortly.

"Sizeless," Moe replied.

Jonathan took note of Nathan's physical condition and that bolstered his confidence. "Burgess Marshall," he said, using the formal title only used in the Republic, "I was wondering if you would care to join me for refreshments at the campus coffee house. As my guest of course."

"That is very kind of you Burg..." Nathan cleared his throat. "Thank you, Jonathan, but I have another engagement." Her Athenian upbringing and regard for good manners would not allow her to tell him the truth. Her polite white lie came into conflict with the unofficial Athenian mandate of never telling a lie. Truth after all, had set Athens free and elevated her above the rest of humanity. That conflict caused her to be a terrible liar and Jonathan immediately saw through her sham.

A great sulking scowl covered his face. "So, you Athenians too good to sit down with us colonials aye?" he growled.

Nathan appeared beside her. He had removed his arm from the sling and it hung at his side. A typically gutsy move from Nathan. There was no way he could use the damaged arm no matter how much he might want to. Of course, Jonathan did not know that.

"She's having coffee with us, Jonathan." Although he made his tone conversational, the sparkling blue flecks in his eyes transmitted a different meaning. The two of them had history. After a few seconds Jonathan reconsidered his position. His large shoulders drooped as if supporting a weighty load.

"My apologies Burgess Marshall," he mumbled.

"Your apology is accepted," she said. "And please, call me Olivia." She looked back at Nathan. "I believe that you were going to show me around?"

Nathan grinned. "Yes indeed, Olivia," he said, then remembered his best friend. "Ready to go, Moe?"

"I've got things to do." From experience Moe knew when she became a fifth wheel. "I'll catch up with you later." She received no argument from either of them as they walked off together.

Jonathan scowled after them. "What's he got that I haven't," he moaned.

"Her." It was a thoroughly ancient line, but Moe suspected that it held more than a grain of truth. She considered it odd that such a realization would make her feel so sad.

CHAPTER 14

Time: 22nd December, 315 (ASC).
Position: Penkovsky homestead. Mullally province. Planet Kastoria.

Nathan gazed through the window to where the sun spilled down the valley. The undulating spirals of coffee trees came to life as the light glanced off the early morning dew clinging to the leaves.

He could scarcely believe how much he had changed the last three years. Over that time, slowly, with times of painful lessons learned he had come out of his shell. He could never forget the past but he could concentrate more of his attention on the future. Then there was Livy. *I never sought her out, I tried to dismiss her as I'd dismissed so many others, but despite my best efforts she won my heart. Thank goodness.*

A thought popped into his head unbidden. It surprised him but also brought a smile to his face. "I'm happy," he whispered to the waiting valley.

He hung his weapons webbing across his shoulder and reached for his bow.

"The mighty hunter of the Kastorian rain forest." Livy returned from the bathroom and ran her eyes across his taut body. "I suppose I could do worse." She rested her hands on his chest and kissed him deeply.

Nathan's head swam, as it always did when she was close. "You take my breath away," he whispered into her ear.

Livy rested her head on his shoulder. "When do you think you'll be back?"

He stroked her thick chestnut hair. "Why darlin', you used another contraction. We'll have you sounding like a colonial in no time."

She beat playfully on his chest and giggled. "When?"

"Hard to say. If we get lucky we might be back by lunch, but I wouldn't make plans."

"Already have. Bernie, Lucy and I are going into town after lunch. There are a few things we have to pick up for the celebration."

"Ah yes, the New Horizons night." Nathan lowered his voice and quoted, "With graduation behind us the hopeful future beckons."

"I hope it's half as good as last year's."

"Hmm." *And the future with my lovely Livy beckons.*

The whine of an approaching air-car broke Nathan from his thoughts.

"Moe's here," Livy said.

"Yep. We better get to the breakfast table before she eats everything."

Hand in hand they wandered into the dining room.

"Mornin' you two," Caleb said. Nathan could never understand how Caleb could be so chipper at this time of the morning. *My father was right. The Penkovskys are such good people.* The thought of his lost family caused a heaviness to rest on his heart so he brushed the memory aside. Again.

"Good morning, Caleb," Livy said.

Nathan pulled out the heavy wooden chair for Livy.

"I hope you two slept well," Bernie said.

"Fine." Livy blushed slightly.

Nathan took the chair beside Livy and noticed his kid sister trying to hide a smile.

"Mornin' Lucy," Nathan said.

Fourteen years old and fully aware, Lucy's room was next door to Nathan's.

Lucy giggled.

"What's so funny little sister?" Nathan asked.

"Nothing," she said, her eyes remaining on her plate.

Lewis could not leave well enough alone. "The walls aren't all that thick, you know."

"But you are ... Lewy," Nathan teased.

"How many times do I have to tell you? My name is Lewis, not Lew, not –"

"Mornin' all," Moe said. She dropped into the seat beside Nathan. "So Bernie, what treats do you have for breakfast today?"

"Nothing special Moe, just pancakes."

"Not *just* pancakes, but Bernie's best on Kastoria pancakes. I'd walk the twenty clicks from my home for your pancakes."

Moe glanced past Nathan to Livy. "So, did you two wake the rooster again this morning?"

Livy's ears burned bright pink as polite laughter filled the room.

"Behave yourself, Moe," Nathan warned playfully. He squeezed Livy's hand and winked. *Moe's tomboy attitude won't last long at the academy.*

The breakfast continued in the same easy vein until the time came for them to leave. They walked onto the verandah and while Nathan and Livy lingered Moe continued onto the gate. He did not want to leave her, not even for a few hours.

Nathan knew Livy loved him and that she knew he loved her, even if he could never say those *exact* words. In his rattled mind everyone he loved died. Within the crazy notion dwelt a fear with a history he dared not ignore. *I loved my family but in the end my love did not spare them from their ghastly deaths.*

"I've got to go," Nathan said.

Livy hugged him and stared into his eyes. "I love you."

"Right back at you." He gently stroked her hair before forcing himself to leave her.

Nathan fell into step beside Moe and together they passed through the broad front gate.

CHAPTER 15

Time: 22nd December, 315 (ASC).
Position: Mullally province. Planet Kastoria.

Moe's gaze locked onto Nathan, awaiting his next signal. He stood motionless in the middle of the deathly-quiet clearing fifty meters upwind of her position. She smiled, recalling the first time she set eyes on that skinny, reticent boy. Since arriving in the province three years ago, he had filled out very nicely indeed. A rigorous physical regime guaranteed not a gram of fat touched his muscular frame. From firsthand experience she knew how fast and dangerous he could be. Yet today he had been distracted. *Probably daydreaming about Livy.*

Throughout the morning they had tracked the rogue boar from the high equatorial escarpment to this glen, a few kilometers from the Penkovsky homestead.

Moe brushed a trickle of sweat from her upper lip.

Nathan's relaxed pose had remained unchanged for the last ten minutes. His attention focused on a thicket of tall reeds about a hundred meters in front of him. Moe detected nothing but if he suspected the boar lurked within the silent thicket she would bet her life on it. Within the province's hunting fraternity his freakish hunting instincts had gained him respect beyond his years.

Using hand signals Nathan directed her to the best firing position with a clear shot at the creature's forequarter when it broke from cover. Being upwind also positioned her in the safest spot. Noiselessly, he moved twenty meters to her right. Moe nocked an arrow and waited. No hunter would be stupid enough to wander into a dense thicket in pursuit of a wild boar. Certainly not Nathan. Years ago when she asked him why he preferred a bow instead of a modern pulsar hunting rifle, his answer never varied: "When one shot determines your fate, you pay attention."

Still no movement, no sound. Nathan remained stock still, his bow hand casually by his side. His body angled toward a spot in the tall reeds. His head slowly rotated until their eyes met. A wry smile creased the left side of his mouth making Moe tense. He winked. *Oh shit.* Nathan deliberately stepped onto a large, dry twig. The crack of wood shattered the silence like a thunderclap. Moe's heart missed a beat when a deep roar rumbled across the clearing. A great swathe of reeds parted frantically. Nathan's bow hand remained down.

Seconds later the boar erupted from the undergrowth. Seven hundred kilos of insane aggression stormed toward Nathan. Its half-meter long tusks could disembowel a four-tonne plains buffalo with a single swipe. Moe drew a deep breath, raised her bow, led the target and fired. The shaft flew directly for its heart. An instant before contact the charging beast rocked to its left. The arrow buried itself in the hard bone and gristle of its right shoulder. She blinked in disbelief when the boar continued its headlong charge.

Nathan's bow hand did not move. The charging mass of death closed to fifty meters. This was not the first time Nathan waited until the last possible moment to shoot. Foolhardy in the extreme; infuriatingly gutsy, but idiotic.

"Shoot, you stupid bastard." Her words rasped between clenched teeth. "Shoot!"

The beast closed to ten meters. With measured poise Nathan crouched slightly, drew back the sixty-kilo bowstring and fired. The shaft scythed through the beast's chest and sliced into its heart. The boar's tremendous momentum drove it on until, with a final tortured grunt, it staggered and collapsed to the ground. The enormous body kicked up a cloud of fine brown dust, temporarily obscuring Nathan from view.

Moe heard him sneezing as she broke into a sprint. With her blood boiling she rushed to the felled boar. As the dust cleared Nathan sneezed again as she rounded on him.

"What is it with you?" she shouted. "Do you have some kind of death wish?"

He rested on one knee and paid homage to the kill, placing his hand respectfully on the boar's immense head. His eyes tracked to her, his head at a curious angle. "If you never challenge yourself, Moe, you never grow." His expression remained serious for a few moments before a wry smile cut the left side of his face.

Relieved Nathan was unharmed, her scowl melted away. Moe shook her head.

"You know Nate, if you try this sort of shit at Mount Kratos, they'll kick you out."

"Why Moe," his voice feigned surprise, "I thought you knew that controlled aggression is the most desired quality in Monitor Corps captains."

She snorted. "I don't know how to break this to you, but you're not a captain."

"Yet."

Moe rolled her eyes in resignation. Their acceptance into the academy had been confirmed. Once there, four years of backbreaking work stood between them and their dreams of graduating as junior officers.

"Just don't forget your friends when you make admiral."

The odd angle of his head returned, this time accompanied by a wrinkled brow. "Who are you again?"

Moe lunged forward, knocking him off his haunches. They hit the ground with a vigorous thump. Her mother's fiery temperament surfaced as she beat playfully on his solid chest. "Who's your best friend? Who's your very best friend?"

"You are, Moe Okuma," he laughed between gasps. "You are my very best friend."

"And don't you forget it." She stared into his beautiful grey eyes. *So close and yet so far.*

"I will never forget. Now, would my very best friend please remove her knee from my balls?"

"Oh, sorry about that." Subduing a smirk she struggled to her feet and offered her hand, hauling him to his feet.

"Thanks, very best friend." With exaggerated care he massaged his groin. "You know Mary Ann, you need to watch where you put your knee."

"Hey, I've warned you before about using that girlie name." Moe's resolutely threatening tone was softened by her smile.

He yielded surrender with raised hands. "All right, don't get your knickers in a knot. Mary Okuma Esquire, it is."

An explosion thundered down the valley and they pivoted to the east. The rumbling echo could only have come from the Penkovsky homestead.

CHAPTER 16

Time: 22nd December, 315 (ASC).
Position: Mullally province. Planet Kastoria.
Status: Under siege.

Caleb Penkovsky surfaced through an ocean of pain. *Still alive! Should be dead.*

His last memory was of sitting down to lunch. *What the hell happened? An explosion.* His marine training had taken command without conscious thought. With the blast still ringing in his ears he had pushed back from the table and sprinted to the gun cabinet. The sound of splintering timbers as the front door crashed open, the stomping of hard boots on the stone entrance resounded as he grabbed his hunting rifle. Searing pain racked his body before the blessed relief of oblivion. Finally resurrection restored him to a world of piercing anxiety.

His back felt like it had been scrubbed with a jagged rock dipped in lava. Scavengers rarely used the stun setting on their weapons. At least not on males.

How the devil had these backward scavengers penetrated his hi-tech defenses? Somehow they crossed the two-kilometer zone covered by the defensive net without setting off the alarms.

Low mumblings came from nearby. Caleb kept his sagging head motionless as he forced his eyes open. Through slits he glimpsed Lewis' unconscious body slumped in the chair beside him. The same coarse, tough rope used on him secured Bernice, Lucy and Livy to sturdy wooden chairs to his left.

Caleb saw that gags had rendered them mute. They were conscious, their faces unmarked and clothing intact. With relief washing over him, he closed his eyes. Everyone was alive. For the time being at least.

Odd. Perhaps the bastards are branching out from their usual hit-and-run atrocities. Kidnapping Livy, the governor's daughter, could in their tiny minds bring great rewards. If that were the case, surely they would have fled with her by now and his family would be dead. Caleb opened his eyes, raised his head and scanned the room.

At his first movement the women's eyes swung to him. His wife and daughter's eyes revealed understandable fear but resolute determination. Livy tried to do the same but could not pull it off. He nodded to them.

Two roughnecks stood to one side of the main room talking in low, urgent whispers. From their garb Caleb immediately recognized how the scavengers had neutralized his security. Wafers of micro circuitry designed to mask the wearers from sensor detection were embedded into every centimeter of their black harnesses. High stakes military hardware like sensor suppressor harnesses were never made available to the public, let alone to these mongrels. *Must have smuggled them in from off planet.*

A scavenger noticed Caleb was conscious.

"Hey boss," he yelled to a man who stood by an open window.

A tall, ruggedly built man with a scruffy red beard turned from the window and strode to Caleb. Something about this man set Caleb's nerves on edge. He cleared his throat after red beard yanked the gag from his mouth.

"Where's the boy?" red beard asked without preamble.

Caleb feigned surprise. "Boy? What boy?"

"Caleb Penkovsky." His finger jabbed Caleb's chest. Red beard identified everyone else with the same pointed finger. "Your son Lewis, your wife Bernice, your daughter Lucilla and your guest Olivia Marshall. Nathan Telford is missing. Where is he?"

Caleb shrugged, displaying a false listlessness. *This prick is unusually well informed.*

To emphasize his deadly serious intentions, Red stepped behind Caleb's fourteen-year-old daughter. With his gaze locked onto Caleb, he unsheathed a short-bladed dagger from a scabbard attached to his left wrist. Lucy's eyes bulged when the blade pressed against her throat, drawing a thin scarlet trickle.

"He's hunting pigs." Although terrified for the safety of his daughter, he could *not* show weakness to this kind of man. Caleb set his face with the most gruesome smile in his arsenal. "Nathan wouldn't have bothered leaving home to kill pigs if he knew you and your pals were going to visit."

Red's steely gaze remained fixed on Caleb. A slight glint of respect briefly touched his hard features. Caleb breathed again when red sheathed the dagger.

"When will he return?"

"There's no way of knowing." Red's expression turned menacing, prompting Caleb to continue. "If he tracked his quarry somewhere close to the plantation he would have been back by now. The fact that he isn't probably means he's ranging far out along the lower plains. If that's the case he won't be back until after dark." Caleb hoped the latter were true. Every hour Nathan stayed away increased his chance of survival.

Red said nothing. His eyes defocused as the thousand-meter stare set in.

Another scavenger, short and stocky, marched up to him.

"What are we waiting for boss?" His voice betrayed fear, bordering on panic. "No amount of money is worth hanging around here. Marines could be on their way. Let's finish up and clear out." The scum glanced at the women.

Red shot him a murderous scowl.

"Shut your mouth, Kroener," he snarled. "You're in deep enough shit as it is."

Kroener's face darkened. "I told you before, I did exactly what you ordered me to do."

Red bared his teeth. "I told you to *disable* the communication net, not *blow it up*." Red's long finger jabbed Kroener's chest with enough force to stagger him. "If this mission turns to shit because of your fuckup, I will personally skin you alive."

The blood drained from Kroener's face.

Caleb had fought scavengers for most of his life and had questioned prisoners at length. Red didn't fit the type. Caleb's years as a marine taught him to recognize a professional when he saw one. Red was no mere scavenger. The mystery surrounding this day deepened.

Red, apparently lost in thought, stepped to the open window. Caleb had never met a scavenger known for deep thinking.

What the devil does Red want with Nathan? Caleb foresaw one absolute certainty from today's bizarre nightmare: many answers written in blood. Whose blood was yet to be determined.

After a brief interval Red straightened his back. "We wait," he said to no one in particular.

CHAPTER 17

Driven by a burning fear Nathan and Moe fell to their knees at the top of the rise. Still struggling to catch his breath, Nathan pulled his eyeglass from a leg pocket and scanned the valley.

From two kilometers away the high, sand-colored compound walls stood empty. Careful inspection confirmed both the comm. tower and sensor feeds remained intact. Nathan detected no movement from the compound walls and the solid front gate remained open. Outwardly, the homestead remained as it had been when he left there this morning. Despite what his eyes told him his Prep screamed a warning. He pushed himself to his feet and wiped sweat from his brow.

He followed Moe's lead and drank deeply from his canteen.

Breathing raggedly Nathan gasped, "Moe ... get to Abner's ... raise the alarm."

"I won't ... leave you ... alone," she responded around panting gulps. She yelped when he grabbed her roughly by the arm and hoisted her to her feet.

"I've no time ... to argue. Get going."

Moe staggered off in the direction of Abner's cabin. Nathan sprinted down the valley toward the homestead. Through the undulating plantation he pushed his exhausted body until his tortured lungs burned and orange splotches marred his vision. Topping the last rise before the compound he staggered and dropped to his knees. For precious seconds he choked down air until his vision cleared.

The ache in his heart battled with the bitter recognition that he had failed to listen to his instincts. A sense of apprehension had troubled him all morning. He finally understood why the spot between his shoulder blades burned with such intensity. His premonition of danger, his Prep, had sharpened since it first saved his life six years ago. Today's warning was stronger than anything he had sensed before. Nathan had wrongly assumed the danger related to the hunt. Now he understood that this new sensitivity not only warned *him* of personal danger but also extended to others. He cursed himself for failing to read the signs correctly. Nathan pushed the recrimination away. Today he had a man's work to do.

Closer inspection of the homestead revealed no signs of disruption. He detected no movement from the high compound walls. Despite the apparent evidence he dared not ignore the knot of hot coal burning between his shoulder blades.

Nathan cranked his eyeglass to maximum. He breathed deeply, forcing his thundering heart to slow. This time, with exacting care he scanned the compound. The roof and general structure of the building showed no damage. The shutters stood wide open, odd for this time of the afternoon but otherwise normal. His gaze tracked along the western wall, panning past the comm. shack. Without his eyeglass' military grade optics he may have missed the vital clue. Charcoal scorch marks smudged the shack's door and adjacent wall. Someone had blown the door off its hinges before clumsily propping it in its frame. Walking home from a day's hunting with thoughts of family and Livy on his mind, he would have missed it.

Closer scrutiny showed indications of two men hidden behind the front wall. If not for the telltale wisps of smoke rising from the parapet at regular intervals he would not have spotted them. The light breeze carried the unmistakable scent of Mascar to him. This illegal noxious narcotic made cowards feel courageous.

Scavengers.

His stomach lurched. By now his family was dead; and Livy.

Orphaned twice in one lifetime.

He shoved the ugly thought aside. Scavengers regularly took their time with the women. His stomach lurched and again when he swallowed bile.

Nathan had personally witnessed the aftermath of scavenger attacks. Murdered farmers, burned properties and women, whose suffering before the release of death made grown men vomit. Outlaws, raiders from a distant province who had defied attempts to eradicate them for years. These were not men but vile creatures draped in human form.

A long shuddering breath partially calmed him for what came next. Nathan focused his rage to serve, not hinder. His breathing steadied as a soft chill settled onto his clammy skin. In this state of white cold self-control he considered his options.

Nathan couldn't expect help for at least an hour even if a distress call was sent and marines were en route. Too long.

At least two scavengers covered the frontal approach to the homestead. Almost certainly more were inside. From the homestead's interior he detected only shadowy movements.

His first priority must be to get inside the compound's walls.

Rows of coffee trees hid him from view as he circled the compound. At the rear wall he saw no movement. No wisps of smoke rose from the parapet. *No sentries or no weed?* With no time for a second plan, he relied on his instincts.

Slinging his bow across this back freed his arms. For weeks Caleb had told Lewis to trim the Plocklar tree where the great sagging limb drooped over the back wall, ending barely two meters above the ground. Fortunately, Lewis had considered it a low priority and ignored the order.

Nathan took another deep breath, broke from the protective umbrella of coffee trees. Bolting down the embankment he leapt, seized the tip of the branch and struggled to the top of the wall. With his nose level with the wall, he inspected the area. No one guarded the rear parapet. Muffled voices wafted across the rear courtyard from the homestead. Silently he dropped onto the parapet. Bow in hand, he slid over the parapet's rough timber edge. Nathan hung by one hand before dropping noiselessly to the ground.

The murmurs heard earlier had grown rowdy. They guided him to the back verandah. Through a small gap in the trees he spotted two scavengers. Beneath the verandah's shady roof they sat at a table smoking Mascar and drinking wine. Nathan withdrew two arrows, planted one in the ground at his feet and nocked the other. Drawing a deep, cleansing breath, he forced himself under control. If one of them sounded the alarm.

Nathan pivoted side-on to the verandah. His eyes locked onto the first target, held it for a moment, raised the bow and fired. The shaft tore through the scavenger's back and pierced his heart. The piece of shit died before his head hit the table.

The second scavenger barked a raw laugh. "You drink like a virgin school girl."

Nathan's second arrow struck the target in the center of his chest. The astonished grimace on the scavenger's face produced a soft rippling growl from Nathan's throat. The scavenger pitched forward, the protruding arrow propping him in place.

Nathan edged along the narrow path toward the main gate. Rows of white-barked Plocklar trees growing around the inside of the compound walls hid him from view. The homestead's open front door came tantalizingly close. The temptation to charge through the door gnawed at him but he pushed the suicidal notion aside.

Stopping twenty meters from the front gate, he closed his eyes and concentrated. A subdued murmuring flowed from the parapet. *Good, the two I spotted earlier are still there.* Nathan worked his way silently forward until he stood directly beneath the pair of guards. They were sitting on their heels, smoking Mascar. If they glanced through the two-centimeter gap between the planks they would spot him.

Nathan sighted through the opening and fired. The arrow whistled between the planks, pierced the soft skin under the scavenger's chin, tore through his palate and embedded itself in his brain. He stepped from under the parapet. His second arrow ripped cleanly through the scavenger's left eye, exiting with sufficient force to pin his twitching body to the wall.

Nathan crept to the break in the tree line that marked the homestead's entrance. A few perilous meters of open space. His head snapped toward the house when an unfamiliar voice reached his ears. The incoherent words came from the main front room. The sun had shifted to the west and now light spilled into the room through the open windows and door. Through the glaring haze he just made out a large, red-bearded man. His heart skipped a beat when he caught sight of Lucy, alive and tied to a chair. The red-bearded scavenger pressed a dagger to her throat. A shiver dashed down Nathan's spine. He could not move. Interminable seconds later red beard stepped away from his kid sister. Fear fled before renewed hope. If Lucy was alive Livy and Bernie might be too.

Nathan released a breath he had not realized he was holding. His jaw ached with the effort to restrain his anxiety. He battled against the insane urge to charge through the front door and rescue his loved ones. *Got to be smart. Have to get into position before I attack.*

Four meters stood between him and the tree line on the other side of the open gate. He could cover the distance in seconds. But if someone spotted him in the open he was dead. No option. Nathan flexed his muscles and focused his mind and body on the task. He sprung from cover and dashed across the exposed gap. As the comforting tree line engulfed him he slid to a stop and awaited a shouted alert and a hail of pulsar fire. When none came he crept forward.

He reached the small gap in the tree line and broke from cover. A frantic sprint brought him to the heat-baked wall in seconds. He hugged the building's north wall while he glanced around the corner. *Front verandah clear.* After slipping over the railing he glided noiselessly toward the windows and the open door beyond.

***

The leader paced the homestead floor, impatience eating at him. He rubbed his red beard. Although he had numerous successful covert assignments to his credit he could not dismiss the nagging disquiet regarding his current assignment. Despite his concerns, playing the role of the nameless mercenary required him to maintain a neutral expression. One sign of indecision on his part would have the scavengers shitting their pants.

For the last two weeks he'd struggled to pound some sense of discipline into his clueless recruits. Sometimes he thought it might be easier to train stone slabs. At least slabs would stand still and listen. Their marksmanship had improved and he finally taught them the proper way to don the sensor suppressor harness. *Something at least.* Despite his misgivings they had accomplished the first stage of their operation without it turning into a complete fiasco.

A bad feeling settled in his gut. His informant had been wrong when he said the boy would be here. Then that idiot Kroener complicated matters by blowing the comm. shack.

Why is this boy so special? Immediately he corrected himself. No one ever questioned the Family elders. They wanted the boy and that was all he needed to know. As an Advocate of the Family he felt shame for allowing the thought.

He stopped pacing and turned toward the front door. The fresh air might help to clear his head.

***

Nathan edged toward the nearest open window, his feet silent on the wooden verandah. He froze when a large, red-bearded man sauntered through the front door and stopped at the top of the short flight of steps. *That's the swine who threatened Lucy*. Red beard gazed into the compound, apparently lost in thought. Nathan had an arrow nocked but could not move without exposing his vulnerable position.

If the scavenger turned his head, even slightly to the right ... *Can I kill him before he screams for help?* A sliver of sweat ran down Nathan's face as he continued to play the part of a statue. Nathan tried to slow his pulse. Finally, Red shook his head and turned back to the house.

Then, as if alerted by some inner sense of danger, Red blinked and turned his head. Seeing Nathan standing so close, his eyes bulged with astonishment. Red charged for the safety of the nearby door. Nathan fired a hurried, crudely aimed shot. In his haste, Red beard stumbled. His clumsiness saved his life. The scavenger screamed as the arrow - intended for his chest - pierced his left arm below the elbow. Red lurched through the open doorway into a room that erupted into panicked uproar.

"Rear guard, get in here." Red's voice cut through the turmoil.

Dismayed howls fueled the frenzied cacophony when the guards failed to answer.

"Shut up!" The same unwavering tone silenced the chaos. "Show some backbone you gutless turds. Form a line on me. Weapons on stun."

Nathan's stomach knotted into an angry fist as he slipped beneath the open windows then stood next to the doorway. He darted a glance around the door jamb and quickly pulled back. A barrage of automatic fire ripped into the doorframe. Stone and plaster disintegrated under the deafening volley. The stinging cut to his forehead proved how close he had come to dying.

From inside a muffled thump was followed by an angry bellow. "I said weapons on stun you piece of shit."

Nathan's fleeting view of the room showed three scavengers including the one he shot. If they were as scared as their voices suggested, there was a good chance they had frozen in place. *Risky. No time for refinement.*

Nathan upended the long wooden bench and propped it gingerly against the wall. He stepped to the window. The bench obediently froze in place for two seconds before sliding across the doorway. Under a furious volley of pulsar fire the bench disintegrated. Nathan stepped to the window and fired. The first scavenger stared in disbelief at the arrow buried in his chest before collapsing to the floor. A second joined him moments later. The last of the scavengers reacted instantly, swinging his sidearm toward the window. A fierce torrent of energy shredded the window frame beside him. Nathan pressed his back against the wall as debris exploded around him.

The firing stopped followed by an ominous silence. Nathan edged back to the door as the silent seconds ticked by. His sweaty skin turned to ice when a woman screamed. Livy!

Nathan burst into the room swinging his bow from side to side seeking a target. The red-bearded scavenger crouched behind Livy. Red's injured left hand enfolded her long chestnut hair, wrenching her head back. The barrel of his pistol dug into her jaw under her right ear.

Nathan swiveled his body to present a narrower profile. At this range his tactic counted for nothing against an assault weapon. He focused on the small fragment of the scavenger's head. Too close to Livy. If he mistimed the shot by a fraction he would kill her. He maintained his stance, awaiting the searing pain of an energy blast.

"Drop your weapon or I'll kill her." Unlike the other scavengers, Red's voice did not betray the slightest hint of indecision or panic.

Nathan wanted to scream that he would gut him like a swine but did not trust his voice. Only one of Red's eyes was exposed and he longed to take the shot.

"Listen boy. Everyone can come out of this in one piece. You drop your weapon, I walk away. You get your girlfriend back. I get to live. My way, everyone wins. Your way –" He shrugged.

Nathan knew better than to trust one of these creatures. *Why is red negotiating with me? He could cut me down without effort.*

"You're quick boy, but not fast enough to save this pretty thing," he tugged Livy's hair, "and some of your family as well. Is it worth the price?"

A dozen crazy ideas whirled through Nathan's mind. Each one led to the same tragic ending. Through the open front door Nathan heard the distant cry of a Kastorian mallard – a distinct, strident squawk. Mallards were out of season. The bird protested again, an almost urgent cry. Male mallards made such sounds only during the mating cycle. Kastorian mallards were out of season.

The setting sun poured through the open door, burning against Nathan's back. Taking the biggest risk in his life he lowered the bow and threw it aside.

"And the knife," Red ordered, from behind his sanctuary.

Nathan meekly unsheathed his hunting knife and tossed it aside. Red released his grip on Livy. He stood before Nathan keeping well out of arms reach.

"Smart boy." He smiled benignly. "You will soon know the joy that is service to the Family." Red held out his open, bloody hand. "Take my hand and your journey to a life of service will begin."

Again the urgent sound of the mallard's cry. A mallard. A duck. A big duck. *Duck!*

Nathan dropped to his knees.

"No need for that Nathan, I'm not going to k ..."

A frayed twelve-millimeter hole darkened red's forehead above his nose. The bullet's impact snapped red's head backward, throwing his body across the room in the same instant the rifle's boom cracked the air. The back of the scavenger's head splattered against the far wall forming a grisly curtain of bloody bone and grey shards of brain matter.

Retrieving his knife Nathan sliced through Livy's bindings. She threw herself into his arms so ferociously she almost knocked him over. Nathan melded her body to his and smothered her face and lips with kisses.

"Shhhh, it's over now," Nathan whispered. "I'll never let anything harm you."

Livy clung to him. "I knew you'd come for me." His fingers explored her shoulders and back to confirm she had no injuries.

"When he threatened to kill you I ..." Emotion cracked each word Nathan uttered. "Are you sure you're all right? Did anyone hurt you?"

She sniffled. "I'm fine, but they scared me half to death." Her chest heaved as she gasped for breath. When her trembling body eventually calmed, she broke their embrace.

"I'm fine darling," Livy said. "Your family needs you. Take care of them."

Her plucky composure startled Nathan. His family had spent their lives fighting for survival, so he expected such grit from them. His heart swelled with love and pride.

Nathan freed Bernie and placed his hand gently on her shoulder. "Are you all right?"

"I'll live." While rubbing her wrists to restore blood flow she surveyed the carnage. "I'll never get that bloodstain out of the rug."

After cutting Lucy's bonds he removed the tight gag. "How are you?"

She brushed a thick curl from her face. "I'm fine, big brother. How did you know to – "

"Not now, Lucilla," Bernie interrupted. "Help me in the kitchen."

Nathan glanced in Livy's direction to convince himself she really was all right. Her reassuring smile calmed his concerns as he moved to the men.

"Where's your precious Monitor Corps when we need them?" Lewis' sarcasm resounded the instant Nathan removed the gag.

"For that comment, you can wait your turn." Nathan bypassed him and released Caleb.

"Leave it, Lewis," Caleb barked. To Nathan he said, "You took your time getting here." He winked at Nathan.

Nathan reassessed the situation. Satisfied his family was safe, he wrapped his arms snuggly around Livy. "I'm so sorry this happened," he said. "It's my fault."

Livy's mouth dropped open. "How could this possibly be your fault? Don't be silly."

"My fault," he mumbled. *No way can I tell her. It would put her in danger far worse than today. This raid was obviously after me. I brought this down upon my family.*

The crash of Abner bursting into the room frightened Lewis so badly he tried to jump out of his bindings.

Tall and broad, Abner's weathered face and thick, blond hair reflected the setting sun. His alert brown eyes scanned the room, the huge hunting rifle tracking his movements.

"Any more?"

"There's a couple out back, and two on the parapet. They've attacked their last homestead." Nathan glared at his stepbrother. "To answer your stupid question, Lewy," Nathan said, "may I present to you, Sergeant Abner Lawrence, *Monitor Corps Marine Special Forces,* retired."

Abner's mock salute acknowledged Nathan's grin. Caleb slapped his old friend on the shoulder. For a few seconds he stared at Red's prone form before making his assessment.

"Nice shot."

"A smidgen high."

"Is anyone going to free me?" Lewis whined.

Caleb and Abner exchanged a silent contact. With his enormous hunting knife Abner released Lewis.

Exhaustion overwhelmed Nathan and he slumped onto the floor, pillowing his head on Livy's knee. To the former marine, Nathan asked, "How did you get here so fast?"

"Ran into Moe." Abner was always economical with words.

Bernie and Lucy returned from the kitchen with pitchers of ice-cold, homemade lemonade. After hours of sitting in the room with gags in their mouths, everyone drank thankfully. Nathan quaffed the last of the pitcher's contents in a single gulp.

"Nathan, I'm dying to know," Lucy said. "How did you know to drop, so Abner could shoot that bastard?"

"An old hunting trick. Taught to me by a cunning, albeit ancient, hunter."

Abner snorted.

Behind his smile guilt gnawed at Nathan. At that moment a cold hand touched his heart. This had been the third attack on the property in the last two years, each one coinciding with Nathan's return from school. *Today's raid was too professional for scavengers to plan and execute. Someone has discovered my secret. Will they ever relent?*

CHAPTER 18

Time: 5th June, 316 (ASC).
Position: The capital city of Athens, planet Attica. Athenian Republic.

Livy stepped into the early spring sunshine outside the Athenian Central Arts Center. She stopped by the statue of Athens' first president Julia Beresford and read the bronze plaque: Where Athens leads others follow. A little arrogant but historically accurate. As the first to colonize the space-locked region of the galaxy known as the Tunguska Fault, it was natural that those who followed the first fleet into the region would adopt similar views and look to the senior member for guidance. So it had been for three hundred years.

Her first months at teacher's college had been remarkable. Although she missed Nathan terribly the pace of life within the Athenian capital helped to –

"Olivia?" The shrill voice cut through the lazy afternoon like a trumpet. "Olivia Marshall?"

A trio of identically clad young stylists congregated in a tight group at the bottom of the steps, bouncing on the toes of their elegantly styled shoes. For several moments Livy did not recognize the young women but smiled indulgently as she continued toward them.

"Olivia, do you not remember me?" The young woman answered her own question before Livy could respond. "Mona. Mona von Steer." She rushed forward to touch cheeks.

Livy trimmed the speaker's weight by fifteen kilos and dressed her in the uniform of a senior at the Anastasia Kimbrough Academy for Young Ladies.

"Mona! I hardly recognized you. How are you?"

"Why I am just peachy my darling," she squawked. "And look at you. All brown and ... oh my, look at what you are wearing. What did those monsters out in the colonies do to you? You have lost so much weight you poor darling," she said in mock sympathy.

The other young women Livy remembered as Chelsea and Philippa. They continued to bounce excitedly on the toes of their expensive shoes. Their incessant squealing augmented their childish behavior. The group of effervescent jellybeans wore matching outfits; undoubtedly the latest in Athenian fashion for young ladies of elevated social means.

"Oh this is so wonderful," Mona gushed. "Now that you are back from the horrors of the colonies the four of us can pick up where we left off."

Not even if hell freezes over.

"Remember what we used to call ourselves, Olivia?" As usual Chelsea answered her own question. "The four princesses of AKA." This triggered another round of high-pitched squealing from the trio. Their behavior began to attract attention from the passing patrons.

"Come along my darling," Mona said, "we've slummed enough for one day. Let us find somewhere a little less ... um, common than this refuge for the masses. I know this darling little bistro that just opened and I am dying to catch up with you, sweetness."

"Well that would be nice Mona," Livy lied, "but I have work to do."

"Work!" Philippa squealed. "Work?"

"Oh, do not listen to her," Chelsea yelled. "She is joking with us."

"Well, no, actually I do have a lot..."

"The only work for us," Philippa said, "is to have fun and spend as much of our parent's money as we can." A three-bar giggling chorus ensued.

Livy struggled to control her rising exasperation.

"As a matter of fact, I've a lot of work waiting for me. I took the afternoon off to see the exhibition but now I've got to make up for it."

"Oh my, you have developed one of those awful colonial accents, have you not?" Mona squealed. "Oh, how divine. You never know, you just might start a new trend amongst the better people in town." The asinine trio giggled at the prospect. "Come along darling, go home and change into something civilized. We will all meet for lunch. Time for you to stop slumming, sweetness."

Livy agreed to meet with them later and they cheerfully believed her. If her time on Kastoria had taught Livy anything it was how to survive in a hostile environment.

Thank goodness those blue bloods did not represent the average Athenian. There were eight 'Republicans' in her classes. Yes, they would proudly boast that their ancestors arrived on the First Fleet, and yes, their abhorrence of contractions was annoying, but they were decent, hard-working people, polar opposites of that trio of disingenuous simpletons. Their scrupulous honesty was another aspect to deal with.

Nine generations of Athenians had lived under the influence of the AVU, which resulted in the creation of a thoroughly honest and polite society. The Aletheia Verification Unit, Athens' unbeatable lie detector, governed not only the political apparatus of the Republic but everyday life. The AVU, used exclusively within the borders of the Athenian Republic, gave false credence to outsiders' notions that Athenians were incapable of lying. At its best interpretation that view was an extreme exaggeration.

Livy boarded the Bay Commuter for the journey to the other side of Beresford Bay. The abrupt reminder of who she had once been, before discovering the intrinsic Livy hidden behind the pretense, prompted a surge of gratitude. And it all started on Kastoria.

Livy could not remember a time when she felt happier. The friends she had made on Kastoria were friends for life and her enemies few, the enmity short-lived.

Livy debarked from the commuter and walked toward her apartment.

A smile touched her lips. She held no doubts that Nathan loved her. At first his inability to say *I love you* annoyed the hell out of her. These days she loved to watch his face as he painfully and unsuccessfully struggled to express his feelings with that one simple word.

Livy recognized that his natural reticence coupled with occasional mood swings were Nathan's way of dealing with a tragic past. He was adamant from day one that his past was a closed and locked book. If she persisted he tapped the bump above his right eyebrow to confirm his loss of memory.

When Livy entered her small apartment she strode to the computer. The red message-received light flashed. She tapped the play button to activate the holo screen. It showed straight text rather than an audio-visual presentation. Nathan preferred the intimacy that hid within the detail of the written word.

I wonder what unbelievable nonsense he'll expect me to believe today?

My darling Livy,

Life at the academy is so much more than just another resort vacation. The friendly and attentive staff cater to the every whim of their guests twenty-four hours a day. No request is too much trouble for them and they bend over backwards to see that each plebe feels as if the academy has been created just for them. The cuisine is extraordinary with three courses per day of something no recruit will ever forget.

We are in the best physical condition of our

```
lives thanks to the kindly, soft-spoken physical education instructors and the dietary geniuses who spare not a moment of their precious time to seek out the odd kilogram of unhealthy flab and attack it with gusto. Health spas throughout the Republic cringe in shame when they attempt to measure their successes against the academy's robust program.
```

Livy broke from the text laughing. "Oh Nathan, you rascal."

```
Yes my darling, life at the academy isn't anything like the horrors you may have heard about. The personnel here are so in tune with our needs they know what we need before we think of it ourselves.
   The upperclassmen are kindly and attentive to our every need and nothing is too much trouble for them. Yes, life at the academy is just full of such surprises.
   Well, I hear the dinner bell ringing for one of chef's cordon bleu specials so I must away. Moe says hello.

   Missing you constantly
   Nathan.
```

She giggled as she disengaged the screen. A year ago she would have believed everything he said without question. These days each of them read the words *and* the meanings between lines of text. When he returned there would be no awkward silences between them, only times when they had little to say and were simply content to be together.

Who was this young man who had captured her heart so completely? They still had battles ahead but Livy knew with absolute certainty they were destined to be together until death ripped them apart.

Livy took the hard-copy picture of Nathan from the desk and hugged it against her heart. *Another whole month until I see him again. Each day will seem like a month. Oh, but what a homecoming it will be.*

CHAPTER 19

Time: 2nd August, 318 (ASC).
Position: Dryad freighter *Maluku*. Francorum Union.
Status: Approaching orbital insertion to the planet Saffron.

Orson took his first life at fourteen. He found the experience to be the most profoundly gratifying of his life. It just felt ... right. One of his fellow trainees had shown an unhealthy regard for the so-called sanctity of human life. Orson demonstrated his first genuine flare for initiative when he snapped the weakling's neck. His callous act earned high kudos from his instructors and earmarked him as a student of note.

By the age of twenty-two he had established himself as an exceptionally promising Family Associate. Years of rigorous training in the high arts of death and covert operations had paid off. Now he wanted to do more, to prove himself more worthy, to achieve far more. He would never dare to voice his opinions to those he served. He owed everything to the Family.

This relatively straightforward mission was his first as a solo operative. The insidious product he smuggled into Francorum space would have a decidedly negative, long-term influence on their society. Still, he longed for the primary missions the Advocates undertook. For the time being he employed his talents into playing the role of Biers.

The most junior officer aboard *Maluku*, Lt David Biers had earned the reputation of being 'mister enthusiasm'. By deliberate intent, Biers made for the perfect disguise for someone of Orson's true calling.

The real David Biers had been a minor obstacle on Orson's path. Minimal computer alteration to Biers credentials and disposal of his body presented little difficulty.

For the last five months Orson had played the role of the eager young officer with sufficient dedication to impress a drama critic. He considered his performance deserving of an acting award, if one existed for those of his profession.

Orson inspected the cargo container's customs seals one last time. The seals were expensive but well worth the cost.

Francorum customs officials had the most lackadaisical reputation in Tunguska. Getting a consignment through the entry port was easy, as long as the customs tags were sealed. In a worst-case scenario, bribery of Franc officials was possible.

Orson snapped from his thoughts as he rounded the corner to container Sierra seventeen. The seal had been broken then hastily stuck back in place. Repairing the damage presented little difficulty. He had a duplicate seal. He opened the container and checked the contents. All of the cylinders remained undisturbed, except for one on the lowest tier, which rested at an odd angle. After prying off the cap he checked the contents. Someone had tampered with the merchandise. A problem but not an insoluble one. After returning the cylinder he secured the container and tagged it with the spare seal.

Orson had a better than fair idea who had been sticking their nose into his business. Planetary insertion was minutes away and connection to the Orbital Space Dock within the hour. He needed to deal with this predicament quickly.

Orson sensed the presence of the other man well before he spoke.

"Everything all right, lieutenant?" The mocking tone of Demarti's voice confirmed Orson's suspicions.

He was a typical example of a Dryadian crewmember. Overweight, unshaven and possessing a crude animal cunning. Demarti was too dense to fully comprehend how dangerous his game was. However, degenerates like Demarti usually responded to money.

"Do you know anything about this?" Orson held the torn seal before him.

"Maybe I do, maybe I don't."

"Meaning?"

"Meaning, I don't mind turning my back for the right price, but what you've got in that container deserves a second look at our deal."

Orson nodded thoughtfully. If money would buy his cooperation then money it would be. He had prepared for such contingencies.

"How much did you have in mind?"

"Well now, let's see." Demarti leaned casually against a container. "Considering the Francs have an open death penalty on the books for anyone smuggling drugs across their borders, I think double is fair." He smirked and held his hands out to his sides. "Let's face it, lieutenant, with what you'll make on this shipment of Kesium you can afford to be generous."

The cretin had a point. However, Orson worked for a much higher authority to whom money was nothing but a means to an end. A fool like Demarti was incapable of fathoming such lofty aspirations.

Again, Orson nodded thoughtfully. "Very well, Demarti." Orson employed his weakest, most reasonable tone. "I would appreciate it if next time we make a deal you stick to it."

The idiot grinned like a triumphant dog that retrieved a thrown ball and stubbornly refused to relinquish it. "Aye-aye, lieutenant." His self-assured smile hardened, as did his tone. "But I want my money before I go ashore. Remember, I can get a sizeable reward from the Francs for identifying a drug trafficker. I make the same money and you get a speedy trial and a firing squad. So I get paid up-front."

"I appear to have little choice in the matter."

The Dryadian fool smirked again. As with numerous fools before him, Demarti had never seen Orson's true face, his real intent. He saw what Orson wanted him to see. A young man from the outer colonies, naïve, fidgety and harmless. A novice with a ridiculously boyish face who simply wanted to make some quick money.

"Let's go to my quarters and take care of business."

Demarti relaxed and made the mistake of turning his back. Orson struck a piercing blow to the base of the brain stem, snapping the vertebra connection to the brain. He dragged Demarti's limp, lifeless body across the hold and dropped it headfirst down an access shaft. He hit the bottom of the five-meter drop with a satisfying crunch. Orson sucked in a deep, shuddering breath and forced the smile from his lips.

"Help," Orson cried. "Somebody please help. Poor Demarti."

CHAPTER 20

What we have to learn to do, we learn by doing. Aristotle (384-322 BC) Greek philosopher. Nicomachean Ethics (4th cent. BC).

Time: 5th April, 320 ASC
Position: Athenian Republic Extraterrestrial Naval Academy, Mount Kratos, Attican moon Peloponnesia, Athenian core system.
Status: Fourth year.

Nathan strode from the mess and reached Amelia Hall a few minutes later. Unlike the plebes he had access to the lift, but chose to use the stairs, taking them two at a time. Turning left at the fourth-floor landing he walked along the corridor, stopping when he reached room 4/219. Nathan touched the call button. When the hatch slid open a midshipwoman snapped to attention.

"Room inspection plebe. Step aside."

The seventeen-year-old 4/C straightened her back against the wall. When the hatch slid shut he scanned the room briefly before directing a cold stare at the middy.

"Well plebe, what do you have to say for yourself?"

"Sir, I do not understand. Sir."

"Oh, you don't eh?" Nathan unclipped his left epaulet to signify the suspension of rank, grinned and spread his arms wide.

Lucilla Penkovsky hurled herself at him with enough force to stagger Nathan. After a few seconds they broke from their fierce embrace. He pecked her on the cheek and sat beside her.

"How are you coping, Lucy?"

"Piece of cake, Nathan," she said. "And my hair has grown back."

"So I see." Nathan gave the trimmed, curly mass a good ruffle. "Your one-time visit to the *hair stylist* serves tradition."

"Yeah, it was fun." Lucy rolled her eyes. "And the last four months have been *really* great." She giggled at her own foolishness.

"Plebe year is tough, but I knew you could handle it."

"Yeah, I ... hey, did you catch Aletheia's Friend today?"

Nathan scowled. "Yes. Thoroughly disgraceful." He smiled despite his best effort not to.

"He's been getting away with posting on the academy web for years," Lucy said.

Most people considered the regular column posted by the serial prankster known as Aletheia's Friend to be harmless fun. The comments ranged across topics as diverse as the weight gain of the commandant's bulldog Princess, to the upperclassmen who were most unpopular amongst plebes, to what bit of mischief may have taken place, when, how much and to whom.

"Yeah, the cheeky bugger has been posting his version of the truth despite the concerted efforts of everyone from the commandant, to the head of the computer sciences department, right up to the master chief petty officer of the academy."

"How could he have known about Lieutenant Duffy's condition?" Lucy asked.

Nathan snorted. "How AF discovered that Duffy had fallen pregnant has baffled everyone. Some of the more conservative readers thought it to be in poor taste when the net humorist described the situation as: Duffy up the duff. The majority of readers found it hilarious, even though most publicly frowned at the article."

Their smiles froze as the hatch opened behind them.

A midshipwoman bolted to attention. "Give us the room, middy," Nathan ordered.

The startled plebe quickly backed away and the hatch snapped shut.

"Your roomie?"

"Yeah," Lucy said. "I wonder if Aletheia's Friend will report this?"

"I wouldn't worry about it." He smiled. "You're really starting to grow up Lucy. I can't believe you're the same scrawny kid I first met when I came to live on Kastoria."

She returned his smile fondly. "I'm not, Nathan. I'm a big girl now. And I can't believe you're the same screwed up kid who kept venturing into the rain forests even though father told you not to."

Nathan chuckled at the recollection. "Yeah, Caleb and Bernie got a bit upset about that. But I proved I can take care of myself."

Lucy stroked the side of his face. "Yeah, you've never needed anyone's help, have you? Always the lone wolf." Her wry smile looked awfully familiar to Nathan. "Anything you want to share with me?"

Nathan cleared his throat. "I was in a different place then. Thanks to your family, and especially you, I got past it."

"Me? What did I do?"

"You reminded me of what it was like to be a kid. To laugh and play as if nothing could ever touch your perfect world." Nathan cleared his throat again. "You helped me just by being who you were. But you're not a kid anymore, are you?"

"No *sir.*"

"I should be going," Nathan said, rising from his chair. "Judy Parnell is a damn good company commander so if you have any major problems take them straight to her. All right?"

"Sure Nathan, but I don't think it will be necessary."

Nathan felt the back of his neck grow warm. "Lucy, I'm sorry I took so long catching up with you but it's been pretty hectic since I got back from summer cruise." He cleared a small lump from his throat. "Lucy, you're as good as my kid sister, but ..." he squirmed.

"I know, I know." Lucy rested her hands on his shoulders. "You have nothing to worry about. I might be new but dad told me how things work here. I won't embarrass you in public or attempt to contact you. I'm a plebe and you are a regimental commander. Even though you're my brother, in every real sense, we don't share the same surname and that could be the cause of tongue wagging. I get it, Nathan."

Relieved, he hugged her. Lucy would be fine. "I'll touch bases with you as often as I can. And I expect you to drop in and visit Livy on Athens when you're on leave." He reset his epaulet and Lucy copied him. "But for now you'd better snap to, plebe."

Lucy drew herself to rigid attention. Nathan winked and stepped through the hatch.

CHAPTER 21

Date: 28th May, 320 ASC.
Position: Mount Kratos.
Status: Awaiting mid-term results.

Nathan's opponent struck at his exposed throat. He quickly raised his sword to block the killing blow. Harada countered by shouldering Nathan off balance then sweeping his feet from under him. Nathan crashed to the mat and rolled away. As he tried to regain his footing a sharp agonizing pain flared from his thighs when Harada's sword struck. Fighting the pain through clenched teeth Nathan again tried to stand. He groaned as Harada's blade smashed across his armored shoulders, dropping him to the deck. On his knees Nathan swung his blade at Harada's ankles and missed. Pain stabbed through his arm when his opponent's parry struck his sword from his hand. Harada's sword thundered onto the back of his helmet stunning him. Unarmed, his body and mind roiled as blows rained onto his writhing body.

In a display of leniency rarely seen from Master Sokoi Harada, the beating ceased before the medics were required. Nathan was thankful the master swordsman used a dull practice sword. If Nathan were an enemy combatant Harada would find the gaps in his armor and cut him to pieces. Today's beating had not been the first time the dangerous old swordmaster had taught him a harsh lesson.

Nathan struggled to his feet, feeling as though a plains buffalo had trampled him. He joined Harada in the center of the training square and sat before him, his legs folded under his buttocks. Nathan bowed slowly until his head touched the training square. Ignoring the piercing pain that throbbed through his body he sat without moving, awaiting the inevitable rebuke.

When Harada removed his helmet Nathan followed suit. Sweat rolled down Nathan's back and flowed from his sodden hair stinging his eyes. He resisted the urge to wipe his face. The Nihonese swordmaster sat impassively, unmoving, disconnected and totally dry. Harada brought his soulful black eyes to bear.

"Where are you, Telford?"

Nathan's obvious confusion prompted Harada to continue.

"You are not here in this moment, not focused. Not one with

body and mind. Your technique remains but you are not here. So Telford, where are you?"

As if to answer the question Nathan heard the comm blare across the academy training ground.

"Midshipwoman Commander Okuma, report to Commander Zoehrer's office at 1400 hours. Class A's. That is all."

An odd mixture of emotions struck Nathan. Moe had qualified for the special cruise. Fantastic. Nathan knew Moe would make the cut and was overjoyed for her. However, only ten middies won their way into the exacting mid-year cruise. Moe's name was the tenth and final name called.

"I apologize, Master Harada." Nathan's low tone reflected his sincerity. For a swordmaster of Harada's repute to give personalized time to a student was unheard of. Nathan had squandered his gift by allowing his mind to wander to an undeserved hope.

"Perhaps you should place mud in your ears?" The severe lines on Harada's face softened fractionally, removing twenty years from his age.

Of course he was right, mud in the ears. The old man missed nothing.

"Yes, Master Harada."

"Do you believe I have treated you harshly, Telford?"

"No sir, of course not."

"The universe will provide all that you need, Nathan."

"Yes, Master Harada." *The old man's going Zen on me again.*

"And what you need right now is a shower."

Nathan, more through surprise than good judgment, stared at Harada. An expression dancing on the edge of lethal amiability greeted him. For the first time Nathan smiled in the swordmaster's presence.

"You are my best student, Nathan, but such lapses in concentration will get you killed where you are going." His finger pointed lazily to the sky. "You know this to be true, do you not?"

"Yes, Master Harada. Again I apologize for my disgraceful behavior. It will never happen again. I give you my pledge." Harada had referred to him by his given name twice during his time at the mount, both within the last ten seconds. *Does he know something I don't?*

"As you should," he said, with contrived gruffness. "Go and hit the showers."

"Yes, Master Harada." Nathan bowed to the deck. He jumped to his feet ignoring the darting pain in his leg.

"And Telford ..." Nathan glanced over his shoulder. "If you ever again waste my time I shall not be so lenient."

Nathan nodded once and left, knowing from painful experience how much Harada meant what he said.

***

As mid-afternoon approached, time dragged for Nathan. His index finger massaged the bump at the corner of his right eyebrow. The mass of numbers scrolling across his comp pad could not distract him from his unease.

His entire naval career did not depend on the results of his upcoming assessment. However, he would feel justifiably irritated if all the hard work counted for nothing. Nathan had become accustomed to meeting challenges and attaining his goals. His failure to qualify for the special cruise hit hard.

"Go for a run before you implode," Roger suggested.

"I'm fine." Nathan replied while trying to make sense of the navigation problem mocking him from the screen.

"You're ready to jump out of your skin."

Nathan looked up. Roger's boyish grin had not changed since they first became roomies. Nathan snorted and shook his head.

"So you missed out on the special cruise," Roger said. "So what? There are hundreds of middies trying for ten slots. We both know what you've been doing instead of hitting the books. You've put too much time into your regiment. Listening to every kid with a problem. You can't be the big bother to all of them, you know. So you dipped out. Get over it. As for your mid-terms, don't worry. If you get a good passing grade, great. If you don't, bad luck. Either way, having kittens over it is a blatant waste of energy. Yes?"

"Once again my friend, you are the voice of reason in a world of noisy disarray." Roger did not precisely represent the steadfast yin to Nathan's passionate yang but at times Nathan admired his friend's logical mindset.

"Then listen to your friend. Get off your orifice and go for a run for an hour or so. If any breaking news arrives I will run as fast as my chubby legs can carry me to the training field to tell you."

Nathan nodded and stood. As he opened his locker the wall-mounted comm buzzed. Nathan's hand reached for it, his finger poised over the button. This would be his mid-term results.

He stabbed the answer button. "Room eight dash four five. Midshipman Commander Telford."

"Ah, Mister Telford, just the middy I was after," Cmdr Zoehrer said.

Aletheia's Friend had done a series of articles on how much the commander's silkily resonant voice sexually aroused most male middies, together with a small contingent of females. Apparently 'Zenith' Zoehrer had not responded favorably to Aletheia's jest.

Today her throaty tones carried in the background buzz of the comm speaker, an additional spoonful of honey.

"Report to my office at fourteen-thirty hours. Class A's."

"Aye-aye, commander, fourteen-thirty in your orifice. Class A's. Telford out." Nathan froze in place, staring at the silent comm.

"I think you got away with it," Roger said, breaking the chilling silence. His dubious expression suggested otherwise.

Nathan groaned. "In your *orifice*?" his head hit the locker with a sound thud. "What was I thinking?"

"You were thinking what every red-blooded middy has been thinking since plebe year."

"This isn't funny, Roger," Nathan growled. "I have to front Zoehrer in fifteen minutes."

"In her *orifice*." Roger laughed so hard he tumbled off his rack. "Well," he said, choking back a laugh, "if things go well between you and Zoehrer it couldn't hurt your reputation, you know?"

"My rep is fine, thank you." Nathan's fingers fumbled as he struggled to tie the thick black cravat to his high-collared white shirt.

"You're a good guy Nathan, but over the years you've taken too many truly risky chances. You can push the envelope just so far, you know?"

If you want risky chances, try escaping from the Pruessen Empire in an unarmed freighter being torn to pieces by an attack boat.

Nathan straightened from the mirror, the cravat in place. He was aware of his reputation as a walking talking advertisement for Monitor Corps. Had his desire to be one of the best become obsessive? Livy didn't think so and their discussions rarely ventured into his naval aspirations. They regularly laughed about all sorts of things.

"We will talk further on this subject when I return. In the meantime I shall, as an old friend suggested, attempt to lighten up. All right?"

"Make me proud, Nathan."

Nathan winked conspiratorially before stepping over the coaming.

***

Nathan paced the waiting room floor. He stopped before the huge transparent globe that floated within the faintly shimmering anti-grav fields. As he had done countless times before, he examined the three thousand star systems and over two hundred habitable worlds that comprised the sphere of the Tunguska Fault.

An irregular line encircled its circumference marking the frontier with the northern quarantine zone. Established after the first Franco-Pruessen war, the border had torn the map of Tunguska in half, after diplomatic negotiations with Pruessen collapsed. The fortuitous separation helped to restrict the spread of the terrible disease to the south during the final weeks of the second war with Pruessen. Worlds north of the frontier had not been so lucky. The infected worlds stood out from the map as ugly black dots.

To the south of the frontier one black dot marred the many systems of the League of Allied Worlds. Delos.

To the west of the Athenian Republic the border with the north, and the protection of the independent worlds therein, became the responsibility of the Bretish Commonwealth. The Brets had a fine modern navy crewed by aggressive commanders who held the line against all who would intrude into League space. To the east the Francorum Union was accountable for protecting the many independent worlds bordering the frontier. Their reputation had repeatedly been found lacking. Nathan felt his blood rising. *My family would still be alive if the Francs hadn't abandoned their duty and left the Iberian system without protection. Fucking Francs, little better than Pruessens.* He shook the ugly thought aside and steadied his breathing.

One anomaly not shown on the globe was the Ebony Corona, a solid hyper depression surrounding Tunguska to a depth of six light years. Vessels were incapable of making hyper-transitions within the depression. This factor transformed Tunguska into a space-locked environment. At the best speed of the fastest vessel, a one-way journey through the corona took twelve years.

This effectively made the region a non-commercial enterprise. Terra Corp had ignored Tunguska, preferring to continue its headlong exploitation of every system they encountered. This made Tunguska the ideal place for those rebellious types who had become sick of T-C's despotic rule.

Three hundred years ago, the first colonists to arrive in Tunguska must have viewed this broken region of space as if it were a new Eden. A chance to start over, a new hope. It was not surprising, therefore, that they named their new world after the first democracy in human history. Humanity brought into the Fault a determination to do better, thousands of years of art, literature, philosophy, technology and high hopes. Sadly, humanity also carried the baggage of ancient passions and an unquenchable proclivity for mayhem. Two wars in the last fifty years proved that things never changed. Nathan was studying for his minor in ancient Earth history. He sighed and wondered if humanity would ever evolve sufficiently to learn from the catastrophes of its past. *We cannot escape the nature of our lesser selves.*

"Midshipman Telford," the secretary said, "Commander Zoehrer will see you now."

Nathan nodded, straightened his waistcoat and stepped to the hatch.

***

Commander Constance Zoehrer scratched at the ghost itch on her left arm. "Bugger," she grumbled and discontinued the futile gesture. Modern prosthetics were good but they did not itch.

The hatch chimed. "Ad-mit."

Her eyes remained glued to her screen as Nathan snapped to attention before her desk.

"Midshipman Commander Telford reporting to the commander as ordered, ma'am."

She spared him a glance. "At ease, commander. Take a seat."

Constance Zoehrer showed favoritism to no one. However, from plebe year onward she had been Nathan's year supervisor and knew him as well as anyone. Unlike other military institutions, Mount Kratos earmarked exceptional leaders from day one. This young man stood out from his written reports to his behavior through plebe year and every year since.

But she never played favorites.

Zoehrer finished her pseudo screen activity and examined the middy. Although Nathan had longed to be one of the elite special cruise candidates he did not show a trace of what must be a crushing disappointment. *What do I have to do to rattle him?*

"The results of the mid-terms have just been released. I thought you might like a heads-up before they're posted." The middy's forehead and upper lip remained free of perspiration. *Dammit.* "I'm pleased to see your grade point average is up again this term. Once again, commander, you have placed within the top ten percent in your year. Well done."

"Thank you, ma'am."

"Results from your classes on tactical analysis, problem-solving scenarios, civil and military history are outstanding. I see you are still having difficulty with shipboard administration and theoretical navigation. However, your persistent arguments in Professor Mollard's moral philosophy class are counterproductive." Her eyes narrowed as his lips formed a smirk. "Yes, Nathan? You have something to say?"

She harbored a small hope that he would be smart, for a change, and keep his big mouth shut. The hope vanished as soon as his jaw set.

"Respectfully, ma'am, we have had this discussion before. Professor Mollard may be well regarded within the academic community, but as far as I'm concerned he is a pretentious windbag who has not earned the right to discuss such life and death matters. His lack of real-world experience is appallingly obvious."

"That is impertinent, middy. What the hell would you know about it?" she snapped. "Do you think because you killed a handful of bandits on Kastoria it gives you some special insight into the complexities of moral ambiguities?"

As usual, his obscure expression masked his thoughts.

"It might come as a terrible shock to you, but you don't know everything." Now and again he deserved a sound kick in the backside. *Though I shouldn't have mentioned his civilian record.*

"Again, you are missing the point," she continued with greater moderation. "There are no absolutes in either moral philosophy classes or your exercises in moral ambiguity. That's why it's ambiguous. Morality classes are not a contest about right or wrong but an exercise in coming to grips with new concepts. Not everyone at this facility has faced death in the eye, as you have." A slight flicker at the corners of his eyes. "We are not in the business of producing stone-cold killers. Whether *you* like it or not, moral philosophy classes are part of the overall regime of studies to ensure that levelheaded, morally correct decisions are made in high-pressure situations, by those graduating this academy. Or do you disagree with my assessment, mister?"

Zoehrer knew he respected her, but did he see her point? As she had seen him do on countless occasions he exercised inhuman control over his emotions. His eyes softened and the harsh line of his jaw relaxed.

"I would never dream of disagreeing with you ... Commander Zoehrer." They maintained neutral expressions until his peculiarly wry smile creased the left side of his face. Despite her best efforts she failed to restrict a snicker.

"You're incorrigible." She tucked her smile in. "Now, back to business. You have been spending an inordinately disproportionate amount of your time in the flight simulators. It might be fun, but fun won't get you into Flight Training School, certainly not at Metier level. Furthermore, the time spent with your Kendo squad, whereas commendable, will not advance your chances of graduating within the top hundred graduates. And the less said about you working out with the marine detachment the better. Once again I must remind you to balance your time. Your final-year thesis will require more effort than you can imagine. Time management is also a quality desired in a command officer."

She straightened her waistcoat and fought to keep her grin in check. "The special cruise candidates ship out in sixteen days time. You are aware of that I assume?" The corners of his mouth tucked in as though he had bitten into a lemon. "Oh, how I remember my special cruise. Would you like to hear about it?"

Nathan seized an imaginary dagger, plunging it into his abdomen then upward in a silent parody of an ancient suicide ritual. They laughed at his nonsense.

"Competition has been as ferocious as I have ever seen," she continued. "You've heard about the successful candidates?"

He nodded slowly. "Yes ma'am and I could not have selected a finer group of middies for the cruise. They will do us proud."

"Yes, I believe you know them all from your Kendo and Aikido teams?" From his rigid expression, his sense of humor on this subject had waned. "Pity there are only ten places. But that's the way the system has always operated ... until today."

Zoehrer smiled internally as his forehead wrinkled.

"For the last forty-eight hours a debate has raged between the naval and academic tutors ..." her finger stabbed the air between them, "concerning you."

Nathan's eyes widened and his mouth dropped open.

Finally.

"Apparently, because your name is affixed to the Tactical and Strategic Excellence plaque, the military tutors consider it a factor worthy of consideration. The academics disagreed and so an impasse ensued."

Nathan remained mute – a history making event in itself.

"To cut a long story short, Commodore Ponsford stepped in

and broke the deadlock. As he's often said, being Commandant of the Brigade of Midshipman might not make him God but within the walls of Mount Kratos it comes close enough.

"The academy produces more than its fair share of geniuses, but high quality, instinctual leaders have always been the rarest and the most highly prized vocational assets. This facility exists to identify, produce and nurture exceptional leaders. It is my opinion and that of every senior officer at Mount Kratos that this agenda will be best served by the inclusion, for this year only, of an eleventh place on the special cruise."

Nathan's genuinely flummoxed expression pleased her no end.

"Anyway," she continued, "an opening on the special cruise has become available." Zoehrer paused, her smile curling. "Interested? Or should I invite the next candidate into my ... orifice?"

An uncontrollable grin split Nathan's face. His pressure release valve cut in. He threw his head back and laughed as if he were a man reprieved from a death sentence.

***

The sun had fallen well below the peak of Mount Kratos. Midshipwoman Moe Okuma pushed her exhausted body up the final ten meters of steep incline to the summit. Her well-muscled legs had turned to lead-weighted rubber pegs. Her throat rasped air into her ferociously burning lungs. *Damned if I'll let this hill beat me.*

With a final tortured surge she lurched onto the flat-topped summit. The other nine middies sprawled, in varying states of sweat-soaked exhaustion, around the perimeter wall. Their broad grins acknowledged the arrival of the final candidate. She smiled back while dragging her aching body to the stone monument. Moe fell against the chest-high dedication slapping both hands onto the polished plaque. The academy's motto stared back at her.

"Take the High Ground," she whispered. Moe often wondered if the academy's architect had also been a wannabe comedian.

When she supported herself against the monument, Janine Gilchrist, captain of the Brigade of Midshipmen, started clapping. The others joined in although some of the recent arrivals had trouble sustaining the applause. Moe returned the ovation, nodding to them as she did so.

The academy's student population numbered over eight thousand, but all of the faces surrounding her were familiar from

Kendo class.

"They'll let anyone onboard a monitor these days." A familiar barb from Meta Kaspowitz.

"Obviously," Moe said, as she dropped next to Janine. Unhooking her canteen Moe drank greedily. Only one thing dulled the joy of her achievement. Nathan's single-minded devotion to his regiment had diverted far too much of his time. As a result his grades suffered and he missed the cruise. Of all people, he should be part of this elite group.

Moe's heart rate slowed and she limbered up for the slow jog down the mount.

Janine heard the footfalls first, tilting her head to pick up the sound. By tradition the mount was theirs for the afternoon. If some errant plebe had ignored the decree, the senior middies would tear the youngster a new one.

They patiently waited as the grunting and panting grew louder. All eyes focused on the final hump leading to the summit. As the runner's head came into view every jaw dropped.

Nathan limped to the plaque and slapped both hands onto its cold shiny surface. Like the rest of them his shirt was soaked through. Meta found her voice first.

"Well, bugger me!"

Nathan smiled crookedly. "Thanks for the offer, but I'm a little tired right now."

Meta chuckled and the others joined in.

"Nathan, please don't take this the wrong way," Janine said, "but what are you doing here?"

Moe noticed a few of the middies shaking their heads and she resisted the temptation to join them. Intense rivalry between Nathan and Janine resulted in the formation of a less than conventional friendship. In a sense their mutual respect had created a more binding glue than any social affection.

"I got lucky," he said, slipping into his lazy Kastorian drawl.

"Well now, isn't that just like Nathan Telford," Meta chimed in. "He sits back having fun with his regiment, doesn't do the real work and still gets pegged for the cruise. Must be great being the commander's pet."

Nathan answered her good-natured barb with an easy smile as he dropped next to Moe. As with everyone else he had long since learned to allow Meta's brand of acerbic humor to wash harmlessly over him. Moe offered her canteen and he took several large gulps.

"Come on, Nathan," Osmond Hayden said. "Tell us how you pulled *this* one off." Ozzie's grin cut a startling white line across his broad ebony face.

"I'm not entirely sure, Ozzie. So, what did everyone get?" As usual Nathan chose to deflect the conversation away from himself.

The middies took turns describing their assignments. Some were destined for duty in Command Eastern Quadrant, some to Southern and some to Western. Meta and Ozzie had pulled the plum assignment, *Truculent,* out of Northern Quadrant, where the real action happened.

Nathan raised his eyebrows inquisitively at Moe.

She did a drum roll on her thighs. "Truculent." The group groaned at her good fortune.

"Me too." The good-natured groans swelled.

They sat for some time without talking. Neither found the silence uncomfortable. Eventually Moe asked, "Have you told Livy?"

Moe caught his slight wince. "We've considered the possibility and she's fine with it."

"Surrendering all but three days of your leave? And she's *fine* with it?"

"She's used to being a naval widow by now."

Yeah, sure she is.

A burst of laughter interrupted their conversation. The eleven of them were about to embark on missions usually reserved for experienced commissioned officers. The impact of their incredibly good fortune struck at the funny bone of one of their number. Of all the people to let their luck get to her, Meta was the most unlikely. Her laughter's therapeutic qualities drained away Moe's fatigue. Some middies had the energy to start whooping, until they fell back against the wall panting in delighted exhaustion.

CHAPTER 22

Date: 5th June, 320 ASC.
Position: Imperial Pruessen Naval Base Virtus, Pruessen Empire home system. Orbital Docking & Refit Facility Beta Ten, in orbit around the moon Virtus Two.
Status: Preparation and training ongoing.

Captain Foss examined the latest reports on the condition of his current command. Calling this poorly armed, worn out pile of junk a sad joke. Not even a regular navy warship but a fucking headhunter. He reached again for the bottle of Sorrenson brandy. He sipped the vile brew, grimacing at its bitterness. At least it dulled the pain, a little. *Where did it all go wrong?*

Foss' brilliantly distinguished fifty-year career had long since earned him Pruessen citizenship. An imperial citizen merited benefits unavailable to the masses, most notably the zealously craved genetic treatment. Known as the GT, the treatment guaranteed an enhanced lifespan free from ill health. At seventy-two Foss had a spring in his step the envy of any forty-year-old. However, without the treatment booster due within the next four months his body would quickly degenerate to match his actual age.

Foss swallowed another nip of brandy and reflected yet again that life was rarely fair. A lifetime of service obliterated because of one mistake. In the days of the old Republic, showing mercy to a helpless enemy was the expected norm. Then came the war, the president's insane release of the Derwent Plague and the implosion of the Republic. From the ashes of the old republic the Empire rose and everything changed. Too late Foss learned the error of continuing to employ his antiquated moral values. The HRS fell upon him like an avalanche wearing long black boots. In the case of the Human Resource Service, Foss could not imagine a more benign euphemism for such a malignant, all-powerful entity.

The HRS gave him a taste of his changed circumstances. Six months as an ordinary seaman attached to the reclamation teams crushed the last of his stubborn resolve. At the mercy of petty officers handpicked for their hatred of former officers, he endured countless brutal humiliations. These too he survived. Finally satisfied that they had purged the last traces of pride and resistance, they offered him command of *Picaroon*.

He chuckled mirthlessly at the term 'offer'. *As if I actually had a choice?* So he drank, sometimes to excess. If he completed this preposterous mission to his superiors' satisfaction they might forgive his one mistake. Perhaps restoration to duty in the regular navy? Foss clung to that hope as a drowning man clings to a small lump of wood. Only hope kept him from eating his pistol.

Mad men must have planned this mission. It would probably get him killed. Draining the glass of brandy he reached for the bottle. The call chime sounded. Foss hid the bottle and glass under the table and straightened his waistcoat.

"Ad-mit."

The hatch slid aside and Lt Saxon stepped over the coaming. He looked far too young to hold the rank of lieutenant jg. Foss knew who he was and suspected *what* he was.

The lieutenant snapped to attention. "Good morning, captain."

"Lieutenant." Foss gestured to the nearest chair. "What can I do for Pruessen Naval Intelligence today?"

"Same thing as last time I'm afraid." His rueful smile failed to hide the lethal nature of his eyes. Eyes that did not belong on such a boyish face.

Foss spread his hands wide. "If you're having trouble training the crew in your new techniques you're on your own. You know what these headhunters are like."

"Yes, Captain."

Saxon's nose twitched, undoubtedly detecting the brandy on Foss' breath.

"I will have another word with my executive officer and see if we can reach an accommodation of some sort. Perhaps I can buy his cooperation with a case of brandy."

"Any assistance will be appreciated, captain." Saxon snapped to attention and left.

Under his breath too low for the pickup to capture, Foss said, "And there goes the future of the empire."

***

"Another mission, another pseudonym," Orson mumbled as he left Foss' cabin.

The Family's orders were abundantly clear but his concerns over the likely outcome of this mission caused his head to throb.

From the thousands of vessels available to the Pruessens they chose *this* ship. Not a warship, not even one of their svelte e-boats but a great hulking mass. *Picaroon* was little more than an armed freighter formerly used by pirates.

Orson wanted the hand-picked finest from the Pruessen navy. He got headhunter dregs. He required a year of intense training. They gave him four months.

What the hell is the Family thinking? In a rush of shame he bit his lower lip. Orson loved the Family. Without the Family he would be nothing more than a Pruessen slave.

Although doubts remained he understood the reasoning behind the strict mission parameters. However, pitting *Picaroon* and her miserable headhunter crew against the best of the League Navies carried extreme risks. All League worlds treated headhunters as nothing more than pirates. The penalty for piracy was death.

The Family could not allow technology of this advanced type to fall into enemy hands. Orson's junior status and expendability made him ideal fodder for this potential suicidal mission. Regardless of the high-risk nature Orson knew he would return from this assignment. He vowed that nothing would stand between him and his true destiny. He would prove his worth to the Family.

Orson reached the gray metal door and read the bronze plaque: Commander Bannister, Department of Planning and Infrastructure. Orson tapped the call button and stepped into the room when the hatch opened. The small, sparsely furnished room contained nothing to distract from its utilitarian function. Behind the single desk sat a man about thirty years old. Tall and broad-shouldered he showed the benefits of years of tough physical training. Bannister glanced from his screen, severe disinterest clouding his features.

"I'm busy Saxon. Make it quick."

"Sir, we have a problem and we need to discuss it."

"Very well." For the first time in weeks Bannister's expression changed to one of acute interest. "What's the problem?"

"You are."

Bannister's curious expression turned lethal.

"For the last three months I have done everything you've asked of me, accomplished every task assigned to me. Despite this you treat me like a piece of shit stuck to your boot. I accept I am the junior member of this team. But it is essential that we work in concert to accomplish the mission. This will not do ... sir. This is a vitally important mission and – "

"I don't need to be lectured about the mission, certainly not by you." Bannister leapt from his chair his hands supporting his weight on the table. "I will not have you bursting into my office making demands. Let's get something straight, Saxon, I did not request you. Nor do I want you here. However, when those we serve give me an order, I obey. But that doesn't mean I have to like it."

Bannister waved impatiently at the only other chair in the room.

"We're stuck with each other so we'll have to make the arrangement work, somehow. But understand me, lieutenant, I don't trust you."

"I've never failed to complete a mission."

"You're missing the point. You, are, reckless. You think your way is the only way and damn everything else. Your intractable, bigheaded attitude is fucking unacceptable." His voice had not risen but his tone remained frosty. "You have great potential, Saxon, but a flaw in your psyche will seriously impede your chances for further promotion. Do you know what your flaw is?"

Orson failed to suppress a sigh. "No sir."

"I think you do," Bannister snapped. "I sense the rage in you but I cannot fathom its origin. Directed rage can be a useful asset. An out-of-control sadist like you introduces a dangerous element to any mission you are part of. Since early youth we have trained you in the arts of our profession. Despite this, your obsession for mayhem overcomes your better judgment."

"So I enjoy my work." Orson smirked. "So what?"

"*So*, if you continue to favor that type of negative, short-sighted attitude it will impact on your effectiveness. Remember your training and control your passions. Failure to do so will eventually lead to your downfall. Do you read me, son?"

"I don't understand why you'd say this. My record – "

"I know about your record. On the surface it's impressive. But it's what is not on the page that's the problem."

"I don't know what you mean."

"Of course you do," Bannister snapped again.

Orson groaned internally when the Advocate held out his hand. He followed the unspoken order of his superior. When their hands touched he sensed the other man's mind merging with his, the tendrils of thoughts intertwining. An Associate was incapable of resisting the power of a white level Advocate. Or so the story went.

Bannister's mind reached into his, probing aggressively. But he could not breach the walls of the dark place Orson kept hidden from all. After a few seconds of intense probing Bannister broke contact. His mouth tightened as he nodded.

"Yes, *there* it is," Bannister said. "Your escalating ambition, your resentment of authority, your belief that you are better than your place within this organization. And of course, your rage."

Orson had devoted his life to the Family but all Bannister could do was complain about his spotless record. He felt his anger mounting.

"Yes, you accomplish your missions. Do you expect a pat on the back for doing your job?"

"No," Orson said through clenched teeth.

"You say *no*, but I sense more." Bannister's eyes bore into him. "You think this mission is a joke, don't you?"

"No, not a joke. But an ill-conceived plan relying on deficient resources."

"I had similar reservations and I expressed my concerns to those we serve."

Orson took a sharp breath.

"They told me what I'll tell you. This mission will proceed on schedule and with the resources provided." Bannister's mouth curled into a pout. "If the mission succeeds under these circumstances we will have done our duty. If it fails ..." he shrugged.

"So, that's it," Orson said.

Bannister stared at him for a long moment before nodding.

"Since you're here you may as well bring me up to date," Bannister said. "How goes the training?"

"What the headhunters lack in brains they make up for in aggression."

"And the retrofitting?"

"At least that's on schedule. But the crew, ha crew, are another problem."

"Perhaps if you chop a few of our noble crew into little pieces the others will become properly motivated?"

"You have no idea how much that idea appeals to me. But with the clan mentality of these *people* if you kill one of them the whole pack will mark you for death."

"You afraid of dying, lieutenant?"

"You should know better, sir." He shook his head. "I suppose if I can't kill a few of them I will have to try a different approach."

"I don't care what you have to do. Slap them into shape."

"I have never failed in my duty to the Family and I won't start now." His anger began to rise and he fought it down. Perhaps

Bannister had a point. In his current infuriated state he referred to the Family aloud.

"Indeed, to date your work has been satisfactory. Your efforts have not gone unnoticed by those we serve. Control, Saxon, is the word for the day. Maintain your control and you could have a bright future." Bannister smiled grimly. "If we return from this mission, of course."

Orson resigned himself to waste no more time trying to change the Family's decision. On the plus side, if he survived this mission he would be in line for promotion to white level Advocate. Gone would be the days of smuggling Kesium into League space. With Advocate status he would contribute significantly to the fall of the League of Allied Worlds. Once they had scaled that high pinnacle ... the Family had plans.

"Very well, commander, thank you for your time." He stood and straightened his waistcoat. "I'll get back to thumping some sense into these numbskulls."

Bannister nodded curtly before returning to his screen.

***

When Orson reached the training area he was not surprised to find the headhunter trainees playing with the swords as if they were toys. Their lax attitude threatened to endanger the mission. These dregs understood only one language. He sought out the toughest of *Picaroon's* crewmen.

Spicer lounged against a cargo container and spared Orson a token glance as he approached. Like the rest of the crew he wore the obligatory beard and carried an unhealthy stink. Spicer ran the ship, his size and natural brutality placing him at the top of the food chain. This made him the ideal candidate for Orson's much-needed demonstration.

"Petty Officer Spicer, finished for the day?"

"Looks like it, doesn't it." Having been top dog for so long Spicer saw no threat from someone half his build.

"So, there is nothing else you can learn about this weapon?"

"What's to learn?" Spicer finally spared him a glance. "Chop into the other man till he stops moving."

"Really?" Orson said. "Why don't you demonstrate how to do that?"

"I'm busy."

"What's the matter?" Orson adopted an arrogant pose to match his tone. "Scared?"

The headhunter laughed roughly. Most of the sycophantic crewmen joined in.

"I'm scared of nothing." The great oaf pushed himself to his feet and seized the broadsword. "Who do you want me to kill?"

"Me." Orson hands rested on his hips, smugness playing across his face. Spicer's obvious irritation was just what Orson hoped for.

The headhunter snorted and shook his head. "You don't even have a sword. And besides, when I kill you I might be brought up on charges."

Orson showed his back to the killer and addressed the fascinated crew. "Now hear this," he shouted. "This training demonstration between Petty Officer Spicer and myself is an open bout. No rules, no rank." The crew smiled at the prospect of a fight between one of their own and an officer.

Anticipating Spicer's next move Orson stepped aside as the blade passed by his left shoulder. When the sword struck the deck Spicer used its momentum to slide it across the metal deck and swing it around to take Orson's head.

Orson ducked under the killing blow. Catching Spicer off balance Orson's heel struck the crewman's exposed right knee. The light kick would hurt but not disable the headhunter. Orson had a point to prove and ending the bout too early would soften its impact.

Spicer grimaced and limped away from his opponent. The oaf approached Orson with greater care this time, one foot sliding after the other, as his training demanded.

Spicer made tentative thrusts at Orson's body while circling him. *I don't have the patience for this game.* He allowed Spicer to step into position behind him.

Orson heard the headhunter's hurried attack as if it were a stampede. This time he slipped inside the reach of the raised sword before it descended. Orson drove the heel of his right hand into Spicer's nose. The sound of splintering cartilage echoed around the hold. Spicer staggered back but to his credit kept his sword raised.

As Orson stepped forward to finish the bout, Spicer swung at his head. Orson caught his arm above the right wrist, twisting it back and around once.

Spicer groaned and the sword dropped from his hand. Orson could have snapped his wrist without effort but settled for a severe sprain. At the end of the day this scum had his uses.

Orson left Spicer to nurse his wounds and addressed the flabbergasted crewmen. "Does anyone else think they know everything about this weapon and its proper use?"

Orson scanned the crew, pleased to see only downcast eyes. *Good, I've made my point without inciting retribution from the clans.*

CHAPTER 23

Date: 1st June, 320 (ASC).
Position: Sentinel Artemis, Planet Carina, Northern Quadrant. Athenian Republic.
Status: Monitor *Truculent* undergoing pre-embarkation preparations.

Commodore Donatella Waugh examined the holo display projecting from the briefing room table. Red and orange status icons peppered *Truculent's* image but were significantly fewer than they were yesterday. Waugh had no doubt all icons would be uniformly green well before their morning departure in five days.

Pleased with the condition of her boat she reclined in her high-backed chair. After so many years, the black leather had contoured to enclose her body. A warm sense of familiarity flowed through her. Waugh chose to ignore the forthcoming unpleasantness.

A smile touched her lips when she faced the stern bulkhead. Dozens of full-color hard copies festooned the wall. John and her four daughters, two granddaughters, associated family and friends smiled back. Official functions with old comrades and new allies. In pride of place in the center of the wall, a large print of her entire crew, taken six months ago on the day of her surprise fiftieth birthday bash. Of course she knew about the *surprise*. Waugh knew everything happening aboard her boat. For the crew's sake she feigned a wonderful display of surprise when a cheer went up as she walked into the boat bay.

That day marked the beginning of a less than subtle change from her D-O, Luis Demianski. With the greatest respect he began referring to her as the Old Lady. Luis never missed an opportunity to remind her she was no longer the young firebrand he had known since they were youngsters. Thoughts of the academy brought her back to her immediate problem. Before the thought festered, the hatch chimed.

"Ad-mit," she said, to the omnipresent Shipboard Management Computer. Waugh steeled herself as the hatch slid noiselessly aside.

A tall, narrow man in his mid twenties bobbed his head awkwardly under the coaming as he entered. He must be at least three centimeters above the maximum height requirement for an attack boat. Anyone possessing a modicum of experience in monitor operations would know to step through the hatch sideways.

His head dipped to clear the low overhead. He snapped to bent-necked attention at the head of the briefing table. Unlike everyone else on her boat, this buffoon wore a class A uniform to better separate himself from lesser beings.

"Lieutenant Stephenson Tivendale, reporting to the Commanding Officer 27th Flotilla, Monitor Corps Third Fleet."

Waugh extended her hand. "Welcome aboard Truculent, lieutenant."

"Thank you, commodore."

Waugh indicated the nearest chair.

His well-rounded Athenian accent assaulted her ears as a tutored afterthought rather than a consequence of proper breeding. *Another social climber.*

Waugh fought the urge to reach across the table and slap the conceited expression from Tivendale's face. *How dare he come aboard my boat pretending to be a qualified officer?* Oh, she knew Tivendale all right. Not personally of course, for they had never met, but she knew his type. She shuddered to think of how many of his ill-deserved ilk wore the uniform of the Athenian Naval Service. Just how much more damage would these amateurs inflict on the Service before people woke up and dealt with them?

"I'm glad to have someone of your experience joining us."

"Thank you, commodore."

"No thanks required, lieutenant." Her stomach lurched. "Admiral Jardine provided an extremely flattering report regarding your time aboard his flagship. You will find life aboard a monitor will take some getting used to. I'm sure someone of your obvious skills will have little difficulty in making the leap."

"I am sure you are correct, commodore."

"Now we come to a relatively minor point. I have a little problem. Perhaps you can help me out?"

"Problem?" Finally his smirk slipped.

"Nothing major I assure you," Waugh continued, somehow containing her rising ire. "We are taking onboard four middies for the next deployment. Do you believe it, *four*. This is where I need your help. An officer of your redoubtable background could take these young officers under your wing and keep them out of mischief. I need your experience as Midshipman Training Officer. So, what do you say? Do you think you can help me out?"

The worm squirmed. “Commodore, with my twin duties in the supply department and Damage Control I do not see how I could possibly find the time to babysit middies.”

“Oh, really?” She examined the overhead as if in deep thought. “Hmm, I understand your position. I certainly don’t wish to monopolize your time. However, I truly believe it would be in the best interests of everyone aboard this boat if you accept your appointment as Midshipman Training Officer. But I see your point and most certainly don’t want to overwork you. So, effective immediately, you are relieved of all responsibilities relating to the Damage Control Department of this boat.”

Tivendale's face dropped. His mouth opened and closed twice before sound came out. “Commodore, I must protest. I naturally assumed my posting to this ship would entail carrying out those duties pertinent to my training. Not to nursemaid a group of children. I must insist –”

“Insist?” Waugh said with menace. “What makes you think you can come aboard my boat and insist on anything?”

“Commodore, Admiral Jardine assured me my posting to this ship–”

“Boat!”

Stunned by the interruption to his well-rehearsed speech Tivendale needed a few seconds to adjust. “I beg your pardon?”

“This is a boat, lieutenant, not a ship. I am a commodore, not a lieutenant. Don’t ever insist to me again.”

His naturally pallid complexion turned pink.

“With all due respect, commodore, I believe that looking after the middies is a voluntary position. As such I prefer to maintain my current postings.”

“What you prefer is of little interest to me, Tivendale. In case the fact has escaped your attention this is not a democracy.

“Your transfer orders come directly from Command Northern Quadrant. As such, I have no choice in accepting your appointment to my boat. Whether or not you like it, while you are aboard my command you will carry out whatever tasks I assign to you. Cross me Tivendale and I will destroy you. Have I made myself clear, mister?”

He raised his chin defiantly and glared down his long nose. “I do not believe Admiral Jardine will be pleased to learn you have treated a serving officer with such disrespect.”

“Well then, why don't you contact your father-in-law and tell him what a bad, bad person Commodore Waugh is?” Under her wilting gaze he examined his hands. "Oh, that's right. He already knows, doesn't he?" Waugh waited until his head snapped up. "Nice chatting with you, Tivendale. You are dismissed."

When the hatch slid shut Waugh slapped her forehead with a flat palm.

"Stupid," she muttered. "All this time in uniform and I still haven't developed the skills to suffer fools gladly."

The bridge hatch slid open and Cmdr Luis Demianski stepped inside. He assumed his usual position in the chair to her immediate right.

"From the red in your cheeks, I assume everything went swimmingly?"

Despite her poor mood she managed a short laugh.

"Even from here I can tell your blood pressure is up. A woman of your age should watch her temper."

Waugh shook her head. "Never again ask me why I accepted promotion at such a young age."

"Young?"

Her eyes narrowed. "As I recall, Luis, you are three months older than me."

"Yes, but aren't I looking grand for it? You however, if you don't mind my saying so – "

"I do mind, commander, I *really* do." They laughed at their shared silliness. "Honestly, Luis, Tivendale will be a problem. He's arrogant enough to be dangerous."

Luis grinned. "Monitor duty is the most dangerous in the Service. Accidents happen to idiots all the time."

"Belay that talk, commander." Her harsh reply was tougher than she had intended.

Probably because the same thought crossed my mind.

"Aye-aye, ma'am." Luis said. "We can handle him."

"Yes Luis, I'm sure we can. But it's not *us* I'm worried about."

CHAPTER 24

Date: 5th June, 320 (ASC).
Position: Sentinel Artemis, Planet Carina, Northern Quadrant.
Status: Embarkation.

Nathan rubbed his dry eyes and looked through the commissary's broad window. Their boat awaited them on the hangar below. The monitor looked like a matt black turtle, resting on her three main skids. The design might look odd to some but Nathan knew that her smooth lines made her the most stealth-capable vessel within Tunguska.

He glanced around the table. Meta counted the floor squares. Ozzie read from his comp pad with eyes long since turned red. Moe snoozed, her head resting on the table.

"Anyone up for a Q & A session?" Nathan asked.

"God no," Meta groaned. "Not another one?"

Moe awoke with a start. "Is it time yet?" She rubbed the sleep from her eyes.

"No. Nathan wants to do another Q&A," Ozzie said.

"Good idea," Moe said. "A Q&A will sharpen us up before we report aboard. Who's going first?"

Stony silence met Moe's suggestion until Meta smirked.

"All right teacher's pet, I've got one for you," Meta said to Nathan. "Who is Aletheia's Friend?"

Nathan and Moe pointed at Ozzie. He leaned back, placed his hands behind his head and grinned.

"Hook me up to the AVU and find out," Ozzie said.

"Yeah, you Thracians are such religious zealots you can probably beat the unbeatable lie detector," Meta said.

"Yeah right," Moe said, "and Salamisians never lie."

"Hey," Meta said, "I don't come from a garden world like Kastoria. We Salamisians have a history of fighting for our very survival on a daily basis. So yes, we might tell the odd fib."

"The odd fib?" Ozzie shook his head. "You almost got expelled for violations of the honor code."

"That was never proved," Meta said.

"And all of those insubordination charges were misunderstandings?" Ozzie asked.

"I don't like taking orders from idiots," she said with finality. "A condition we all share." Her index finger jabbed at Nathan. "Especially you."

"I have no idea what you're talking about, Meta," Nathan said. He had a moment of reflection. People really *do* change. Meta was the most prominent example of change he had ever seen. The wild woman of Salamis had matured in the last three and a half years. They all had. It had taken years of merciless teasing but Ozzie, a native of the Athenian core world of Thrace, had finally been convinced to use contractions. Even Moe had shed the last of her tomboy behavior. *Damn they're good people.*

Nathan checked the time and perked up. *Not long now.*

***

First Lieutenant Jakovich slid down the ladder onto tier two before striding to where Sergeant Redpath guarded the monitor's port side, deck two gangway. Redpath reminded her of the proverbial immovable object. Well within the height limit for attack boats, his broad shoulders and superbly robust physique exemplified the image expected for Marine Special Forces. *Now* that's *how a Spartan should look.* As Jakovich approached him, Redpath gestured with his eyes to a point over her right shoulder. Jakovich resisted the urge to glance back, waiting until she turned to stand next to Redpath.

Four middies approached the boat in an orderly if not precise formation. They had eyes only for *Truculent.*

"God damned grommits," Redpath growled under his breath.

The sergeant did not dislike middies, exactly, but he showed little respect for anyone who had not proved themselves in combat.

"No eating the youngsters on their first day, Rusty," she warned playfully.

Redpath snorted. "Aye-aye, LT."

Jakovich could scarcely believe how young they looked. She knew they were senior middies but the ridiculous youthfulness of the lead middy made her wonder. Something in the young man's gait singled him out from the rest. A combat veteran would walk that way but not a middy.

When the middy drew closer she saw the truth in his eyes. *Yes, it makes sense now.* Those soft gray eyes had seen death at close quarters. His gaze locked onto her as he snapped to attention.

"Midshipmen Hayden, Kaspowitz, Okuma and Telford reporting for assignment to the Monitor Truculent, ma'am."

In no way did his voice match the fresh-faced youth who stood before her.

"At ease, ladies and gentlemen." Jakovich took the comp pad from him, slipping it into the mainframe port. As the verification process took place young Telford made the mistake of eyeballing Sergeant Redpath. Technically a midshipman outranked anyone below the rank warrant officer. Jakovich knew Redpath did not care for such distinctions. Confirming Telford's orders she returned his pad, which now contained his roster and berth allocation.

A vigorous tapping on Telford's shoulder diverted his attention. The black-haired girl behind him pointed to the entrance to the port-side torpedo bay.

Jakovich followed the middies stares. Displaying her usual swagger, Commodore Donatella Waugh marched into the forward bay. The middies stared after her. After all, a living legend did not cross their paths every day. The youngest captain in Monitor Corps history, Waugh had rewritten the rules for combat sorties on the Frontier. Her tactics were required reading at the academy.

"Ma'am, that *was* Commodore Waugh wasn't it?"

Jakovich eyed the middy's nametag. "Yes, Miss Okuma, it certainly was."

The middies grinned like idiots.

"The commodore believes staff officers should not spend all of their time behind a desk. As such she leads by example, taking her boat out on regular patrols like every other skipper."

"The commodore is commanding Truculent, ma'am?" Okuma asked.

Jakovich nodded. "Thumb please," she said.

Telford placed his thumb on the DNA verifier. It beeped once and presented a single green light.

Telford snapped to attention. "Permission to go aboard, ma'am."

"Permission granted. Carry on."

"Aye-aye, ma'am."

He took three precise paces to her right then marched along the gangway as if he had done it a hundred times before. *I'll have to keep my eye on that one.*

***

Passing through the outer hatch Nathan ducked to avoid hitting the low overhead. The boat's sleek profile enhanced her stealth capability and high speed through normal space. The crew paid the price for her impressive credentials.

At a slight crouch he made his way through the corridors, falling into the rhythm of crab-walking through the open pressure hatchways. As the officer's quarters came into view he stopped, leaned against the bulkhead and took a deep breath.

After a moment to calm his nerves he examined his comp pad. Confirming his berth he turned left onto the longitudinal corridor, stopping when he reached the hatch marked 2/29. He tapped the call button and waited.

When the hatch slid aside he stepped sideways over the lip into the room. A spare room, smaller than a middy's quarters at the academy. Two permanent, tiered racks stood against one wall with two lockers in the far corner. Against the opposite wall were two fold-down racks locked into position against the bulkhead. Opposite the lockers, squeezed into the space between the computer station and the wall, was his footlocker. Nothing better illustrated the cramped conditions aboard a monitor than fold-down racks in a room measuring three-square meters. The Corps preferred to think of the quarters as snug.

An officer stood at the far locker and glanced at him.

"You must be Telford." He couldn't have been more than two or three years Nathan's senior.

"Aye, sir." Nathan forgot himself and snapped to attention.

The ensign winced when Nathan's head struck the overhead. "You can cut that out for a start. Middies are reputed to have few enough brain cells without battering what little they have."

Nathan rubbed his head, smiling awkwardly to cover his embarrassment.

Doubled over, the ensign offered his hand. Nathan kept his grip firm but unchallenging.

"Ensign Leonard Saunders," he said. He motioned Nathan to the room's single chair. The ensign sat on the lower bunk. "For the next ninety days I will be your running mate. Outside this hatch it's ensign, Mister Saunders, or yes sir. Inside the hatch and in private, Leo. We aren't as spit and polish as our senior colleagues in the Athenian Naval Service but we work in far closer proximity to one another than in any other warship type. So try to get the stick out of your backside and relax. Understood?"

"Aye-aye ..." Nathan caught himself in time. "I've got it, Leo. I'm Nathan."

"Very well, Nathan. You've been on a monitor before?"

"Third year cruise on the monitor *Audacious*. Hot racking with the ratings."

"Ah, I remember it well. Makes our little digs here seem quite luxurious don't you think?" His accent sounded Republican but had a languid quality common to the worlds of the outer core.

"Absolutely."

"All right, Nathan, in case you haven't researched this cruise in finite detail, here are some of the rules." Nathan had done his homework but remained silent. "When not in your rack you will secure it to the bulkhead. You have access to the boat's database through the terminal. Your running schedule is posted on the database so familiarize yourself with it. The showers and head are forward, Wardroom sternward, both off the longitudinal corridor. Free time is a rarity for the crew but middies will be given ample downtime to continue their studies. Once we get underway someone, I'm not sure who at the moment, will give you the grand tour.

"One last thing." His mouth tightened. "Do not, under any circumstances, borrow my socks. I had a roomy on my first deployment who frequently borrowed my socks. It drove me bloody crazy, so don't do it." He winked. "Any questions?"

"May I ask what your postings are?"

"Apart from keeping you out of mischief I am the boat's Auxiliary Operations Officer and fourth assistant engineer."

With a compliment of only ninety-seven, everyone multitasked. Nathan's eyes tracked to the silver wings above Leo's left pocket.

"You're a flyer?"

"Flight Training School class of 317. I graduated forty-fifth in my year. They offered me a posting to a picket boat in the outer core or this," he said, raising his hands. "Sit in orbit around a safe Athenian world or serve with Commodore Donatella Waugh. A no-brainer, right?"

Nathan nodded. "Have you served with the commodore for long?"

"Third cruise," he said. "Aren't you the lucky middy? Not only do you get to go on an actual Combat Interdiction Patrol but your first skipper is Donatella Waugh."

Nathan felt his idiotic grin return.

"Have you ever – " Nathan stopped as Leo held his hand to his right ear.

Leo made a short swallowing motion. "Saunders." Leo nodded as the thousand-meter stare set in. The hands-free larynx and audio implants were standard issue for monitor crews. Nathan could hardly wait to get his. "Aye-aye, sir. On my way. Saunders out." From his locker he retrieved a sealed container and removed the external communications set. "I assume you've used these before?"

Nathan inserted the earpiece into his right ear and strapped the larynx mike to his throat.

"A tip. Never remove the earpiece, even when showering. Don't fail to answer a hail. There are no excuses."

"I've got it, Leo."

"Very well, settle in and I will catch up with you later."

"Thanks for the heads-up."

"No problem." Leo paused briefly at the open hatch as if he had something further to say, reconsidered, then left. Nathan couldn't be certain if he caught a brief touch of concern on Leo's face.

CHAPTER 25

Date: 5th June, 320 ASC.
Position: Monitor *Truculent*. Moving out of the system.

By the time *Truculent* had ascended from Carina and left orbit Nathan had squared his kit away. He brushed at an imaginary spot on the gray-colored academy flight suit. The soft-soled footwear felt springy underfoot.

Nathan tied into the computer and memorized the names, ranks and faces of every crewmember. The exercise had reaped benefits during his third year cruise, convincing him of its worth. With that task completed he examined the midshipman's running sheet. Nothing until boat orientation at 1400 hours.

Nathan fell onto his rack, impatience eating at him. Monitors scoured the frontier looking for trouble. Pruessen trouble. *This is a lucky boat. Maybe, if her luck holds, we'll see some action. Kill some Pruessen swine even if they're only headhunter raiders.*

He stood and paced the room before dropping onto his rack. Nathan closed his eyes and breathed deeply. "Calm down, relax," he said as he began the meditation exercise. Although he tried to reach a level of controlled relaxation he felt hindered by a curious sensation. *I'm aboard a monitor, surrounded by professionals, so why is Prep warning me.* It didn't burn as it would if he faced imminent, life-threatening danger but pulsed with a slight, but unmistakably steady hum. *Prep mark two?*

Nathan's eyes snapped open. His body buzzed like a plebe on his first day at the mount. *Me, of all people.*

He pushed away from his rack, carefully stooping to clear the low overhead. Nathan locked the rack into position before stepping into the corridor. With the crew at their duty stations preparing for hyper ingression he encountered no one.

The uniformly gray hatches passed by, identified only by stenciled numbers. A locked hatch stood before him, emblazoned with bold red lettering: Maneuvering. Authorized Personnel Only. A drop shaft marked DS 2/5 lay open beside the hatch.

Nathan reached into the shaft through the meter wide portal. His skin tingled as he passed through the environmental force field. He seized the recessed handholds and pulled himself inside the drop shaft. Nathan took a moment to adjust to the null gravity.

The same iridescent green used on the corridor's overheads coated the drop shafts. On his third-year cruise some middies considered the large black arrows to be funny until they lost their orientation and headed 'up' instead of 'down'.

Nathan tucked himself into a ball and rotated his body so his head pointed 'down.' Recalling an unfortunate incident while onboard *Audacious*, he made certain to push away with the most gentle of taps. At deck three he slowed his feeble momentum, reached into the corridor, seized the external handholds and dragged his body into the corridor's normal gravity.

When his feet hit the deck he stood motionless until the queasiness passed. During training the instructors told him to expect the sensation and not to rush things. It would pass in time, they assured him.

Nathan headed aft until another hatch barred his entrance. Maneuvering occupied the greater part of deck three and a large section of deck two. For the next ten minutes he floated within the boat's drop shafts, reacquainting himself with this remarkable vessel. The entrance to the boat bay loomed. Although tempted to examine the hangar areas he thought better of it. In the eyes of the crew, middies were all young idiots who were more trouble than the valuable boat space they occupied. Having familiarized himself with the drop shafts, he navigated to the port side of the boat then down to deck two and back toward the longitudinal corridor. Nathan swung from the shaft, landing firmly on the deck outside the wardroom. His navigation had been accurate to the centimeter but his moment of self-congratulation was short-lived.

***

For the past five days Tivendale fought against his sense of outrage. Yet he could not control his seething anger. *That bitch Waugh will be sorry. My father-in-law will see to her once I have finished this silly deployment. Three months on this little boat will do wonders for my naval resume. Might even get me my fourth star.* When this mission ended he would return home to his darling wife. He shuddered at the thought. But a man with his background did whatever he had to in order to advance. If that meant bedding a sow, so be it.

Admiral Jardine had assigned him to this particular ship for a reason. He wanted dirt on Waugh. Jardine had never specifically said so but Tivendale knew his mind. Jardine and Waugh had some kind of falling-out in the distant past. Tivendale suspected Waugh had gotten the better of him.

The crew was not what he expected. Their overall indifference toward proper discipline appalled him. Even his assistant, CPO Argento, displayed an unhealthy familiarity toward someone of his rank. He put *her* in her place.

Tivendale glanced around the otherwise empty wardroom. *Where could the rest of the crew be?* The ship was underway but surely the services of the entire crew were not required.

When he stepped into the lateral corridor a body dropped onto the deck. Startled, he jumped back.

"You there, what do you think you are doing?" he shouted. "Midshipman, I asked you a question."

The middy swayed as if disorientated before finding his balance.

"Just taking in the sights, sir."

"Are you trying to be funny, mister?" The boy looked too young to be in uniform, even academy grays.

"No sir." Although outwardly respectful there lingered within his appalling accent a hint of weary impudence.

"Stand to attention when you address a superior officer," Tivendale snapped. "What the blazes do you think you are doing playing around in the drop shafts?"

The middy slowly straightened his back as far as he could without hitting the overhead. Even in the slightly hunched position his stance lacked conviction. *Did he just sigh?*

"Familiarizing myself with the layout of the boat, Lieutenant Tivendale."

"Who authorized you to go wandering around the ship?"

"Well, lieutenant, you did."

"What?"

"It's on the running sheet, lieutenant."

Running sheet? Oh yes, of course. He had not found the time to examine it so he used the previous MTO's running sheet.

This middy's accent was going to drive him insane. So slow, such an irritating drawl.

"What is your home planet?"

"Kastoria."

Tivendale nodded knowingly. A colonial *and* an academy senior midshipman. *The universe is definitely conspiring against me.*

"What do you call yourself?"

The colonial brat raised his eyebrows. "I call myself Midshipman Nathan Telford."

"Do not be impertinent. You know perfectly well what I mean. Are you Republican or colonial?"

"Athenian."

Tivendale wanted to slap him. "You were born on a colonial world. Yes?"

"Some people have all the luck."

"Are you trying to be clever, Mister...?" he glanced at his nametag, "Telford?"

"That was never my intention, lieutenant. Merely trying to defuse an awkward situation with a little levity."

Tivendale caught in Telford's lethargic tone the gist of what he left unsaid. The dullness in the eyes. The barely veiled disinterest and his insistence on avoiding the use of the honorific 'sir' was now blatantly clear. *Well, no middy will ever get the better of Stephenson Tivendale.*

"How would you like to be put on report, midshipman?" The boy stood there, the same dull-eyed expression unchanging. "I asked you a question, Midshipman Telford. Are you refusing to answer my question?"

"Please forgive me, lieutenant," he said, with the exaggerated innocence of a five-year-old. "I assumed you were asking a rhetorical question. But apparently not so." He squinted, as if in thought. "What was the question again?"

Tivendale bounced on the balls of his feet.

"You are confined to quarters until further notice."

"Aye-aye, lieutenant." Telford made no attempt to hide his smirk as he turned away.

Impudent wretch.

CHAPTER 26

Date: 5th June, 320 (ASC).
Position: In orbit, Planet Carina.
Status: Awaiting clearance to inner marker, for hyper ingression.

From his position at the Auxiliary Operations Station, Leo Saunders observed how the *real* professionals performed like a well-oiled machine.

"Thank you, harbormaster, we are proceeding now." Cmdr Demianski glanced up from his readouts and nodded once to the captain.

"Helm, set course for the Inner Marker," Waugh said.

"Captain, course is laid in to the I/M," Lt Cmdr O'Donnell replied.

"Very well. Both ahead half, thrust engines only."

"Aye, captain, both ahead half."

"Captain, time to Inner Marker is four hours sixteen minutes."

"Very well." Waugh leaned close to the D-O and whispered something. He nodded and partly stifled a snort.

Leo considered *that* to be a well-oiled machine. Those two had served as captain and operations officer for so long rumor suggested they could read each other's minds.

During the dreary four-hour journey to the I/M the crew stayed alert by conducting checks and counterchecks. Tactical and helm stations kept a wary eye on the surrounding space. The Auxiliary Operations Station provided additional backup. Leo ran his checks but dedicated one of his screens to sweeping the surrounding space. Commercial shipping was unlikely to venture anywhere near an Athenian naval vessel but human beings were flawed creations and mistakes happened. It would reflect poorly on their files to have a wayward civvy plow into their state-of-the-art boat. Leo felt every minute of the next four hours but paid attention to everything happening around him.

"Captain," O'Donnell said, "I/M ETA thirty seconds."

"Very well. D-O, confirm our clearance out of system with harbor control."

"Aye, captain," Cmdr Demianski said.

Leo stifled a yawn.

"Captain, permission to ingress has been granted," the commander said. "We have a clear run to the Outer Marker. All departments report ready. I show green across the board. Full shield power is at your command."

"Very well. Helm, prepare to ingress."

"Aye, captain. Stealth engines on standby. Thrust engines are at your command. Standing by to ingress."

"Thank you. D-O, final systems check."

"All systems optimal, captain. The boat is fully pressurized and buttoned up. All departments report ready. Maneuvering department reports hyper generator buffer at maximum. Awaiting orders to ingress. Shields are at optimal for station keeping and navigation. I confirm we are green across the board."

"Very well, bring shields to Alert Condition one status."

"Aye, captain, shields are at A/C one status."

"Very well. Helm, standard hyper ingression procedures."

"Aye, captain," O'Donnell said, "activating hyper generator, now."

Leo focused the forward optical scanners at the point directly ahead of the boat. The perforation into hyperspace created by the Hydro Magnetic Wave Form generator caused a circle of golden light to form within the darkness of space.

"Captain, ingression point opened."

"Very well. Both ahead dead slow."

"Aye, captain. Helm is responding. Both ahead dead slow."

Crossing the invisible barrier between normal space and hyperspace was indistinguishable to human senses. Some old hands said they could physically sense something during transition but Leo could not.

"Captain, hyper ingression achieved."

"Very well, helm. D-O, confirm shield status."

"Shields are at optimal A/C one status, captain."

"Very well. Helm, secure hyper generator. Both ahead full. ETA to Outer Marker?"

"Aye, captain. Hyper generator is secured. Both ahead full answering. ETA to O/M is one zero niner minutes. Suggest standard roll over and braking commence in fifty-five minutes plus or minus one."

"Very well, helm."

With shields at optimal level a protective energy barrier stood between the boat and the destructive forces of hyperspace. Any vessel entering hyper without adequate shielding would have their hull fried in very short order. *Like sticking your finger into a beaker of undiluted pressic acid.*

One hundred and nine minutes later *Truculent* egressed into normal space. Leo checked his navigation plot and shook his head. O'Donnell had been within thirty-five seconds of the marker. It was an outstanding example of dead reckoning navigation. O'Donnell, like the captain, wore the gold wings of a command pilot. They were not only remarkable pilots but, by absolute necessity, equally talented navigators. They had to be, for once a course had been laid in all variables had to be accounted for before entry into hyper.

Having passed through the outer marker and now free of the restraints of the Carina system, *Truculent* set course toward her northern patrol area.

"Captain," O'Donnell said, "recommend ingression on course 325 by 165 by 289. Recommend roll over for egression in eight point two five hours."

Leo scrutinized the captain and helm officer intently. This was one of the most critical standard procedures any vessel could undertake. A half-degree variation in course could result in an awkward situation at best and a fatal outcome at worse.

"Very well, helm, I concur with your recommendation. Prepare for ingression. Both ahead full after transition on a course of 325 by 165 by 289."

"Aye-aye, captain."

Once the vessel ingressed into hyper Leo checked his panel one last time before CPO Rocca relieved him.

Now, time to feed the inner man.

He should also touch bases with his middy.

***

Nathan looked up from his reader when an officer, about his age, stepped through the hatch. Silver wings adorned his left breast pocket but he did not wear an academy ring. *Probably an OCS graduate awaiting a fighter berth.*

"Allan Mattich," he said, extending his hand. Allan had a nasal twang peculiar to residents of the colony world of Koufos Laurium in Western Quadrant.

"Nathan Telford."

"Settling in all right?" Allan dropped onto the bottom rack.

"Fine thanks."

"Good." Allan glanced at the hard-copy images affixed to the wall above where Nathan rested on his rack. "Family?" He stood to take a closer look.

"And friends." The Penkovsky family, Moe and Livy stared back.

"Wow! Who's this beauty?"

"My fiancée."

"I thought middies weren't permitted to marry."

"We're not married yet. We plan to, the day after graduation."

"Who's that?" Allan said pointing at the image. "She looks familiar."

"That, Allan, is Midshipwoman Moe Okuma." Nathan said.

"Moe? Strange name."

"Her given name is Mary Ann, but I wouldn't recommend calling her that."

"She's *really* attractive. Are you two ...?"

Nathan laughed. "Moe and me? No, she's my best friend. More like a sister than anything else." Nathan noted that Allan's eyes remained fixated on Moe's image. "She's aboard Truculent you know. I could arrange an intro if you like?"

"Ah, well, I –"

Leo stepped into the now-crowded room. "What are we looking at?" After examining the image of Livy, Leo whistled. "You dog, Nathan."

Make that lucky *dog.*

Leo squeezed past Allan, removed a holo cube from his locker and activated it. An image formed of a pretty young woman with short dark hair. The little boy in her arms emulated her soft smile. "Mary-Lyn and James Saunders." Leo swelled with pride. "We got married straight out of the academy and junior arrived a few months later."

"Nathan's planning to do the same thing," Allan said. "I don't know about the baby but the marriage bit. That's right isn't it, Nathan?"

"Yes Allan, and as for starting a family ..." He smiled. "If we did everything right before I shipped out I could be getting some good news when we disembark."

"Good for you," Leo said. "A sound tactical approach. If the academy won't let us marry for some silly fear it will distract us from our studies, that's their call. But they can't stop anyone from starting a family."

"How about you Allan?" Nathan asked. "Any special someone waiting back home?"

Leo took advantage of Allan's awkward delay. "Our young ensign has more than he can handle. A girl in every port, isn't that right young man?"

When Leo shook Allan firmly by the shoulder the young officer blushed bright crimson with astounding speed.

Nathan smiled at Allan's obvious embarrassment. Moe would

love to get her lustful hands on an innocent like Allan. *I wonder if I should hook them up?*

"Enough of this frivolity gentlemen. Shall we retire to the mess to see what disaster Cookie has dreamt up for today's repast?"

Allan, only slightly less red, mumbled his agreement. Nathan leaned against the bulkhead. At the hatch Leo glanced over his shoulder.

"Coming?"

Nathan shook his head.

Leo's eyes narrowed. "I'll catch up with you in a minute, Allan."

Allan nodded before the hatch slid shut.

"What happened?" Leo's asked.

"I have been ordered to remain in my quarters until summoned."

"Why?"

"I spent a little time familiarizing myself with the drop shafts. Mister Tivendale did not approve."

"Tivendale." Leo's single word said all Nathan needed to hear of his opinion of the Midshipman Training Officer.

"I can't remember the last time I was sent to my room without supper. Would I be correct in assuming the lieutenant has no bloody sense of humor?"

Leo choked back a laugh. "You work fast, Nathan. On the boat less than two hours and you've already run afoul of the MTO. Impressive."

"You get that."

Leo sighed. "Did he place you on report?"

"He asked if I would *like* to be put on report." Nathan shrugged.

"What happened?"

Nathan explained to him the gist of the encounter. Leo shook his head. "You're not backward about coming forward are you?"

"I had experience with Tivendale's kind when I was ... in the north." He snorted. "He's an amateur compared with the Pruessens but I recognized his type within a few seconds of meeting him. I'll never bend knee to that sort of power abuse again."

"I thought you'd lost your memories of that time," Leo said.

Damn. "I have. But I get flashes, images of some of what my family went through."

"I see."

"Besides," he added in a lighter tone, "I've heard bad manners are most un-Athenian."

"That's generally correct but there are always exceptions to any rule," Leo said. "Just watch your step with him."

Nathan nodded.

Leo stared at him for a long moment. "He *is* the MTO so I can't overrule his decision. But I will have a word with him and see what I can do."

"I'd appreciate it if you didn't interfere." Leo's startled expression told Nathan to soften his harsh tone and force a smile he did not feel. "I thank you for your concern but I've had to deal with Tivendale's type before. I don't want you or anyone else getting caught in the cross fire. Please say nothing to him. All right?"

Leo sighed. "Are you sure?"

Nathan nodded.

"Very well. Is there anything I *can* do for you, middy?"

"As a matter of fact there is a small matter I would like you to run past Commander Demianski."

CHAPTER 27

Nathan leaned against the bulkhead outside the wardroom hatch. In the twenty minutes since Tivendale had summoned him, several officers passed by, their expressions curious. When Commander Demianski stopped before him Nathan snapped to attention.

"What are you doing here, mister?"

"Waiting for the Midshipman Training Officer, sir."

"Can't you wait inside the wardroom?"

"That would undoubtedly be the sensible thing to do, sir, but the MTO has ordered otherwise." Nathan caught the barest twitch at the corner of the commander's eye before he entered the wardroom.

Less than a minute later the middies spilled out of the wardroom. They pinned themselves against the wall next to Nathan. Moe rolled her eyes. Tivendale stepped through the hatch still licking his lips.

"One of the best meals I have ever had," Tivendale said. "Pity you missed it, Midshipman Telford."

You petty little rodent.

"You have something ..." Nathan pointed to Tivendale's mouth. As the lieutenant checked for refuse clinging to his teeth, the middies drew on their years of self-control training to maintain neutral expressions.

"Today, middies, I will show you how a monitor works. Pay close attention and do not touch anything. Follow me."

Tivendale stepped through the first pressure hatch headfirst. The clod stumbled over the coaming and barely retained his balance. Meta held her thumb and forefinger slightly apart. Nathan cleared his throat. After a few near falls Tivendale took the lift to deck three. They arrived at the entrance to the maneuvering department. Tivendale entered the security code, opened the hatch and stepped inside.

"Maneuvering," he said, with a derisive snort. "On a proper Service warship this would be called by its correct name. Engineering. Why would anyone call it maneuvering?"

"It's a tradition dating back to the old Earth wet-navy days," Ozzie said. "In those times a type of stealth ship had its engineering area called maneuvering because – "

"If I wanted a history lesson I would ask for it," Tivendale snapped.

Some of the crew shot the group inquisitive glances as

Tivendale led them toward the reactor room. A short woman with hard-boned features blocked his path.

"What can I do for you, lieutenant?" Her tone told Nathan she wanted nothing to do with him.

"Nothing, thank you, Commander Chanderpaul," Tivendale said. "I am showing the middies around the ship and thought I would start here."

"Think again," the senior engineer snapped. "It is customary for the MTO to request a time to tour his middies rather than stumbling into my department unannounced. Your blatant disregard for professional courtesy aside, there is the larger issue. This *boat* is currently transiting through hyperspace. The last thing I need is a bunch of grommits cluttering up my department." The commander softened her tone as she addressed the middies. "We egress to N space in two hours. Have your running mates contact me for an appropriate time to tour the department. But one at a time. Later, I will have time to give you a proper overview." Her scowl reappeared when she turned on Tivendale. "For now, lieutenant, take yourself and your middies out of here." She stalked off.

Tivendale bounced on the balls of his feet before clearing his throat noisily. "Apparently we are not welcome here." The middies maintained neutral expressions. "Does anyone have a preference for what we see next?"

"I'd be pretty keen to see Damage Control, lieutenant," Moe said, exaggerating her lazy Kastorian accent.

"Yes, lieutenant," Meta added pleasantly, "let us check out DC."

"I have always been fascinated by the workings of Damage Control," Ozzie said.

Tivendale's face darkened. Not surprisingly, they did not end up in Damage Control. They spent the next three hours in the supply department hand counting inventory.

Back in the wardroom they sat and drank coffee.

"I'd be pretty keen to see Damage Control, lieutenant," Nathan mimicked, causing subdued chuckling from the middies. "You shouldn't antagonize Tivendale like that," he said, addressing them as one.

"Look who's talking," Moe said. "We could hear the blast he gave you through the bulkheads. What did you do to upset such a sweet fellow?"

"I told him thanks very much but I'm seeing someone at the moment."

The middies roared with laughter.

"Hey, Moe," Nathan said, "you're the one who keeps telling me to lighten up."

"Yeah, life is so unfair," Moe said.

CHAPTER 28

Sergeant Redpath was a marine not a nursemaid. He examined the last middy's v-suit and was pleased, though surprised, to find a fault. "Do you want to suck on vacuum, girlie?" he growled. "Tighten your O ring."

"It's Miss Kaspowitz to you, *sergeant*," Meta snapped.

Redpath's face hovered millimeters from the middies. "Tighten your O ring, Miss fucking Kaspowitz." To her credit she did not flinch and dutifully tightened her O ring.

Lt Jakovich stepped in and finished off. "On this boat middies do not rank this sergeant." She set her grim stare on each of them. "Am I being clear, people?"

"Aye-aye, ma'am."

"Very well. Let's take in the neighborhood."

Lt Jakovich led the middies into the starboard airlock with Redpath bringing up the rear. The sergeant made one last check to ensure suit integrity before nodding once to the officer. *If one of these academy kids gets spaced it will seriously bugger up my day.*

"What is the number one rule for dealing with a serious suit breach?" Jakovich asked.

"Don't hold your breath," the middies recited.

Redpath had seen professionals panic during a suit breach. Those who followed protocols stood a chance of living through the experience. Those who panicked and held their breath died or survived with severely ruptured organs. In either event they never went into space again.

Depressurization went smoothly, the hatch was cracked and the middies followed the LT as instructed. Although they had undergone v-suit training at the academy, Hayden's pale face and labored movements caught Redpath's attention.

They walked 'up' the hull to the topside following the running lights to the midships position above the bridge before heading toward the bow. The group kept well clear of the shield blisters. When they reached the leading edge above the torpedo bays they fanned out. In the blackness of interstellar space reading their faces became difficult. Redpath kept close to Hayden. The forward shields flared occasionally as minor spatial debris impacted.

"Lieutenant Jakovich, we are ten minutes from ingression."

Redpath recognized the voice as Cmdr Demianski. A good man.

"Thanks for the heads-up, commander," Jakovich replied.

She's a good man too. She should be. After all, he had taught her everything she knew. Well, almost everything. Still, Jakovich had saved his third stripe after the unfortunate, semi-violent incident at the Iguana Bar on Carina. With his ill-deserved reputation he would be lucky to be a lance corporal if she hadn't run interference for him over the years. *Yeah, she'll do.*

The six figures leaned forward as the boat slowed for ingression. Then Redpath heard the sound he had been dreading. The great pre-transit yack.

Young Hayden doubled over as the nauseating sound of vomiting echoed through their earpieces. Redpath had once seen an entire squad of grommits set off by a single yacker. One of Hayden's teammates broke ranks. The lieutenant beat Redpath to the punch.

"Hold your position, Mister Telford."

Redpath edged toward the stricken middy. "Come on laddie, follow your training," he said to the heaving middy. Redpath did not touch him or tell him how to clear his helmet. As a senior midshipman he should know the routine by heart. Within seconds the heaving subsided and the foul mess flushed into space. Hayden breathed normally and his visor was clean again. Such could not be said for his reputation. The other middies would terrorize him for embarrassing the team. In front of the marines no less.

The marines would not be involved in this training if the middies had a half-competent Midshipman Training Officer. Telford had asked his running mate if they could undergo EVA orientation and his running mate asked the MTO. Tivendale said he did not care one way or the other as long as he did not have to participate. Mister Saunders referred the matter to the D-O who asked Lt Jakovich, who said yes. With Mister Saunders and the other running mates at duty stations the task fell to the marines.

"Very well, lieutenant, time to bring your lambs home," the D-O said.

"Shall do, commander," Jakovich replied. "Sergeant, take up the rear, thank you."

"Aye, LT."

Redpath closely examined Hayden as he passed. His face was pallid and drawn but the color was slowly returning. Telford fell back far enough to check on his friend. They touched helmets, to speak confidentially. Hayden's helmet nodded and they continued on their way back into the boat.

CHAPTER 29

Shortly before midnight Nathan entered the Environmental Control Center. Tivendale had posted an amendment to his running sheet. ECC substituted for the more stimulating environment of bridge orientation.

The environmental control officer looked up from her console.

"Welcome to my parlor of miracles," Cmdr Barbara Grimmett said, spreading her arms wide to encompass her domain. She sat comfortably before a huge instrumentation console spread across the starboard wall from deck to overhead.

"Thank you, ma'am. I'm pleased to be here."

"Rubbish." Her good-natured smile set his mind at ease. "You young people want to be anywhere else on the boat except boring old ECC. But thanks for the polite bull."

Her accent definitely came from a colony world. A large, solid woman of late middle age, her robust physicality evoked images of a kindly aunt with a killer right cross. Her eyes checked his nametag. "So handsome, you're the one who's been upsetting our supply officer?"

"I couldn't help myself, your honor."

Grimmett roared with laughter.

"Come over here, sit on my lap and tell me all about it."

She adopted a grief-stricken expression when he declined her kind offer and took the only other chair in the room.

Grimmett chuckled occasionally as he recounted his tale. "I assumed you were asking a rhetorical question," she parroted. "I bet you're going into flight training after you graduate."

"Cor-rect." He frowned. "How did you know that?"

"Figures. Fighter pilots, all balls and bravado and little in the way of common sense. My third husband was a fighter jock. Magnificent bastard."

"What boat is he on now?"

"Got killed, eight years ago. Headhunter wolf-pack on the frontier. But he nailed the bastard before they got him. A genuine hero." Her eyes bore into him with an intensity that surprised him. "But the silly bugger didn't stop to consider the odds he was facing."

Her attention returned to her readouts. "You need to watch your step around Tivendale. The prick can be a nasty bit of business.

His record is one of unbridled ambition punctuated by fits of sadism against anyone he perceives as a threat."

"So I've heard," Nathan said.

"And why am I telling you this?" Grimmett asked.

Nathan suspected this too was a rhetorical question.

"Bottom line son, he is a commissioned officer and you are a midshipman. So do not antagonize him further, no matter how much fun it is. I can get away with it, you can't." She cocked an eyebrow. "Don't take on an opponent who outguns you. It could kill your career."

Nathan managed to nod.

CHAPTER 30

Date: 6th June, 320 ASC.
Position: Monitor *Truculent*, en route to the frontier. Officers Wardroom.
Status: Morning Mess.

Chief Belsky greeted Nathan. "Mornin', Mister Telford. And what gastronomic feast can I tempt you with today?"

Nathan had repeated this ritual every day since coming aboard.

"Gastronomic feast, Belsky? Rumor has it you can burn water. But no matter. I'll have three eggs, sunny side up, three prime rashers of bacon, a beef sausage, toast and a jug of Kastorian coffee."

"Certainly, sir." Belsky slid a bowl onto the counter. It contained neither eggs, bacon, toast nor anything else distinguishable as food. K ration packs were one of the biggest drawbacks for crews serving aboard monitors.

"I think I'll try something else," Nathan said.

A rumor had been circulating throughout the Corps for years. The story told of a monitor captain in a desperate fight against overwhelming odds. With the boat at condition Winchester, all torpedoes expended, the situation looked dire. In an act born of desperation, the skipper loaded all six forward tubes with Monitor Corps porridge and fired them at the enemy. The salvo, so the story went, created such a foul layer on the hulls of the enemy vessels that they broke off the engagement and fled back across the frontier.

Nathan poked his spoon into a bowl of the legendary porridge staring as the spoon stood by itself. The attending officers chuckled at Nathan's perplexed expression.

No matter how much milk he added, the ferro-crete-like compound refused to soften. Nathan spooned the pasty yellow porridge into his mouth and sighed with relief. It tasted nowhere near as bad as its reputation suggested. *Just like Rhodesian snails.*

When one ate K-pack supplement thirteen - colloquially referred to as bog stew - five times a week, the temptation to assassinate the blameless cook grew in the minds of the crew.

Leo and Allan sat across the table from Nathan. Moe took the seat next to him with her running mate, Ensign Iris Ahrens, beside her.

"How was your watch?" Leo asked.

"Illuminating," Nathan said.

"ECC was illuminating?" Moe said, wrinkling her nose.

"It's all part of the great mosaic that is duty aboard a monitor. Besides, Commander Grimmett is a riot. She's *forgotten* more about the ECC than I will ever learn. Grimmett has done everything on a boat worth doing, short of captain. I can learn so much from her." Nathan prepared to spoon another portion of the gluey porridge into his mouth. "How about you?"

"Great," Moe said. "Commander Matrakas ran a simulated torpedo loading with an emergency jam in the number two tube. The weapon's crew is so good, fast, unfazed by anything. Real professionals." She glanced at Leo. "I suppose the crew has been handpicked by the commodore?"

"For the most part," Leo said.

"Leo and I came aboard at the same time," Ensign Ahrens said. "I still feel like a bit of an outsider, but as Leo said it's to be expected."

As they contemplated the thought the hatch opened.

"Good morning everyone."

Every head turned as a short, elegantly fit woman stepped into the wardroom. Her long, blonde hair was tied back in the regulation manner but tufts of unruly strands hung loosely to frame a pair of inscrutable, pale blue eyes. The officers responded while the two middies sat in open-mouthed awe. Nathan recovered quickly, leaned across and tapped Moe's mouth shut.

The commodore filled her mug and faced the crew. "Bucking for a medal, Mister Telford?"

Nathan fought to maintain an unfazed expression. "Captain?"

"Your first deployment and you're trying the porridge? Action above and beyond the call of duty."

"I live for danger, ma'am." Beside him Moe wriggled nervously.

Waugh's strong Athenian inflection remained but had evolved into a type of trans-Republican accent. Years of working with predominantly colonial crews had to have some positive upshot.

"That's the spirit," Waugh said, holding Nathan's eyes for a few seconds. She glanced around the wardroom. "Where are the other middies?"

"They're on yellow watch, ma'am," Nathan answered.

"Why?"

"Respectfully, ma'am, you will have to ask the MTO."

"What a splendid idea."

Waugh held her hand to her right ear and keyed her L-M. "Supply - captain." A short pause. "Mister Tivendale, I am in the wardroom and am missing two middies." For nearly a minute the commodore sipped coffee and with a steady cadence tapped her foot onto the deck. "You are aware of the regulations concerning midshipmen aboard this boat so comply with them. I expect all middies to be back on the same watch by 1200 hours. Captain out."

During the exchange the commodore never raised her voice or adopted a threatening tone.

"Mister Telford, you are currently assigned to ECC are you not?"

"Yes, ma'am. I'm back on duty during blue watch."

"Watch out for Auntie Babs. She has a reputation for deflowering young middies."

Moe giggled like an adolescent.

"I'm quick on my feet, captain."

He expended enormous effort to prevent his bottom lip from quivering.

Waugh chuckled before turning her attention to Moe. "And how are you finding life on a monitor, Miss Okuma?"

Nathan nudged Moe under the table when she failed to respond. "Ah, fine ... just fine. Ah commodore, captain ... ma'am."

"Good for you."

Waugh's inscrutable smile was identical to the images Nathan had studied at the academy. *My God she's impressive.*

The captain drained her mug, placed it in the tray and left.

As soon as the hatch snapped shut Moe's head fell in slow motion to the tabletop. She repeated the process, each time producing a hollow thud when her head hit the table.

Nathan looked across the table. "Allan Mattich, may I introduce you to Moe Okuma."

CHAPTER 31

Date: 12th July, 320 ASC.
Position: Monitor *Truculent*, on station: Ibis Nebula.
Status: Alert stand down.

Nathan had been under the shower for less than a minute when his earpiece beeped. Stepping from under the water flow he held the L-M to his throat and keyed it.

"Telford." Nathan made sure to hit the stud after making his transmission.

"Midshipman Telford, report your location." Tivendale's tone suggested a good mood for a change. *Moron.*

"Officer's head, lieutenant."

"Very well. Carry on."

Odd. Back in his quarters Nathan hit his rack and fell asleep instantly. Sometime later his comm beeped, waking him from a deep slumber. Nathan recalled Leo's warning. *There is no excuse for not answering your comm.*

"Telford," he croaked.

A slight pause. "Mister Telford, this is Chief Petty Officer Argento, supply office." Her deep voice carried a disconcerting undertone. "Under orders from the supply officer I must ask you for your location, sir."

"Mount Olympus," he said. Then Nathan thought better of it. Argento undoubtedly had little choice in the matter. "I'm in my quarters, chief."

"Thank you. Good night, sir."

The interruptions to Nathan's sleep increased with two or three calls disturbing his rest during every six-hour downtime shift. Unlike Moe, Nathan took time to get back to sleep after each disturbance. As a result he averaged only three hours of fitful sleep per downtime shift.

CHAPTER 32

Date: 13th July, 320 ASC.
Position: Monitor *Truculent*, on station: Ibis Nebula.
Status: Alert stand down.

Waugh contemplated the star map that floated within the holo field. She keyed her larynx mike to connect with the Shipboard Management Computer.

"SMC, zoom out."

The image expanded to encompass the entire Tunguska Fault. The northwestern approaches into League territory were the responsibility of the Bretish Commonwealth. The Francorum Union covered the northeastern approaches.

Athens plugged the huge gap in between. Due to the elongated nature of this section of the frontier, jutting as it did well into the north, it had acquired the colloquial name of the Slot. This was Monitor Corps patch.

"SMC, zoom in." After a few seconds, "Stop."

The Ibis Nebula hovered slightly off the dead center of the Slot, one point two light-years from the Rio Grande. Unlike other nebulas, Ibis contained trace quantities of Boronium isotopes that effectively scrambled sensors efforts to penetrate it. The effect worked both ways so a string of small, powerful sensor buoys was seeded from the ingression point to their location. *Truculent* hovered within the nebula biding her time until an unsuspecting interloper crossed her path.

Waugh wondered about her decision. Scarcely half a light year from their position was the Poseidon Shoals. Only an insane captain would venture into it. Within the shoals, intense gravity sheer was the norm, together with massive ionic disturbances and hyperspace antimatter eruptions capable of wiping a ship from existence. Waugh played a hunch that greed would overcome the better judgment of certain rapacious captains.

So *Truculent* lurked in total secrecy. With sensors set to passive mode and all unnecessary systems shut down, no energy telltales betrayed her position. Day in, day out, *Truculent* noted the passage of various types of shipping, ranging from foolhardy pleasure yachts to heavy bulk freighters and general-purpose shipping.

Thirty years in the business of defending the Republic's borders had failed to curb Waugh's impatience. She had taken a chance, played a hunch, but a month of patient waiting had failed to glean anything close to a positive outcome. Waugh did not care to think about her last patrol being the most disappointing.

She paced the briefing room before stepping onto the bridge. With tactical sensor functions funneled to the Ops Station, the nearly deserted bridge gave the forlorn impression of a party where all the children had left early.

"Anything happening, Maggie?"

Lt Lehmann leaned back in her chair and rubbed the back of her neck. "Not so much as a stray rock, skipper." Her bored tone matched Waugh's mood.

"Very well. If you need me I will be on the Parade Ground."

"Aye-aye, skipper."

Minutes later, clad in a fighting suit, Waugh slipped from the drop shaft onto the boat bay deck. She arched her back, relieved as the vertebra popped.

The largest open space on the boat, the boat bay and its adjoining hangars were the only areas on *Truculent* where crew members taller than 170 centimeters could stand erect. With a respectful nod to the academy, while being used for this purpose, the boat bay was referred to as the Parade Ground.

Waugh took in the scene around her and nodded her approval. Activities ranged from one end of the bay to the other. Under the watchful eyes of Senior Chief Petty Officer Scaroni, the CPO's ran the enlisted crew through a dynamic calisthenics program. Officers performed standard unarmed combat exercises, others practiced the lethal Aikido. Pilots kept their reflexes sharp with Kendo exercises. The marines used the long, cold steel bayonets for the same purpose.

In a corner on the starboard side of the bay the middies stood in a tight circle. Telford held the rapt attention of every eye and ear in his small group. As captain of the academy Kendo team they deferred to him in all matters pertaining to the ancient art of two-handed sword fighting.

Telford clapped his gloved hands and the circle broke up. Okuma and Hayden found a clear area for themselves while Telford and Kaspowitz took up positions in a corner. They bowed to one another and drew their swords. The sword tips almost touched.

Unlike in her day the middies carried their swords strapped to their backs rather than on the left hip. Perhaps this indicated a new trend for a new generation of middies. Or could it be that one of them chose to do it and the others followed?

The bout had been underway for nearly a minute when Kaspowitz's impatience showed. Telford remained immobile as if baiting her. She tried circling him but he mirrored her every movement. Kaspowitz advanced aggressively and tried for a head shot. Telford ducked under her wild swing and as she passed he rapped her on the rump with the flat of his sword. From across the Parade Ground Waugh heard her anguished cry.

Telford smiled at the enraged middy and tapped his left shoulder. As Waugh had observed, Kaspowitz dropped her left shoulder when she attacked. The middy's grimace indicated her disapproval of having her shortcomings pointed out. A curt nod acknowledged his instruction. Again she approached her opponent but this time showed greater circumspection, one foot ahead of the other in short, sliding increments. Kaspowitz leaped forward and a fierce parry ensued. Failing to find an opening in Telford's defense she backed away. Next she attacked with speed and took a wild swing at his head. Telford ducked under the murderous blow, dropped onto one knee and struck upward. A dull buzz confirmed he had found the heart sensor with the tip of his blade.

Waugh blinked in astonishment. Telford had read his opponent's movement, apparently before she thought of it herself. And his reactions were bloody fast. Another anguished howl from Kaspowitz. Telford shook his head and tapped his left shoulder.

"Fast isn't he?" Luis said.

Waugh had become used to his stealthy approach. Her threat to tie a bell around his neck had fallen on deaf ears.

"Hmm."

"You could take him, skip," O'Donnell said.

Luis snorted.

Over the next three minutes Telford tagged his opponent four times without registering a return hit. Kaspowitz had all the requisite skills but even with her blood up was outmatched. In a contest between ice-cold control and passionate fire, control always won.

After the fifth kill Telford's attention drifted to the other two middies. He said something to Kaspowitz, she objected with a vigorous shake of her head and he acquiesced. Within sixty seconds he had *killed* her five more times, ending the bout. After a short bow he walked to the other middies.

Waugh glanced at the boat's command pilot whose mouth hung open. “Still think I can take him, Scobie?”

“That young man is going to make one hell of a pilot, skip,” O’Donnell said.

“He could dice you like a blender,” Luis said.

Waugh set her eyes on her old friend. “Care for a bout, Luis?”

“I don't have a sword.”

“You can borrow mine,” O'Donnell offered.

“No I can't,” Luis said hastily.

“Suit up, commander. Let's see how your Aikido skills are holding up.” She grinned and added, “Old man.”

CHAPTER 33

Date: 14th July, 320 ASC.
Position: Monitor *Truculent*.
Status: Dog tired.

Nathan returned to his quarters after morning mess and unhooked his rack. As much as he hated to admit it Tivendale's childish campaign was taking its toll. Tivendale had abandoned any pretense of professionalism and openly increased pressure onto the middies. No task was too loathsome, too dirty, too humiliating. No opportunity to make the middies' lives miserable was missed. Yet they refused to capitulate and fought him right to the edge of insubordination. *Babs had said don't take on an opponent who outguns you. Maybe she was right.*

Although he longed for sleep there was a problem that had been bothering him for days. He placed his rack in the upright position and made for the hatch.

Allan was sound asleep while Leo reviewed some notes. "Nathan," Leo whispered, "where are you going?"

"Need to check on something," he said, in an equally low whisper. "Be back in a minute." Nathan slipped through the hatch before Leo could respond.

Nathan passed the wardroom and hit the hatch call-button to the enlisted quarters. Forty-one ratings rotated through the quarters every six hours. They were crammed into the small area in racks three high with only a few centimeters of headroom between them. When one watch left their racks to go on duty the next watch took their place. Hot racking at its worst.

When the hatch slid open the stench struck his nose like claws. Nathan began breathing through his mouth. A handful of NCOs sat on the deck playing cards. A petty officer with the nametag Dearkov appeared to be the senior rank.

"Has someone smuggled a cat onboard the boat?" Nathan grimaced.

"I don't understand your meaning ... *sir*." A large-framed, solid young woman with bad skin, Dearkov's scraggily black hair reminded Nathan of a rug stolen from a mangy dog.

"My meaning is the stink. What the devil is that?"

"That'd be us ... *sir*."

"Excuse me?"

"There are forty of us crammed into this area. Sorry if our odor offends you ... *sir.*"

Nathan's jaw tightened but he ignored Dearkov's rudeness and stepped to the nearest air filtration scrubber mounting. He reached up and unbuttoned the housing. Nathan recoiled as the stench made his eyes water. Shutting the housing he addressed the card players.

"How long has it been since these scrubbers were replaced?"

"I wouldn't know – "

"Has anyone reported this to the ECO?"

Dearkov shrugged.

Nathan resisted the urge to tell her what he thought of her attitude and left. A minute later he slipped from the drop shaft onto deck three. Before entering the supply office he forced his breathing to calm. Fortunately, Tivendale was apparently catching up on his beauty sleep.

"Good morning, Chief Argento."

"Good morning, sir." Her expression indicated a restive mood.

"Good to put a face with the voice at last."

The face was attractive in a plain sort of way. Argento's large brown eyes took on a wary set.

"How may I assist you, sir?" Her colonial accent did not sound as pronounced as it had over his earpiece. To have been promoted to chief petty officer at such a young age she must be very good at her job.

"I'd like thirty air purification scrubbers, thank you," he said. No reply. "Is there a problem, chief?"

"I am unable to comply with your request, sir."

"Because?"

Argento cleared her throat. "Sir, our stock of those items was not replenished during our last layover."

"Are you saying there are no spare scrubbers aboard this boat?"

"There are a few, sir."

"Good. I'll take all you have."

"I can't do that either, sir."

Nathan stared coldly at Argento. Until this moment he assumed she hadn't volunteered to be Tivendale's Judas.

"Sir, I am under orders from the supply officer not to touch the stock without his express permission."

Nathan exhaled slowly as he dropped into the spare seat. He snapped the stud from his epaulet, allowing it to drop over his shoulder. "Talk to me, chief."

The knot left Argento's shoulders, a relieved smile forming as she unbuttoned her epaulet. "Off the record, sir?" Nathan replied with an impatient nod. "Firstly sir, the supply officer neglected to order the required stores, even though I had prepared a complete inventory. I highlighted those stores requiring the most urgent attention. When he finally discovered there is actually a need for scrubbers he decided to stash away the few we have for the exclusive use of the senior officers. I guess he thinks if he kisses up to the officers no one will twig to what a screw-up he is." She smiled uncertainly until Nathan nodded. "But I guess you already know that, Mister Telford."

As he reset his epaulet he nodded and made certain his voice did not reflect his inner rage. "Thanks for the heads-up, chief."

"Anytime, sir."

Nathan left the office and headed back to his quarters. *You're going to earn your pay this week, Nathan.*

CHAPTER 34

Date: 18th July, 320 ASC.
Position: Monitor *Truculent*. Environmental Control Center.
Status: Condition stand down. Grey watch.

Barbara Grimmett smiled. "I sincerely hope you showered since your last watch, Nathan?"Her expression of exaggerated trepidation brought a smile to his lips.

"I soaked for an hour in a solution of pressic acid." Nathan sniffed under the armpits of his freshly cleaned flight suit. "Like a rose garden in spring time."

"I am relieved beyond words." Grimmett cautiously leaned forward to take an exploratory sniff.

It had taken Nathan four six-hour shifts, spread across three days, to return the air in the enlisted quarters to a tolerable state.

Since no fresh scrubbers were available Nathan took a different approach. The cargo holds saw little use so the scrubbers were in fair shape. He removed them from the holds and gave them a thorough cleaning before placing them in the enlisted crews' quarters. Nathan took the filthy scrubbers from the crew quarters to a small corner of the maintenance bay. Nathan soaked the scrubbers in a solution of industrial strength solvent before scouring the bulk of the foul mess from them. They were so badly degraded that the cleaning process was not entirely successful. He fitted the inefficient scrubbers to the cargo holds. Undoubtedly the air in the holds would become unpleasant but that couldn't be helped. The crew always came first. He smiled at that thought.

Yesterday he stumbled upon two ratings sharing an intimate moment in cargo hold two. He turned his back while they slipped back into their flight suits. They stood to attention awaiting the expected reprimand. No regulation forbade the crew from *interacting* with one another, as long as they observed military proprieties. He deliberately took his time while forming an appropriate response.

"Where are you, Chief Petty Officer Rocca," he asked the young non-com.

"Sir?"

"Petty Officer Allenby," he continued, "Where are you?"

"Cargo hold two, sir?" she ventured.

"Under whose authority does cargo hold two fall, Chief Petty Officer Rocca?"

"Yours sir?" Although his accent bespoke a colonial upbringing his attitude needed readjustment. Nathan's expression said as much.

"Aw, come on Mister Telford. The crew have been using cargo two, for ah, get-togethers, for years. It's accepted practice."

"And how acceptable do you think it will be if the supply officer catches you two numbskulls in flagrante?" Nathan allowed a few moments for the thought to sink in. "Send the word out. The cargo holds are off limits. Forthwith they will be known as the forbidden zone. Tell me you understand my meaning."

"Aye-aye, sir!" they intoned as one.

"You two should show a little restraint," Nathan continued, showing a stern expression not matched by his mood. "Try playing cards or something." Their expressions were priceless.

"When I was posted to *Audacious* a lot of the crew played cards." He leaned forward and spoke in a conspiratorial tone. "Apparently the coolant exchange room on deck two, had been used for ... the occasional game of cards. I wouldn't know myself but that's the rumor. And, from what I've heard it's sufficiently cool so the cards, don't stick together." The two non-coms smiled. "Now follow me and keep quiet."

Nathan repeated the grimy business of removal, cleaning and fitting until he completed the disagreeable task. During the process the stinking residue adhered to his hair, skin and clothing with the tenacity of industrial grade adhesive. No amount of scrubbing could remove the final hint of foulness. Despite employing his best cleaning skills his flight suit reeked of such vileness that the ward room officers kept their distance. Help arrived from an unexpected source.

He returned from his watch to find a stack of disposable coveralls sitting on his trunk. CPO Argento had undoubtedly smuggled them out of the supply department at great personal risk. Without delay he changed into a pair of the clean coveralls and soaked his filthy flight suits overnight in the small laundry. Only senior officers had their clothing cleaned for them.

Returning the crews quarters to a livable standard made him an overnight success with the ratings. Instead of being largely ignored, greetings flew at him from all quarters. "Good morning, Mister Telford." "How's it going, Mister Telford." One particularly cheeky young petty officer, "Smelling good, Mister Telford." Even Petty

Officer Dearkov nodded respectfully, stepped aside for him in the lateral corridor and produced something distantly akin to a smile.

His rotation through the ECC had almost ended. His next posting would be a return to maneuvering. Over the past six weeks Nathan had served in every department on the boat, except for bridge orientation. The MTO had kept that prized posting from him.

With only days left in ECC he could not deny he would miss Auntie Babs. With Tivendale riding his coattails at every opportunity her backing meant a lot to him. Always there with a supportive word for him and a nasty set of expletives for his nemesis.

"Oh shit," Grimmett said.

"What's up?"

"Damn air flow tube in weapons bay one is blocked again."

"Is there anything I can do?"

"Yeah. Mind the store, will you?" She headed for the hatch.

"Me?" Nathan said, to her retreating back.

"It's not hyper science, Nathan. Remember, while we're at alert stand down the SMC will take care of most of the operations automatically. See all those green lights?" Nathan nodded at the enormous bank of telltales. "If any of them turn orange or red contact me. All right?"

"Aye-aye, ma'am."

"Now cut that out," she snapped facetiously.

Nathan busied himself keeping his eyes fixed onto the array of green lights. He made certain to keep his hands folded in his lap to avoid the chance of touching any of the controls. His concentration on the task caused time to pass rapidly. When the hatch slid open behind him Nathan spun his chair to face it. His contented mood fled.

"What are you doing, Telford?" Tivendale asked.

"My job ... lieutenant." Nathan had stopped disguising his jaded tone when responding to the MTO.

Tivendale's eyes widened and his complexion darkened with alarming haste. Four strides brought him towering over Nathan.

"Stand up when I talk to you," he screamed.

Nathan sighed wearily as he dragged himself to his feet.

"Stand to attention. How many times must I tell you?"

To avoid insubordination charges Nathan adopted his most uninspired stance.

"Now, what are you doing? Where is Grimmett?" Tivendale stood so close Nathan could tell what the lieutenant ate for breakfast.

"*Commander* Grimmett left me in charge of the ECC while she attends to an urgent matter elsewhere on the boat ... lieutenant."

"You? She left *you* in charge?" He sniggered in a particularly irksome fashion, even for him.

"That's correct, lieutenant." Nathan barely stifled a yawn.

"In that case, Mister Acting ECO," he said, "I will direct my complaint to you. There is a disturbing odor emanating from the cargo holds. I want the problem fixed immediately."

"You've been into the cargo holds?" Nathan asked innocently.

Tivendale's skin prickled. "Do not dare speak to me in such a disrespectful manner or I will have you brought up on charges. Now do your job, Mister ECO." His chin thrust into the air as if enticing Nathan to refuse.

"Certainly, lieutenant." Nathan kept his expression neutral as the idiot's face drooped. "As soon as I am relieved I will pick up new scrubbers from supply and take care of the problem for you."

Tivendale bounced on the balls of his feet. "There are no scrubbers available so you will have to take care of it some other way. Now, follow me."

The lieutenant got halfway through the hatch before realizing Nathan had not moved.

"I said follow me," he roared.

"I am unable to comply with your order, lieutenant."

Tivendale got back in his face. "Are you refusing to obey my orders, Midshipman Telford?"

"Lieutenant, I have been ordered to stay at my post until the ECO returns. To do otherwise will be a dereliction of duty." Nathan stared squarely into his eyes. "You wouldn't want one of your middies getting into trouble ... would you, Lieutenant Tivendale?"

"You will do as I say, you will follow my orders you insolent colonial brat."

Nathan passed his sleeve across his face to remove a few drops of spittle. "No, lieutenant. I will not abandon my post."

Nathan's body stiffened but he did not react as Tivendale punctuated his words by poking him in the chest. "You will follow my orders or I will have you brought up on charges of insubordination and have you removed from this ship." Poke, poke, poke.

"Boat."

"I am the midshipman training officer and you will show me the respect due to me." Poke, poke, poke.

"Lieutenant, your current actions could be legally construed as assault on a fellow officer," Nathan said quietly.

"You are not an officer, boy. And you do not give me orders, I give the orders. Do you hear me?" Poke, poke, poke.

"Last chance."

"Sir," poke, "you will address me as sir," poke, "do you hear me?" Po...

Nathan brushed Tivendale's hands away from his body with a fast upward sweep of his forearms. A heartbeat later the heel of his right hand struck the center of the MTO's sternum. The lieutenant staggered back grabbed his chest and winced. For a moment Nathan regretted pulling his punch. As Tivendale backed away, the pain fled from his face. In its place, a triumphant grin.

"I have you now, Telford," he squeaked. "Striking a superior officer. You are finished." He panted heavily, the pure delight causing his face to glow.

Aunty Babs stood in the hatch jam, her expression obscure. Tivendale finally noticed her.

"Ah, Grimmett, good," Tivendale panted. "Did you witness what happened? Did you see what this midshipman did to me?"

"Yes, I saw everything," Grimmett said quietly. "Do you wish to lay charges?"

"Of course I do."

"I wasn't talking to you, lieutenant." Tivendale's face sagged. "Well, Mister Telford, do you wish to lay charges against this officer?"

"Are you insane?" Tivendale shouted. "He struck a superior officer. You said you saw him do it."

"Yes, I did, didn't I?" Babs winked at Nathan, too quickly for the dim-witted MTO to catch. "As a matter of fact I saw everything. If you hadn't been shouting so much you would have heard the hatch opening before you attacked the middy." Tivendale's jaw dropped open. "To be perfectly honest, Mister Telford's level of restraint to your unwarranted attack was quite frankly remarkable. I would have decked you the first time you put your paw on me."

"But, but, he, he struck me." Tivendale hovered on the brink of a meltdown. "I am an officer, and he, he, does not respect me. He calls me *Mister* Tivendale, he calls me *lieutenant*, but never calls me *sir*. He should be court-martialed. He ..."

"Shut up you twit." Bab's disgust disappeared as she turned to address Nathan. "Mister Telford, do you wish to file charges against Lieutenant Tivendale?"

"No ma'am."

"What?" she cried.

“Lieutenant Tivendale was good enough to show me a few Aikido moves. Right, lieutenant?”

Through his expression of stricken misery Tivendale managed a jerky nod. Babs stepped closer to Nathan, her mouth a tight line.

“What are you saying, middy?”

“What I’m saying, ma’am, is clear enough.” Nathan leaned in closer to her and whispered, “Please Auntie, let me handle this my way.”

She shook her head ruefully before rounding on Tivendale. “What are you doing here, Tivendale?” she growled.

Totally flustered Tivendale took several moments to partially recover his composure. “The smell,” he finally stammered. “The smell in the cargo holds. It is quite unpleasant. I want it remedied.”

“Oh you do, do you? Very well, supply this department with thirty air filters and I shall consider it.”

Tivendale's face flushed. He spun on his heel and stormed from the ECC without another word.

CHAPTER 35

Date: 19th July, 320 (ASC).
Position: Monitor *Truculent*. Briefing room.
Status: Captain's mast.

Waugh sat passively at the head of the table. Luis took his place to her immediate right with Tivendale two seats away from him. The middies entered the briefing room dressed in immaculate gray class A uniforms, as befitted the occasion. They took their seats beside Ensign Saunders.

Luis raised his computer pad slightly. "SMC, record. This captain's mast is now in session." For the record he read the full names, ranks and postings of all participants, careful to correctly note the midshipmen who stood accused. "The charges brought against the accused are, A: Gross insubordination. B: Dereliction of duty. C: Gross disrespect of a serving officer." He sighed faintly. "How do the accused plead?"

Saunders straightened his back. "Sir, for the record I have been asked to plead on behalf of all accused, not guilty."

"Lieutenant Tivendale, describe the incidents leading to your request for a captain's mast," Luis said.

"Certainly, commander." Tivendale's confident tone flowed as smoothly as treacle over a knife's blade. "Since being appointed as Midshipman Training Officer I have witnessed these midshipmen flagrantly disregarding authority. I have repeatedly ordered the accused not to contact me during my rest time but they have ignored my orders. Because they are only children I have tolerated the matter in the hope they will see reason. But it has become blatantly clear that they have no respect for the lawful chain of command. The situation has become intolerable and moreover confirms my belief that academy children should not be permitted aboard a serving warship.

"They refuse to call me *sir*, as is my right. This untenable situation is exacerbated by their generally poor attitude, their disrespect for authority and their poor work habits. Such misbehavior is one thing, but when they deliberately disobey the orders of a superior officer they go too far. Insubordination, plain and simple.

"I respectfully submit that the accused are guilty as charged. When found guilty they should be relieved of all duties, confined to quarters and returned to the academy at the earliest opportunity. Furthermore, the Superintendent of Midshipmen should be notified of these proceedings together with a recommendation that these four people be dismissed from the academy." His self-righteous smirk loitered until he recalled the protocol. "That is my statement of charges for the record, sir."

"So noted," Luis said. "Ensign Saunders, do you care to respond to these charges on behalf of the accused?"

"Yes sir, I sure would."

Waugh kept her smile in check.

"Might as well get the big one out of the way first," Leo continued. "Lieutenant Tivendale, tell this hearing of an instance of this alleged insubordination."

"Certainly, ensign."

"Midshipman Telford, did I not order you and the rest of the middies not to contact me during my downtime?"

"Yes, lieutenant, you did give such an order."

"There see, he admits it. I told you so."

Tivendale addressed his remarks directly to Luis. Recalling the chewing out she had given him, his eyes avoided her.

Spineless slug.

Saunders remained unfazed. "Can you cite any other occasions where the accused refused to follow a direct order from you, no matter how ludicrous your order might have been?"

"That is an impertinent remark, ensign. You are addressing a superior officer." He tugged at his waistcoat. "I do not need to cite other instances of insubordination. One is quite sufficient."

Leo leaned back, his easy smile hanging like an accusation. "So, Lieutenant Tivendale, the charges of insubordination are based solely on the proposition that the middies contacted you during your downtime. Is that correct?"

Leo's remorseless droning dulled Tivendale's former confidence.

"Lieutenant Tivendale?"

"Yes. I ordered them not to contact me and they ignored my order."

"Very well lieutenant. Let's move on shall we? The matter of their quarters not being up to scratch. In what way was this so?"

"Bunks not made properly; clothes strewn about the quarters. Kit not kept in the storage area provided and general messiness."

"Really?" Leo sighed wearily. "Midshipmen are taught from day one to keep their quarter's neat and tidy at all times. Mister Hayden, during your first month at the academy you were cited on a number of occasions for the messy condition of your quarters."

"Yes sir. It saddens me to admit that was the case."

"What was the punishment for this messiness?"

"I marched punishment parade during midsummer until I learned the error of my ways."

"Thank you, Mister Hayden. I will waste no more of the captain's mast by having the rest of the accused cite similar stories of their time at the academy. For my part I have observed no such tardy behavior from my running mate. I submit for the record affidavits from all running mates." He slid a data chip across the table to the D-O. "Suffice it to say senior middies would not be aboard this boat if they were not housebroken. You should know that Lieutenant Tivendale." Leo smiled shrewdly. "Oh, my apologies lieutenant, you didn't attend the academy did you? No matter. Let's move on."

Tivendale's face flushed. Waugh chose that moment to rub her hand across her mouth. Luis' left eyelid twitched. Saunders continued in the same remorselessly languid tone.

"Now let us address your allegations of poor attitude, disrespect for authority and bad work practices. Again, lieutenant, could you cite an instance of each of these supposed misdemeanors?"

Lines of irritation creased Tivendale's face. "My response to the previous charge covered disrespect for authority. And as for bad work practices," he shrugged, "you cannot have one without the other."

Leo waited for a moment as if expecting more. "So, lieutenant, you cannot cite one instance to back up these charges. Is that correct?"

"All of this is of little consequence, ensign. I have submitted my word under oath. The word of a serving officer."

Leo nodded slowly before addressing the D-O. "Sir, I respectfully submit that charges B: Dereliction of duty, and C: Gross disrespect of a serving officer, be dismissed due to lack of corroborating evidence."

"Lieutenant Tivendale?" Luis asked.

Tivendale squirmed in his seat and nodded with a sharp jerky movement. "Very well, commander, I agree to drop those two charges. However, I insist charge A remains."

"So noted for the record. Ensign Saunders do you have anything else you wish to add?"

"Yes, thank you, sir." Leo slid another computer chip across the table. "This chip contains endorsements from every department head on the boat." He cleared his throat. -"With the obvious exception of the supply department. They unanimously attest to the high work ethics of each middy. They also state that they encountered no instances of disrespect for authority, tardy work practices, poor attitudes or insubordination."

"Their statements mean nothing," Tivendale grumbled.

"Submitted as rebuttal evidence to show the character of the accused, sir."

"So accepted and entered into the record."

"It does not matter what little tricks you try, Saunders. They disobeyed my orders and that stands."

Leo tugged on his bottom lip.

"Commander Demianski, do you recall a meeting we had about three weeks ago?"

Tivendale sat bolt upright in his chair as if he'd been goosed.

"Refresh my memory, Ensign Saunders," Luis said.

"With pleasure, sir. You were good enough to grant Mister Telford and myself a few minutes of your valuable time. We met in this very room in fact. I mentioned that the MTO had ordered all middies not to contact him. I wondered if this was strictly in order. I asked how are the middies to be supervised if they cannot contact him."

"Ah, yes, it comes back to me now." Luis said. "And I believe I said balls to that. Does that sound about right, Mister Telford?"

"Balls to that? Yes sir, that's my recollection." Telford maintained a neutral tone. Tivendale's jaw dropped.

"I believe I said you should disregard such a stupid and obviously inappropriate order, on my authority as operations officer, and pass on the instruction to the other middies. I said I would have a word with the officer who demonstrated such gall."

"You did not contact me," Tivendale shrieked. "You've never contacted me."

"It slipped my mind," Luis said, with arid dryness. "Will you forgive me?"

"Sir," Leo said, "under the circumstances I submit that the final charge of Gross insubordination be dismissed."

"This is an outrage," Tivendale howled as he rose from his chair. "A travesty of all proper decency. On a properly run Service ship this sort of behavior would never be tolerated. I demand the immediate removal of these children from this ship. They have disrespected me. They have plotted against me at every turn. They ..."

"Sit down, lieutenant." Waugh's acerbic tone left no room for misinterpretation. Tivendale's mouth froze half open. After protracted seconds he clamped his mouth shut and slumped into his chair.

The commodore's steely gaze softened. "Mister Saunders, take your middies outside while we consider the disposition of this hearing."

"Aye-aye, captain." When the hatch shut behind them, Waugh turned a dark eye onto the supply officer.

"Lieutenant Tivendale, you are new to Monitor Corps so perhaps you do not fully appreciate the seriousness of requesting a captain's mast."

"But captain," he whined, "they do not show me respect. They are all plotting against me."

"If, for the moment, I accept your proposition, why do you think this group of middies would act in this fashion?"

"Why? They are ill-disciplined children is why. These academy types think they are so special. But they are the most junior officers aboard and I am a full grade lieutenant. I deserve the respect due to my rank. Perhaps you disagree with this most basic principle of military discipline, captain."

"I don't care for your tone, lieutenant. But your disrespect aside, let us ask ourselves why you have had so much trouble with the middies." She glanced at the readouts flowing across the comp pad in front of her. "Within two hours of the middies reporting aboard you confined Midshipman Telford to his quarters. You kept him there throughout mess then had him stand outside the mess awaiting your arrival. Correct?"

"If he was one of the enlisted drones I would have placed the impudent boy on report," Tivendale growled. "I caught him playing around in the drop shafts. I disciplined him accordingly. As MTO, is it not my job ... captain?"

"Once again, lieutenant, your tone is doing your cause no good." Tivendale examined his fingernails. "Certainly as MTO you are responsible for the fair maintenance of discipline with regard to the middies. However, confining Telford to quarters for showing the initiative to acquaint himself with the layout of the boat does not serve that purpose. Browbeating the middies at every possible turn does not serve – "

"I never did that. Who said I did? I have always treated them with more respect than they deserved. Captain I protest in the strongest measure to your assertion that – "

"Lieutenant Tivendale." Waugh fixed him with a searing glare. "I will not warn you again about your attitude. And don't ever interrupt me again. Are you reading me?"

Tivendale's jaw hardened but he managed to nod.

"Excuse me?"

He snapped upright in his chair. "Aye-aye, captain."

"Intimidation is something I will never tolerate aboard my boat. Don't even think about protesting your innocence. Unlike those big ANS ships, on a monitor we record everything. Including all internal communications."

Tivendale's shoulders sagged.

"Yes, I know everything that happens aboard my command. So perhaps you would care to explain to me what you were hoping to achieve by this exercise. Or do you prefer to be questioned under Aletheia verification when we return to base?"

Tivendale blanched at the notion. The Aletheia Verification Unit had an irrefutable reputation for exposing liars. "They needed to be shown discipline. They should have learned their lesson but they kept disrespecting me. Damn arrogant academy brats."

"I wish you would refrain from referring to those who have attended the academy in such unflattering terms, lieutenant. All of the senior officers, including the D-O and myself are academy graduates." She turned a lazy eye on Demianski. "Doesn't that sort of talk hurt your feelings, D-O?"

"If only I had operational tear ducts, captain," Luis drawled.

***

Nathan adopted the slanted way of leaning against a bulkhead, his feet angled from his body and his back flush against the wall. Within the tight confines of the corridor his friends took up the same stance. Nathan sighed. *What have I done to them?*

"What do you think the commodore will do to us?" Ozzie asked.

Immersed in his own thoughts Nathan shrugged. *It could go either way.*

"We did what we had to, in order to protect ourselves from that idiot," Meta growled. "This isn't fair." Her tone became a little more reserved as she asked no one in particular, "You don't think they'll kick us out, do you?"

Nathan shrugged. *If they do, it's my fault. You just couldn't let it go could you Telford?*

"I bet the skipper is chewing a big chunk out of Tivendale's backside." Moe tried to sound upbeat but fell short of achieving the effect.

Nathan never wanted to get Leo involved in his mess. Leo knew what had been going on and had ordered Nathan to join him when he approached the D-O. Under the commander's gaze and no-nonsense interrogation he could do nothing but recite the truth. Even with the commander onside the serious nature of a captain's mast could not be ignored. Their collective fates still hung in the balance.

The hatch opened and Tivendale tripped over the coaming into the corridor. His shoulders slumped as if carrying a heavy burden. He did not make eye contact as he passed.

Cmdr Demianski poked his head out. “Lieutenant Tivendale has withdrawn his charges.” The middies sighed in a combination of relief and satisfaction. “You will report to the wardroom in twenty minutes for an update to your running sheets. Carry on.”

“Aye-aye, sir,” they said and turned to leave.

“Not you, Mister Telford.”

Here it comes.

Back in the briefing room he took the offered chair. Nathan had instigated the counterattack against Tivendale and involved Leo and the D-O in it. If he had gone too far, he would be the one to pay the price.

“I suppose you’re pretty pleased with yourself, mister?” the commodore said.

“I did what I thought best for all concerned, ma’am.”

“Yes, according to your record you make a habit out of doing what you believe to be right and damn the consequences. Any more of these childish vendettas and you will be looking down the barrel of career suicide. Well, what do you have to say for yourself?”

“It has been my experience that every time someone backs away from a bully, their position is weakened and the bully’s is strengthened.”

“A sound point but not one that will save a promising career.” Waugh sighed and shook her head. “There will always be someone in a position of authority who is less than fair or reasonable. That’s the way life works. You’d better learn to deal differently with the Tivendale's of the world. If you continue these outrageous frontal attacks on those whose opinion you disagree with, your luck will eventually run out.” Waugh paused for a moment and stared at him. “What are your long-term military ambitions, Nathan?”

“I want to be a boat jockey, ma’am.” This conversation was sounding all too familiar to Nathan.

“Well I'm here to tell you, young Mister Telford, considering your recent actions that will never happen. It takes more than talent and guts to rate a command. A monitor captain must be a leader who possesses sufficient political savvy to use force as a last resort. Captains do not indulge in this type of disgraceful schoolboy vendetta. They find ways around confrontations wherever possible." A faint smile touched her mouth. "You should be ashamed of yourself. Allowing yourself to be goaded into brawling with a senior officer. What did they used to say about that sort of confrontation, Luis?"

Cmdr Demianski's eyes remained focused on his comp pad. "It is not considered sporting to engage in a battle of wits with an unarmed opponent."

"That's the one. Now-hear-this, Telford. You will cease all harassment of Lieutenant Tivendale. I don't care what he does to you and your friends you will grit your teeth and take it. Do I make myself clear, Midshipman Telford?"

"Aye-aye, ma'am."

The captain tapped her epaulet. "Tivendale may be a poor excuse for an officer but he is also a person with friends in high places. If you are to survive and prosper in the Corps you need to consider such factors. And it wouldn't kill you to call him sir now and again. Remember, it's the rank you acknowledge not the man."

"I shall take all of your advice onboard, ma'am."

"See that you do," she scolded. "I shall expect to hear no more reports of such outrageous behavior. Now, get out of here."

As Nathan slipped into the drop shaft he wondered if the commodore actually said what he thought she said. Perhaps he had misinterpreted her meaning. His mind still worked the problem when he entered the wardroom.

Urgent appeals assaulted him. "What happened?" "Did you get in the shit?" "What happened to Tivendale?" "Are we in the clear?"

Their chatter died when the hatch opened. Leo Saunders stepped into the wardroom. He nodded amiably to the middies as he poured himself a cup of cold lemon juice from the dispenser. Taking a seat next to Nathan he ran his gaze over the middies.

"You miserable lumps of bovine droppings," he said, his lips tightening. "For those unacquainted with the vernacular, I believe the colonial equivalent to the expression is turds." His mouth turned grimace-like when his teeth locked together. "You turds have dropped me right in it, haven't you?"

In the six weeks Nathan and Leo had shared quarters he had never heard Leo curse, even mildly. He rounded on Nathan.

"I suppose you are the ringleader of this insolent, mutinous mob who so vilely tormented poor Lieutenant Tivendale?"

"I care to think of it as a team effort."

Leo snorted. "Well *thank you* so very much. You really shorted Tivendale out, didn't you? And guess who's been appointed as the new midshipman training officer?" All four middies grinned at the news. "Yes, well you might smile. Starting right now there will be changes to your training schedules. Tivendale let you four pirates get away with murder. That ends, right now. And don't even think about contacting me during downtime unless the boat is on fire. Now get out your comp pads. We have much to review."

CHAPTER 36

Date: 20th July, 320 ASC.
Location: Monitor *Truculent*.
Status: Marine orientation.

The day following the captain's mast, Nathan reported to the marine detachment. For some reason, known only to the former MTO, none of the middies had cycled through marine orientation. Nathan wondered if Tivendale harbored a prejudice against marines as well as those from the academy.

There were very few marines who survived the ninety-day ordeal known as Marine Special Forces training. Their reward came when they affixed to their left shoulder the patch with the black five on a grey background, denoting the elite Fifth Marine Division. Spartans. Although small in number, their reputation for being the masters of bedlam was unequaled.

Nathan stepped through the pressure hatch into the marine section. Both marines sat on short stools examining a 'droid that lay face down on the two-meter-long bench. Sergeant Redpath made fine adjustments to a long narrow probe he had inserted into the CPU at the back of the 'droid's head. Lt Jakovich monitored the variations on a screen.

"That's got it Rusty. Button him up."

Redpath grunted a confirmation.

Nathan browsed the marine's quarters, failing to find a space not occupied by some form of marine accoutrements. 'Droids, suits of armor and masses of weapons lockers were packed deck to overhead.

Nathan had been so fascinated by the marine's lair he forgot the etiquette. Lt Jakovich glanced at him.

"Reporting for orientation, Mister Telford?"

He snapped back from his inspection. "Aye-aye, ma'am."

"Take a seat."

Nathan looked around the room. The other twenty-three 'droids ranged around the walls, laying on horizontal platforms stacked four high. Finding a chair in a nearby corner he took his place beside the marine officer. Her strong jaw and attentive eyes marked her as someone who took control of the moment.

"What do you know about the inner workings of the type K 14 combat 'droid, Mister Telford?"

"Only the basics, ma'am."

"And I dare say a young man like you with his eyes set on a future of combat flying has little interest in such mundane activities."

"Everything that happens aboard a monitor is of interest to me, ma'am."

"Good to hear." Redpath finished fitting the armored cover plate to the back of the 'droid's head. The marines wrestled the machine onto its back. The eyes stared lifelessly at the overhead. Although manufactured to approximate the veneer of their human masters, 'droids were not equipped with the luxury of eyelids.

"'Droid eight, sit up." The huge machine complied, its head barely clearing the overhead. "Rotate head right. Rotate head left." The 'droid responded. "I think your nimble fingers have once again sorted out the bug, Rusty. 'Droid eight, return to your station."

"Aye-aye, ma'am," the machine voice said. It slid off the workbench, doubled over and moved to a vacant berth.

"So Mister Telford, you have a rudimentary knowledge of 'droids?"

"Yes, ma'am."

"Tell me what you know."

Nathan massaged the bump above his right eyebrow. "They are extremely strong and fast. They are assigned to duties considered too high risk for humans. They have multitasking abilities but they are primarily at their best deployment as combat units. Their programmable adaptability, combined with no requirement for bunk time or consumables make them ideally suited to a boat of this size." For a moment he paused to consider anything he may have forgotten. They were an integral part of a monitor's makeup but as the lieutenant pointed out his interests lay elsewhere.

"Considering the advances in AI technology," the LT said, "why do you think 'droids operate with such limited mental capabilities?"

"Superstition, ma'am."

"Explain."

"'Droids could be designed and manufactured to incorporate thought processes closely equaling human beings. They could, but they are not. During the technology explosion on Earth during their late 20th century there was an almost paranoid fear, in some ways justified, that machines would take the jobs of human beings. The economic and technological realities of the time precluded such an eventuality but still the fear remained. That same apprehension has lingered within human beings ever since. As they used to say, machines make fine servants but poor masters.

“Although I don't advocate creating artificial sentience, I believe 'droids could reach their full potential by fitting them with a rudimentary AI brain. Even though the benefits would be great, the old fears lock the 'droids within these painfully tight parameters. It is my belief that, so-called moral issues aside, the ancient superstitions with regard to the rise of the machine haunts the process of fully utilizing what could be an extraordinarily useful asset.”

“So why don't we do as you suggest and program 'droids to do all the work for us while we sit back on the beach?”

“You cannot program instinct into a machine, no matter how sophisticated it is. If you could do so you would probably be giving birth to a sentient machine. Something I do not advocate, as I said, ma’am.”

“Do you believe instincts separate us from machines?”

“I believe a range of special qualities separate us from machines. But in so far as our occupations go, a soldier without superior instincts may as well be a machine for all the good he can do. As a Spartan I'm sure I don't need to tell you, ma’am.” He felt the corners of his mouth tuck in. Nathan contained his amazement when Redpath snorted. Until that moment he had been all but invisible. *I didn't know the old troll had facial muscles.* .

“I think we've got a live one here, Rusty.”

“If you say so, LT,” Redpath mumbled.

“So, Mister Telford,” the marine continued in an easy tone, “now you have elucidated your sterling knowledge on the morality of 'droid sentience and your obviously strong views regarding their utilization, perhaps you would care to learn how they work?”

“Of course, ma’am.”

“Rusty, roll out number twelve. Let's see if Telford can figure out how to fix that gyro problem.”

CHAPTER 37

Date: 27th July, 320 ASC.
Position: Monitor *Truculent*.
Status: Ambivalent.

Nathan fully appreciated that Leo Saunders did not possess a hidden capricious side to his nature. However, someone had to be the first into the fire and Nathan's name was next on the roster.

Nathan exited the drop shaft on deck three and made his way to the supply department. He caught himself dragging his feet and corrected his pace. Nathan took several deep breaths, hit the hatch chime and after a lengthy delay the hatch opened. After stepping over the coaming he stood to attention before the desk.

"Midshipman Telford reporting for supply orientation ... sir."

Tivendale's head snapped up from his screen, his eyes narrowing.

"Sir? You are calling me *sir*?" The high tone of his voice held an incredulous lilt. "I suppose the commodore ordered you to say that, eh? Oh, forgive me, midshipman, please, stand at ease. I do not wish you complaining to the commodore that I brutalized you by expecting you to show respect for a senior *boat's* officer. Please, feel free to lounge about my office in any manner you like."

Nathan had not expected a 'hail and well met my hearty', so the tirade washed harmlessly over him. However he did not expect to see the lieutenant in his current miserable condition. On closer scrutiny Tivendale's overall body language showed as beaten an individual as Nathan had ever seen.

"I presume you are quite proud of yourself?" Tivendale whined. "I tried to instill some proper discipline into you and your associates and this is what I get for my trouble."

Although truly delusional, Nathan found the bitterness of his recrimination to be pitiful. Despite his natural dislike of the man, he felt an obscure sense of remorse.

"I thought I would be, but is hasn't worked out as I expected."

"Oh? The mighty superstar of the academy is admitting to a mistake? I do not believe my ears."

"Well you should. You were right. I failed to show correct respect for your rank. For that I owe you an apology, sir."

"Again with the sir? Is this another of your so-called jokes, Telford?"

"No sir. You were right and I was wrong. It's that simple."

Tivendale eyed him skeptically for a time before slumping into his chair, his rage spent. Lost for words he brushed a dismissive hand through the air.

"May I ask what my duties are?"

"Duties?" he said dully, "Oh, I do not care. Do whatever you want."

"I was born and raised on a freighter. Perhaps I could make some small suggestions that might, with your approval, increase efficiency?"

"So now you want to take over the supply department?"

Nathan pushed down a flash of anger. "That's not what I meant."

"Oh, I no longer care what you do. Do whatever you want. Just leave me alone."

"May I have access to the inventory and manifests?"

"I said you can do whatever you want, Telford." The anger had left his voice along with any sense of self-respect. "Just leave me in peace."

"Aye-aye, sir."

Nathan spent the first two hours of his watch laboring over the manifests. Even without the requisite organizational courses he had undertaken at the academy he recognized a deranged mess when he saw one. Friends in high places or not, this idiot should never have been commissioned. A first-year plebe could organize the distribution of supplies better. He examined the prescribed routines for onloading containers as detailed on the computer readout. Tivendale couldn't have done a worse job if he were a saboteur. No wonder the department heads were baying for Tivendale's blood.

For the rest of his watch Nathan inspected the cargo holds, checking the manifests against the container numbers and making regular corrections as needed. The stink in the holds came back to haunt him. At the end of the shift he reported back to Tivendale who told him not to bother doing so in the future. Nathan lingered in a nearby drop shaft until Argento relieved Tivendale. When the supply officer stepped into the stern lift, Nathan entered the office.

Argento leapt half out of her chair before recognizing Nathan. He dropped into the chair opposite hers, tapped his left shoulder and laid his hands flat on the desk.

"What's your name, Argento?"

A smile touched her lips. "Heather, sir."

"Nathan," he said, offering his hand. *She's been around long enough to know the drill.*

"Very well, Nathan."

"This isn't a date Heather, we have work to do."

She blinked in surprise. "Work? I don't understand, sir ... ah, Nathan."

"Work, Heather. It's what we do for six hours, twice per shipboard day. Remember?"

The chief snorted."Nathan, I am under orders from the supply officer to do nothing other than my usual requisition duties unless otherwise ordered."

"Ah, but the supply officer has given me permission to, and I quote, *do whatever I want*. Therefore, if I wish to work your tail off until we get this department into some kind of order, I will." Grinning wolfishly he added, "And Heather, I do indeed wish to work your tail off. Professionally speaking of course."

"That would make a damn fine change. What have you got in mind?"

CHAPTER 38

Date: 5th August, 320 ASC.
Position: Monitor *Truculent.*
Status: Downtime.

Nathan fell into a deep sleep as soon as his head hit the pillow. The double shifts were starting to get to him. It felt as if mere minutes had passed when the alert alarm blared. He sprung from his rack and crashed into the overhead.

The internal gravity was off and the room was in complete darkness. Nathan pushed against the overhead to regain his footing. In the absolute darkness he kept bumping into Leo and Allan but could not tell them apart.

The hatch slid open allowing dim green light from the corridor's overhead to spill into the room. Somehow Leo had found his way to the hatch and activated the override.

"What are you waiting for, Nathan?" Leo said.

Allan was already half into his flight suit, pressing himself to the deck by pushing his head against the overhead. Nathan donned his flight suit and slipped on his shoes. Leo and Allan had far more experience than he and beat him out the hatch by half a minute.

Nathan stepped into the corridor and made his way forward. Within the zero G environment he kept his feet planted to the deck by sliding his hands along the overhead. Reaching the forward drop shaft he made a quick check to ensure no one blocked his passage then hauled himself inside.

He reached his destination and swung from the shaft, onto the deck. The starboard torpedo bay was his assigned alert station. CPO Veivers noted his arrival with a short nod. Nathan remained where he was to allow the professionals do their jobs. In the time it had taken him to struggle into his flight suit, the pros had done the same, got to their duty station and loaded all three tubes. *Yes young man, you still have a lot to learn.*

Nathan strapped into the jump seat to observe how real experts conducted themselves. Such calm proficiency is what he expected on a boat commanded by Waugh. As he plucked a ball of sleep from the corner of his eye he absently checked the time: 0412 hours. At least he had gotten three hours sleep.

The gravity returned with a jolt and full illumination flooded the bay. Nathan blinked rapidly to adjust to the change. The weapons engineering officer stepped into the bay.

"Well done everyone," Lt Cmdr Matrakas said. "Secure from alert. The drill is over." He noticed Nathan. "So Mister Telford, you made it to the party?"

"Not as rapidly as I would have liked to, sir."

"Never mind, it all comes with time. And I think the crew could manage without you for a while."

"I dare say they'd struggle by."

"You have another six days with us so perhaps you might pick up a few tips?"

"I'm sure I will."

"Good. Now you may as well get back to your quarters. I will see you back here at 0600 hours on the dot."

"Aye-aye, sir."

Nathan retraced his path down the drop shafts, but at deck two he kept going. With the residual adrenaline in his system he was unlikely to get back to sleep. It had been a drill but he didn't know it at the time. At any time of the day or night he may need to react to a genuine threat.

When he stepped into the supply office, he noted CPO Argento's absence. *She must still be at her combat post in Damage Control.* He slid behind the desk, activated the computer and examined the records. Heather had far more experience in supply than he, but had patiently listened to his suggestions, accepting some rejecting others and making her own practical recommendations. Between them they had devised a plan to tackle Tivendale's disaster. Although it entailed many hours of hard work the benefits were beginning to show.

Heather stepped into the office. "Checking on me, Nathan?"

"You bet. Since I was already up I thought I would see how things were progressing."

"What do you think?"

"It's coming along nicely. I hope Moe isn't getting under your feet?"

"Moe's been great. She was happy to pick up where you left off."

"Sounds like Moe," Nathan said, rising from the chair. "Have you heard anything from your esteemed leader?"

"Surprisingly not. Tivendale has lost all interest in his department. Hasn't even tried to put me on report this week."

Again, the odd stirring of guilt. “Very well, Heather, I will leave you to it."

“Call in any time, Nathan.” The return of her sultry smile had Nathan wagging his finger at her.

The hatch opened and Moe stuck her head in. “What's happening?”

“Midshipwoman Okuma. I was about to pay you a visit.”

CHAPTER 39

Two months on station without enemy contact had Waugh pacing the briefing room like a caged tigress. Her wretched mood had gotten the better of her and she caught herself nearly snapping at her crew. This would not do. It had been years since she walked the boat but perhaps it would help to clear her mind.

Waugh began her *walk* in the Maneuvering Department. The senior engineer, Cmdr Chanderpaul, was still on duty.

"Good morning, Jocelyn."

"Good morning, skipper," Chanderpaul said. "Is there anything I can do for you, ma'am?"

"How's everything going?"

Jocelyn's eyes narrowed for a moment."Are you walking the boat, skip?"

Waugh cleared her throat.

"You haven't done that in years."

"Hmm."

Chanderpaul leaned in close. "Truculent's luck has to change soon," she whispered. "Why, right now there could be a big juicy headhunter on her way to us."

"Nice thought. All right, Jocelyn, I'll leave you in peace."

"Enjoy your walk, skipper."

Half a minute later Waugh slipped from the drop shaft into the boat bay. She froze at the sight before her. Half an hour after stand down Telford and Okuma were still up, which surprised her far less than what they were doing.

Telford drew back on the bowstring and as soon as the weapon reached eye level, he fired. The arrow flew the full length of the boat bay striking the holo target dead center of the bull's-eye.

Okuma took the next shot, her fast firing technique identical to Telford's. Her arrow landed fractionally off center. Telford slapped her on the back. He noticed the commodore approaching. Before they snapped to attention she waved them down.

"Good morning, middies."

"Good morning, captain," they responded. *They make an odd couple these two.* Waugh found it odd how lifelong friends stood out from the crowd. All of the middies were friends but these two displayed a deeper, more profound familiarity.

"Don't you two ever sleep?" she said cheerfully. "I do not recall seeing two more hard-working middies. What do you do for fun?"

They exchanged wry smiles before transforming back into respectful young middies. Waugh sighed internally. *Surely I was never this young?*

"We like going to the movies, ma'am," Okuma volunteered.

"So do I. Did you catch last night's flick?"

"No, ma'am," Telford said. "We had a gouge session."

"Academy gouge sessions." Waugh felt a reminiscent warmth. "I am pleased to see you are not ignoring your studies."

"No ma'am," Telford answered.

"What's your favorite movie, Mister Telford?"

His forehead creased. "It's hard to say, ma'am."

"Try."

He rubbed at his right eyebrow. "Well, *The Sea Hawk* comes to mind."

"Ah yes, Errol Flynn. Great fun."

"And the good guys always win."

"Unlike real life?"

"As you say, ma'am, great fun."

"And you, Miss Okuma?"

"Anything with Laurel and Hardy. They break me up, ma'am."

"Yes, I have always found them to be dryly amusing."

"I can't believe the vids are more than five hundred years old," Okuma said.

"Quite amazing isn't it? They only came back into vogue thirty-odd years ago and the effect they've had on the idiom has been remarkable. Subtle but remarkable." She thought of explaining to the young officers just how much the movies had changed the speech patterns within Tunguska since she was their age, but assumed that another lecture from the old lady would put them to sleep.

Waugh extended her hand to Telford. "May I?" Holding the bow in her left hand she pulled on the draw string. It took all of her effort to pull it all the way back. Light glanced off the smooth polished wood. She returned the bow, noticing for the first time the calluses on his index and middle fingers. No fancy shooting gloves for these colonials.

"Keeping your eye in?"

"Yes, ma'am," Telford said. "We get in what practice we can manage."

"I have seen archery contests during the Olympics. Those

archers raise the bow the way you two do but hold, aim carefully and fire. I have never seen your technique before."

Telford glanced at his friend.

"Well, ma'am," Okuma said, "when you've chased your quarry through the rain forest for two hours and are ready to drop from exhaustion you don't have time to consider Olympic etiquette. You usually have only one shot at your prey." She appeared pleased at the commodore's interest. "A bull's eye won't see you coming and go to ground."

"I see. So were you two sports hunters on Kastoria?"

Okuma glanced at Telford. "No, ma'am, when we hunt we do so either for food or to rid ourselves of a rogue animal. Usually a plains buffalo or wild boar that's wandered onto our plantation. They can do a lot of damage if left unchecked. Of course these are target bows and not the type we use back home. We had to save our pennies for two years to afford these babies." A smile formed as she examined the bow. "Apart from loving archery we are hoping to be considered for Kastoria in the Olympic team trials in twenty-three. Nathan has won a number of archery contests but I'm starting to catch up with him so we think we might have a chance. And by then we will be representing the Corps as well as the Republic."

"Outstanding." Waugh was relieved to see such fine young people were the real future of the Corps. Whether they could counter the other more negative influences infecting the Service would be decided by their future endeavors. "Well, I shall leave you to it for now."

"Aye-aye, ma'am." They successfully fought the urge to snap to attention.

CHAPTER 40

Date: 11th August, 320 ASC.
Position: Pruessen Headhunter *Picaroon*. Within League space.
Status: Operation ongoing.

Orson followed Bannister onto the bridge.

"Very well, lieutenant," Bannister said, "you say everything's ready, so let's run one final test."

"Aye-aye, commander."

Orson sat before the EDF console and prepared to dazzle his superior. "Initializing EDF test field, now." He flipped the switch. Nothing happened. Orson flipped the switch again, then once more to be certain. No lights registered on his panel. "Fucker," he whispered. "Everything was in the green w1.42hen I checked it yesterday." From over his shoulder Orson heard the barest sigh from Bannister. "We will need to overhaul the entire system and do a complete diagnostic."

"Not so fast, Saxon," Bannister snapped. "You know how touchy this technology is. We'll first check out the hardware in the EDF transmitter compartment."

"Sir, I guarantee it isn't a hardware problem," Orson said defensively.

"We'll see about that." He stroked his chin, his eyes revealing genuine concern. "If we can't get this buttoned down quickly we may have to abort the mission."

"A problem gentlemen?" Captain Foss asked.

"A glitch, captain," Bannister said.

"Should we return to Imperial space while you fix your glitch? I don't like the idea of running into an enemy patrol if this thing is going to blow up in our faces."

"Yes, captain," Bannister said, his voice laced with a poisonous inflection, "that wouldn't look good on your record would it?" Orson followed him from the bridge.

Two bored guards waved them through the hatch. The ship's crowded engineering deck stank worse than the rest of the ship. If that were possible.

Bannister strode to the stern of the reactor room and into the compartment assigned to the EDF transmitter. For a few minutes Orson checked the external leads and relays.

"Lieutenant?"

Bannister had an unusually dangerous lilt to his tone. The Advocate motioned him to the transmitter. Orson followed his pointing finger. Behind the recently removed cover plate a small feeder conduit hung loosely from its fitting. This single conduit threatened to terminate their glorious mission.

His jaw tightened. He stared at Bannister.

"Well?" Bannister asked.

Orson's mind raced. Could he have missed it? He had run exacting checks of the systems to ensure something like this never happened. When he examined the locking clamp his heart raced. The scratch marks around the receiver had not been there yesterday.

"Someone's fucking with us!" Orson spat.

Bannister's face hardened.

Orson breathed heavily to control his rising fury. "Some motherless piece of headhunter shit has sabotaged the transmitter. Why? Why would anyone do such a thing?" He shook his head. "I don't care who did it. And damn the clan mentality. When I find the fucker I will kill him with my bare hands."

"Control yourself, lieutenant. Rank has its privileges. The kill is mine. Now pull yourself together. Remember who you are and who you serve."

Orson sensed the presence of someone behind him. In four broad steps he marched to the hatch and dragged the crewman inside. If Orson's anger had not gotten the better of him he would have sensed him earlier. *Control, must have control.* He pinned the crewman to the bulkhead locking a thumb and forefinger around his windpipe. The scum tried to knock his arm away so Orson kneed him in the crotch. All resistance drained from the headhunter. Orson loosened his grip to let him breathe.

"What are you doing here you piece of filth?"

"Nuttin' sir, nuttin'."

"You were listening to us, weren't you?"

"No sir, no sir," he squeaked, "I didn't hear nuttin'."

"You're lying to me you shit eater." Orson hit the man squarely in the nose causing an immediate bloody response.

Through tear-soaked eyes the pathetic animal bleated for his life. "Honest sir, I was just passing by, that's all, sir."

"Lying dog." Orson knew he had to dial it down a notch. A dead suspect would do them no good. *Control.*

"What's going on here?" Cmdr Weiss said from the hatchway.

Before Orson could spit out a vile reply Bannister stepped to the hatch. "Someone aboard this ship has sabotaged the EDF."

Cmdr Weiss smirked. "And you think this pathetic fool is responsible?" His snigger made Orson's blood boil. "This weedy creature is the captain's steward. He's not capable of sabotaging anything short of the captain's dinner."

Bannister locked eyes with the scrawny headhunter and held his terrified gaze for a short count of ten.

"Let him go."

Orson released his grip on the crewman who slumped to the deck.

"Someone on this scow has been in this compartment without authorization," he yelled.

"The crew was ordered to avoid this area, commander," Weiss said. "You must be mistaken."

"I see."

How the Advocate could maintain his control at times like this constantly amazed Orson. Bannister shouldered past Weiss and Orson followed. Bannister examined the congested engineering department. A crowd had gathered to see what the fuss was about. The curious onlookers became the immediate focus of Bannister's attention. Like an arsonist who lingers after a fire, the culprit might be among these putrid crewmen.

Some of the crew avoided eye contact. Others stared back, daring him to confront them. After scrutinizing the group for a full minute Bannister's attention focused on a single crewman. His finger struck like a javelin.

"You!"

The headhunter jumped as if the finger had impaled him.

Bannister strode toward the crewman, a murderous blaze in his eyes. With the crowd packed tightly around him the crewman could not escape. He slid a long-bladed knife from his boot. The surrounding crew frantically tried to distance themselves from their shipmate.

Bannister calmly stepped sideways as the knife thrust at his chest. Using the crewman's momentum he snapped the man's arm across his knee. The crewman shrieked as his elbow shattered. Bannister flung him to the deck and pressed his foot on his neck.

"Look at me, fucker." Finally he released some of his pent-up rage. When the crewman failed to respond Bannister stomped onto his shattered elbow. The headhunter's shriek echoed around the engineering deck. Orson smiled.

"Look at me," Bannister repeated, through set teeth.

The whimpering crewman complied. Bannister held the crewman's gaze for half a minute.

"I know you did this. You will tell me why you did this. I *promise* you." He turned to Orson. "Lieutenant, take this piece of garbage to the brig then report to the bridge. Contact me when you arrive and we'll try the EDF test again. I will run a hardware check from the EDF compartment."

"Aye, sir."

Orson was none too gentle with the saboteur en-route to the brig. He hoped Bannister would let him participate in the interrogation.

Arriving at the bridge Orson opened the channel to the EDF compartment. "Commander Bannister, I am at the EDF console. Ready to proceed."

"Very well. Everything here appears to be in order," Bannister said. "I have reattached the conduit and it's looking good. Commence the initiation sequence."

"Aye sir, commencing initiation sequence."

The flow regulators displayed the minimal amount of energy flowing into the transmitter.

"We are green across the board, commander."

"Very well," Bannister said. "Charge up the capacitors and see how we go."

"Aye sir, feeding mains power to capacitors."

The flow rates were nominal and the capacitors slowly filled with the power required to initiate the transmitter.

"Commander, capacitors filling, flow rates nominal. Do you wish to conduct a comprehensive test of the system?"

"Negative," Bannister said. "I believe we've solved our problem. And we have unfinished business to attend to do we not, lieutenant?"

Orson smiled at the prospect. "That we do, sir." Through the speaker he heard a loud clang. "Everything all right, commander?"

"Hold on."

Coldness settled onto Orson's stomach. The seconds ticked by interminably.

"We not only have a saboteur onboard but a clown. Someone's locked me in."

Orson shook his head. *If this were my crew* ... bile stung his tongue at the thought of what he would do to these dogs.

"Everything looks good here," Bannister said. "How about at your end?"

"All green across the ..." *What was that?* A flicker from the number two inlet gauge.

"Lieutenant?"

Then the universe went mad. Feedback from the capacitors flowed into the reactor. Alarms wailed throughout the ship.

"Commander ..."

"I see it. And I see what's causing it. Damn." Bannister's voice grunted from the speaker as he grappled with the problem. "We need to eject the power build up from the capacitors. I tried doing it manually but it's non-responsive. Damn."

Orson's gut twisted. *If we fail to stop the feedback it will overload the reactor. The ship will disappear into a fiery ball. The only way to stop the reaction is to discharge the excess energy into the EDF compartment.*

"Captain Foss," Orson yelled. "Get someone in engineering to unlock the door to the EDF compartment."

"Weiss, get the hatch open," Foss barked.

"Already tried, captain," Weiss said. "The engineers mate reports the hatch has been jammed solid. He is about to cut through the lock and release Commander Bannister."

"Belay that order commander, there is no time." Not the slightest timbre of regret or fear entered Bannister's voice.

"Commander Bannister," Foss cut in, "we need to purge the power from the capacitors. If we don't do it within sixty seconds the ship will explode."

"I'm aware of that captain." The briefest of pauses. "Lieutenant Saxon, I am placing you in command of this mission. Remember who you serve."

"Aye-aye, commander." Orson fed the dangerous power from the overloaded capacitors into the EDF compartment. He struck the ignition switch detonating the explosive bolts. The emergency hatch fitted to the outer hull of the EDF compartment blew out. The potentially fatal power surge discharged safely into the vacuum of space. The power levels fell rapidly below the red line.

The ship survived. The mission survived.

All for the loss of only one man.

CHAPTER 41

Orson drove his foot into the sleeping man's stomach. Muttering a curse the prisoner curled into a fetal position on the deck of the brig.

"Sit up." When the prisoner took too long to respond Orson kicked him in the shattered elbow. The crewman screamed, rolled over and propped his back against the bulkhead. He cradled his broken arm across his chest.

"Grunberg, that's your name isn't it?"

The prisoner nodded.

"Here's what's going to happen, Grunberg." With an extraordinary effort he maintained a low and even tone. "Very soon I am going to start hurting you. I will continue to *hurt* you until you tell me what I want to know. Do you understand me?"

"Fuck you," he snarled. "I'll tell you nothing."

Orson smirked at the crewman's defiance. *There is more to Grunberg than meets the eye.*

"Believe me Grunberg, you'll tell me everything I want to know. The only question is, how much suffering you choose to endure?"

From the sheath on his left forearm he gripped the small hilt of the finely honed knife between his index fingers. The blade, a mere six centimeters long and two wide, was strong enough to cut through bone and sharp enough to slice silk in mid-air. To anyone not versed in the art of death it would look like an inoffensive toy.

Grunberg stared at the knife but remained stubbornly mute. His obstinate attitude pleased Orson. He would hate to interrogate a coward.

Orson seized Grunberg's throat with his left hand pressing it against the bulkhead. His knee pinned the prisoner's legs to the deck. Orson drove the knife under the crewman's right kneecap and twisted the narrow blade. Grunberg screamed. The saboteur grabbed for Orson's face. Orson twisted the knife, wrenching another pitiful shriek. Grunberg refused to talk despite writhing in unbelievable agony. The prisoner remained resolutely silent, except for his screams, for longer than Orson expected.

Less than thirty minutes later Orson left the prisoner in the blood-spattered brig. Grunberg had been a tougher nut to crack than he had believed possible. The saboteur had blacked out several times during the interrogation but the outcome was never in question. He had shown guts but no one withstood Orson's brand of torment. In a detached way he almost admired the gutsy bastard. Many of the scum on this ship would have pissed their pants as soon as they saw his blade.

The productive session filled him with a powerful sense of accomplishment. *No, more than that. I really enjoyed torturing Grunberg.* Orson's considerable experience in such interrogation techniques convinced him Grunberg had not lied to stop his agony.

Orson considered washing his bloody hands but impatience drove him on. He would shower later.

When he marched into the engineering section the guards gave him a wide berth. At the far end of the reactor room Cmdr Weiss oversaw the repairs to the EDF compartment. Crewmen in v-suits had patched the area where the hatch had blown out and were installing new explosive bolts.

"Find out anything useful?" Weiss asked.

Orson ignored him and strode through the engineering department.

"Lieutenant Saxon, I asked you a question," Weiss yelled.

Orson glanced around the compartment until his gaze fell on the chief engineer. His eyes tracked to Orson's bloodied hands.

"I need to find two of your crew. Shattock and Nehmer."

"Lieutenant Saxon."

"I'm busy Weiss."

"You will report on your interrogation at once. As executive officer it is my responsibility – "

Orson struck with the speed of a snake, pinning Weiss against the bulkhead by his throat.

"It's your responsibility to make certain saboteurs don't get aboard this ship. It's your responsibility to ensure the safety of the crew, including Commander Bannister. Thus far you have fucked up in every way imaginable. So now I will do your job for you and you will keep the fuck away from me." Orson stared into the dark, terror-filled eyes. "Cross me again, Weiss, and I will bleed you dry." He released Weiss who crumbled to the deck. Orson set his focus on the engineer.

"Shattock and Nehmer, where are they?"

"Ah, I'm not certain." He turned to the chief petty officer beside him. "Any ideas?"

Only by remembering the mission, now *his* mission, did Orson control his rage.

"They're off duty until sixteen hundred," the CPO said. "Last time I saw them they were heading to the mess."

Orson strode past Weiss who remained cringing on the deck.

Picaroon was a fairly large ship but driven by a need for vengeance Orson reached the crew's mess in less than five minutes. When he stepped into the mess a mixture of curious stares and total disregard greeted him.

"Crewmen Shattock and Nehmer, on your feet," he yelled. Most eyes rose to glare at him. Some remained down and a few wandered to the two crewmen sitting at the rear of the mess. As he strode toward them they exchanged tentative glances.

"Shattock and Nehmer?"

"I'm Shattock, so what?" said the larger of the two. The other examined his hands.

Orson stared into Shattock's eyes. The crewman neither flinched nor looked away. His defiance sealed his fate.

From behind him Orson heard armored boots clattering onto the deck. Without glancing behind he sensed the pulsar rifles aimed at his back.

"Lieutenant Saxon, what are you doing?" Captain Foss demanded.

"Remember, *captain*, exactly who is running this operation."

"This is still my command, Saxon."

So the dog has found some teeth. Orson stared over his shoulder, past the heavily armed guards and into Foss' eyes.

"Very well, *captain*, perhaps you can explain to me how three members of the Peoples Liberation Front got aboard *your* command."

Unlike the rest of the crew Foss was a professional. He stared at the two crewmen.

"You can prove this?"

"Grunberg gave them up."

"Grunberg's lying," Nehmer snarled, finally finding his voice.

"Could Grunberg have been lying?"

Orson grinned in a way he knew would chill the heart of any headhunter. "No one lies to me for long."

Foss glanced at Orson's bloodstained hands, grimaced and nodded more as a confirmation to himself than anyone else.

"Very well. We'll interrogate them."

"Death to the empire," Shattock screamed, as the two saboteurs leapt to their feet. Each produced a mini pulsar from under the table.

Orson had the knife in his left hand. Not his preferred hand but good enough. His high left kick shattered Shattock's forearm. The mini pulsar dropped from his hand. Orson lunged forward, opening Nehmer's jugular with his dagger. Shifting his balance he slashed the blade across Shattock's exposed throat. Under twin geysers of spurting blood both saboteurs collapsed to the deck.

Orson glared at Foss and his dumbfounded guards. A warm glow surged through him.

"We could have interrogated them for intel, lieutenant," Foss said.

"PLF members operate in small cells with no discernible command structure. So what kind of intel do you think they would have given you?"

"Well yes, but still ..."

"I need to shower."

The crew hastily cleared a path as Orson strode from the mess.

CHAPTER 42

Date: 11th August, 320 ASC.
Location: Monitor *Truculent*, on station: Ibis Nebula.
Status: Alert stand down.

Nathan could not escape his boyish delight when he first stepped onto the boat's command deck. Like a kid in a candy shop, the old saying went. Nathan reflected that he had never been into a candy shop but assumed it would feel this good.

His second watch found him at the Auxiliary Operations Station, running through drills. In the jump seat beside him Leo observed, commenting as required.

From the Operations Stations, Cmdr Demianski ran checks on the overall condition of the boat. As was SOP during alert stand downs most of the crew station were vacant. At the tactical station Lt Hookes concentrated on her readouts. Her bored expression matched the commander's. Leo stifled a yawn.

Nathan's body tingled with anticipation. *Calm down Telford.* He took a deep breath.

Nathan's console, slaved to the tactical readouts, focused on the northern approaches into League space. The sensor array, calibrated to maximum long range, performed passive sweeps which remained free of contacts.

Nathan started to ask Leo a question. His screen flickered momentarily, before stabilizing. Nathan's heart thundered when five giant warships egressed from hyperspace. They converged on *Truculent's* position.

Nathan froze for a full second. "Contact! Multiple contacts bearing..." he began, and glanced at Leo. He reclined in his seat, his hand covering his mouth. Tears glistened and he made small snorting sounds. Cmdr Demianski's head bobbed behind the ops station. Turning his attention back to his readouts Nathan found a single word projecting from the blank screen:

NERVOUS?

The officers' constrained chuckling slowly petered out. Nathan took several deep breaths to slow his pulse rate before seeing the lighter side of the initiation. Back at the academy this sort of good-natured joking was referred to as being fried.

"Good one, lieutenant."

Hookes' eyes remained diligently on her console but her thin smile betrayed her. "The classics never fail to please. Anyway, it broke the monotony, don't you think?"

"I suppose you could say that, ma'am. Unless you think me nearly soiling my flight suit is monotonous."

Raucous laughter exploded across the bridge. Leo slapped Nathan's shoulder. "Welcome to the club, Nathan. All grommits, including me, go through this sort of initiation to bridge operations. Your three cohorts suffered something similar. They handled it well enough. Although Miss Kaspowitz took a little longer than the rest to see the humor of the exercise."

"Nice of my friends to warn me in advance."

"They were under orders to remain silent. We didn't want to spoil the surprise for you."

"How considerate of my friends." Nathan knew it was the lot of junior officers to suffer this sort of good-natured teasing until they completed their first combat operation. *Still, I should have seen this coming.*

On his screen a flashing red icon caught his attention. The ship had egressed from hyper on a course running directly from the Poseidon Shoals. Her helm officer must be a genius or a madman to try such a maneuver. Although an admirable piece of navigation, no sane skipper would permit something so fundamentally dangerous.

Leo tapped his shoulder. "Step out, Mister Telford." Nathan took the jump seat.

"Commander," Lt Hookes said, "I have a bogey, sir. ETA shortly."

"Very well," Cmdr Demianski said. A moment later the Alert Condition two alarm sounded.

From the corner of his eye Nathan watched as Waugh marched onto the bridge and took her chair adjacent to the operations station.

"Report, commander."

"We have a bogie, captain. Popped in through the shoals."

Waugh grinned, her eyes coming to life. "It's about bloody time. Tactical, what do you make of her?"

"The range is still long captain but I would bet a week's pay on her being a Line Runner." Hookes' grin edged around her green-tinted hood. "If she maintains her current course and speed she'll be on top of us in seventy-five minutes."

"Excellent." Waugh rubbed her hands.

Lt Cmdr O'Donnell stepped onto the bridge.

"She's approaching at flank speed." Hookes smiled wolfishly. "Captain, she's maintaining course directly for the Ibis Nebula."

Cmdr Demianski chuckled as the captain turned a wry grin on him. With raised eyebrows Nathan shot Leo a question. Leo shrugged.

The commodore noticed the curious interaction.

"It would appear, gentlemen," Waugh said, "that our friend is planning to emulate our actions." She noted their perplexed reactions. "She is going to utilize this nebula's interference to hide from, well, us."

Their grins matched those of the bridge crew.

"Captain," Hookes reported, "she is a Bretish, Culver class fast haulage ship."

Nathan ran the class through his head. As with a monitor she had a third of her displacement dedicated to her power-plant. If she reversed course quickly enough and matched harmonics for ingression into hyper, she would escape. *Pity she's not Pruessen.*

During the next hour the crew donned v-suits and light armor. The captain never took possible enemy action lightly. Even with a lowly Line Runner.

"No Culver class vessel has lodged a flight plan for this region," the Commander said. "I am classifying her undesignated."

Nathan continued watching as Waugh nodded and adopted a relaxed semi-slouch. She received regular updates on the bogie as it blithely continued on course for the nebula. If they could prove she had violated quarantine regulations, her captain would lose his masters certificates, his ship and his freedom. After a Line Runner had infected Delos the penalties for incursions into the Quarantine Zone were significantly increased.

Nathan tensed as the captain's back straightened. No doubt at a time determined by years of experience Waugh came to life.

"Tactical, report when the bogie is thirty seconds from nebula insertion." Hookes acknowledged. "Helm, prepare to go to maximum intercept speed on my mark."

"Aye, captain."

"Captain," Hookes reported, "the bogie is thirty seconds from insertion... now."

"Very well. D-O, Alert Condition one if you please."

"Aye, captain," Demianski said. The bridge lights died. The iridescent glow from the overheads cast a dim green tint across the command deck. At almost the same moment the dull, pulsing alarm sounded.

"Helm," Waugh said, "go get her."

"Aye-aye, captain."

The main engines engaged with force enough to press Nathan into his chair.

On his screen a kaleidoscope of brilliant colors rushed by as the monitor breached the outer edge of the nebula. When the stars reappeared Cmdr O'Donnell slewed the boat viciously to starboard, before straightening from the seven gee turn. Pumped on adrenaline, Nathan ignored his harness as it dug into his shoulders. The bogie had detected *Truculent* as soon as she fired her engines. She had already come about.

"Ship to ship, commander," Waugh said.

Cmdr Demianski, as with any good D-O had anticipated his captain's needs. "Channel open, captain."

"To Culver class transport. This is Commodore Waugh of the Athenian warship Truculent. You have been classified undesignated. Cut your engines and prepare to be boarded. Respond to my signal."

The Culver responded by raising her shields and increasing speed. Waugh shook her head making sharp tish, tish sounds between her teeth.

"Commander, I'm going downstairs."

"Aye, captain."

Waugh unhooked from the command chair, walked the short distance to the centrally located combat chair and strapped in. Nathan watched intently as she tapped the stud under the right armrest. The iris beneath the chair dilated and the combat chair dropped through the opening. When the commodore's head disappeared from view, the iris snapped shut.

From the combat sphere Waugh said, "Helm, it's my boat."

"Aye, captain, it's your boat." O'Donnell relinquished helm control to the captain.

The beep of the comm. channel sounded through Nathan's earpiece. "Culver class transport this is Truculent. Cut your engines or I will fire into you," the captain said with finality.

"Commodore Waugh," a deep rumbling voice replied, "this is Captain Maloof of the Bretish commercial vessel League Trader. Your records must be in error. We filed our flight plan as per League of Allied Worlds provisions. If you dare to fire at this ship I will make the most profound protests to the ... ahhh!"

The squeal from the weapons tracking system targeted the fleeing vessel.

"Damn, she locked him up."

"That's what he gets for trying to stall her," Leo said.

"Don't fire, don't fire," Maloof cried. "I am cutting my engines now."

"Good for you, captain." Waugh said.

The transport ship applied full power to her forward grav plating. Her speed rapidly diminished.

"Helm, the boat is yours," Waugh said.

O'Donnell replied while the iris dilated and the captain surfaced from the combat sphere. Waugh swiveled her chair to face the Operations Station. "Some people cannot be reasoned with in a civilized manner." Demianski snorted as Waugh unstrapped. "Do you have the LT for me?"

"Waiting in the briefing room, captain."

"Very well." She disappeared through the hatch.

The atmosphere on the bridge had transformed from one of dull routine to an electrically charged condition Nathan could feel on his skin. He wondered if *Truculent's* prize crew still suffered from the same butterfly attacks as him.

"They are rarely so easy," the Commander said, his eyes peering over the console. "This character was too lightly armed to dare fighting back and too far in system to escape into hyper. Bear in mind gentlemen, this isn't over yet."

Lt Jakovich followed Waugh onto the bridge. The marine wore a camouflaged uniform and a light sidearm. Dealing with a league registered vessel required them to follow a conservative doctrine. *League Trader* was innocent until proven guilty. Armor and heavy weapons were discarded to avoid possible claims of provocative overreaction.

Commodore Waugh nodded to the D-O who instantly opened the channel to the suspect vessel. "League Trader this is Truculent."

"This is Captain Maloof," said the gruff voice.

"Captain, open your boat bay doors and prepare to receive our boarding party."

"We are having a small technical problem with the doors commodore," he said uncertainly. "It might take some time to get them open."

Waugh shook her head. "Want me to open it for you, Maloof?"

After a short delay Captain Maloof replied sullenly. "That will not be necessary commodore. We have managed to correct the problem."

"How convenient," Waugh said. "Truculent out."

She eyed the Auxiliary Ops Station. "Care to stretch your legs, Ensign Saunders?"

"Yes, ma'am."

"LT what is your threat assessment for the League Trader?"

"Minimal, skipper. They know they can't escape."

"In that case, Ensign Saunders, you may as well take a middy with you. Got anyone in mind?"

A spark flickered along Nathan's spine when Leo grinned at him.

"I believe Midshipman Telford could be coerced into volunteering, ma'am."

"Mister Telford?"

"Aye-aye, captain."

"Very well. You two know the drill. Remove your armor and report to the boat bay in four minutes."

"Aye-aye, captain." Nathan dashed to the bridge hatch with Leo on his heels.

CHAPTER 43

Through the landing boat's forward view-plates Nathan watched *League Trader* grow rapidly as they approached. The Chief of the Boat, Senior Chief Petty Officer Scaroni, peered into the cabin. "One minute, LT."

"Very well, COB." Jakovich unbuckled and turned to the junior officers.

"Mister Telford, you are along on this little jaunt as an observer only. Understood?"

"Aye-aye, LT," Nathan said.

"Very well," she said. "Sergeant Redpath, prepare for embarkation."

Redpath nodded and headed aft.

"We're not expecting trouble from these people but we take no chances." Jakovich set her eyes on both Nathan and Leo. "Keep your eyes open and follow procedures."

"Yes, ma'am," Leo answered for them both.

As the marine stepped to the back of the boat a slight bump marked their landing. The port and starboard hatches slid open. Three 'droids leaped out of each hatchway. They carried standard sidearms still sheathed in their holsters.

Apart from two shabby landing boats the bay was deserted. Nathan detected movement from behind a clear panel at the end of the bay. Undoubtedly *League Trader's* Landing Control Center. A tall, narrow woman stepped from the LCC.

Sergeant Redpath stopped before her and a brief exchange took place. Two 'droids accompanied him while he followed the officer. Suspect Line Runners had been known to kill boarding parties by dropping the boat bay's environmental force field.

"LT, the boat bay is secured," Redpath reported.

The LT stepped through the hatchway. Nathan dutifully followed behind Leo who stayed on her heels. Unlike *Truculent, League Trader's* overheads were nearly two meters from the deck. The marines, who were a good head taller than Nathan, would undoubtedly appreciate the headroom.

"Commander O'Brall," the Bretish officer said. "First Officer of the League Trader." As protocol demanded she shook hands with the marine.

"Lieutenant Jakovich of Truculent. I wish to speak with your captain."

"Certainly lieutenant. He is awaiting you on the bridge."

Sandwiched between the LT and three 'droids in front of them, Redpath and three 'droids behind them, Nathan followed the procession forward. The midships lift took them to the bridge, three decks up.

The command deck was a large cluttered space showing clear signs of neglect. A tenacious stench made Nathan's nose twitch.

Captain Maloof was no taller than Nathan but easily three times his weight. A fine coating of sweat glistened on his pasty forehead.

"Your captain locked her weapons onto my ship," he complained. "I demand an explanation."

"You should be used to it by now, Maloof," the LT said.

The Bretish captain's brow creased for a moment before his piggish eyes widened. "Lieutenant ... Jakovich? Yes?"

"Nothing wrong with your memory."

"When was your visit? Two years ago?"

"Yes," she said, "I was assigned to the Monitor Arrant at the time."

"I remember. Another trigger-happy Athenian captain. You found nothing then and you'll find nothing now. We are a legitimate Bretish registered trading vessel."

"Captain Maloof, we can take care of our business in a speedy fashion if you are willing to cooperate."

"Of course lieutenant, anything you want."

"Thank you," the marine said pleasantly. "Firstly, I want to see a copy of your flight plan which you claim to have filed before departing Bretish space."

Maloof rubbed at a whiskered chin. "Unfortunately we suffered a major technical malfunction to our navigation computer. The copy you request was inadvertently wiped from our records during our attempt to bring the system back online."

"Let me take a wild stab in the dark, captain. The same difficulty wiped all navigational information from your computer?" The LT's mocking tone revealed her opinion of the Bret captain. Nathan suppressed a derisive snort.

"Regrettably so, lieutenant." Maloof's outstretched hands punctuated his obvious lie. "We have only recently solved the problem. We were heading for the safety of the Ibis Nebula to finish repairs when your ship attacked us. We suspected you were a headhunter and took flight."

"Are your external sensors operating, captain?"

Maloof's brow wrinkled. "Yes."

"And you mistook a monitor for a headhunter?"

"We were startled. To be frank, I don't believe your captain's action in locking her weapons onto my ship is in the best interests of intersystem relations between our two societies. We are, after all, both members of the League of Allied worlds, are we not?"

Nathan held back a sneer. Maloof could make a snake oil merchant blush.

"I would like to see your manifests, captain."

"And I would like to show them to you, lieutenant. Unfortunately…"

"Let me guess," Jakovich said dryly, "computer ate your manifests?"

"Regrettably so."

Now things will get interesting. Without conclusive proof they had crossed over from the Northern Quarantine Zone, *League Trader* would slip through their fingers. A hefty fine for failing to lodge a flight plan might be the most they could get them for.

"Very well, captain," the LT said wearily. "I guess we'll have to do this the old fashioned way."

***

Leo rubbed at the knot that had grown at back of his neck. *What a bloody day. League Trader's* cargo holds had undergone a painstaking inspection. Lt Jakovich brought all twenty-four 'droids aboard together with six supervising CPO's. They opened and inspected every cargo container on the ship. They checked for the usual false bottoms and found nothing. The LT ordered a check of the crew's quarters, including the officers, for contraband. They found nothing. They sensor swept *League Trader* from bow to stern and discovered no incriminating evidence. *League Trader* might well be what she claimed to be. Or these could be the cleverest smugglers in the business.

Three hours had passed since the inspection began. Leo slumped onto the cold deck next to Nathan.

Maloof and his first officer stood to one side of the bay observing the proceedings. His oily smile displayed an overly smug confidence.

Nathan stood and stretched. From his thoughtful expression, and lengthy silence, Leo could almost hear his mind working the problem. Nathan paced for a while, stopped, stared at the overhead, then slapped his forehead with an open hand.

"Nathan?"

"Stupid."

"What?"

"Four years of being put into a box at the academy and this occurs to me *now*?" Nathan spoke to the overhead as if addressing another part of himself. He dropped to his knees and locked eyes with Leo.

"Ensign, I know I'm only an observer but I think I can contribute more. Because of my background."

Leo felt his brow furrow for a moment before the light of understanding came to him.

"Go on."

"As you may know, I was born on a vessel not dissimilar to this one." Leo kept his expression neutral. "During my time in the north the crew hid contraband from the guards all over the ship. I only vaguely remember it but I think that experience might be of use here. I don't think the marines are ready to take advice from a middy at this stage. So why don't we take a wander and see what we can find?" Leo eyed him warily. "If we find nothing, no harm done. But if we stumble across something germane to this investigation we'll be able to pique the LT's interest. Yes?"

"Where do we begin?"

"Where indeed?" Nathan's glassy eyes stared into the distance for a few seconds. "Let's start in their engine room."

"Very well." They disengaged from what had turned into a congregation of Monitor Corps personnel and 'droids and made their way aft.

***

Nathan panned his sensor pad around *League Trader's* huge engine room. After making a thorough scan examination of the area he stepped into the reactor room. Even with heavy shielding to protect the crew, residual energy emissions scrambled his sensor readings. Nathan pocketed his pad and scrutinized the base of the reactor.

As a child aboard the enslaved *Bellinda* he had regularly hidden precious contraband from the Pruessens. Dark visions of his perilous childhood returned. He pushed aside the sadness that accompanied the ghostly imagery and concentrated on the immediate problem.

The reactor operated in automatic standby mode, producing sufficient power to maintain life support. With the crew insolated, he and Leo were alone in the large compartment.

"Now if I was illegal contraband where would I hide?" Nathan said to himself. Finding the tools he needed to test his theory he dropped onto his knees and worked his way along the reactor's base. As he prized the cover plate off, he sensed Leo bristling beside him.

The cover plate took a concentrated effort to remove. He shone a light into the hollow space finding nothing out of the ordinary. Replacing the cover he moved to the next. Each of the following five cover plates required muscle-straining effort to remove. Behind each he found no cache of illegal contraband. The sixth cover plate was unexpectedly cooperative. *That's more like it.*

As he had done with the others he shone the light into the recess. He examined the cavity in exacting detail. He found nothing. Despite proof to the contrary his best instincts warred against the evidence. Nathan lay on his stomach and continued to stare into the darkness. After a minute he put the light aside and reached inside. Running his fingers around the perimeter of the cavity he detected nothing but a smooth interior lining. His fingers brushed a tiny flange he knew should not be there. Nathan clawed at the thin strip of metal until it slid from its housing.

"Pay dirt." Nathan extracted the gray-colored cylinder.

"I'll be damned." Leo gasped. Nathan pried at the lid. "Hold on a minute, Nathan. We don't know what's in there, do we?" Nathan shrugged impatiently before reconsidering. Leo was right. Death in large doses could await the reckless investigator. Besides, had they followed correct procedure according to the law? Nathan thought they had, but the LT would be the final arbiter of their unauthorized sortie.

"I think it's time to call in the marines," Leo said.

Nathan nodded with short, rapid motions. "I should return this to where we found it, don't you think?"

"Good thinking, middy."

Leo keyed his LM. "Marine one - Saunders."

Two more times he tried to contact the LT. "Damn reactor interference is scrambling my signal."

"Very well, you go and get the LT and I will take care of the evidence."

"Aye-aye, sir." Leo grinned before sprinting away.

When the hatch snapped shut behind Leo, Nathan strode from the reactor room and stood the cylinder on a work bench. His sensor readings duly noted that the cylinder measured thirty-three centimeters in length with a diameter of six point two centimeters. It was composed of duraloy composite and weighed one point eight kilos, including the contents. The readings detected nothing further so the stubborn mystery remained unsolved. He considered scanning it further away from the core but chose to leave such in-depth investigations to the marines.

A sudden cautionary stab of pain flared from Nathan's back. He pivoted to face the danger, his right hand reaching for the sidearm that sat on his left hip. In the hatchway Maloof aimed down the barrel of a blunt-nosed needle gun. Nathan's right hand froze, well short of his sidearm. Maloof jerked the gun up. Nathan slowly raised both hands. The needle gun might contain a harmless tranquilizer or a far more malignant concoction. *Damn, I wish I was still wearing my armor.*

Maloof eyed the canister in Nathan's raised left hand. His callous gaze fell onto the midshipman.

"What am I to do with you, boy?"

"Surrender?" Nathan had a fair idea what Maloof had in mind for him. Smuggling drugs into league space carried, at best, a mandatory life sentence.

The Bret captain snorted without humor and gestured with his free hand. "Step that way."

Maloof guided him through the bowels of the engineering department until they arrived at the superstructure and the adjacent airlock. Now it made sense. When they found Nathan's lifeless body floating in space, the natural assumption would be that a novice officer had wandered off alone and gotten himself killed. But if he was missing his sidearm it might provoke suspicion.

"Open it."

Nathan complied while every fiber of his being tensed for attack. He needed an edge, a small distraction.

"Step into the airlock."

Nathan walked meekly into the lock then faced the Bretish captain.

Maloof eyed the cylinder in Nathan's raised left hand.

"Give it to me, boy."

Nathan tossed the cylinder to him, in a high arc. He kept his right hand raised but allowed his left arm to follow the arc. Maloof tracked the falling container, waited, caught it after a minor juggling act and clutched it to his ample stomach. The glee ran from his face. Nathan had drawn his sidearm with his left hand. He fired once, hitting Maloof squarely in the chest. Captain Maloof and the cylinder hit the deck together.

Nathan stared at the inert body and smiled.

"Don't call me boy."

CHAPTER 44

Date: 12th August, 320 ASC.
Position: Monitor *Truculent*, on station: Ibis Nebula.
Status: Alert stand down.

Waugh considered the report submitted by Lt Clementine Jakovich. The Bretish vessel *League Trader* was boarded and searched for contraband without initial success. Ensign Saunders reported to Jakovich that he may have stumbled upon something of interest.

Telford awaited the marines in engineering and directed them to the starboard airlock. Maloof's body lay sprawled on the deck. Midshipman Telford explained that the Bretish captain had pulled a needle gun on him. He said that he had been 'obliged to defend himself.' Rusty Redpath detailed a 'droid to carry Maloof's unconscious body to the brig where he was corralled with the rest of *League Trader's* crew. When he awoke from the stun blast he would find his circumstances had taken a decidedly downward turn.

Telford explained how he and Saunders had discovered some anomalous readings in the reactor room. The LT detected no such readings from her sensor pad. The midshipman could not explain the irregularity but urged the LT to examine the indicated cover plate. Maloof would not pull a weapon on a Monitor Corps officer if he had nothing to hide. Telford, obviously feigning surprise, removed a long gray cylinder from the hidden recess. Waugh shook her head.

Jakovich believed if one illegal item could elude their sensor sweeps so could others. Because of his sterling sensor reading abilities she put Telford in charge of the search team. He proved, in her words, to have a unique approach to unearthing contraband. His methods had little to do with sensor readings.

Off the record Lt Jakovich had more to add. "He broke protocol by not checking in with me first."

"Did he offer an explanation for his actions?" Waugh asked.

"Telford said he did not wish to bother me with what was essentially a hunch. I suppose that's a reasonable excuse. But I suspect there was more going on between those young gentlemen than they're letting on. Don't get me wrong, skipper, I think they both have tremendous potential but going off by themselves that way could have ended badly. Rusty checked Maloof's needle gun. The darts contained a lethal concentration of curare.

"Telford said he 'had been obliged to defend himself', but skirted the issue of how he brought down someone who had gotten the jump on him. He has guts, but only a fool stares down a needle gun lightly. He's no fool so ..." Jakovich shrugged.

As Waugh knew from Telford's academy record his firearm's proficiency was good but not *that* good. Nevertheless, the middy had drawn on Maloof using his weak left hand and hit the target dead center. Perhaps Telford, like any true professional, needed an adrenaline boost to function at his best.

"Do you wish to include these ... irregularities, in your official report, Clementine?"

"No, skipper. I don't believe that will be necessary. It was a productive operation. We confiscated a significant quantity of drugs, captured a Line Runner and everyone came home alive. I'm simply noting my slight concern."

"Very well. We'll leave it there for the moment."

***

Commodore Waugh examined the briefing room's elliptical table. Two hours ago she and her senior officers had gathered around the table, holo screens blazing, computer predictions and star maps projecting above the black top. During the past hour the pragmatic nature of the apparatus had undergone a transformation. Almost everything on a monitor had more than one use. This included equipment as well as personnel. A stark white tablecloth draped over the table's protective cover disguising its obsidian practicality. Silverware marched along the dining table at uniform intervals, the crystal glassware reflecting the mellow candle light.

Seated to her right, Luis took occasional sips of his wine. His eyes stared sightlessly at the bridge hatch. She knew him well enough to appreciate when to leave him alone with his thoughts. No doubt he would be monitoring data over his earpiece while simultaneously enjoying the social occasion. The old axiom still held true: A good operations officer was akin to a dual brained octopus. The daily administration of the boat fell squarely on his shoulders and the responsibility preyed on him around the clock.

The hatch chimed. "Ad-mit," she said.

The marines, resplendent in their black, high-collared class A uniforms, stepped through the hatch. The young marine lieutenant presented a fine picture, with a lean row of medals and Corps awards glistening against the black material. In contrast Sergeant Redpath could not fit another service decoration onto the chest of his immaculately pressed uniform.

"Good evening, marines."

"Good evening captain, commander." Jakovich said. They took their seats to her right.

Waugh stared toward the room's far corner from which the smell of scrumptious treats wafted. Tonight's meal represented an all-too-rare occasion for Chief Balski to show off.

"Have you finished defiling our meals with your vile toxins, Cookie?"

Balski poked his grinning face around the jam. "Any time you're ready, skipper."

"You can start poisoning us shortly."

Waugh's mood had improved appreciably during the last day. After cooling her heels for the better part of two months on station, they had finally attained a positive result. Not as rewarding as bagging a headhunter but better than nothing.

The kilo of Kesium discovered by young Telford proved to be the beginning of a highly valuable confiscation. A half day of tearing *League Trader* apart garnered another nine kilos of the drug. Ten kilos of misery destined for the drug-afflicted streets of the Bretish home world. To the layman, ten kilos sounded like a trifling quantity. However, once refined it would have supplied the needs of half a million addicts for a year. Illegal drugs like Kesium adopted constantly changing names: Light Bright, White Star, Solar Dust, K, Soft Anvil. By whatever name it was called the salient fact remained: it killed people and destroyed lives.

The hatch chimed. "Ad-mit."

Ensign Saunders stepped through the hatch, the elegant cut of his class A uniform suggesting hand tailoring. The immaculately pressed, long-tailed black coat was crisp, as were the bone-colored trousers. The light-beige waistcoat complimented the white shirt and black cravat to complete the ensemble.

Midshipman Telford followed, his standard issue, gray class A uniform dull by comparison. Once again Waugh found herself drawn to his eyes. The shadow behind those innocent eyes reflected an ageless distinction separating soldier from civilian.

"It's only fashionable to be late on Athens, gentlemen," Waugh said with a cordial grumble. She motioned them to the chairs on her left.

Petty Officer Dearkov, wearing a white steward's coat over black pants, stepped from the kitchenette.

Has she washed her hair?

Telford shot her a tiny, obscure nod. Dearkov opened the wine bottle and offered the cork to the commodore.

"I believe you will enjoy this. Thessaly Chateau Ruemont, 299. It's been sitting idle for three patrols so it's had time to mellow." When the glasses were charged she raised her glass. "Ladies and gentlemen, the Republic, duty and the Corps." The returning toast echoed from her guests.

"And," she added, "to a successful mission." She granted Telford a short nod of acknowledgement. Once again he refused to respond in a typically overwhelmed midshipman-like manner. However, the tips of his ears changed color dramatically, giving her hope.

"Very well, Cookie," Waugh said. "Let the ordeal begin."

Balski was the best cook in the fleet but naval cooks throughout the ages would turn in their graves if one of their number were hit with a stray compliment. Dearkov served the first course with practiced ease. The leek soup had a mild flavor and wonderful aroma.

"I believe we have worn out our welcome in the Ibis Nebula," Waugh said. "We need a new hunting ground." She cast her gaze around the table. Waugh had already made up her mind but enjoyed these harmless games. "I'm open to suggestions."

Luis snorted. The marines examined their soup without comment. Leo's head wrinkled in concentration. Nathan's expression remained neutral. Waugh nonchalantly sipped her soup.

"What do you think, Leo?"

The young ensign hovered on the brink of making a suggestion but wisely chose to abstain. "I'm not sure captain."

"Oh? Pity." Waugh set her gaze on the middy. "What about you Nathan? Any ideas?"

Nathan paused, his soup spoon poised below his mouth. Half squinting, as if in deep thought, he said, "I suppose Virtus is out of the question." As he sipped his soup the rumble of laughter began with the commodore and spread around the table. A crooked smile wrinkled one side of Nathan's face causing Redpath to bark a hollow laugh.

Yes, after the life he's had, attacking the most heavily guarded military target in the Pruessen Empire would *appeal to him.*

The main course arrived much to everyone's delight. Wild game hen from Corinth. Luis caught Balski's attention.

"Cookie," he said, while biting into a portion of the delicate bird, "this sauce isn't making me as nauseous as most of your foul concoctions. Would you care to share the recipe?"

"Not a chance, commander," said the grinning CPO. "It's going to the grave with me."

"Probably just as well," Luis mumbled.

Throughout the boat the crew were enjoying the benefits of better food and an open bar. Waugh always rewarded a successful operation.

The meal progressed in a mood of easy conversation. Even the grommits loosened up after a few glasses of fine red cabernet. Leo toyed with the remains of his meal. Waugh read his body language as he mustered all the false indifference he could and plunged in at the deep end.

"Captain," he said, "I was wondering about the disposition of the League Trader?"

Waugh tucked the last of her meal into her mouth. Leo knew perfectly well what the disposition of the captured Line Runner would be. What he really wanted to know was who would get the privilege of captaining her back to Sentinel Artemis. With a skeleton crew of capable non-coms, she rated only a junior officer for the fast journey into Athenian space.

"She is being returned to base in the morning." Waugh knew she should not take such delight in torturing the young officer but rank did have its privileges after all.

Leo nodded gravely.

"Has an officer been chosen to command her, ma'am?" Nathan asked.

Waugh soaked up the last of the extraordinary sauce from her plate with a fresh roll. "Yes," she said before popping the roll into her mouth. Guilt prompted her to put Leo out of his misery.

"I want you to know, Leo, I gave serious consideration to appointing you to the command of the League Trader. But I didn't." Leo nodded stoically. "I even considered dropping you into the captain's chair, Nathan." His head snapped back with a jolt. *Gotcha!* His startled expression, though short-lived, proved he was human after all.

"However, in the final analysis I chose an officer whose appointment would best serve the interests of this boat." She sipped her wine. "Lieutenant Tivendale." The young officer's jaw muscles tightened.

"The massive improvement in the efficiency of the supply department prompted me to reward the person responsible." Nathan examined his meal. "Unfortunately the loss of Lieutenant Tivendale leaves a hole in the command structure. I don't know what we will do without a supply officer of Lieutenant Tivendale's caliber. I guess we'll struggle on." The thought crossed her mind: *You are a bad, bad person Donatella Waugh.*

Dearkov placed a huge silver dessert tray onto the table. Cookie had concluded the meal with chocolate mousse, Waugh's favorite. After she spooned a generous portion onto her plate Dearkov passed the serving tray on to the next in line. Nathan begged off.

"You don't know what you're missing," Waugh said to him.

Nathan tapped his flat, muscular abdomen. Following the luscious dessert, port and coffee arrived. Waugh produced a narrow pouch from an inside pocket. She brought the panatela to her lips. Luis accepted a cigar from her and waited for her to pass the cutter to snip the end. "Smoke them if you have them." The antique gold lighter clicked several times before igniting the long, dark brown cigar. The marines produced the thickest cigars she had ever seen. Clementine Jakovich snipped the end of her cigar with a small knife. Rusty had gone the traditional route, using his teeth. But in a very gentlemanly fashion.

"Cookie, would you mind turning the air extractor to full?"

"Just did, skipper."

"Thank you."

Rusty blew an enormous cloud of smoke across the table, temporarily engulfing Nathan. As the cloud dissipated, Redpath held the smoking cigar out to him.

"Would you care for a cigar, Mister Telford? I have a spare."

"Thank you, sergeant. I'll pass."

"Mister Saunders?" Redpath was determined to get one of the youngsters.

"Why thank you Sergeant Redpath. Don't mind if I do."

Redpath bit down on his cigar, reached into a pocket and handed Leo the long, thick roll of leaf. The marine leaned back puffing mildly while anticipating the young ensign's forthcoming distress.

Leo produced a small pocket knife and snipped the top and bottom from the gigantic cigar. He dipped the end in his glass of port and used the candle's flame to light up expertly. Waugh covered her mouth with her napkin as the sergeant's smile wilted. Leo made a face as he drew the first draft of smoke into his lungs.

"My Lord, you marines really *are* tough, aren't you? Back on

Crete, my family has been growing their own leaf for two hundred years. This," he said, examining the cigar with mild disgust, "tastes about that old."

Nathan fought back a coughing fit as the extraction fan battled to clear the room of the thick smoke cloud. When the coffee arrived Waugh sampled the fine blend from the silver coffee pot and nodded to Dearkov. Nathan begged off. The smoke had obviously blocked his sense of smell.

"Dearkov, pour," Waugh ordered.

As soon as he smelled the fresh aroma, he smiled. A contented sigh escaped his lips after the first sip of the Kastorian-blend coffee.

"Oh, by the way Nathan have you completed your rotation through the supply department?"

"Yes, ma'am, two weeks ago."

"What's your opinion of Chief Argento?"

"First class, captain. She'll make a great supply officer."

"Agreed," Waugh said. "Pity she's not an officer. We really need someone who has a firm understanding of the department's current situation. Wouldn't you agree?"

Guardedly he said, "I suppose so, captain."

From the sound of the badly concealed chuckling, Luis and the marines caught her meaning.

"Better go easy on the port, Nathan. I want you bright-eyed and on the ball when you report for work in the morning. As interim supply officer."

Nathan's air of blasé restraint failed him miserably.

"But captain," Luis said, right on cue, "surely you're not going to appoint a mere midshipman to such a responsible position?"

"Why thank you, commander. Correct as always."

Waugh reached into a waistcoat pocket and removed the small shiny object. She stepped behind Nathan and pinned the silver star onto his left epaulet before returning to her seat.

"I shall expect that back at the end of the cruise, Acting Ensign Telford."

Nathan gawked at her. His initial attempts to form words failed. Finally, he cleared his throat and addressed his running mate.

"May I borrow that disgusting thing?"

Leo handed him the monster cigar. Nathan inhaled a huge draught into his virgin lungs.

Rusty grinned in anticipation of the inevitable outcome.

CHAPTER 45

Date: 13th August, 320 ASC.
Position: Monitor *Truculent*, on station: Ibis Nebula.
Status: Alert Condition three.

Nathan strolled into the wardroom, his easy saunter reflecting a mood lightened by the previous night's celebration. He received a prompt reminder that very little happened aboard a monitor without everyone hearing about it.

"Atten-tion!" Meta ordered. The middies snapped to attention. "Good morning Acting Ensign Telford, sir."

"Shit," he muttered.

"Acting Ensign Telford, sir," Ozzie said. "Permission to continue breathing, sir."

Nathan clamped his hands behind his back and ran a critical eye over the three grinning middies.

"Your deportment is thoroughly deplorable middy."

"Yes sir, sorry sir, acting ensign, sir," Meta replied.

"Get a shine on those shoes middy."

"Yes sir, Acting Ensign Telford, sir." Ozzie's grin underscored the absurdity of the moment.

"And as for you Midshipwoman Okuma," Nathan shook his head, "I don't see any hope for you at all."

"Whatever you say acting ensign, sir."

"I will now give you clowns my one and only order. Knock it off."

Too late Nathan realized his mistake.

"Yes *sir*."

"Of course acting ensign, sir."

"Oh, my deepest and most profound apologies acting ensign, sir ensign acting, sir."

"Everyone's a friggin' comedian," he muttered.

"Whatever you say, acting ensign sir." Moe slapped him on the back. They all fell about laughing. Thankfully the novelty had worn off by the end of the day. They finally stopped the *sir* nonsense, even resisting the temptation to buff his new star. His friends were happy for him, which made the promotion all the more rewarding.

Truculent departed the Ibis Nebula three hours later and for two days escorted *League Trader* toward Athenian space. Regardless of the relative capriciousness of *League Trader's* temporary captain, *Truculent* left her within three hyper-transitions of the Oceanian System before altering course northward. *I'm sure CPO Instelle will pull Tivendale into line if he tries anything stupid. Although the last time I saw him he looked like a whipped dog.*

Reliable scuttlebutt suggested that, on the captain's most judicious recommendation, Tivendale would never again set foot aboard a monitor.

The deployment was almost over. In nineteen days they would disembark at Sentinel Artemis and the great adventure would end. And with it Nathan's hope for retribution. For the first time in thirteen years he made a wish. He shook his head irritably. *Wishes are for children and dreamers.* Even if, by some dark miracle, his wish came true, would it lessen his dreadful guilt?

CHAPTER 46

Date: 16th August, 320 ASC.
Position: Monitor *Truculent*, running along the Fenchurch Depression.
Status: Landing boat orientation.

The tractor beam manipulated the small landing craft as if it were a black fish at the end of a high tensile line. The forward view-plate automatically tinted, adjusting to the beam's glare. Chief of the Boat Scaroni had tractored aboard in this fashion so often she had little concern for having handed her life to another human being.

"Landing Boat three, this is the LCC, I have you on the beam," the Landing Control Officer said. "Sit back and enjoy the ride."

"Three acknowledges."

Truculent's boat bay doors stood open, the fantail extended at a slight downward angle. The young man beside her revealed a glimmer of apprehension.

"Mister Telford," the Chief of the Boat said, "I understand you dined with our captain recently."

"I was privileged to do so, COB."

"How was everything?"

"Fine."

He kept his tone informal but his eyes remained glued to the steadily growing boat bay.

"Now that you've broken bread with her, what do you think of our commodore?"

"She was everything I imagined she would be."

"Meaning?"

"I've never met anyone quite like her. Sure, I've read everything written about her but no words can convey ..." his eyes narrowed and stared into the starfield, "her sense of being. It's as if the room isn't big enough to contain her energy. You know what I mean?"

Yeah, I know what you mean. "So, you shared your feelings with her?"

"What? And sound like every other heroine-worshiping, gibbering middy?"

The Chief of the Boat chuckled. "Well, you're not a middy anymore are you?"

Telford sighed. "It's largely symbolic, COB."

Scaroni showed mercy and said no more on the subject.

Truculent skirted the edge of the Fenchurch Depression, its mild interference helping to mask her signature. Fenchurch was a characteristically large hyper depression covering an area that lapped from Athenian space across the Rio Grande and into the north.

"Mister Telford, have you tractored aboard a monitor before?" Scaroni had read his file but today's exercise was about more than landing boat orientation. The middies, regardless of rank, came within her sphere of responsibility.

"Yes COB, many times."

"In that case how would you like to try a fast trap instead of this boring old tractor nonsense? Hey? What do you say?"

"Sure." As with most grommits he employed the sort of false indifference that made Scaroni feel warm and fuzzy inside.

"Good for you." Scaroni keyed her larynx mike. "LCC, we're going for a fast trap approach. Drop tractor on my mark."

"Roger that LB three."

"Three, two, one mark!"

The tractor dropped. Scaroni pushed the LB into a tight three gee turn. Telford's Adam's apple bobbed up and down appreciably. She could almost smell the salty taste in his mouth. She had seen this so many times before. His perplexed expression said much. Surely this should not be happening to him? No words escaped his slightly parted lips but she would bet a month's pay he was reciting the academy anti-yack mantra in his mind: 'It's all in your head, all in your head, in your head, your head, head.'

The slight nausea affected the best of the grommits their first time on Combat Interdiction Patrol. The environmental and gravity fluctuations took time to adjust to. Rusty Redpath had mentioned to her that one of the middies yacked in his helmet. Would this be the next candidate for the hall of shame? The others had managed to keep their lunch down, although Hayden was a close-run thing. He had been lucky that Doc Kelso prescribed medication to aid his equilibrium.

Telford swallowed hard and stared past her through the starboard view-plate. At dead slow speed *Truculent* ran parallel to the depression with LB three matching her speed. She continued to prowl for business, stealth engines only. The power emissions from a single landing boat would not jeopardize the even running of her stealth patrol.

Scaroni had received nothing but good feedback about this young officer. He had garnered a lot of supporters from within the ranks as word of his mismatched confrontation with Tivendale spread throughout the boat.

Even Dearkov, usually too surly and self-absorbed to be interested, had become a fan. Apparently, a certain senior rating, name withheld, had been informing Tivendale on Telford's movements. Although no fan of junior officers, Dearkov chose to intervene. The multiple bruises on the anonymous rating's face suggested Tivendale's inside card had been removed from the deck.

If Telford could get someone like Dearkov on side, perhaps miracles were possible.

"Chief, is there any chance of ..." Telford eyed the controls hopefully. He officially outranked her but in reality he knew better than to push his luck.

Scaroni snorted. If he hadn't asked to pilot the boat she would have been extremely surprised. She examined the external scanners and except for *Truculent* found clear space in all directions. "How many flight hours do you have?"

"I have eleven hundred and fifty-two hours in sims."

No doubt he thought it would be extraneous to mention he had spent all but forty-nine of those hours in fighter simulations.

"How many real flight hours?"

"Nearly fifty."

"Do you believe you can pilot this craft?"

"Not up to your high standards, chief," he said.

"Very well, Mister Telford, the boat is yours." Scaroni leaned back and folded her arms.

Telford pounced on the controls and adjusted for the expected shift to port. He made small experimental adjustments to pitch and yaw. A curious expression crossed his face when he glanced out the starboard view-plate. *Truculent* had disappeared. He checked the sensors and found her, two point seven kilometers astern.

Running parallel to a hyper depression created some interesting conditions. Such as encountering a hyperspace fluctuation while still in normal space.

"Was that a class four hyper eddy?"

"No Mister Telford that was only a class three. Interesting sensation isn't it."

"Ah, yeah. Permission to come about, chief."

"Granted."

Telford glanced at the COB, noted that she stroked her chin with a rabbit's foot, and snorted.

Scaroni braced herself. Telford would have few opportunities like this during the remainder of the cruise. He would undoubtedly push the envelope.

"Coming about to port, now!"

Scaroni's chest compressed as the weight of the four gee turn pressed against her. She showed no outward signs of concern and continued to stroke her chin with the rabbit's foot. She loved messing with a grommit's head.

"Chief, permission to barrel-roll the craft."

"Granted."

Telford kicked the boat onto her side and held it for a count of two before rolling onto the topside and holding it for a count of two. Telford's anguished growl accompanied the third maneuver. As he slid the boat onto her starboard side she slipped off the line. Half inverted he over corrected. The boat dropped onto her belly with a decided bump.

"Shit!" His eyes dropped to the sensor readouts. The landing boat had slid off course and was now two kilometers closer to *Truculent*. Although still within safety tolerances he should not have allowed it to happen. Scaroni knew he had studied, in minute detail, the effects of flying this close to a depression, knew how they could push a vessel even the size of *Truculent* off course, had trained like a demon to avoid and counter it and still failed to correct for the variation. Telford pushed the LB back on course, irritation written across his face.

"Have we learned something today, Mister Telford?" The COB asked.

Telford gritted his teeth. "As exacting as simulators are they cannot prepare a pilot for every contingency."

"Wonderful, straight out of the manual. But what have you *learned?*"

"I have learned that flying this close to a hyperspace depression takes hands-on practice and should never be underestimated."

"And?"

A sickly smile formed as he glanced at her. "Don't fuck with the Chief Of the Boat?"

"There is hope for you yet. Head for the barn and take it easy."

"Roger."

Telford brought the landing boat about, setting course for the landing pattern. Five clicks from the boat he faced her. *No, you can't land the boat.*

As he opened his mouth to speak, Scaroni heard the flight deck alarm blare Alert Condition one.

CHAPTER 47

Nathan pressed his back firmly against his chair. The burble from *Truculent's* engines vibrated through the seat of his v-suit. Scaroni's face remained rigid as the landing boat hurtled toward the boat bay. Nathan fought against the instinct to avert his eyes.

The landing boat breached the environmental force field. The skids struck the boat bay deck with a bone-jarring jolt. Heartbeats later it slammed into the arrester field. Nathan's seat belt dug painfully against his shoulders and chest. He unbuckled, opened the hatch and jumped from the craft. With the COB on his heels he raced for the drop shafts. Nathan felt the boat's acceleration building.

The COB took the starboard drop shaft to her combat station in maneuvering. Nathan swung into the drop shaft and passed through two pressure hatches before swinging onto deck one. A short walk brought him to the final hatch. He punched in the code before stepping onto the bridge. While he strapped into his jump seat he quickly scanned the crew. No joking today. A glint of excitement sparked in Leo's eyes. He motioned Nathan closer and whispered into his ear.

"We've received a distress call from the Francorum freighter Genevieve. She claims to be under attack by a headhunter."

"A Franc?" Nathan said in an incredulous tone.

Leo's face hardened. "Ensign, she is a civilian craft with a crew of eighty-seven and the capacity to carry thirty passengers. You of all people know what headhunters do with captives."

"Yes," Nathan said. "Sorry." *Even* Franc *civilians don't deserve that fate.*

Nathan examined his readouts and nodded to himself. *Genevieve's* captain had foolishly chosen to enter the Fenchurch Depression. At its narrowest point a fast ship could cross it in thirty-two hours. For the dubious benefit of saving a day's flight time the Franc captain had exposed his ship to indefensible risk. A headhunter had run her down and attacked. Within the hyper depression *Genevieve* stood no chance of escape.

"Helm, report," Waugh demanded.

"Reactor is at eighty-seven percent and climbing, captain. Primary engines are increasing to flank speed," O'Donnell said. "ETA with Genevieve is five point three minutes."

"Damn," Nathan whispered, "we're that close?"

"The boat's been overdue for a change of luck," Leo replied.

"Captain," the D-O said, "I have comm from Genevieve's captain."

Her bearing reminded Nathan of a badly beaten dog.

"Captain," Waugh said, "what is your status?"

"We've been boarded, captain." Her glassy eyes reflected terrible misery. "We fought them but were overwhelmed by their numbers. Ten of my crew are dead. They detected your approach and fled."

"What is your ship's condition?"

"Our shields are still down, one engine is damaged. Both are repairable. But there is something else." The Francorum captain paused, as if dreading her next words. "They have taken my passengers, captain. Twenty-three men, women and children."

"Do you require our assistance, captain?" Under space maritime law she had to ask.

"Thank you captain, but no."

"Then I will bid you good day, captain. Truculent out." Waugh swung to the Tactical Station, expectation burning in her eyes.

Lt Hookes kept her eyes fixed on her readouts. "I have her, captain. I confirm she is a headhunter." Her eyebrows arched. "Badger class. She's running for the Rio Grande at top speed. Feeding course and speed to the helm."

O'Donnell's hands flew across his console controls. "Course set, captain."

"Both ahead flank at your earliest," Waugh barked.

Nathan sensed an inner suspicion about their luck. *The Badger class ship is one of the weakest assets available to headhunters. What would it be doing this deep into league space?* Even though he knew Waugh would be thinking the same thing, the spot between the shoulder blades began to ache.

Within twenty minutes Nathan felt the slightest of vibrations through his console.

"Captain," O'Donnell said, "we are about to hit the compression barrier."

"Very well, helm," Waugh said, "maintain speed."

"Aye, captain."

With each passing minute the vibration increased as the monitor fought against one of Tunguska's most challenging anomalies, the compression barrier. In Tunguska it caused similar problems as old Earth's sound barrier.

Minute by minute they gained on the enemy ship.

The chase continued for five more hours, with the monitor shaking vigorously as the strain on her systems increased. Finally the gap between the two vessels closed.

"The enemy ship is at extreme torpedo range, captain," Hookes said, breaking the long silence.

"Very well." The captain straightened her back and unknotted her neck. "Helm, time to optimal range?"

"Nine minutes, captain."

"Very well. Shut down the primary engines."

As soon as the engines stopped pushing against the compression barrier the vibration stopped. Nathan's ears popped.

The captain addressed the Auxiliary Operations Station.

"Feel like getting your feet wet, Ensign Saunders?"

Leo's face lit up like an aurora. "Yes, ma'am."

"You observe on this one, ensign. Do not leave the landing boat. Clear?"

Showing far less enthusiasm, Leo said, "Aye, ma'am."

"On your way." Leo sprinted for the hatch as the captain's eyes settled on Nathan. "Do you think you can handle Auxiliary Ops, Mister Telford? Or should I get CPO Cairns to assist you?"

"I'm familiar with the systems, captain."

"So I've been led to believe." She paused for a moment, her inscrutable gaze unblinking. "But how will you react when they start shooting at us?"

"I've been shot at before, captain."

Waugh nodded once before turning away.

Nathan carried out an immediate diagnostic of all systems. Within four minutes it confirmed that all systems were green across his board. Happy with the results he realigned his sensors to the bow opticals.

His main screen gave him his first live view of the huge enemy ship. *Yes, there you are, you Pruessen bastard.*

"One minute to optimal firing range, captain," O'Donnell said.

"Very well." Waugh slipped into the combat chair. "D-O, ship to ship."

"Channel open, captain."

"To Badger class Pruessen vessel. This is Commodore Waugh of the Athenian warship Truculent. I order you to cut your engines and prepare to be boarded. If you fail to do so I shall fire into you."

"This is Captain Foss of the independent trading vessel Picaroon." His tone was atypically civilized for a headhunter. "I am holding twenty-three Francorum civilians aboard my vessel."

"I am aware of that, Captain Foss. Heave to immediately and prepare to be boarded. Consider this your last warning."

"Typical Athenian arrogance, but no matter. If you want the Francs come and get them."

Waugh drew her hand across her throat. "D-O, I'm going downstairs."

Demianski acknowledged with a short nod as the captain dropped into the combat sphere.

"Captain, optimal torpedo range," O'Donnell said.

"Very well helm. It's my boat."

"Aye, captain, your boat."

Minutes ticked by as the captain positioned *Truculent* for attack. A flash erupted from *Picaroon's* single stern launcher. Waugh fired a three second pulsar burst. *Picaroon's* torpedo disappeared in a blaze of silver fire.

"WEO - captain."

"Matrakas," said the Weapons Engineering Officer.

"Type thirteens in all tubes thank you."

"Aye-aye, captain."

Nathan nodded to himself. The low yield type thirteen's would easily neutralize *Picaroon's* shields, but were not powerful enough to endanger her interned passengers.

The squeal from the targeting computer confirmed the lock-on to the enemy ship. The boat bucked as six torpedoes burst from the forward tubes. They tracked the fleeing vessel's every sluggish avoidance maneuver. Pulsars struck out from *Picaroon* but headhunter technology could not match the torpedoes' sophisticated evasion countermeasures. The torpedoes surrounded the enemy and detonated simultaneously. Nathan averted his eyes as six thermonuclear explosions flared from his screen.

Sensor readings indicated that more than sixty of *Picaroon's* shield blisters had been overloaded by the massive blast.

Picaroon maintained course for the Rio Grande. She rotated through her longitudinal axis, bringing her bow to bear on *Truculent*. Two flashes erupted from *Picaroon's* nose. Without altering course Waugh picked off the incoming torpedoes with pulsar fire.

Closing to energy weapons range with any vessel involved inherent dangers. Although the Badger was an obsolete vessel, it retained the capacity to hurt *Truculent*. After all, a drunk holding a knife could do far more damage than a drunk without a knife.

The captain methodically picked away at *Picaroon's* defenses while deftly evading the headhunter's pulsar fire. One by one *Picaroon's* weapons fire trickled to a splutter then died. Nathan would never forget one moment of Waugh's virtuoso performance.

"Tactical, report," Waugh ordered.

"All offensive and defensive weapons destroyed," Hookes said. "Hard radiation on the hull makes internal sensor readings foggy but I confirm zero plague emissions. There are five internally shielded compartments on Picaroon. It is likely one of them contains the civvies. I am collating readings and will transmit same to the boarding party."

Nathan switched through his menus until he located the marine detachment. They had slipped out of the boat bay, slid their LB under the monitor's shields and latched onto the topside. There they applied full engine power until their speed matched *Truculent's.*

"When you're ready, LT," Waugh said.

"Departing now, captain."

Two marine Spartans did not constitute an army. However, two marine Spartans and twenty top-of-the-line type K14 combat 'droids, armed to the teeth with the best light weaponry in the League, came damn close.

Three minutes later the packed landing boat latched onto *Picaroon's* port midships hatch. COB Scaroni would use her universal tumbler to unscramble the locking code of the enemy's outer hatch. Then, may the Lord have mercy on their souls. The marine's code with headhunters was one of giving no quarter. Nathan's teeth set. *Go for it marines. Kill them all.*

"Hatch cracked," Jakovich reported. "Opening now." A short pause. "Corridor clear. Boarding vessel, now."

"Watch your step marines."

"Always, captain."

Contrary to the marine's suppositions, headhunters were warm-blooded mammals indistinguishable from human beings on sensor readouts. The marines relied on Hookes' educated guesswork to lead them to the civvies.

Nathan followed their progress on his sensors and imagined the scene in his mind. Nathan picked out the individuals from their comm emissions marked by green icons. The COB and CPO Lerner on the landing boat's flight deck. Leo standing by the hatch with pulsar rifle in hand, observing. Next, a great mass of green mechanical signatures marched relentlessly through the corridors, occasional red icons falling to bursts of fire. Within the storm of metal bodies, two humans directing the mission.

The standard complement of a Badger class varied between having fifty to sixty crewmen. The marines were justifiably confident of their ability to deal with the larger force.

So far resistance had been surprisingly moderate. The marines expected to take care of business with little difficulty. After all, the enemy were nothing more than a ragtag bunch of pirates. Nathan frowned. *Why is my back throbbing so painfully?*

"LT," Hookes said, "I detect a large concentration of warm bodies in section one-niner on your current deck. I read no energy emissions. It could be the civvies."

"Roger that," the marine acknowledged. "Proceeding to section one-niner."

Nathan's back flared, causing an involuntary gasp to escape his lips.

"Are you all right, ensign?"

Nathan had been concentrating so intently on the unfolding scene he had not noticed the captain step behind him to observe the mission on his more-detailed screens.

"Yes, captain." The fire between his shoulders continued to burn ferociously. *What should I do? Tell the captain? Tell her what? I have a* sense *of impending disaster?* Nathan knew danger lurked in the shadows of the very near future. Not for him, but for the boarding party.

"Something's not right here, captain." His eyes stayed locked to his readouts.

"Are you exercising another hunch, ensign?"

"I can't explain it." He committed the cardinal sin, abandoned his screen and stared at the captain. "This *feels* wrong."

If anyone could appreciate the value of good instincts it would be Donatella Waugh. Nathan had his premonition pain to warn him and she had thirty years on the deck of a monitor. Her eyes narrowed.

"Lieutenant Jakovich, report."

"Approaching section one-niner, captain."

"Lieutenant Hookes, is there anything out of the ordinary?"

"Captain, I read twenty live bodies. No weapons signatures." Hookes paused briefly before adding, "In fact I detect no energy emissions at all on that deck."

Nathan caught the fleeting exchange between the captain and D-O. It was as if two minds connected for an instant. The commander's head shook ever so slightly.

"Lieutenant Jakovich, withdraw to the landing boat."

"We're almost there, captain."

"Lieutenant, withdraw immediately."

"Very well, captain, we ar ..." The transmission ended with a forbidding abruptness.

Nathan gaped at his screens. The energy signals from the landing party had vanished. Astonishingly, all signs of life had disappeared from the enemy vessel. *What the hell?*

"Lieutenant, respond."

Nothing.

"Tactical, what's happening?"

Bewilderment replaced Hookes' normally composed features. "I'm not sure, captain. I'm detecting nothing from Picaroon's interior. I can't explain it."

"Luis?"

"Nothing," he said bitterly. "I have tried every channel, all overrides. I can't raise them."

Nathan examined his screen to assure himself that *Picaroon* had not self-destructed. Landing Boat one remained tethered to *Picaroon*. From the outside everything appeared normal.

Several silent, agonizing minutes passed before a scratchy attempted transmission came through. The D-O's face creased in frustration as he attempted to clean up the signal.

LB one disengaged from *Picaroon*.

"... one respond. I say again, Truculent, this is landing boat one." The distress in Scaroni's voice made her words difficult to read. "Am returning to the boat now. Require immediate medical assistance. I have wounded aboard."

"Bring her home, COB," the captain said, "we'll be ready for you."

"Roger that. LB one out."

CHAPTER 48

Orson fought to control his temper. He longed to slowly garrote every idiotic headhunter aboard. *Picaroon's* bridge crew grinned like panting dogs. Foss scowled at their behavior. At least *he* knew the score.

"Helm," Foss said, "ETA at the frontier?"

"Sixteen point two hours, captain."

"Captain," Weiss said, "permission to secure from Alert Condition one."

Foss bared his teeth. "Why in God's name would I do that?"

"We beat them," the XO said. "They won't follow us across the border, so we're clear. The crew has been at Alert Condition one for six hours and I think – "

"I don't give a fuck what you think." Foss' infuriated voice thundered against the bulkheads. "Comm Officer, pipe me throughout the ship. All departments, including crew quarters."

"Aye-aye, captain. Inter-ship channels open."

"This is the captain," Foss continued in the same uncompromising tone. "We *still* have an Athenian monitor on our stern and I for one do not take these Athenians for granted. They have an exceptional reputation. All platoon leaders prepare for boarding party action." He paused and sighed heavily. "All departments will remain at Alert Condition one until further notice. That is all."

"Captain," the xo said, "you don't seriously think they'll attempt another boarding after the pasting we gave them?"

"There is nothing more certain in the universe. They are Monitor Corps."

"In that case we'll capture or kill them," Weiss said. "Either way we'll get a good bounty from this mission."

Foss ignored him. Orson suspected that, like himself, Foss resisted the urge to agree. With what *Picaroon* had up her sleeve the Athenians were as good as dead.

CHAPTER 49

Commodore Waugh rested her hands on the briefing room table. She had lost people before but never like this. Sergeant Redpath sat to her immediate left. His dark, rigid façade could not disguise his monumental rage. Doc Kelso had treated Redpath's superficial wounds and Waugh spared him what recovery time she could. She had never seen the veteran marine so shaken.

"All right Rusty, let's have it."

"It was a standard boarding op. Any of the pricks who stuck their heads up, lost them." His eyes glazed over as he recounted the nightmare. "Resistance minimal. Our scans showed zero weapons emissions, no booby traps, nothing out of the norm. It was too easy. I should've known something was wrong.

"We got your comm. and began pulling back to the boat. Picaroon's internal power went down. The 'droids froze. Their power readings were in the green but they didn't respond to commands." Redpath drew his sidearm and tripped the selection stud to stun. Officers leapt aside when he raised the weapon and fired. The energy dissipated harmlessly against the far bulkhead. "On Picaroon this did *not* fire. A full charge in the mag but nothing happened when I pulled the trigger. Same with my rifle."

"Energy dampener?" Waugh suggested to her D-O.

"Sounds like it. We've been trying to develop one for years. How could a pack of savages get their hands on such advanced technology?"

"We'll leave explanations to the science division," Waugh said. "Go on Rusty."

"Lieutenant Jakovich and I fixed bayonets and began to withdraw. The hatch to section nineteen opened. There must've been twenty of them. It reminded me of one of those old Gothic horror vids. They were armed with swords. *Swords* for fuck's sake. They came at us in waves, screaming like wild animals. The landing boat was within sight but we couldn't break free of the surrounding pack. The LT took a blade to the chest but fought on. We were barely holding our own but we couldn't win against those odds. We were dead meat. Then the boat crew came out for us. The COB, Chief Lerner and ... young Mister Saunders. They punched a hole through the pack and held them off while we made a run for the boat. The LT had taken another hit to the arm and was bleeding out. I dragged her into the LB. The boat crew were bloody magnificent. They used their rifles as clubs and fought like warriors. They almost made it back to the hatch when Mister Saunders fell.

"They hacked into him like wild beasts." Rusty's haunted gaze dropped to the deck. "If we tried to rescue him we would have been overrun and lost the boat. We had no choice but to seal the hatch and withdraw."

Luis slid a tumbler of rum along the table to the marine. The double shot of courage disappeared in a single gulp.

A deathly silence enveloped the crowded room.

Waugh took in the room. The faces of *Truculent's* senior officers were set in uniformly grim, determined casts. "Does anyone feel like going home?"

Redpath's back straightened, a murderous glint lighting his eyes. Waugh saw the same spark burning from every eye in the room.

"Very well. We'll finish what we started. Now that we know what we're up against we'll make the bastards bleed." She rubbed her eyes. "It's time to review our available assets."

***

With Lt Hookes in the briefing room, Nathan occupied the Tactical Station. Ensign Allan Mattich had the helm, Lt Alderman took up the Operations Station and had the Conn. Everyone was vigilant to any change from *Picaroon*. Allan grimly concentrated on his readouts, his fingers never far from the firing studs. The sinister side of Nathan's mind hoped *Picaroon* would try something. Allan and Leo had been friends for three tours. In Allan's current mood he would likely obliterate the headhunter from existence if she twitched. That was fine with Nathan. *As for the civilians? Far better they die quickly now than to spend the rest of their lives as slaves.*

Leo's smiling face intruded into Nathan's thoughts. The image brought with it a terrible pain Nathan had not experienced in many, many years. He forced the tragic picture from his mind and worked the problem.

Nathan examined *Picaroon's* sensor logs while absently rubbing at the bump on his right eyebrow. The dampening field had been disengaged. Throughout the enemy ship pockets of sensor darkness confirmed various sections had been security sealed. A level one security field surrounded the engineering section as well as the bridge and forward weapons bays. Somehow the enemy found a way to generate the energy soaking field without affecting gravity and life support. Throughout the rest of the ship red icons indicated roving patrols.

Five key areas had been marked as possible sites for the missing civvies. What lay behind the double-ply battle armor and internal shielding was anyone's guess. Only a direct assault would provide the answers. The enemy's energy dampener field awaited them. If they could not solve *that* problem the boarding parties would be massacred. For Nathan the real impact came not from the discovery of a new form of technology, but in the reality that Lt Jakovich would probably die from her wounds, and Leo was dead. The image of Leo's young wife and tiny son pushed into Nathan's thoughts. With an angry shake of his head he pushed the picture aside.

Nathan rubbed his hands across his face, digging the heels of his thumbs into his eyes. *What's taking them so long?* The senior officers had been locked in the briefing room for hours. Talk, talk, talk. The headhunter would slip across the Rio Grande into the safety of Pruessen space in less than fourteen hours. They needed to return to *Picaroon* and kill every last headhunter. Nathan held his head in his hands, taking deep, steadying breaths until he brought his murderous rage under control. As his hands slid from his face the bridge hatch opened.

Moe stepped onto the bridge followed by Meta and Ozzie. They leaned against the tactical console. Moe stared at him reading his confirmation. She spoke for all of them in a low, morose voice.

"The rumor's true then. Leo ..."

Nathan nodded. The middies hung their heads.

"Don't you dare!" Nathan's savage tone caused his friends to recoil. "Don't you dare grieve for him. Not yet! Not till we trade blood for blood."

"I'd like nothing more than to get my hands on the bastards who did this," Meta said. "But you don't seriously think they'll take us on a boarding mission do you?"

"They better not try stopping me." His comm beeped and he keyed the larynx mike. "Telford."

"Have the middies arrived, Ensign Telford?" the D-O asked.

"Aye, sir."

"Show them in."

"Aye-aye, sir." He glared at his friends, knowing full well how they reacted when his fury surfaced. *Well bad luck. They'll have to get over it and grow up real fast.* "If anyone wants out of this, say so now."

His friends shook their heads. “Good. Let's see what the skipper wants.”

Nathan led them across the bridge to the briefing room hatch, stopping by the Operations Station. “Sir, permission to leave my post.”

Lt Alderman glanced over the rim of the console. “Permission granted.”

They stepped through the hatch into the briefing room. Nathan’s skin tingled in a most unfamiliar way.

CHAPTER 50

Once more unto the breach, dear friends, once more;
Or close up the wall with our English dead.
In peace there's nothing so becoming a man
As modest stillness and humility:
But when the blast of war blows in our ears,
Then imitate the action of a tiger.
William Shakespeare, *Henry V.*

Date: 16th August, 320.
Position: Monitor *Truculent*. One hundred & sixteen minutes from the Northern frontier.
Status: Alert Condition one.

Redpath huddled on the landing boat's deck surrounded by his team. He had selected the members of Alpha team for their physical strength and steely nerve. They were also the six most notorious brawlers aboard *Truculent*. They enjoyed a good scrap and Redpath would throw them into the fight of their lives.

The violent specialists who comprised Strike Team Alpha opted for the same primary weapon that hung from his shoulder strap. Axes were not standard issue aboard a monitor, as the new supply officer pointed out. Until a few hours ago this weapon did not exist.

Petty Officer Limpski's saving grace, and the reason the skipper kept him aboard, was his transformational genius in the maintenance workshop. Within hours of hearing Redpath's terse demand for a battle-ax in the tradition of barbarian warriors, Limpski had produced a dozen weapons tailored to the sergeant's specifications. The one-piece, case-hardened, battle-steel ax boasted double-edged blades and a swing radius close to a meter. Limpski gave no guarantees how it would fare against enemy body armor. However, he *did* guarantee that if a marine of Redpath's robust physique were to deliver a full-blooded impact, the kinetic energy alone should take his opponent down. Despite the marine's foul mood the lethal news incited a gruesome smile.

Augmenting their medieval arsenal, all combatants carried a sidearm or a shoulder-slung pulsar rifle. The sergeant looked forward to chopping into headhunters with case-hardened steel but did not want to be caught with an ax in his hands if the power was restored. They were inventing tactics for this kind of combat on the run. Only time would tell how well their planning worked.

Redpath examined the middies who clustered against the aft airlock hatch. The eager beavers, false bravado could not mask their fidgeting. However, the middy with the killer's eyes appeared genuinely unfazed by the forthcoming conflict.

Telford spat on the sharpening stone before running it along the sword's newly honed edges. He sighted along the blade. His lips compressed as he examined the keen edge.

Swords! Redpath could barely believe the captain agreed to send academy kids into combat armed with swords. In his twenty years in Marine Special Forces he could not recall a more bizarre situation.

All operational personnel wore the same kit: fighting suits under light, body armor and standard combat helmets. The only people not so equipped were the medics and the hares. Used as runners, the hares relied on their speed and agility for protection.

Telford and Okuma sported a quiver of arrows over their right shoulders. The marine had serious reservations about how effective the toy bows would be against armored troops. The captain insisted they could be of use. Redpath never argued with the captain.

He eyed Telford again, wondering if he would risk this wild card if things got dicey. As if Telford did not carry enough weapons, a bone-handled hunting knife hung from the webbing under his left shoulder and a bayonet under his right. The acting ensign glanced at him as if sensing the marine's eyes.

Although Telford nodded and forced a tight smile he could not hide his smoldering hostility. He had become noticeably livid when Redpath assigned Telford's team to Tactical Reserve. Telford did *not* want to watch from the sidelines. Yet if the speedily fashioned plan stood a chance of working, Redpath did not want untried amateurs getting under foot.

Next to Telford, Dearkov lovingly stroked the head of her ax. Redpath had been quietly astonished when she volunteered to keep an eye on the middies. She stayed close to Telford, saying little, but ready to act, even eager to please.

Cmdr Demianski caught Redpath's attention and held up one finger. "Listen up people, one minute to go," Redpath yelled. He struggled through the crowd and squeezed onto the flight deck.

Through the view-plate, *Picaroon* loomed large as *Truculent* closed the gap between them. Much larger than the pursuing monitor, she followed the basic design of most space-going warships. A long, broad, wedge-shaped vessel, four decks higher than the monitor and eight times her displacement.

Truculent fired two torpedoes. At a preprogrammed point on either side of *Picaroon's* sensor array, the torpedoes detonated. Instead of a massive wash of nuclear fire, a ripple of Weapons Counter Measures discharge washed over the headhunter. Until the enemy physically carried out repairs she would be as blind as a drunk in a closet.

"We have a go, sir," CPO Stokes said from the pilot's seat.

"Very well, chief," Demianski said, "proceed."

Redpath headed aft as the engines increased to full power. Seconds later, Stokes disengaged the magnetic skids and the landing boat broke away from *Truculent's* topside.

While Redpath checked the hatch controls he noticed Okuma lean in to Telford's ear.

"Well Stanley," she whispered, "here's another fine mess you've gotten us into."

Not for the first time Redpath considered that within the tight confines of a landing boat, secrets were as impossible to hide as a fart in a v-suit. Okuma was right on the money. They had all fallen into one shit-hole of a *fine mess.*

***

Nathan shrugged at Moe and forced a smile.

Tactical Reserve! What the hell does that mean? Somewhere to put the middies so they didn't get in the way? The teams were facing odds of at least three to one. They needed every trained body they could muster. *But nooooo, Redpath would rather go into combat with four fewer bodies than suffer the possibility the middies might actually prove to be useful. Frigging stubborn ground pounder.*

Nathan dismissed the thought of telling the jarhead what he thought of him. Probably inadvisable with a man like Redpath. The veteran marine was reputed to be able to kill a grown man with a buttercup. At least the mission was on track.

Nathan grabbed the overhead hand-hold and limbered up. Within the crowded LB he kept bumping into Dearkov's bulky frame. She had recently become his shadow and kept darting short, awkward smiles in his direction. What had come over her? With eye gestures he asked Moe what was going on. Moe shrugged and turned away.

"Twenty seconds," the commander said. "Truculent reports the dampening field is *currently* non-operational. Check your energy weapons."

The medieval weapons slid into improvised sheaths and pulsar rifles came to hand.

"Ten seconds."

"Tactical Reserve, go forward," Redpath ordered.

Nathan's jaw tightened as he led his team through the crush.

Redpath stood by the hatch, rifle in one hand, combination tumbler in the other. Chief Petty Officer Rocca covered the other side of the hatch. A slight bump indicated a successful docking maneuver. A dull metallic clunk confirmed the universal locking clamps had sealed the two vessels together. The boat hatch snapped open. The marine attached the tumbler to the locking mechanism of the headhunter hatch. Redpath's weapon settled into his shoulder as the locking combination cracked.

When the inner hatch snapped open the marines glanced cautiously into *Picaroon's* interior. They stared into the ship for about five seconds. Over Redpath's shoulder Nathan saw Rocca's face turn pink.

"Fuckers," Rocca whispered. A grimace covered his face as he averted his eyes.

Redpath's hard, unflinching eyes sighted along the barrel of his rifle. "Flankers out. Secure the area."

Four of Redpath's brutes poured through the hatch and in less than a minute gave the all-clear.

"Medics out." Redpath's voice became as hard as granite.

A knot twisted into the pit of Nathan's stomach. He followed the two medics and stopped at the hatch. Nathan peered into the headhunter ship. His stomach lurched.

Leo Saunders hung from the side of the corridor. His arms had been welded to the walls of the corridor in an X pattern crucifixion. What they had done to him was ...

"Cut him down," Redpath growled.

Nathan pushed back tears that threatened to blind him. He needed to do something. As if walking through a waking nightmare he stepped through the hatch. Redpath restrained him within a firm grasp. Nathan bared his teeth and wrenched his arm free with a savage twist.

Nathan stared into Leo's lifeless eyes. Blood ran down his cheeks. His eyelids had been sliced off.

Redpath grabbed his shoulder. "We all have our duty to perform, son. Are you capable of protecting the landing boat?"

He cleared his throat. "Yes."

Redpath nodded and turned to his team. "What are you killers waiting for. Let's go."

Alpha Team followed him into the ship.

The medics had to use laser torches to cut the body free.

As the bloody lump of butchered flesh fell, Nathan scooped it into his arms. *Redpath was wrong. Leo did not die during the ambush.* His naked body still retained slight warmth and rigor-mortis had not fully set in. *These fucking animals had hours to work on him. Leo had been alive when they crucified him.*

Battling against grief and rage Nathan carried Leo into the LB.

Nathan took special care not to bump Leo's head against the coaming. He placed his body gently onto the airlock deck. The lifeless eyes stared at him. *Where were you,* they cried. *Where were you while they tortured me to death?*

Nathan's body shuddered as he forced his fury under control. *Pull it together Telford, it's time to get bloody.*

CHAPTER 51

Date: 16th August, 320 ASC.
Position: Headhunter *Picaroon.* One hundred & five minutes from the northern frontier (Rio Grande).
Status: Awaiting implementation of Operation Ensnare, phase two.

Weiss smirked. "The enemy has cracked the port midships hatch," he said. "Four enemy boarders are scouting the corridors."

"Can you get an internal reading on the LB?"

"Negative, captain."

Foss' day of redemption had finally arrived. He felt light-headed at the probable outcome.

"The first boarding party has entered the ship."

"How many?"

Weiss sniggered. "Seven."

Foss knew the captain of this monitor. Not personally of course, but intel reports on Donatella Waugh had seeped from the south over the years. She was by far their best line officer. With the external scanners knocked out he could not be sure what she was up to.

"Hatch cracked, starboard bow. Another boarding party."

This successful operation would change his fortunes. Restoration of citizenship and perhaps more. Today he would show no mercy.

"The second boarding party is aboard. Another seven fools into the net."

Weiss was a coward and a fool. Earlier he had taken matters into his own hands with the atrocities he committed against the civilians.

"Enemy teams are moving toward deck five," Weiss said. "As expected."

Foss nodded slowly.

From the periphery of the bridge he sensed the officer's presence. Saxon said little, simply waiting for the captain's order to activate the energy dampener. Lt Saxon might wear an IRN uniform but Foss knew him for what he was. Foss did not care. To get off this ship and regain his life he would deal with the devil himself.

Saxon's ruthlessness had hidden behind a civilized façade for months. The bloody aftermath of Grunberg's interrogation brought about a dramatic change to that benign impression. Saxon's coldblooded murder of the two saboteurs was done with ease, confidence and pleasure. *Yes, perhaps not Satan, but a damn close relative.*

"Both enemy teams are on deck five," Weiss reported. "Should I activate our platoons, captain?"

"You'll do what I say and no more," Foss bellowed.

In another life he might feel sorry for the Athenians. In this life they were a means to escape his misery. Damn the rules of war. And damn the Athenians.

CHAPTER 52

Lt Cmdr Scobie O'Donnell led Beta Team to deck five without incident. *So far so good.* Scaroni took point, rifle in one hand sensor pad in the other. Lt Alderman covered her.

"Scobie," Demianski called, "we have small groups of hostiles on decks three and four, directly above your position. They're static for now but that could change so watch your six."

"Roger."

There was no easy way of accomplishing their mission. O'Donnell had memorized the schematic showing possible locations of the civvies. *Truculent's* sensor sweeps indicated that deck five housed the ship's cargo holds. They contained replacement parts, food stocks, general supplies and an indeterminate number of sensor traces. In a best-guess scenario the cargo holds presented the most promising starting point. His team moved cautiously aft sensor-scanning each compartment, wary that death could lurk behind any hatch. The lack of headhunter activity increased his edginess. He had expected an attack when the internal hatch slid open. As with any soldier he feared the waiting far more than the actual combat.

Scaroni slowed her pace and examined her sensor pad. She pointed to the next hatch on the port side. The internal hatches on a ship of this vintage were old style, round-handle type. She un-dogged the hatch and took a cautionary peek inside. Scaroni nodded to O'Donnell and stepped through the hatch. The COB examined one of the eight men who lay sprawled on the hard deck. They were all neatly dressed and did not stink of headhunter sweat. Their glazed eyes expressed the Francs' intense agony. They hissed and groaned when Scaroni touched their wounds. The COB stared bleakly at O'Donnell.

"The bastards broke their ankles," Scaroni said.

O'Donnell nodded, his feelings pensive. The deliberately brutal nature of the Francs' injuries contained a degree of atypical headhunter ingenuity. His team was supposed to find these damaged men. If his small squad was attacked they would be burdened with eight civilians incapable of independent mobility. Their one true advantage, speed, had been shattered as cleanly as the sixteen purposeful fractures.

While the medic worked on the Franc civvies, O'Donnell reported to Demianski.

"Unusually clever for brutes." The commander's tone held none of its usual dryness. "Did you copy that, Rusty?"

"Yes sir. We're double-timing it to his position."

O'Donnell sensed a nervous stirring in his gut. Headhunters might be little more than savages but they possessed animal cunning. Hauling these shattered men back to the boat would take time they might not have.

***

"Hold on Sarge."

Redpath nearly plowed into Petty Officer Tokunaga.

Her eyes remained fixed to his sensor pad. "I have warm bodies, two hatches down, port side."

"Shit!" As much as he needed to reach O'Donnell's team he could not leave his flanks exposed. He raised his rifle and stepped to the hatch. Down on one knee he un-dogged the hatch and pulled it open. He risked a quick glance into the dimly lit room. Redpath took in the sight, fell back against the bulkhead and sighed. They had found the Franc women.

When the women saw him standing in the hatch they began to cry, some whimpering pathetically. This was not the first time he had witnessed such an outrage. Redpath detailed two female teammates to care for the distraught women. Sensor scans indicated that the women ranged in age, with the oldest in her early sixties down to a girl in her mid teens. Redpath's lips compressed as the pitiable weeping resounded from the room.

CPO Sal Rocca shook his head, disgust written across his face. "I can't wait to catch up with the fucking heroes who did this, Sarge."

Minutes later the pitiful sobbing gradually diminished. His people patiently explained that danger still threatened. With gentle insistence, they got the women to their feet and moving. They emerged in twos, clinging to one another, bruised bodies, torn, bloody clothing held together with trembling hands.

One of the women stumbled and Rocca reached out a supporting hand. The woman cried out and cringed away from him. Rocca held his hands in supplication and backed off.

Into Redpath's ear Rocca whispered, "I thought we were the good guys."

Redpath suppressed the rage threatening to overcome his professional detachment. "I doubt if any of these women will look at a man and see a good guy for a very long time."

Something does not add up. Headhunters were beasts in human form but they were also businessmen. The bottom line always dictated their actions. This sort of obscenity went contrary to their basic imperative. In the Pruessen tradition since the end of the war, their ships carried no female crews. So yes, they might have a taste of the product, but brutalizing their merchandise to this extent was extremely uncommon. This had not been the usual selective reward for the officers. It was a deliberate, systematic process designed to break the women physically and spiritually.

Redpath reported his situation to the commander.

"The way is open to evacuate the civilians directly to the LB one," Demianski said. "The troops above you are making no moves to collate or intercept either of your teams. I don't like the smell of this, Rusty."

"Me neither, sir."

"I'm sending the Reserves to assist you. No arguments Rusty. Like it or not you need them. I will – "

The comm snapped off. In the same instant every light went out.

CHAPTER 53

The landing boat's sensor suite was a toy compared to *Truculent's* power and sophistication. However, the LB had the advantage of proximity. It had taken the techs fourteen hours of meticulous tinkering to modify the LB's sensors to cut through the interference. The readings were scratchy and distorted but gave a fair indication of the unfolding situation.

From his position beside the sensor suite Nathan heard what Cmdr Demianski told Redpath. He made it halfway to the hatch.

"Hold on, Telford," the commander yelled. "Look at this before you go off half-cocked."

Nathan's forehead creased when he stared at the readouts. Headhunter reinforcements flooded from the shielded forward weapons bays. A macabre ballet played out on the sensor screen. The little red dots formed into much larger red dots, those dots bonded with others. They would attack O'Donnell's small force as soon as they formed into a single body. At least fifty headhunters against seven Athenians burdened with wounded civvies.

"Archibald," Demianski snapped. The young rating ran to the commander's station and listened attentively. "Report to Sergeant Redpath on deck five, corridor two and inform him there are fifty-plus hostiles about to attack O'Donnell's position. Got it?"

Archie repeated the message.

"Good lass, now run like the wind, run."

Archie leaped from the boat with the agility of a startled deer.

"What are your orders, sir?" Nathan asked.

"Prepare to repel boarders," Demianski said, while he tracked Archie's running green icon.

"Look sharp," Nathan said, as he stepped through the hatch. For no apparent reason his conversation with Cmdr Zoehrer sprang to mind. "No moral ambiguity today," he whispered.

Moe nocked an arrow while Meta and Ozzie drew their swords. Dearkov caressed her ax. Nathan returned to the command station.

From the shielded engine room a second group of enemies emerged. Another fifty combatants had hidden behind internal shielding, awaiting the attack signal. With fifty charging from the bow and this huge group from the stern, *Truculent's* Strike Teams were about to be cut off and overrun.

One hundred armed combatants represented more personnel

than a Badger class vessel normally carried. The second group divided. Thirty took the stairwell to deck three. A smaller group of twenty continued toward the midships-lateral corridor.

Nathan strode aft. A grin would have split his face but rage held it in check. *Stay angry. Stay angry.*

"Ladies and gentlemen, we're about to entertain guests. Helmets on." His helmet would get in the way of his shooting so it remained attached to his webbing. Moe assumed the position beside him.

"They're pretty damn brave against unarmed civilians," Nathan bellowed. "But we are not unarmed and we are not civilians."

"Aye-aye sir," they roared.

Nathan sensed their trepidation so began the old mantra.

"Headhunters," Nathan called. "What are they?"

"Animals in human form," the team replied.

Nathan heard the enemy well before he saw them. A raucous, shrieking cacophony that grew in intensity as the horde charged along the midships corridor.

He leaned into Moe's ear. "Nervous?"

Moe poked her tongue out. She knew what to do, where to fire. They had ten arrows each. Unlike their barbed hunting arrows, the target arrows had only a snub nose of composite material. A fragile wooden shaft against headhunter body armor.

"Headhunters. What are they?"

"Scum under our boots."

Nathan glanced over his shoulder at the commander and nodded once. If the enemy overpowered Nathan's small group of defenders the commander would have no alternative but to disengage the boat.

"Headhunters. What are they?"

"Child molesting motherless dogs."

The deck under Nathan's feet trembled as the enemy force rounded the far corner into the lateral corridor. Although fifty meters away, the headhunters looked huge. Their dark brown body armor did not show the individual tailoring of the Corps issue. Dark patches marked lovely big gaps at the joints of the headhunter's armor. Including at their torsos and necks. Nathan glanced at Moe. They both grinned.

"What do we do with animals?"

"Kill them quick and move onto the next."

"On my signal, cut them up."

"Aye-aye, sir."

Stay angry. This one's for you, Leo.

Nathan waited, waited. On a silent cue he and Moe fired at almost the same instant.

CHAPTER 54

Leorna 'Archie' Archibald slid down the ladder to the ship's lowest level, rolling as she hit the deck. Up and away in the same movement she ran as if her life depended on it. Which, in fact, it did. Archie did not see them but heard the terrifying roar of the enemy's second wave charging from astern. Unlike her, cumbersome body armor and heavy weapons weighed them down. *I am the swift gazelle and they the plodding rhinos. Mind you, if the rhinos catch the gazelle ...*

Her heart raced so fast she thought it would burst. What bayed at her heels drove her on. Ahead she made out the flankers from Alpha Team. Their weapons drawn and ready to cut her down. She waved her hands frantically – her headlong charge had taken her voice. When she reached the team she fell into their arms.

"What kept you, junior?" said one of the brutes.

She staggered past them and fell to her knees before Redpath. She wanted to make her report but only heaving gasps escaped her dry lips. Redpath patted her on the back.

"There you go lass, take it easy now."

"Headhunters," she managed to wheeze.

"Yes lass, where?"

She swallowed hard, held up five fingers, pointed forward and hit her palm quickly.

"Fifty-plus coming from the bow, fast," Redpath interpreted.

"Many ... from the stern. Don't ... know how many. Lots." News that they were surrounded and cut off from all assistance should have produced a grim response from the marine sergeant. Instead a canny grin crept onto his face. Archie decided right then she would never understand marines.

"Did they see you, Archie?"

"No ... too quick ... for them." *Redpath knows my name?*

"All right lass, they'll be coming for us now," Redpath said. "They don't know you're down here so hotfoot it to corridor three and hide. When you can, make your way back to the boat. Tell the commander the entire enemy force is at our position. Have you got that Archie? The *entire* enemy force."

Archie nodded and Redpath turned her sweating body around and pushed her down the side corridor. While she staggered away from the doomed team Redpath's voice grew to a bellowing crescendo.

"We will move forward and link up with Beta Team." A slight pause. "Now damn you! Run!"

CHAPTER 55

Nathan stood shoulder to shoulder with Dearkov, careful to avoid being hacked to pieces by her swinging ax. He parried the Headhunter's blade and struck into the opening beneath his chin. Dearkov's ax smashed another brown clad enemy with a horrendously violent blow to the helmet.

Meta and Ozzie covered the gaps from behind. A huge headhunter charged. Moe shot him in the stomach with her last arrow. The six remaining combatants gave ground. Through their visors terrified eyes said they wanted nothing to do with the crazed Monitor Corps demons. For the first time in the remarkably brief battle the odds were almost even.

When arrows started cutting them down the headhunter troops had been first surprised then shocked into inaction. Their broadswords were uncivilized weapons wielded clumsily by a barbarous species. They were no match for skilled exponents of the blade.

"You outnumbered us four to one and *this* is the best you can do?" Nathan roared.

The enemy's nerves broke, they ran for their lives. Apparently Dearkov disliked running. She pulled Nathan aside, hoisted her ax over her head, swung it three times and hurled it spinning toward the fleeing soldiers. The heavy ax smashed two headhunters across the back of their helmets. Their limp bodies dropped to the deck.

Nathan leapt over their inert bodies and sprinted after the remaining Pruessens.

The last four headhunters were fifty meters from the entrance to engineering. Safety was almost within their reach when Nathan caught up to the straggler. He struck under the straggler's armor. The blade smashed past ribs to rip into the lung. When the enemy fell Nathan twisted his sword free from the body. Nathan swung his blade, catching the next enemy behind the knees. The headhunter screamed as he collapsed to the deck. Nathan ran on.

The last two glanced back at the blood-soaked devil who closed on them. Headhunters were opportunistic raiders used to attacking defenseless civilians. The sight of what pursued them caused them to whimper. They were ten meters from the engineering hatch when Nathan drew level with them. He swung his sword at the enemy's head. The headhunter dropped to the deck, avoiding the blow. The sword continued, slicing the throat of the other one. He fell in a bloody heap.

Nathan skidded to a halt and rounded on the one he had missed.

The terrified scum had fallen to his knees his helmet thrown aside, hands raised.

"I surrender! I surrender! You're Monitor Corps. You've gotta accept my surrender." His eyes were huge, his bearded face covered with filth and sweat.

Nathan wrinkled his nose. All headhunters stank but this one had compounded his misery by soiling his armor. Nathan wanted to drive his sword through the wretch's eye. He hung onto a tiny wisp of humanity that hovered at the edge of his bloodlust madness.

"Name."

"Huh?"

"What is your name?"

"Err, Himmel."

Nathan knelt beside him.

"Himmel, I am going to ask you some questions."

The interrogation proved him to be a dense thug, a blunt instrument too stupid to know anything except how to butcher civilians. Nathan leaned in close to him. "If I find you have lied to me ..."

Himmel cringed.

A wave of nausea crashed over Nathan as he stood. Coming down from a massive adrenaline high had sapped his energy. He remembered the headhunter he had taken at the back of the knees.

When he turned around three middies and a blood-soaked petty officer stood in a loose group staring at him. What did he see in their eyes? Respect? Uncertainty? Shock? Fear? Did his friends fear him? He wanted to scream at them: *They're only Pruessens for Christ's sake.*

"Will someone get that for me, please?" he said, hooking a thumb over his shoulder at the cowering headhunter.

Nathan pushed past them and found the headless body of the last headhunter. Dearkov had not been in the mood to show mercy. He dragged his aching body back to the boat.

CHAPTER 56

Archie's heart beat so fast she thought the headhunters would hear it. She had barely slipped up the access ladder when a group of enemy troops passed below. If one of them had glanced up the access tube ... When they were gone Archie continued on, her soft-soled footwear silent on the hard deck plates.

Alert for the tiniest sound, Archie silently jogged to corridor one on deck four. The clatter of tramping boots caused her skin to prickle. Archie spun the dog on the nearest hatch and ducked inside. When the stampeding boots faded, her heart started to beat again. She examined the large, dimly lit room and noted a long control panel positioned before a clear, rectangular view-plate. Totally by mistake she had wandered into the Cargo Control Center. Cautiously, she edged to the view-plate. Below, a scene of frenzied activity greeted her.

Against the starboard bulkhead a five-meter wide loading hatch was the single entry point into the hold. The hatch's smashed locking mechanism hung from the wall. Sergeant Redpath shouted at the fourteen members of Alpha and Beta Teams, officers and enlisted alike. Archie quickly recognized what they were doing. With applied brute strength they were building an artificial corridor out of the available containers.

At the end of the hastily contrived passage they had cobbled together a shoulder-high barricade by stacking the smaller containers together. The headhunters would have to run the gauntlet of the three-meter wide corridor and scale the barricade to get to the good guys. The teams faced odds of more than six to one. By the weight of sheer numbers the enemy would overcome mere courage.

Behind the barricade the eighteen rescued civvies huddled in the far corner.

She repositioned to get a better view and a marine spotted her. Redpath glanced up winked and jerked his head aft. Archie got the message and stepped to the hatch. From somewhere in her memory, a school history class perhaps, the word Alamo came to mind.

CHAPTER 57

In the ten minutes since the battle ended, Nathan's bloodlust had cooled. His exhaustion faded to a numbing lethargy. However the ache in his chest had little to do with the sword blow to his breastplate.

The last time he had killed he employed surgically precise shots fired to stop creatures who were threatening his family. There had been distance to those engagements. This time he had been close enough to smell the enemy's last breaths, feel the shuddering of their bodies as life deserted them. Close enough for their blood to splash across his armor.

Combat had a numbing effect but as the adrenaline bled away pain flooded in. Still, there was nothing to prevent him fighting on.

"Movement," Ozzie said from his sentry post at the open hatch. Nathan leapt to his feet. "Ha!" Ozzie laughed. "It's a female of the genus Lepus."

At the end of the corridor, Archie froze at the sight of the battle's gory aftermath. Her face turned white as she cautiously sidestepped the bloody corpses. Nathan caught her as she staggered through the hatch and cradled her head in his lap as she fell. Archie snatched the offered canteen with both hands, gulping down half its contents. Cmdr Demianski hovered, waiting with inhuman patience.

"Commander," Archie gasped, "both teams ... trapped ... deck five." She took another sip of water and leaned against Nathan's aching chest. "Sergeant Redpath ... says he is ... surrounded by ... entire ... headhunter force. He emphasized ... the *entire* force, sir."

The commander's mouth stretched thin as he slowly nodded his head. He keyed his larynx mike. "Truculent, we have a go for Gamma Team. I say again, we have a go for Gamma Team."

CHAPTER 58

Cmdr Barbara Grimmett spoke firmly. “This is a simple enough plan, but theory doesn’t always follow planning. So we do this by the numbers, people. If we fuck this up many of our shipmates will pay the price.”

The four team members nodded thoughtfully.

Her comm beeped. “Grimmett.”

“You have a go, commander,” Waugh said. “Good hunting, Babs.”

“Roger that, skipper. LB three out.” Grimmett stepped onto the landing boat flight deck and tapped Chief Miller on the shoulder. The boat shuddered when the throttles pushed into the red zone. A minute later, after matching speed, it leapt from *Truculent's* topside.

Landing Boat three docked with *Picaroon* three minutes later. The boat hatch opened and Grimmett attached the tumbler to the headhunter's external hatch. While it worked on the combination she secured flat sensor suppressors to each corner of the external hatch. Without the suppressors set exactly in place her team would show on the enemy’s scans as soon as the hatch opened.

The tumbler clicked into place and the hatch opened. They made their way hastily to deck one without incident and minutes later approached the bridge from the stern. With a blinding flash, lighting came to life as the power was restored. They would now show up on the internal sensors.

“Go, go, go,” Grimmett yelled. Slinging swords and grasping energy weapons the team fell against the bridge hatch.

“Babs, you're going to have a whole lot of company in about three minutes,” Demianski reported.

“Terrific.”

Grimmett attached the tumbler to the bridge hatch. While the last combination engaged, the five combatants steeled themselves to charge into the teeth of fire. With a final click the bridge hatch slid aside.

Gamma team stared with disbelief at the slab before them. Brilliant in its simplicity, the solid section of toughened battle steel stood as an impenetrable barrier between the team and their objective. No outside locking devices were visible.

“Harry, the shaped charge or the cutting torch?”

Matrakas went to work on the barrier with his cutting torch. His doubtful expression did not fill Babs with confidence. For a full minute he applied the torch to the unyielding hatch cover.

A sound reached her ears, stampeding feet on the deck plates, the shrieking cacophony of a headhunter charge.

"One minute, Babs, and you'll be shit-deep in enemy troops," Demianski warned. "Report your status."

"Main hatch open," Grimmett said. "There is a secondary hatch of toughened battle armor held in place by a manual locking system. I will use the shaped charge to try and gain access."

"Hold on that. Harry, will the charge work?"

Matrakas' mouth tightened. "Against battle armor it won't make a dent."

"That's it then."

"Hold on," Grimmett snapped. "We can still – "

"Commander," Demianski said, "you will withdraw your team immediately. Confirm your orders."

With ashes in her mouth Grimmett said, "Aye-aye, sir."

"Get the hell out of there. Hostiles are approaching your position from forward and astern."

"Moving now."

***

When the lights came on Redpath grabbed his rifle.

"Everyone behind the barricade."

A high-pitched squeal began to echo through the hold. A narrow shower of sparks sprinkled from the main hatch.

"Commander, do you read me?"

"Yes Rusty. Bring me up to date with your situation."

"We are in the main port-side cargo hold. The enemy is using cutting tools to get to us. I estimate no more than ten minutes until they get through. How is Auntie doing?"

The commander's update on Grimmett's failure painted a gloomy picture. "Can you hold out, Rusty?"

"Guess we'll have to," Redpath said.

A long pause followed. "You have eighty-plus on the other side of the hatch." Again the silence.

"We'll make sure to take some of them with us."

"Very well. Demianski out."

***

Cmdr Grimmett fired her rifle, bringing down another enemy combatant. Gamma team fell under attack twenty meters from their LB. A desperate running gun battle ensued as the Athenians backed toward the boat. Blazing silver pulsar fire ricocheted off the bulkheads from more than twenty enemy soldiers. The gammas killed five of their attackers and wounded an unknown number. Just shy of the LB Iris Ahrens was hit in the chest. Grimmett dragged her into the protection of the boat.

"Chief, stand by to disengage on my mark," Grimmett yelled.

"Standing by."

Grimmett removed the shaped charge from her satchel and primed it.

"Fall back to the boat now," she yelled.

Firing automatic rifle bursts, the team cleared the corridor of all resistance before diving into the boat. Grimmett pulled the pin on the improvised explosive device, threw it into the corridor and secured the hatch.

"Now, chief," she yelled.

To the accompaniment of severe grinding the LB disengaged from *Picaroon*. Grimmett counted the seconds. She had no idea if the makeshift bomb would work.

Through the forward view-plate she saw a brief burst of orange flames as *Picaroon's* hatch disintegrated. The escaping air turned into fine mist as it bled from the vessel. Most pleasing to the eye were the four mangled bodies expelled into space.

While the medic worked on Iris, Grimmett reported to Demianski.

"Commander, we have egressed Picaroon and are in transit to Truculent."

"Very well."

"So, what do we do now?"

"I suppose we'll have to come up with another plan."

***

From the outset the operation had been plagued by bad luck. Without the ingenious secondary hatch to frustrate their efforts, Gamma Team would have had the bridge crew for breakfast. Redpath reflected that bad luck could undo the best-laid plans.

The COB stood by Redpath's side watching the line of sparks make its final slow cut. The cutting torch spilled the embers onto the deck of the purpose-made corridor CPO Rocca had named Redpath's Run.

"Well Emmett," Scaroni said, "it's been quite a life we've had."

"Wouldn't have had it any other way, Corrina."

In silence he stared at the hatch for some time while contemplating their short futures.

"This is the only way for soldiers to retire," Scaroni said

"Definitely!"

She stepped close and whispered. "I'll take care of the civvies, if you like?"

He snorted without humor. "I'll deal with my responsibilities."

"Fair enough."

The line of sparks stopped when they reached the hatch's lower coaming. Minutes passed before the lights went out. Once again the overheads cast a dull green hue across the hold. *Now we're for it.*

"Switch," Redpath yelled.

The fourteen determined men and women prepared for the final assault.

A great slab of hatch crashed onto the deck. Redpath braced for the sound of the screaming, frenzied attack. Instead, a tall, lean man stepped through the opening and onto Redpath's Run. The cheeky sod marched down the corridor smiling as he examined the makeshift construction. Rank after rank of armored troops followed him. All were armed with broadswords. The newcomer stopped five meters from the barricade while his troops crowded in behind him. He removed his helmet, revealing a long, pock-marked face lacking the usual headhunter beard. His hands went to his hips.

"Who speaks for this detachment?" he demanded.

***

"I suppose we'll have to come up with another plan," Cmdr Demianski said, ending the transmission.

Nathan noted the dull hue of defeat in the commander's eyes.

Demianski glanced at Nathan, did a double take then sighed.

"Very well, Telford, if you've got something to say, get it off your chest."

As succinctly as he could, Nathan patiently explained the bones of his strategy. The commander procrastinated.

"You've seen what we can do to an organized enemy in a confined space," Nathan said.

Cmdr Demianski set a hostile eye on the acting ensign. "I saw everything you did, Telford. *Everything.*" He rubbed his chin. "If they drop the dampening field, they'll detect your team's weapons emissions. Even if your sensor suppressors mask your bio signatures you will show up on their internal sensors. When that happens – "

Nathan slammed his sidearm onto the console. Four more sidearms joined his.

"If this plan doesn't work a few sidearms won't make a shit's bit of difference, will they?" Nathan expelled a noisy breath between pursed lips. "Commander, I apologize for my ... abruptness. I appreciate that the responsibility for this operation falls squarely on your shoulders. But we can't just sit here while our shipmates are butchered. To do nothing is unconscionable, sir."

The commander shook his head.

"I don't like the idea of sending grommits into the teeth of battle." He shook his head again. "But I'll agree to this as long as you stick to the plan. Do you read me, ensign?"

"Aye, sir."

Nathan took the young rating aside. "Archie," he said, "we can find the control room without you but it might take precious minutes Redpath's teams can ill-afford." He placed his hand on her shoulder. "You won't be expected to fight, but I need you with us."

"Of course, sir," Archie said.

They shed their leg armor, retaining their breast plates, arm guards, shoulder guards and helmets.

Nathan led the team stealthily down to deck four with Archie giving occasional directions. As they proceeded to the cargo bay Nathan's back flared.

"Into the access tubes," he ordered. Instantly and without question everyone scrambled into the nearest tube. The team members exchanged mystified expressions. Shortly after they found refuge, hanging onto the ladder rungs, the sound of marching boots passed by their position. Everyone froze, daring to neither breathe nor blink. Gradually the rumble of boots faded, before disappearing.

With most of the headhunters gathered below on deck five their entry into the cargo control room went undetected.

They gathered around the clear screen and observed the unfolding situation. From the cargo hold below the high-pitched squeal of a cutting torch assaulted their ears. Sparks danced across the deck as the glowing line moved inexorably to the coaming.

Dearkov used a cutting torch to remove a section of the view-plate. The sound produced by her efforts was muffled by the enemy's shrieking effort to get into the hold. She completed the final cut just as the headhunters cutting torch fell silent.

Nathan stopped all movement with a raised hand then held his finger to his lips. For several seconds he listened carefully. No shouted alert came from below. It took the efforts of the entire team to pry the section of view-plate clear of its housing and rest it silently onto the deck. As Nathan stepped through the opening the lights went out. Below, a section of hatch crashed onto the deck.

The opening act of a new drama began to unfold on the deck below. However, the behavior of the headhunters did not follow their usual ferocious pattern. A solid wall of enemy troops filed into the hold without uttering a sound. One of them removed his helmet and stepped forward.

"Who speaks for this detachment?" he asked.

"What's it to you, dickhead?" CPO Rocca yelled, followed by jeering from the rest of Redpath's thugs.

"If you want to live you will show the respect due to my rank," the headhunter yelled.

Redpath raised his hand to silence the rabble. "Sergeant E J Redpath, Monitor Corps."

"I am Captain Foss, master of this vessel."

Redpath shifted his ax so that it rested across his right shoulder. "What can I do for you, captain?"

"You can save your life and that of your companions, Sergeant Redpath, by surrendering immediately. I give you my word you will be well treated."

Redpath sneered. "Like the way you *well treated* the civilians?"

"An oversight by a subordinate," Foss said. "Brave sailors such as yourselves deserve better. Spare us this unpleasantness and surrender now."

While the remarkably civil discourse continued, Nathan motioned to Koops, the medic. She carried two satchels; one contained medical supplies, the other their hastily engineered incendiaries.

Petty Officer Koops gingerly handed Nathan the first of the lethal cocktails. He tossed the green bottle to Dearkov who caught it in one large hand.

On the deck below the conversation neared its inevitable conclusion.

"And if I don't surrender, you'll kill us all?" Sergeant Redpath said.

"This doesn't have to end with your deaths, if you are willing to see reason. Is it not better to live rather than die?"

The venomous smile returned to Redpath's face. "Yes, and it

wouldn't hurt your profit margin either, would it? Twenty-three civilians and fourteen captured Monitor Corps personnel would be quite the coup for you. I dare say we'd fetch a handsome price on the auction block at Kulak."

Nathan nodded to Moe and together they stepped through the opening, dropping noiselessly onto the container stack. Dearkov and Archie remained where they were as the academy's finest silently edged along the containers.

"Look around you, sergeant," Foss said. "You are vastly outnumbered and even Athenians cannot win against such odds. Be reasonable. Surrender or die. What do you say?"

"Blow it out your crack," Rocca yelled.

"Go fuck the ship's cat you pantywaist," Tokunaga added, leading a flood of foul-mouthed abuse.

Instead of becoming furious, in typical headhunter style, the captain's face assumed a pathetically weary expression. "Very well, you choose death."

Foss had been good enough to remove his helmet for the exchange. *How obliging.* Nathan's first arrow followed a logical path through his right ear. The wooden shaft struck at an acute angle, partly exiting at the left extremity of the throat.

Everyone froze for a timeless moment, stunned into silence. Seconds later, Foss' eyes rolled into his head and his body collapsed to the deck. At almost the same instant another enemy fell with an arrow in his throat, courtesy of Moe.

The headhunters began to panic, staring in all directions for the source of the death raining down on them. Nathan fired again and while he strung another arrow nodded once to Dearkov.

Archie lit the fuse. Dearkov threw the first Molotov cocktail. The bottle sailed in a high arc toward the torn hatch before shattering just above the opening. Its ignition cast a layer of vile-smelling, sticky burning goo across the exit. The incendiary splashed onto six headhunters who were leaning against the adjacent wall. High-pitched screams echoed from the bulkheads as the blazing headhunters staggered around the exit. The awful noise continued until the flames burned through the weak points in their body armor roasting exposed skin, boiling blood, filling helmets with noxious fumes.

While the archers continued to unleash arrows into promising targets, Dearkov lobbed two more incendiaries onto the same spot, catching a small group of headhunters who were trying to escape.

Nathan caught Redpath gazing up at the middies. The marine grinned like the devil himself. "Let's have at them," he roared and he led his teams from behind the barricade.

The larger headhunter force had deteriorated into a panicking mob.

Dearkov followed the third cocktail and leapt onto the container stack.

Nathan had only two arrows left in his quiver. He ran toward the flaming door. Two more enemy fell to his arrows as they tried to escape.

Within a half minute of Captain Foss' grisly death, four middies and one petty officer stood atop the containers swinging their weapons down onto the rabble. Dearkov's ax cut a bloody swathe through any headhunter foolish enough to come within range. The middies were not faring as well, making impacts only on the helmets.

Nathan was possessed by a demon who denied him his rightful kill. Despite his rage the enemy troops remained stubbornly out of reach of his bloodless blade.

Time and again he struck down at the enemy forces only to have his sword blocked by helmets and armor. The angle was wrong and although he shifted position several times he was still unable to deliver a killing blow. A bold headhunter swung his broadsword, narrowly missing his ankles.

"Fuckers," he yelled.

Nathan slipped his helmet on and stepped to the edge of the container stack closest to the flaming hatch. He surveyed the chaos on the deck below. A small gap had opened between the wall of flames and the frenzied headhunters. Moe yelled to him but he heard only gibberish over the din. He paused for an instant then jumped into the fray.

His feet hit the deck, slipped in fresh blood and he crashed onto his back. Using his momentum he rolled away. A broadsword struck where he had landed. Still on his back, he parried multiple blows and caught one of his attackers in the stomach. Their unyielding attack prevented him from regaining his footing. The heat from the flames burned against the back of his neck. If he gave ground he would burn. If he didn't they would hack him to pieces.

"Stay down," Dearkov yelled. She leapt from the containers.

Her considerable bulk crashed into the three attackers with a crushing force, driving them into the fiery hell. The headhunters staggered blindly through the opening, their armor ablaze. Dearkov swung her ax in wide arcs, keeping the enemy at bay until Nathan regained his footing. Side by side they pressed into the pack.

Nathan's training automatically kicked in. Duck, parry, strike. Duck, parry, strike. Find the openings, legs, abdomen, armpit, throat. Dearkov did not exercise Nathan’s selective method. Chop, club, smash became her mantra. Together they held the line while the middies dropped into position behind them. They gave Dearkov's swinging ax a wide berth, plugging gaps as required.

With Redpath's team on one side and the reserves on the other the headhunters were squeezed into a tight pack. Most of them could not swing their weapons. Line by line fell before the closing ranks of Monitor Corps sailors. On both sides of the shrinking line the odd enemy soldier tried to surrender. Within the blazing teeth of combat, bloodlust overrode any sense of compromise.

The carnage continued, the savage bloody clash of human against human. The screaming of combatants mixing with the shrill cries of the wounded and dying. The sharp clang of sword on sword, sword on armor and the metallic crunch of axes crushing the enemy. Nathan stepped on and over bodies as his team pressed relentlessly forward.

Dearkov took a mighty swing at an enemy soldier, cleaving the helmeted head from the neck. A gush of blood erupted from the neck’s ghastly stump, splashing a coating of thick red goo across Nathan’s visor. Partly blinded, he fought on. He desperately tried to clear the sticky muck from his visor while fending off attackers. A broadsword came at him through a blind spot. He groaned when the impact hit his breastplate. Another struck the sword from his hand. A third thundered into his helmet with stunning force. Meta lunged forward, dragged him from the fight before slicing the throat of the nearest enemy soldier.

Nathan frantically wiped his visor but his meshed gloves only smeared the viscous fluid. His frustration grew. He desperately needed to rejoin the fight. He tore off the helmet and threw it aside. On his knees he groped the deck for a weapon, but found only bodies and the useless headhunter swords.

Meta cut down another two enemy crewmen. She parried brilliantly, holding off three of the brutes. Another enemy fell but the sheer weight of numbers became too much for her. Meta screamed as a broadsword got past her guard and smashed into her shoulder armor. Her sword dropped from her hand. Unarmed, Meta backed away, her useless left arm dangling by her side. Nathan dragged her as far from the fighting as possible. For a moment their eyes met and what he saw in her eyes said everything. They were losing this battle. With two of the team disabled and despite their best efforts his team yielded ground.

No, it can't end like this. Not like this.

Nathan beat his hands against the deck and screamed. He had to get his hands on a decent weapon and rejoin the fight.

Then something happened.

An odd sensation, as if another part of himself hidden just under his conscious surface clicked into place. Like a balloon had popped inside his head. His frustration vanished like the lifting of heavy gravity. Everything became ridiculously clear. Every action absurdly predictable. In a moment of exquisite clarity he acted without conscious control.

Nathan drew the bayonet from his webbing with his left hand and grasped his hunting knife with his right. All the enemy crewmen were tall, broad creatures. He knew he could use their size against them. He charged into the chaotic fight with a clear mind and a single purpose. Keeping low he parried with the bayonet and thrust upward with the hunting knife. He struck at the exposed areas around the throat, under the armor into the stomach and anywhere an opening presented itself. He no longer required a killing blow and concentrated on taking enemy combatants out of the fight. A blade drew a fine red line across his exposed forehead. He ignored it as he cut down another enemy.

His return to the fight bolstered the team but they were nearing physical and mental exhaustion. They continued to lose ground. The flood of panicked enemy pressed his small team toward the flames. Bodies fell, blood spurting from ghastly wounds splattering the deck and containers with obscene dark crimson. He had lost count of how many they had killed. Twenty? Thirty? And still they came. The team formed into line, risking decapitation from Dearkov's wildly swinging ax.

From behind a loud whooshing assaulted his ears. It was the unmistakable sound of a powder fire-retardant appliance extinguishing the flames. The heat on the back of his neck died. He hoped Meta, although wounded, could somehow cover their backs. They were totally committed to full defensive fighting mode. The temptation to glance over his shoulder was compelling but he could not afford to take his eyes from the forward enemy line for a second.

As the flames spluttered and died the headhunters saw a way out. They pressed forward with a power born of desperation and revived hope. They could see the light and only had to overrun his team to gain their freedom. It renewed the enemy and Nathan's team fell back under their last desperate attack.

Dearkov disappeared from his side and another took her place. A firm hand grabbed the webbing on his shoulder and pulled him from the battle. Spinning around he went at his attacker with both blades going for the throat. With a start of recognition he held his strike.

Captain Waugh held her sword defensively. She relaxed only when Nathan dropped his guard. All around her fresh troops from a reformed Gamma team streamed in to fill positions on the line.

"Stand down, ensign." Waugh charged into the battle.

"Yes ma'am." Nathan could barely recognize his strained, raspy voice. *The captain? Here? The captain never leaves the boat. Exception to the rule for an exceptional ruler?* A bleary thought came to him. *If I were captain, would I sit back while my crew was getting butchered?* The answer was too obvious for words.

More fresh troops brushed past him and drove back the panicked enemy. The grisly spectacle mesmerized Nathan. With Redpath's larger force still pressing forward and fresh replacements blocking the enemy's escape, the pack of headhunters shrank as the converging forces cut them to pieces. It took mere minutes of ferocious close-quarter combat to eliminate the last of the once powerful enemy force.

Truculent's sailors stood with bloody weapons in hand. Even the fittest of them breathed raggedly. Nathan's madness had fled, replaced by knee-buckling fatigue. As his heart rate slowed his senses returned. The first was his sense of smell, bringing him the fetid stench of burning flesh mixed with the unique scent of death.

In the background someone vomited.

Nathan staggered through the sea of mangled corpses. *I have to find my sword. Where's my sword?* Down on hands and knees he groped through the carnage until he found it wedged under a fallen enemy. He could barely lift his arm to sheath his sword.

"Mister Telford." Redpath stepped through the crowd of blood-soaked sailors removing his helmet.

"Sergeant Redpath."

The two men faced each other for several mute seconds. "Tactical *reserve.*" Redpath chuckled, shook his head and slapped Nathan on the shoulder.

Nathan had never received a higher compliment.

Medics worked their way around the slaughterhouse, moving from one team member to another. Few were without wounds of some kind. Moe attended to Meta's fractured shoulder. Medics worked on Chief Petty Officers Rocca, Lubar and Tokunaga who lay on the deck.

Cmdr Demianski stepped into the charnel house and froze. His face paled alarmingly when he made the mistake of breathing through his nose. He joined the captain who stood beside Babs Grimmett. Waugh took in the grisly sight and shook her head.

The victors stood ankle deep in the carnage. No one spoke for what felt like a long time.

CHAPTER 59

The hypo hissed as Moe administered the pain medication to Meta's neck. Within seconds Meta's face mellowed from intense agony to glassy-eyed euphoria.

"Meta like," she slurred.

Moe waved to a medic at the far end of Redpath's Run. They could now painlessly strap Meta's crushed shoulder. Moe slipped the hypo into the first-aid bag noting with disbelief that her hands shook. She clasped her unruly hands together. "Stop that," she whispered.

Nathan grasped her right hand in his while slipping his left arm supportively around her shoulders. Meta, Ozzie and Dearkov looked on as Nathan eased her to the deck. Moe felt overcome by a curiously disturbing numbness. She rested her head on Nathan's shoulder and waited for the malady to pass.

From the far end of Redpath's Run the captain appraised her bloodstained crew.

"Ladies and gentlemen, I am rarely lost for words so I trust you will forgive me if I simply say ... well done."

Waugh moved amongst her crew checking in with each in turn.

She looked at Nathan's small, battered team. With a single nod and a tight smile she acknowledged their contribution. Her small commendation almost made up for their savage day.

The captain crouched by the civvies, listening attentively to their heartrending pleas. Moe could not hear her words but could well imagine her response to these people who had suffered so much. Waugh would no doubt placate the traumatized civvies by saying she would do what she could to recover their lost children.

"How long?" Moe asked.

"We cross the frontier in twenty-six minutes," Ozzie said.

"That's it then." Moe felt Nathan's body tense.

They could not remain onboard the headhunter ship. Nor could *Truculent* pursue *Picaroon* across the frontier. Violation of the plague quarantine regulations carried an automatic court-martial for any crew that did. Such was the understandable panic engendered by the Derwent Plague.

The female civilians filled the first landing boat. The Franc males, heavily drugged to dull their terrible pain, followed.

One of the ratings found bottles of clean drinking water in a container. The combatants quenched their parched throats and removed the worst of the bloody residue from their body armor. With their high bloodlust fading to a nightmare memory, a lighthearted mood surfaced. Water fights broke out amongst the combatants who had so recently been embroiled in brutal mayhem. Any hares who failed to demonstrate their fleet footedness got a good soaking.

The operation had been an outstanding success against incredible odds. Nonetheless Moe sensed Nathan's dissatisfaction. Five civilians were still unaccounted for. Most likely they were hidden within one of the *Picaroon's* sensor-blind zones. Behind armored hatches and internal shields the chances of locating and rescuing them in the time available loomed as an impossible task.

Nathan had never tried to disguise his fanatical loathing for Pruessen. After what he had been through as a child slave the thought of leaving children in the hands of such fiends would burn within him. *He thinks we've all fallen for his 'I can't remember anything about my time as a slave' spiel. Nathan may have fooled everyone else with the bull but not us. He couldn't hate Pruessens with such passion if he didn't remember a lot of what happened in the north.*

The time arrived for the teams to disembark. Alpha team had already returned to the boat with their wounded. Beta Team moved to the aft hatch while the newly call-signed Tackies sprawled on the deck by the port-side bow hatch. Moe felt control returning to her hands as she savored the peace and quiet. After the recent massacre the remaining headhunters were unlikely to venture anywhere near the battle zone.

Moe glanced at Meta who stared back through glazed eyes. She had asked to remain with her team. Due to the large number of wounded filling the landing boats, she got her wish. Ozzie moved gingerly to avoid aggravating his cracked ribs. Even Dearkov was content to enjoy a few moments of idleness. Moe opened her hands palms down, pleased that the embarrassing shaking had gone.

Moe was no longer the tomboy girl she used to be and felt justifiably proud of holding her own in any fight. But this had been the real deal. It could not get any more real; dark, cherry-red real.

"The blood," Moe whispered. *Did I say that out loud?*

"The barbarity," Ozzie said, his eyes unfocussed.

"Can't believe how much those animals stank." Meta's lazy half-smile confirmed the drugs were doing their job.

Dearkov's warped expression reminded Moe of a Kastorian leopard. "I really liked the way they squealed when I hacked into them."

Nathan had gone mute. He sat slightly off to one side of the group, his head resting against a bulkhead, his eyes closed. Moe knew when to back away and when to break his morose mood. He should feel good about the mission. They had rescued eighteen out of twenty-three civilians. Pruessens by the score had fallen to them with minimal casualties to their own forces. The team had been cut and bruised but they survived the ordeal. All in all a damn fine result. Nathan had to know there was no chance of rescuing the missing children. Moe sidled over and grunted as she dropped beside him.

"A dollar fifty for your thoughts."

Nathan opened his eyes. He was like a brother to Moe so she knew he would be firmly focused on what had not, rather than what *had* been accomplished today. Being Nathan he chose not to speak of it.

"I was just thinking about a long hot shower and a drink of something non-regulation."

The Tackies groaned in agreement.

"I'm going to sleep for the next week," Ozzie said.

"So what's new?" Meta slurred.

Moe suspected that her friends would be considering the questions raised today. How had Nathan avoided the headhunter patrols? What demon had possessed him during the heat of battle? However, their academy training had prepared them to be not only naval officers but ladies and gentlemen of refined dispositions. No one would be rude enough to broach the subject.

"So, Nathan, what's with the spooky shit?" Meta's eyes were two bleary slits. Her head drooped to one side.

Nathan's raised eyebrows indicated he had no idea what she was talking about. Everyone groaned at his usual response.

"I think what my esteemed and semi-delirious friend is trying to ask you, Nathan, is how did you avoid those patrols?" Ozzie asked.

"That's what I said," Meta slurred.

Nathan tapped his right ear. "Good hearing."

In an instant Ozzie's affable expression hardened, together with his tone. "We bled together, Nathan." A declaration wrapped in an accusation. A gauntlet thrown down.

Moe caught Nathan's slight wince. She knew he would deflect the conversation as he always did.

"I had a gut feeling, Ozzie," he said. "So I followed it."

His frankness stunned everyone into silence. After several awkward seconds Nathan received support from an unexpected source.

"With all due respect, ladies and gentlemen," Dearkov said, "you're all full of shit." Every eye considered the brawny petty officer. "He came up with the plan, he led us to victory over our enemy and he fought with the courage of a Salamisian lion. But all you lot can do is whine about how he saved your collective rumps."

Nathan thought he handled such moments well but Moe noted the prickly rash on the back of his neck as it flared with the prominence of Quasimodo's hump.

The uneasy silence lingered until a distinct clang of metal on metal echoed down the corridor. They were on their feet in an instant, swords drawn. Nathan strode along the corridor, Dearkov his shadow. Moe nocked one of the remaining arrows.

They ventured deep into the lateral corridor. The plaintive cry of a distressed individual guided them forward. Ahead, sprawled on the deck next to an access tube, an enemy sailor cradled his foot in his hands. This genius had apparently fallen out of the access tube.

The headhunter's sword lay on the deck beside him but he did not attempt to reach for it when he spied the approaching sailors. Dearkov raised her ax and went for the kill.

"I surrender," he squealed. His hands covered his head in a useless gesture of protection. Nathan stood before the ax and raised his hand.

"You're not going soft on me are you, Mister Telford?"

Nathan ignored her. He knelt beside the terrified headhunter.

"Name."

"Flencher." His narrow eyes darted between Nathan and the ax-wielding petty officer.

Flencher did not fit the headhunter archetype. A short, spare fellow, Moe doubted if he had the strength to lift the enormous sword resting so close to his hand. His voice had a nasal quality. On closer inspection Moe saw that Flencher's nose had recently been broken. The ill-fitting armor hung off his wiry frame. Obviously, this weak excuse for a man was no warrior.

"Flencher, my name is Telford. I am going to ask you some questions." Nathan kept his voice to a low whisper. "If you answer my questions honestly you will get to keep on breathing. If not, I shall become quite irritated. Do you clearly understand what I have said to you?"

"Will you take me prisoner?"

Nathan cleared his throat.

"No, I will not," he ventured.

"Then no deal," the wiry headhunter said. "If you're going to kill me, get on with it." Flencher tensed and swallowed nosily but his resolve remained firm. Unlike his knees.

"Are you saying you want to be taken prisoner?"

"What do you think I'm doing on this deck? I was trying to link up with any Athenians still onboard. I don't belong here. I was press ganged from Midway ten months ago. I'm a gentleman's gentleman not a killer. You have no idea what these people are like. They're animals. I want no part of this ship. Take me with you when you go and I will tell you anything you want to know."

"You've got a deal, Flencher. When we leave, you go with us. First, there is something specific I would like to know."

***

"What do you mean they're not there?" Waugh slumped into the command chair, sighing deeply.

"Skipper," CPO Stokes said, "I locked onto the hatch right on schedule but the Tackies were nowhere to be seen. I checked the adjoining corridors but found no trace of them."

"Do you have *any* idea where they might be, chief?"

"Sorry, skipper." A long pause followed. "Maybe the team was ambushed and taken prisoner. I mean it's possible, ma'am."

Waugh struggled with an inner turmoil. Her best instincts compelled her to arm every able-bodied combatant and get her people back. Her duty, however, forbade such action.

"Chief Petty Officer Stokes," she said, "unless you come under direct enemy attack, you will remain locked onto the hatch until 1356 hours. If by that time you have not recovered the team you will disengage your boat and return to Truculent. Am I being clear, chief?"

"Aye-aye, captain," Stokes said glumly.

"Very well. Carry on. Captain out."

What the devil could have happen to them? Waugh could not imagine a man like Telford falling into an ambush. Considering the gigantic losses inflicted on *Picaroon's* crew, only small isolated patrols remained. *Where the hell are the Tackies?*

Truculent would hit the Rio Grande in sixteen minutes. The most sacrosanct rule in Corps, the Athenian Naval Service and the forces attached to the Coalition League Navy remained as solid today as it had thirty years ago. For no reason could a League vessel cross the border into Pruessen space.

Like it or not, if Telford and his team did not return to LB three by 1356 hours she would be left with no choice in the matter.

CHAPTER 60

Orson disengaged EDF. With the internal sensors restored they revealed the disastrous truth.

"What the fuck are you doing," Weiss shrieked. "Restore the field immediately." He leaped from the captain's chair and loomed over Orson, his hand caressing the stock of his sidearm. "Saxon, did you hear me? Get that fucking field back up."

Orson could visualize the pure joy he would feel from slowly garroting the cowardly headhunter. The twelve heavily armed bridge guards would undoubtedly dispute his fair-minded reasoning. Weiss might be scum but he was *their* scum. Orson submerged his rage and turned the EDF dial back to the maximum setting.

"Why the hell did you do that, Saxon? There could be Athenians outside the hatch ready to force their way in. Are you mad?"

"We need to have current-time intel, Weiss." Orson had given up trying to conceal his contempt. "We've received zero intel since the insulated line to the captain went down."

"I don't care about intel," Weiss yelled. "Touch the panel again and it will be the last thing you do."

"We're almost at the frontier," Orson said. "The Athenians won't remain aboard. It would violate their most sacred military oath."

Surprisingly, Weiss considered his words. "Helmsman, how long till we cross the border?"

"Fourteen minutes at current speed."

Orson examined the few readings he managed to record. It confirmed his worst fears. These scum should never have been entrusted with such an important operation. But the Family had refused to listen to him.

Weiss strutted around the bridge buoyed by the news they were minutes from safety.

"Tactical, what internal readings do you have?"

"None, commander."

"Didn't you get anything when the EDF was disengaged?"

"No sir," the T-O said. "It was too quick. But Saxon might have."

"What can you tell me, Saxon?"

"It's difficult to say with such a short time to record the data," Orson said impatiently. "However, from what I can ascertain our special platoons have been annihilated by the Athenians."

Weiss' face paled. “All of them?”

“There are a few patrols still operating on the upper decks but nothing on deck five.” Orson could not resist a last jibe. “That’s the bad news. Would you care to hear the good news?”

Weiss nodded, his mouth agape.

“Throughout the engagement the EDF worked flawlessly.” He paused shortly before adding, “But we don’t need it anymore.”

“I don't agree with you, lieutenant,” Weiss said, the fear returning to his eyes. “And you will address me as captain.”

Orson ignored him and returned to his readouts. With this fool in charge, Orson's sense of apprehension amplified.

“We will maintain course and speed to the frontier,” Weiss announced. “When we cross into friendly space I’ll decide what we do next."

Orson's gut twisted into a hard knot.

CHAPTER 61

Nathan faced the team. "I cannot in good conscience leave without the children," Nathan said, his tone endorsing an unyielding tenor. "I *can't* and I *won't*. I'm going to find the civvies, with my new friend here." Flencher smiled halfheartedly when Nathan slapped him on the back. "I am disobeying orders by committing to this action so the rest of you should rendezvous with the landing boat."

"You really need to lighten up, Nathan," Moe said. "You don't have to make everything so bloody dramatic do you? We'll find the civvies, return to Truculent and face the consequences together. All right?"

"Don't even think you're going to get all of the glory for yourself," Meta said.

"I could really use a shower," Ozzie said. "But I suppose I can wait a little longer."

Dearkov slapped the flat side of her ax into the palm of her hand. Her gruesome expression confirmed her acceptance.

"You know, as acting ensign I could order you jokers to report to the landing boat." The team chuckled. He cleared his throat. "Very well. We'd better get to it." He looked at Dearkov and raised an eyebrow. "Feeling fit, petty officer?"

After safely negotiating four decks into the bowels of the enemy ship they approached their destination.

Nathan noted that Petty Officer Dearkov did not appear at all happy with her new assignment. The indignity of carrying the injured former headhunter on her back was testing what little patience she had.

Flencher whispered something into her ear.

Dearkov stopped, plucked Flencher from her back and pinned him to the bulkhead by the throat. Her blazing eyes said much about her restraint.

"Listen to me you scrawny little weasel," she said. "The only reason your head isn't tucked up your arse is because Mister Telford says so. But if you don't stop talking to me I will hurt you so severely that your grandchildren will cry. Are you reading me shit-for-brains?"

With her hand clamped firmly around his throat he could not reply.

"I'd nod if I were you," Nathan suggested.

Flencher nodded, frantic eyes bulging from a red face.

Dearkov swung him onto her back with the ease of tossing back a cape.

The team reached the juncture of two main corridors.

"Which way?" Nathan asked the newly reticent Flencher. "She said don't talk to her, not to me. Now which way?"

"Right." After a dozen paces he said, "Stop here."

Nathan stood before a hatch embossed with the symbol of a skull and crossbones.

This guy has to be kidding.

"You're sure?"

"The captain keeps the best prizes for himself," Flencher said.

Dearkov glared over her shoulder. "Get off me." Flencher instantly dropped to the deck.

Nathan examined the old-style hatch. Unlike the other hatches he had encountered aboard *Picaroon,* this one was fitted with a manual locking bar. Nathan stared at the lock before looking to his team.

"You could probably shoot it off ... if you had your sidearm."

His frown indicated he was not impressed with Moe's attempt at light humor.

"Now *you* know how it feels." Moe said.

Dearkov took a step back from the hatch and swung her ax above her head.

"No!" Flencher cried. He hopped toward the hatch, ignoring Dearkov's blistering glare. "It's cast armor metal. All you'll do is jam the mechanism," he said. "One of the advantages of being the captain's steward is that I know his secrets." Flencher manipulated the tumblers until the lock snapped open. "When you raise the locking bar it automatically disengages the internal shielding."

"Is it sensor-monitored?"

"No, only the externals are covered by sensors. This is a headhunter ship not a battleship."

Nathan reached out with his senses. Prep did not respond. He sheathed his sword.

"Wait here," he said.

Nathan spun the round handle and pulled the hatch open. He slowly stepped into the room. The children, three girls and two boys, ranged in age from about four to eight years. They huddled together on a huge bed, their little chests heaving. He smiled and approached the children slowly, his hands open in a gesture of supplication. Although healthy and unmarked, fear dominated their eyes. At any moment the restrained whimpering would explode into a full-scale panic attack. *How to handle this?*

"Hello children. I'm an Athenian naval officer and I'm here to take you home to your parents." He held his breath as five pairs of huge eyes stared at him.

"Our parents are dead." The pretty blonde girl appeared to be the oldest.

"What's your name, young lady?"

"Simone Garneau."

She reminded him of his kid sister Lucy. Not physically but in the wide-eyed innocence young children exhibited.

"Well, Simone Garneau, that's not true. My crew have rescued them and they are now on my ship."

"You're lying," she cried.

Time for a different tactic. "Mind your manners, Miss Garneau. Athenians don't lie. Now behave yourself."

Tick tock. Simone looked at her hands.

"I want to go home," one of the youngsters whined.

"Are our parents really alive?" Simone asked.

"As I said, my crew rescued them all and you'll see them real soon. But children," he hardened his tone moderately, "you all must do exactly what I say when I say it. Understood?"

The younger children nodded.

"Captain Foss said we couldn't leave our quarters," Simone said.

"Captain Foss has a headache he's not going to get over any time soon. I am captain now. You may call me, Captain Nathan."

He stared at the children. All were rightly apprehensive but far less so than a few minutes ago. Only Simone retained a resolute expression.

"Anyone who wants to go home, jump off the bed." All but one of them leapt onto the deck. Simone stayed rooted in place, her face twisting with fearful uncertainty. Being the oldest she would suspect the danger more than the other youngsters. Nathan got down on his knees, held out his hands to her and spoke with firm but gentle insistence. "Come on Simone. Let's take you home." Again he held his breath.

Her resistance crumbled and she leapt into his arms.

***

Time was running out. Nathan pushed the team to keep going. Each of them carried a child. Flencher limped after them.

Halfway along deck four Nathan's back flared. He wanted to stand and fight but couldn't take the risk of the children being harmed.

He stared at his friends. "Very well, we'll take a shortcut down to the next deck. Into the access tubes."

The team went first and Nathan had just made it into the tube when he heard the sound of armored boots on deck plates. He froze on the ladder. Simone's eyes became wide as the sound grew. Her mouth began to open. Nathan held his finger to his lips. If Simone called out... He locked his eyes onto hers and repeated to himself, *don't scream, don't scream, don't scream.* The girl's chest heaved with the effort to control herself. It felt as if the marching boots would go on forever. Gradually the clatter of the headhunter patrol dimmed then died. He brushed the girl's hair and whispered, "Good girl, Simone." She hugged his chest and her breathing started to return to normal.

They encountered no other patrols as they moved stealthily to the rendezvous. *How the hell have we gotten this far without one of the kids crying or screaming? I guess it's true. Children really are malleable. Or perhaps it's the absolute terror that silenced them.*

Nathan quickened his pace as the lateral corridor loomed ahead. Sensing no danger he jogged around the corner leading to the forward hatch. His momentum slowed before grinding to a stop.

The bow hatch was pressure sealed. The landing boat had left without them.

CHAPTER 62

O'Donnell turned to the Captain. “We are two minutes from the Rio Grande.

“Very well.” Waugh rubbed her dry eyes.

“The last landing boat is coming aboard now, captain,” Luis reported.

The Tackies *were* all dead by now, or in chains.

“Boat bay is secured, captain,” Luis said.

“Very well. Helm, bring the boat to a dead stop as close to the frontier as you dare.”

“Aye, captain.”

Waugh crossed the bridge and leaned over the Tactical Station. “Lois, I want you to track Picaroon for as long as possible. Deploy the long-range array if need be but keep an eye on her.”

“Aye, skipper.”

Waugh dropped into the captain's chair.

“Do you think I'm an idiot, Luis?”

“I think for someone of your advanced years the correct term would be old fool ... captain.” He smiled and added, “And no, I don’t.”

“Why should I think they’re still alive?”

“He’s quite an exceptional young man, don't you think?”

“Hmm.”

So far she had three of her crew dead on this mission and others who could die from their wounds. The loss of her middies ate at her. It had been her decision to attach them to the strike force.

She pushed her recriminations aside. For the time being she could only sit and wait. Clinging tenaciously to an aching wisp of hope.

CHAPTER 63

Nathan stared at the secured hatch. Simone's white-knuckled grip indicated her suspicions, but thankfully she kept her peace. His mind went blank.

"Sir, I believe the landing boat is in the boat bay," Moe said.

"Quite right, middy," he replied.

He stared at his team. They nodded slightly in confirmation. He set off at a light jog with Simone's hands digging urgently into his webbing. Nathan's sense of unease increased. If the landing boat had left, *Picaroon* must have crossed the Rio Grande. However, that was the least of their many problems. At any moment the EDF could be disengaged and the children would show up on the enemy's sensors. Nathan could not understand why they continued to maintain the field.

They made their way to the boat bay entrance without incident. Even though his Prep gave no indication of danger he would take no chances with the children's safety. He placed Simone onto the deck.

Dearkov placed her charges onto the deck with utmost gentleness.

"Very well children, I'm going to leave you with Meta and Ozzie for a minute while I get my boat ready. Please behave yourselves."

Meta and Ozzie ushered them through a nearby hatch and dogged it.

Once the children cleared the corridor Nathan and Moe prepared their bows. They each had only two arrows left. According to Flencher the boat bay was one of the five areas on the ship where the EDF was not deployed.

If armed troops were waiting for them behind the hatch ...

Dearkov held her ax in one hand and undogged the hatch with the other. Nathan charged into the boat bay, his bow at the ready. He winced as the dazzling light from the overheads struck his eyes. Blinking rapidly he sighted along the drawn arrow panning from bulkhead to bulkhead. Moe and Dearkov checked out the hangars while Nathan inspected the bay. No armed troops, no pulsars tearing into him.

If anyone gave the alarm before they were ready to depart they were finished. Bows and arrows against energy weapons would have a poor outcome. For the moment their sensor suppressors would keep the middies hidden from the boat bay sensors, but such protection did not extend to the children. When they left this wretched ship they would have to do so very, very quickly.

“All clear,” Moe said.

“Dearkov, check out the LCC.” The petty officer sprinted up the stairs to the Landing Control Center. Nathan and Moe walked around the hangar examining the poor selection of landing boats. One boat was on the center line ready for launch. Nathan cracked the hatch and they checked it out.

After a careful inspection Moe voiced her opinion. “What a piece of shit.”

“Yeah, but it’s the best piece of shit.”

Moe wrinkled her nose. “This belongs in a museum, Nate.”

“Yeah, but you get that. Start the pre-flight checks will you?”

“Why certainly, Stanley.”

When Nathan stepped from the boat, Dearkov jogged down the steps. “All clear. Mind if I ask a question?” Nathan nodded. “I suppose you plan to steal one of these boats and make a run for it?”

“Sounds good to me.”

“What about those.” Dearkov pointed her ax at the huge hangar doors.

“I'm planning to open those before we leave.”

“Oh ... good. So you know how to operate the controls.”

Nathan gasped and held a hand to his mouth. “I thought you did.” She did not appreciate his humor. “We'll figure it out, Dearkov. Don't worry so much. I mean, how hard could it be to open a couple of doors?” She rolled her eyes. “I'll get Meta to give you a hand. She's better at this sort of thing than I am.”

Dearkov jogged up the stairs while he returned to the corridor. He reached the hatch and heard childish laughter. When he stepped through the hatch Ozzie and Meta reached for their swords. They sat on the deck playing games with the children.

He waved at the kids and they waved back. *Remarkable. Children really are made of rubber.*

Nathan motioned Meta to join him by the hatch. She winced as she got to her feet and joined him.

“You're hurting?”

“The drugs are wearing off.”

“Good,” Nathan said without humor. “I need you sharp. Get up to the LCC and figure out how to get the hangar doors open. Dearkov can assist you. And you know not to actually open them until I say so, right?” For the sake of the kids, she simply nodded. After she left he drew Ozzie aside.

“Keep them entertained by whatever means you have to.”

"I get all the great assignments." As the eldest child of nine siblings Ozzie's qualifications were beyond reproach. "Problems?"

"Nothing that the academy class of 320 can't handle." Nathan maintained his smile for the kid's benefit but his eyes and tone changed. "You need to keep them quiet. I could hear them out in the corridor."

"You're kidding, right?"

Nathan heaved a sigh. "Just do your best."

Nathan walked slowly toward the boat bay, taking a moment to assess their situation. Meta and Dearkov would get the hangar doors open. Moe would prep the LB and Ozzie would take care of the kids. The worrisome, noisy kids who were close to going ballistic. Another reason to get off this ship as quickly as possible.

Flencher slumped on the deck, his legs stretched out before him. As with the children, he did not wear a sensor suppressor.

Nathan set his eyes on the former headhunter. Under his gaze Flencher shifted uncomfortably.

"Flencher, how much do you weigh?"

***

"You're the bloody academy genius, not me," Dearkov spat.

Meta resisted the urge to tell the great lump of a petty officer what she really thought. Her *sister* from Salamis made her feel like a proper lady. They had slaved over the LCC controls for ten minutes. Meta still hadn't figured out how to open the hangar doors.

"This technology is forty years out of date. It's totally dissimilar to the systems I've studied."

"So take a good guess ... ma'am."

Meta scrutinized the broad control panel, struggling to make sense of the mass of unfamiliar controls. Some of them, like the force field activator and the power relays, she recognized, but numerous others remained mysteries.

She tried not to think about leaving without Nathan but if company arrived she might have no choice in the matter.

"The safety of the children comes first, Meta," Nathan had said. "I'll try to divert any patrols away from the boat bay. But if I get unlucky, do not hesitate. Leave as soon as you can."

Alone and unarmed he was playing the biggest bluff of his life. *If a patrol turns up and does not fall for his ploy ...* Nathan could take care of himself better than anyone she knew. He'd walk home if need be.

Meta's impatience got the better of her. She held her breath and struck at a likely series of controls. Power to the main hatch showed green on her board and she shut down the sequence within a second.

"Got it."

"Great!"

"But I may have told someone we're here."

"Jesus wept," Dearkov cursed.

"Get ready to move out."

"What about Mister Telford?"

"He'll be fine. If the bridge officers are as slack as everything else on this bucket we should be fine."

Meta led the way down the stairs, stifling a wince each time her feet hit the steps. She sent Dearkov to guard the hatch while she sprinted to the boat. It hurt to sprint but it would hurt a lot more with a headhunter broadsword in her belly.

She worked her way through the smelly LB and stuck her head into the flight deck. Moe sat in the right-hand seat examining a bank of instruments.

"Please tell me this thing will fly."

"This thing will fly." Moe's impersonation of Nathan's dryness caused Meta to chuckle. "Are we ready to go?"

"Pretty close," Meta said, turning to go.

"Where's Nathan?"

"He'll be along shortly." Meta stepped from the LB and strode across the boat bay to where Dearkov guarded the hatch. *Like the hound from hell.* Meta froze as the hatch swung open. A headhunter stepped into the bay. Dearkov swung a mighty blow at the helmeted head with force enough to cleave it from its body.

The headhunter dropped under the blow and drove a flat-handed strike onto her chest. Dearkov staggered back then launched herself at the intruder. He sidestepped her and ran toward Meta while pulling off his helmet. Nathan stopped before the enraged, charging Dearkov and held up his hands in submission.

"This has been fun," Nathan said, "but it's time to go."

Dearkov checked her next killing swing.

"Meta, the doors?" Nathan asked.

"Done," she said, then added, "I think."

"Moe?"

"Ready to go when you are."

"Very well. Get back to the LCC and stand by."

Meta took the stairs two at a time, the pain from each step making her shoulder scream. She stood by the clear composite screen for nearly a minute before Nathan led the children into the boat bay. *A modern-day Pied Piper.* Nathan urged them not to dally and to disregard their obvious fascination for the old wreck of a LB. As the last little body filed into their escape vessel, Nathan held up his left thumb.

Meta activated the force field and hit what she hoped were the appropriate controls. While the hangar doors rumbled noisily apart she bolted down the stairs and dashed for the boat. By now the enemy bridge would *have* to be aware of their presence. Ozzie closed and secured the hatch after Meta jumped aboard. Together they secured the kids into the seats. Now all they had to do was escape.

***

Nathan dropped his helmet onto the deck and slipped into the left-hand seat of the LB. Through the view-plate, he saw the huge hangar doors struggle open.

Moe had done a fine job of prepping the boat and succeeded in doing so without alerting the enemy. He scanned the controls isolating the more-vital instruments.

Moe finished pressurizing the boat and began the engine start-up sequence. "Strike any trouble out there?"

"Nothing worth mentioning," he said absently.

"Hangar doors are fully opened." Moe glanced over her shoulder into the boat's cabin. "Our passengers are secured."

"Very well."

Nathan tightened his harness. If *Picaroon* maintained her frantic speed, their escape would not be a comfortable one.

"Reactor active," Moe said. "Full power is at your command."

"Very well."

Nathan diverted the maximum-allowable power supplement to the landing gear constrictors, overrode the safeties and pushed both throttles fully forward. Almost immediately the boat began to vibrate as the power built steadily toward the red marker. The hangar area quickly transformed into a maelstrom of blazing plasma. He kept the boat locked in place as the power indicator approached the red line. The hangar doors started to close.

"Ah, Nathan." Moe pointed to the slowly closing doors.

"I see it." The engine power indicator hit the red line. Nathan cut power to the skids. The landing boat leapt forward, streaked from the bay and into open space.

"Clear," he said, surprised by the relief in his voice.

A few moments later the expected buffeting struck the small boat.

The impact tossed the landing boat around like a balloon in a windstorm. Nathan needed a full minute to fight the unruly craft under control. He left the throttles fully open and set a course away from *Picaroon*.

"How does she handle?" Moe asked.

"It's like strapping a saddle on a big old boar. Get on the sensors and locate Truculent."

"Roger that."

If *Truculent* were not within range of their sensors this could be a very short-lived escape. By now *Picaroon* would be aware of their getaway. It would undoubtedly annoy whoever had taken command from Captain Foss.

As with the rest of the boat, the sensor array had seen better days but it clearly showed three icons. A green one astern of them, their own green icon and a red one off to starboard.

"I have Truculent, twelve degrees to starboard. She's maintaining a static position."

"I'm so pleased," Nathan said. "How long?"

Moe squinted as she made a quick mental calculation rather than relying on the crude headhunter computer. "If we maintain current speed and alter heading by twelve degrees to starboard we should rendezvous with Truculent in approximately nine minutes."

"If this heap has anything resembling shields it might be prudent to initiate them, don't you think?"

"I certainly do, Stanley." In short order Moe identified the controls and activated the shields. For a landing boat the shields were pretty good.

"How long before they catch us?"

"Did I hear right before we left the boat? The skipper took out the headhunter's weapons array. Right?"

"I forget."

"You know, Nate, there are times when your sense of humor is totally inappropriate. Haven't I taught you anything over the years?"

"Lighten up, Ollie," Nathan said. "They don't need weapons to capture us. If they catch us they will simply tractor us aboard."

"And this doesn't concern you?"

"If they capture us I'll wait until we are inside the boat bay then blow the reactor."

"Well, I'm glad you've thought this through."

"But it might not come to that. Picaroon's engines are damaged– as slow as this bucket of bolts is we might outrun her. Of course I would know for certain if you gave me a time to intercept as I asked you to." He distorted his face into a rendition of Stan Laurel.

Moe leaned over her sensor readouts. "Some people can't handle stress situations."

CHAPTER 64

With little else to occupy his time Orson glanced around the bridge. *Picaroon's* tactical officer yawned and stretched. His eyes passed lazily across his bank of screens and widened.

"Captain, I'm detecting some strange readings from the boat bay," he said.

"Strange? How so?" Weiss asked.

"I'm detecting ignition from a landing boat engine."

"A landing boat?"

"Boat bay doors are open."

"Override and close them."

"I'm trying, captain," the T-O said, while he frantically struggled with the controls. "Doors closing, captain."

"Good," Weiss said. "Send guards down to – "

"They're gone!" the T-O said.

"What?" Weiss screamed.

"The landing boat got out before the doors closed." The T-O's face sagged with astonishment. "I've never seen anything like that. The pilot must be a madman."

"Who would be using a landing boat?"

"It has to be the Franc prisoners," Orson said.

"So a bunch of children stole one of our boats?" Weiss sniggered.

Orson bit down a curse. "There must be Athenians aboard the LB."

"Impossible," Weiss said.

"It doesn't matter," Orson said, "now that we're across the frontier."

For a few moments Weiss' stood in silence as if he were actually thinking about something.

"Guards stand ready," he said. They gathered at the main bridge hatch, rifles at their shoulders. Weiss checked the manual lock. "Saxon, drop the EDF. Tactical, scan the ship. I want to know if our prisoners are still in the captain's ... my cabin."

Orson dutifully disengaged the EDF.

"I've swept the ship, captain," the T-O said. "There are no enemy combatants aboard."

"And the children?"

"They're not on the ship."

"Scan the landing boat."

"She's out of range."

“Helm, hard about,” Weiss shouted. “Plot an intercept course with the landing boat.”

After a few seconds of stunned silence the helmsman said, "But that will take us back under the monitor's guns."

“He's right, captain,” the T-O confirmed.

Weiss drew his pistol and aimed it at the helmsman’s head. "Carry out your orders or I will relieve you of duty, permanently.”

“Aye-aye, captain,” the sullen helm said. “Coming hard about now.”

“This is madness,” Orson said. “We are in Pruessen space. We have accomplished our mission. The technology works. And you want to wander into a monitor's torpedo envelope for a handful of children. For God's sake let them go.”

“Shut your mouth, Saxon,” Weiss shouted. “I am captain of this ship. Do you have any idea how much those children are worth?” Sensing the potential danger he swung his sidearm to point at Orson’s stomach. “The Athenians won't fire on us. Not while they think we have civilians aboard.”

“That's enough.” Orson forced his rage under control although the urge to kill every useless headhunter on the bridge burned hot. “This mission is under the direct authority of IPN Intelligence. Under that authority I order you to come about and resume course to Virtus.”

“Your authority ended at the frontier. This is *my* ship now.”

“I'll see you hang for this, Weiss.”

“That's mutiny, lieutenant.” Weiss addressed the two largest bridge guards. “Throw this mutinous dog into the brig.”

“You want us to go out *there*, ah, captain?” one of the guards asked.

“Just do it,” Weiss screamed.

Too many guards on the bridge but it's a long way to the brig. Every muscle of Orson’s body flexed for action.

CHAPTER 65

Hookes sounded agitated. "Captain, something's happening," Waugh strode across the bridge and hovered behind the tactical station. She knew better than to interrupt Hookes' concentration. The plot showed two red icons moving toward *Truculent*. Waugh tried to contain her hope.

Hookes' smile crept around the edges of her sensor hood. "I have two craft on an intercept course. A headhunter landing boat with," a pause while she fine tuned, "Picaroon in pursuit."

"How many people are aboard the landing boat?"

"I can't tell with her shields activated."

"Damn." Waugh had a fair suspicion who was aboard the craft.

The satisfied expression bled from Hookes' face. "Picaroon is rapidly closing on them. I estimate they will intercept the LB three minutes shy of the Rio Grande."

Waugh stepped back to her command chair and sat heavily. A headhunter landing boat running from a headhunter warship. It had to be Telford and the civvies.

"Captain," Luis said, "I have a transmission coming in. Putting it onto the command channel."

"Truculent this is the Tackies." Smiles spread throughout the bridge as everyone recognized the voice. "We are aboard a captured headhunter landing boat and we have the – "

A squeal of static ended Telford's report.

"Transmission blocked by Picaroon."

"Damn," she hissed.

"Captain," O'Donnell said, "my navigation console just went down. I have no way of knowing where we are." His eyes expressed a hope-felt plea.

"Captain," Hookes said, "my navigation panel has gone down as well. We could be anywhere."

"Captain," Luis said, "a boat-wide corruption of the – "

"That's enough, commander," Waugh said quietly. Although sorely tempted to follow her crew's deception the price would be far too high. "Lois, time to interception?"

"A little over five minutes, captain," Hookes said.

Waugh nodded slowly while considering her options. "This vessel cannot cross the Rio Grande. That is set in stone. But," she said, "the rules don't say anything about shooting across the frontier, do they?"

On a silent invitation from Luis she leaned across the console. "If you're wrong," Luis whispered, "and even one of the civvies is still aboard Picaroon, and you destroy her, there are people who will use that as an excuse to crucify you."

"Telford said he had them aboard the landing boat."

"His message is ambiguous."

"Perhaps. But I believe he has them. I have larger concerns at the moment."

"No IFF beacon on the landing boat?" Waugh nodded. Luis shrugged. "I suppose it's time to prove your legendary status, isn't it?"

"Pulsar heads in tubes one and six thank you."

"With the greatest pleasure, captain."

Waugh strapped into the combat chair before tapping the stud under the right-hand armrest. The iris dilated and the chair dropped into the combat sphere. She initialized her menu from the holo projector and selected real time image. The sphere's panels shimmered for a moment before displaying an image of the space surrounding *Truculent.*

"SMC-captain. Tie in for combat operations."

"Acknowledged, Commodore Waugh," the Shipboard Management Computer replied.

"SMC magnification one hundred percent."

The headhunter landing boat filled the front panels. "SMC reduce zoom to seventy-five percent and continue to adjust." The LB shrank; the pursuing headhunter came into sight. *Now things get tricky.*

Her screen displayed tubes one and six loaded with pulsar heads. Because of the close proximity of the landing boat she could not risk anything more powerful. Even a clean kill could be problematic for the fragile landing boat. A Badger Class had a displacement of two hundred and fifty thousand tonnes. *Picaroon's* destruction would send a wave of explosive debris against the LB's fragile shields.

"Two minutes to intercept, captain," Hookes reported.

"Very well."

Come on middy. You've studied my tactics at the academy. You know what I want you to do. Perhaps he needs a wake-up call.

***

Nathan glanced at Moe. Her eyes were focused on her sensor readouts but her mouth hung open. "She's locked us up."

"What!"

"Truculent's locked her weapons onto us."

Nathan blinked, equally confused. For a terrifying moment he assumed *Picaroon* had restored her weapons. His mind roiled for a few seconds before understanding dawned.

"What's so bloody funny?" Moe asked.

"The captain's sent us a message. I think." He rubbed his right eyebrow. "How soon to intercept?"

"Eighty seconds."

"Listen Moe, Truculent can't fire at Picaroon with us so close to her. Remember, we'll show up as an enemy craft."

"Yeah, no IFF. So what do we do?"

"I have an idea."

"What is it?"

"You're not going to like it."

"So what's new?"

Nathan made his smile embody true evil.

"I'm *really* not going to like this am I?"

"No. But you get that."

***

Weiss jumped as the officer's voice blared. "Captain, the landing boat is coming about." *Picaroon's* tactical officer had a perplexed tone in his voice.

"Giving up at last," Weiss said. "They can't outrun us and they can't call for help." More importantly they could not reveal the secret keeping *Picaroon's* crew alive. "Weapons officer, confirm tractor readiness."

"Confirmed, captain."

"Captain, if they're surrendering they're in a fucking big hurry to do so," the tactical officer said. "Their speed has increased to flank."

"Huh?"

"I think they're trying to ram us."

"Bullshit. Weapons Officer, snag them as they pass and bring them aboard."

"I'll try, captain, but at flank speed – "

"Do whatever you have to," Weiss screamed, "but get the fucking boat back in the bay."

"Aye, captain."

"Captain, we're now well inside the monitor's torpedo envelope."

"Are we still maintaining the comm blackout?"

"Yes, captain."

"Good. We have nothing to worry about."

***

"They're getting awfully close don't you think?" Moe did not sound at all happy.

"Yep."

"This isn't a razorback boar you know?"

"Same principle."

Through the forward view-plate *Picaroon* grew in size with alarming speed. Nathan maintained an unerring course toward the enemy vessel. He waited until the slow, steady beep of the collision alarm began, counted to five and acted.

He piloted the landing boat under the onrushing warship and slid down her starboard side. The proximity alarms wailed as he skimmed perilously close to *Picaroon's* hull. Nathan steered the craft into a vicious turn to starboard pinning everyone to their chairs. A tractor beam lanced out but missed them.

Nathan pulled the throttles back to zero. "Now!"

Moe touched a single control key. The internal gravity went down and the craft plunged into darkness.

***

"They're gone!" the T-O cried.

"What!" Weiss screamed.

"I've lost the landing boat. She was on my screen then ... nothing."

Weiss rubbed his bearded chin.

"She's probably gone doggo," the weapons officer suggested.

With no power emissions betraying her position it would take a little longer to retrieve her. *A foolish gesture on their part.*

"Helm bring us about. Take us to the landing boat's last known position."

"Aye, captain."

"I'm going to enjoy spending time with the pilot of that boat," Weiss said between set teeth. "I will enjoy it greatly."

***

"Pretty good flying for a grommit," Luis said through her earpiece.

"Hmm." Waugh's attention had been on the landing boat but now it switched to *Picaroon*. She had assumed Telford would try something to separate himself from the enemy ship. His dicey maneuver had been quite spectacular. It reminded her that Telford, among other things, was a risk taker.

Right under *Truculent's* looming weapons, *Picaroon* started to come about. The Badger class had a flaw she intended to exploit.

"Now, commander."

The boat came to Alert Condition one while the captain counted down the seconds. "Come on you big brute. Just a little further." *Picaroon* turned sluggishly, again something the class was renowned for. Waugh quickly calculated the running time for her torpedo. Three seconds from mid-turn Waugh fired. Torpedo one streaked toward the target. The pre-programmed attack pattern positioned at point-blank range before detonating. A narrow, silver beam of focused energy tore through *Picaroon's* thin midships keel. It pierced the bulkheads and sliced through the reactor core's thin shielding. The core breached. A microsecond later, *Picaroon* vanished from existence in a blinding flash of energy.

CHAPTER 66

When the dull ache between Nathan's shoulder blades erupted into fire, Nathan acted.

"Bring all systems back online. Full power to shields. Route back-up power to the keel blisters."

Even as he talked and before Moe acknowledged, Nathan raised the boat's nose rotating it through her axis, presenting her keel to the enemy ship. Nathan averted his eyes when the darkness was illuminated by a blinding white flash as *Picaroon* vaporized.

Seconds later, *Picaroon's* death throes reached out and struck the little craft with a massive, angry fist. The LB spun through her axis out of control. The high-velocity debris slammed into the boat, overloading the shield blisters. More debris continued to hammer the hull, sounding to those inside the boat like house-sized hailstones pounding a metal drum. Systems shorted out and every emergency alarm wailed.

Eternal seconds later the shock wave passed. They were still alive, for the moment at least. Nathan fought the wildly gyrating boat under control, wishing all the while he had spent more time in the LB simulator. Finally the shuddering craft fell silent and grew still. Nathan took a deep breath.

Moe's face had turned white and rigid.

"I don't think we'll try that again," Nathan said.

Moe stared at him for a long moment before remembering how to use her vocal cords.

"Well I'll be buggered. It worked."

"Yeah, I guess our luck ..." Nathan's skin prickled. He glanced around the flight deck. "We're venting atmosphere. I think it would be a good idea to do something about that, don't you?"

Moe unbuckled and went to the emergency repairs locker. While she set to work locating and plugging the various small punctures to the flight deck's hull, Nathan stepped through the hatch to check on his passengers. Meta and Ozzie were working on repairs. The kids remained strapped to their seats, shocked but unharmed.

The middies were plugging the worst of the hull punctures while Dearkov tore a utilities locker apart searching for more sealant. Flencher remained strapped to his seat, a long dribble of vomit on his undershirt.

"Bad enough to be stripped of my clothing and strapped into this death machine," he whined, "but then one of your friends vomits on me."

"Them's the breaks, Flencher." Nathan smiled at Ozzie. "Did you forget to take your medication?"

Ozzie answered with a crooked smile.

"It wasn't him," Flencher said.

Dearkov rounded on the former headhunter with a blazing expression that could sear marble. The small dribble of vomit sticking to the side of her mouth completed the story. Nathan clamped his jaw and returned to the flight deck. Moe had located and plugged the major leaks and was now huddled over the sensor readouts. Nathan began a systems check.

Although the shields – along with most of their attitude thrusters and maneuvering plating – were destroyed by the blast, the LB's hull integrity had held up surprisingly well. Presenting the stronger aspect of her keel to the blast contributed to their survival. Protecting their vitally important engines was a plus. *Now, if our luck can hold for just a little longer –*

Crack!

Nathan cocked his ear. It had been a sharp, distant sound similar to an icicle snapping underfoot. A hasty inspection of the flight deck failed to show where the noise originated.

Meta stuck her head through the hatchway. "We've plugged the larger holes but we're still venting air. The air recycler is not keeping up with the demands of eleven people. Nathan, we need to get back to Truculent fast or we're going to be in trouble."

"Very well. Moe, I need a course."

"I have Truculent. Steer 288 by 351 by 72 and we should make rendezvous in under two minutes."

Nathan punched in the coordinates.

Crack!

"What *is* that?" Moe asked.

"I don't know. And I don't like what I don't know. Let's go home. The comm is in fair shape, try raising the boat. Advise them of our condition and request a straight-in tractor approach."

"You've got it, Stanley. Now that Picaroon has gone to the big shipyard in the sky it shouldn't be a problem."

Nathan engaged both engines and pushed the throttle controls steadily forward. When the starboard engine reached sixty percent thrust the boat vibrated. He eased off and pushed the port engine fully open.

Crack! Crack!

That sound could really get on a person's nerves after a while. The growing ache between his shoulders foretold a far more unpleasant outcome.

"I've got Truculent." Moe reported their condition and requested an immediate straight-in tractor approach.

"Come on home middy," Waugh said. "Commander O'Donnell is in the LCC awaiting your arrival. Please advise ETA."

"One point five minutes, captain," Moe responded.

"Is everyone all right?"

Moe glanced at Nathan and smiled. "Excuse me, ma'am, I have something to attend to. I'll put you over to Mister Telford."

"Very well."

Moe leaned back and hooked her hands behind her head. Keying his LM he said, "Telford here, skipper. We have taken a few bumps but we're in fair shape. And captain, so are the children."

"Outstanding." An unaccustomed pause. "Mister Telford, who is piloting the LB?"

"I am, captain. But don't tell the COB or she'll have a stroke."

The transmission went mute for a few seconds. The captain's voice returned, laced with suppressed amusement. "I will make sure to keep the shocking news from her."

Crack! Crack! Crack!

Nathan glanced at Moe. Her smug expression had distorted into one of dismay. She pointed a shaky finger at the clear overhead view-plate. Nathan leaned across and followed the unsteady finger. A jolt of electricity dashed down his spine.

Crack!

One sound this time but significantly louder than the others.

"Mister Telford, are you still with us?"

"Please stand by, captain, we have a problem."

"Standing by."

The line etched its way across the overhead view-plate starting at the top corner where it joined the hull. A chunk of high-speed debris had missed the view-plate by millimeters but the kinetic force had crushed the upper housing in several places and sent a concussion wave through the clear composite. It resembled a spreading spider web across the plate. Fine, delicate lines in some spots, but critically deep in others. Total decompression loomed if the plate blew out.

"It will hold till we get back to the boat."

"Yeah," Moe agreed, "no problem."

If my expression matches Moe's face then we're not fooling anyone.

"Any sealer left?" Nathan asked.

"I think we used it all."

"Better find some more don't you think?"

Moe sprung from her seat and rushed aft.

The light from *Truculent's* boat bay glowed in the distance. Having built up sufficient momentum to coast home, Nathan shut down the engines.

Crack! Crack!

"No more sealer," Moe shouted through the hatchway.

Nathan cleared his throat. "See if you can find a magnetic patch or something."

"Right." Moe stepped through the hatch into the cabin. Nathan closed the hatch and set the lock.

"What are you doing?" she screamed over his earpiece.

"Get everyone strapped in. We're doing a fast trap."

"Oh shit."

"Truculent, I am declaring an emergency. Flight deck decompression is imminent. I am bringing the craft in manually for a fast trap. Please initiate all emergency procedures. I'm coming in hot."

"This is O'Donnell in the LCC. Follow my instructions and we'll get you down in one piece."

Nathan glanced to where his helmet rolled around the deck. He could not take his hands from the controls to retrieve it. "Roger, sir. If I do not respond to your signals it means I am unable to do so. Do you understand my meaning?"

"Roger."

Crack! Crack!

Nathan could see the boat bay clearly now, a single source of light glowing in the endless darkness. *Truculent* had shut down her engines to avoid any possible interference from her backwash. She had come about to point her stern directly toward his damaged craft. He started hyperventilating. *Don't hold your breath or you'll rupture your organs.*

"You're on the beam but high," O'Donnell said. "Drop your nose."

With the grav plating torn from the hull Nathan used what remained of the thruster controls to adjust his approach. Small, careful thrusts, gentle and considered.

"Still high."

He hit the attitude thrusters three times while increasing his rate of hyperventilation.

“Your approach is good but you are drifting to starboard.”

The boat came tantalizingly close. A few more seconds and ...

CRACK!

The view-plate exploded. Nathan closed his eyes and averted his face. Shards of shattered plate blew out into space but some ricocheted off the boat’s interior and into his headhunter armor and lowered face.

Nathan slowly expelled air from his lungs. With the air in his bloodstream he could remain conscious for about ten seconds. The cold struck him like a million icy needles. He blinked rapidly to prevent his eyeballs from freezing.

“Veer port! Veer port!” O'Donnell shouted.

If Nathan could, he would have cursed. He had slid way off the beam and was in danger of running down the starboard side of the boat – or into it. The image of the boat bay faded in and out of his focus as unconsciousness threatened. He kicked the unruly thrusters and the boat slid to port. *Bad angle, bad angle.* The monitor rushed at his forward view-plate.

Then something happened. It felt like a balloon popping inside his head. He adjusted the LB's pitch minutely, squaring the craft just enough. It was if he had done it a thousand times before.

The craft flew into the boat bay at the right height to avoid disaster but way off the center line. The port skid struck the deck with a bone jarring impact and snapped off. The craft careened off the port-side bulkhead and skidded across the boat bay at an oblique angle. When the boat slammed into the arrester field Nathan was pushed into his harness. He gratefully took a full breath of clean monitor air.

A thin dribble of blood slithered across his cheek.

CHAPTER 67

Date: 17th August, 320 ASC.
Position: Monitor *Truculent*, En route to the Francorum border.
Status: Alert stand down.

Commodore Waugh marched into the boat bay and stopped in her tracks. The stolen headhunter landing boat lay where it had, for lack of a better word, landed. She walked slowly around the old boat running a critical eye over its battered hull. With the grav plating ripped away and most of the thrusters disabled, she wondered if she would have been able to bring the craft home. Stopping before the blown out view-plate she shook her head.

"That's got to be the lousiest landing I've ever seen," O'Donnell said. "But considering..."

Yes, considering. With the vacuum of space having cut off his air, unconsciousness looming and his eyes threatening to freeze shut, Telford had pulled off a miracle. Waugh left the wreck and strode into the hangar.

Due to the large influx of wounded, Doctor Kelso had set up a temporary triage in the port-side hangar. He plucked a piece of view-plate from Telford's head and dropped it into a bowl.

"How are they Doc?" Waugh asked.

"They'll live," he said, continuing his examination. "Kaspowitz has a fractured clavicle, but a little rest and she'll be fine. When I get space in the infirmary I'll reset her shoulder. Telford here has a few cracked ribs, and they all have various degrees of bruising and lacerations. Nothing serious." Doctor Kelso stepped back from Telford and eyed him critically. "You've taken quite a beating young man. Light duties for the next few days. Oh, and try to refrain from chopping off any heads until your ribs heal."

The middy nodded. For the first time since coming aboard he did not meet his captain's eyes. They all deserved the highest accolades for their service to the Corps this day. Nonetheless, they had disobeyed orders and Waugh could not allow that to pass unanswered.

"Get yourselves cleaned up and have something to eat. I shall need to speak with each of you later." She turned to go then reconsidered. "You did good work today. Well done." Waugh walked away before any of the stunned group could reply.

***

An hour had passed since the Doc had cleared them to return to light duties. Nathan spent most of the time under a steaming hot shower trying to wash away the foul stench of the headhunter armor. The steaming water had failed to wash away the numbing fatigue and his mounting emotional turmoil.

"Hey Cookie," Nathan said, "what poison is on the menu today?"

"Whatever you want, Mister Telford." Chief Balski said.

"Well, let's see." Nathan commenced the ritual. "A nice thick steak with lightly steamed vegetables and a fine mushroom sauce would be fine."

Balski's grin broadened when he produced the meal from a heated serving receptacle and placed it on a tray before him. Nathan's eyes bulged. The steak lapped over the sides of the plate, the mushroom sauce releasing a mouth-watering aroma.

Balski's hands went to his hips. "The Corps takes care of our own. I had a suspicion you might order something like this. Enjoy, Mister Telford."

Nathan stared at the superb meal, lost for words.

"Knowing Cookie's reputation the beast is probably shockingly undercooked," Moe said from behind. "But it's not likely to jump into your mouth on its own."

Nathan cleared his throat, picked up the tray and searched the crowded wardroom for a seat. 'Auntie' Barbara Grimmett, true to form, patted the space beside her. After taking his seat he noticed all of the meals were of the same gourmet type.

"The skipper always rewards a successful mission," Auntie reminded him.

Nathan nodded but wondered where his mind had been. The wardroom's wonderful scent should have alerted him. Two days without sleep and two bloody battles must have taken their toll on him after all. Nathan picked up his utensils and examined the meal.

"Watch out everyone," Auntie yelled. "Telford's got a knife in his hands."

The back of his neck burned as the wardroom filled with laughter. Nathan offered Babs a short smile before hoeing into his meal. He finished the superb feast, leaned back and sighed contentedly. The weariness threatened to engulf him so he closed his eyes for a moment. When he opened them again the wardroom was empty. He rubbed his face vigorously in a futile attempt to clear the fatigue.

Nathan's feet dragged along the deck. His bleary mind still struggled with questions and roiled with confusion. The rage and the killing didn't feel as he thought they should. How the hell had he landed the damaged enemy craft? Nathan considered himself to be a fair pilot but by all rights they should all be splatter marks on *Truculent's* hull. Somehow they survived.

There remained the other matter. After ten years of fighting the ghosts from his past until they no longer tortured him, they had unexpectedly returned. '*You're weak, boy, weak. Coward!*' Each word bowed his shoulders and cramped his stomach. "Why now?" he whispered. He staggered against a bulkhead his hands covering his ears in a futile attempt to block their accusations. *Stop, for God's sake,* please *stop.*

Nathan felt himself falling, losing grip of his stubborn resolve. He desperately needed to sleep. Perhaps after a long rest he could silence the contemptuous voices and make sense of all this. Trying to push the unsettling thoughts aside he squared his shoulders as his quarters came into view.

***

Moe sat alone in their quarters bent over the computer. With twenty-three guests aboard, most of the officers were doubling up. Nathan's quarters corralled all four middies. Earlier she had spoken to Meta and Ozzie about her plan.

"Nathan has always been a little ... different," Ozzie said. "But it's part of what makes him such an outstanding leader."

"Can't argue with that," Meta said. "I guess spending six years as a Pruessen slave would have done some damage. But Ozzie's right. He's always been an odd duck. Don't get me wrong, we all like him." She smiled reminiscently. "It's kinda difficult not to like him. But what happened on Picaroon is a completely new level of weird. "

"Have you noticed over the years, that every so often he will slip and say something he shouldn't know?" Moe asked.

"Yeah," Ozzie said. "Now and again he'll state some fact that the rest of us don't know. Something not in the manuals or intel readouts. Something that doesn't make a lot of sense. I thought he still suffered from northern amnesia."

"I've had my suspicions about that for years," Meta said. "He's said he has *flashes of remembrance* but these flashes are bloody convenient. So what's going on with Nathan Telford?"

"What indeed," Moe said. "But that's not the issue at the

moment. I've known Nathan since we were kids and I'm telling you something happened to him today. I need to find out what."

"You're taking a big chance, Moe," Meta warned. "You know what happens to him when he gets a full head of steam."

"Yeah, Moe, watch yourself," Ozzie added.

"He won't hurt me." Confronting him in his current state of mind carried risks, even to her. For seven years she had awaited this day and was determined to do whatever was required to help him. She loved him; as her best friend of course. Moe could not dismiss the notion that under Nathan's civilized shell dwelt an enduring pain. For the sake of her friend she must risk awakening his inner demon.

"So," Meta said, "what are you going to do?"

"Fly by the seat of my pants and see where it lands me," Moe said.

"Make sure it doesn't land you in the infirmary," Ozzie warned.

"He won't hurt me," Moe repeated forcefully. "Now, you two bugger off for a while. I'll comm you when it's time to return."

While Moe awaited Nathan's return she scanned the casualty reports. She was about to log off when a late input scrolled onto the screen. She bit her lip.

When the hatch opened she ran a sleeve across her face to wipe away the tears.

"What's happening?" Nathan dropped his rack into place and sat heavily.

Moe cleared her throat before answering. "We're off duty until yellow watch." She sat on the edge of her rack facing Nathan. Her head fell into her hands.

"Talk to me," Nathan said.

"Iris Ahrens just died. She was wounded during Gamma Team's attempt to neutralize the dampener."

"I'm so sorry, Moe." He rested a hand gently on her shoulder. The silence lingered for some time. "We all liked Iris." He snorted. "Remember the time Tivendale put us into the reclamation bins for some alleged offense. Iris showed up and lied through her teeth to get us out." His hand remained on her shoulder. "I know what you're going through so if you need to talk ..." Nathan apparently perceived her reticence and sighed deeply. "Who else?"

"Sal Rocca."

"But I saw him after the battle. The big galoot had taken a hit but was joking with everyone." He shook his head.

"He was one tough bastard all right. Some kind of complication set in on the way back to Truculent. He was gone before anyone knew it." They fell silent for a short time. "But we did our duty, didn't we?"

"You bet."

"All that blood."

"It was a messy business all right." He stared into the distance, his eyes dull. "Nothing morally ambiguous about today." He rubbed his reddened eyes. "Have we heard anything from the skipper?"

Once again he diverted the conversation to spare her feelings. Always it was Nathan protecting his friends. Always there for others. But who was there to spare *his* feelings?

"Nothing," Moe said. "I suppose she has other things on her mind."

"I guess."

The fatigue etched into Nathan's face told Moe his mind was turning to mush. Even so he still showed some presence of mind.

"Where are Meta and Ozzie?"

"I asked them to give us some space." Moe leaned forward. "We need to talk."

Nathan nodded but chose not to speak.

Nothing new there. "What happened to you on Picaroon?"

"I'm not sure." He rubbed the bump above his right eyebrow, shrugged and said, "I guess I just got mad."

It was a true indication of how much he had changed in the last few days that he abandoned his usual evasiveness.

"I've seen you angry before and it's not a pretty sight. But this was different. The way you ran down those fleeing headhunters, it was ..." she shook her head. "I've never seen that side of you before. I'm concerned for you, Nate."

"You know me, Moe. I've got a nasty temper at times." He punched her playfully on the arm. Moe didn't change her expression so he tried a different tack. "Something changed in all of us today. People who had never taken a life before stepped up to the challenge and it is only because of their commitment that we won the day. As for me? Something took over for a bit. But it's a good thing. It gave me an edge."

Moe's jaw dropped. "Nathan, you jumped into a nest of eighty headhunters with a sword in your hand. You don't find that a tad excessive?"

"They killed Leo."

His sudden rush of anger made Moe blanch.

"Look Moe, I got mad, that's all." Irritation ate around the edges of his words. "I hate Pruessens. You of all people should know why. I guess I went overboard a bit. It's no big deal."

Moe saw in his eyes the waging of a battle. He fought the emotion, struggling to push it aside. For the first time in his life he was losing the fight. She leaned closer to him.

"Going overboard I can understand. But that's not the worst thing that happened today, Nate."

"Very well, great sage, what's the worst aspect of today's little exercise?"

"You enjoyed it."

"Yes, I did!" He spat the words into her face, so close his hot breath brushed her cheek. "Damn right I enjoyed it. And I can hardly wait to kill more of the bastards." Moe gaped at his sinister grin. "If I could get away with it I'd break into the brig and kill the prisoners, slowly, with a knife. How dare you judge me! While you were sunning yourself on peaceful Kastoria my family was going through every kind of living hell imaginable; courtesy of the empire." His eyes widened in fury. "You have no idea what we had to do to survive. You don't know what I ..."

"Nathan ..."

"Shut the fuck up," he screamed into her face. "Shut up! Shut up or I'll fucking well k..."

The words caught in his throat, ending with a strangled cry. Nathan clapped his hands to his mouth. A shudder ran through his body and his breathing became labored. He squinted as if in pain then his head slumped onto his chest.

Holding her heart in her mouth Moe leaned forward.

"If I don't know what you've been through," she said softly, "it's because you've never shared your grief with me."

He refused to meet her eyes.

"I've never pushed you to talk about your past but now is definitely the time to do so, Nate." She took his hands and cradled them in her lap. "Whatever burdens you've been carrying all these years are too much for one person to bear. Even you have your limits, you know."

"I'm sorry, Moe." The quaking rasp revealed a self-loathing she had never seen from Nathan before. "You know I didn't mean ..." Moe bit her lip as hot tears spilled down his cheeks.

"Who's your best friend," she said, forcing a sad smile. "Who is your very best friend?"

His voice cracked as he responded with the old litany. "You are,

Moe Okuma. You are my very best friend."

At that point the stone man cracked. "Oh God, I miss them Moe. I try not to, but I miss them every day. I thought today would make it better but ..." The long-repressed tears streamed down his face. He brushed a sleeve angrily across his face and sniffed. Nathan threw his head back, took a huge breath and expelled it in one giant rush.

"So, Moe, how did you get so smart all of a sudden?"

"Wadda ya mean, all of a sudden?"

"God I'm tired."

"Time for truth between us, Nate. Let me carry some of the load." She nudged his arm. "You know you want to." Moe knew she had never spoken a truer word.

"How much of those six years do you remember?"

"Every single day."

He drew in an enormous breath, expelling it between pursed lips.

He told her of the Francs' failure to protect the Iberian system and *Bellinda's* capture by Pruessen navy units.

"A Pruessen naval commerce raiding party?" Moe said. "They haven't tried anything like that since the war."

"Yes they have, Moe. They've just never been caught." He shrugged. "We came about and made a run for the I/M but no freighter outruns an E boat. Long story short, we were captured and taken into the north. Because of the Francs' failure to meet their League responsibilities we spent the next four years as slaves of the Pruessen Empire. Never again ask me why I hate the Francs."

"Four years, Nate?"

"We played a patient waiting game, luring the guards into thinking they'd broken us. When the time was right, we escaped. A Pruessen escort boat caught us shy of the I/M and shot us up pretty badly but we got away."

"You'll have to tell me how you did that one day."

"Hmm. Our communications were destroyed during our escape so we couldn't call for help. We made for the nearest Athenian world. Our hyper generator blew as we passed through the planet's inner marker. We had no choice. We crash landed on the surface." Nathan's haunted expression sent a chill down Moe's spine. "We'd been out of touch with everything for four years. We didn't know Delos had been exposed."

"Delos? God almighty."

"There's no God on Delos." He rubbed his eyes. "Two years later the Monitor Impudent discovered me." He shrugged. "I then spent a delightful four months at the ANS Bio-Deterrent Research facility on Mylor. The doctors would have killed me with their, how did they put it, oh yeah, their *research*. In the end it was all for nothing. I'm a one in a billion genetic freak who happens to have a natural immunity. To get out of that hellhole I made a deal with the devil. The devil in this case was an Athenian Naval Intelligence officer. If I talked about my time in the north, he assured me it would lead to war with Pruessen. Athens would do anything to avoid entering into a military operation within a plague zone. So he made up the cover story and I went along with it."

"Shit."

"Even after thirty years the thought of bringing the plague back into League space is as feared as ever. Athens would do anything to avoid war with Pruessen because of the understandable fear."

Another thought struck Moe. "How the hell did you survive on your own for two years on Delos?"

"That's because of my Prep." Moe's face inquired for more. "My premonition pain. It's a warning of danger. Before you ask, I don't know where it came from or how it manifests itself. All I *do* know is that without it I would *not* have survived on Delos." He shrugged. "That's the bones of the whole, ugly story."

"And today? Something else happened today."

Nathan rubbed his eyebrow. "Yeah. I have no idea about that. It surprised me more than you."

"You're just full of surprises aren't you?"

Nathan's expression turned dark.

"By telling you this, I've put your life in danger, Moe." Nathan seized her by the shoulders. "You can share this with no one. *No* one."

"But Nate, what about Livy? She has to be told – "

"Are you nuts? Firstly, I will not put her in danger the way I've just done to you. Secondly ..." His eyes stared into her as intensely as she could ever remember. "I want your word, Moe. What we've talked about doesn't leave this room." He held out his hand. "Your word, Moe." His dangerous tone left no question as to his intent. Even the puffiness above his cheeks did not detract from the flint in his eyes.

She nodded and shook his hand.

"After the attack on our homestead I should have broken it off with Livy. But I'm weak and my weakness puts her and anyone else I care about in danger." His self-loathing was heartbreaking. "Now, very best friend, if the inquisition is over I really need to get some sleep."

"Not yet." Somehow Nathan seemed to know what was coming. "There's more, isn't there?"

Hit bit his lower lip so hard he drew blood.

Moe took his head in her hands. "Finish it, Nate."

His eyes became blank his breathing shallow. He cleared his throat with a shudder.

"Delos." A shiver ran through his body. "Day forty-two, on Delos. The incubation period for the plague had been reached. The very young and the very old were the first to be affected. Except for me. It began with the fever, then the muscle cramps, the pustules on the skin, the internal rupturing, the staggering pain. Father had attended the academy and served in Monitor Corps. He recognized the symptoms.

"How are you feeling, Nathan?" he asked me.

"Fine," I said.

A pustule burst on his face.

Within a few hours everyone, except me, was visibly affected. The moaning turned to screaming as internal organs were attacked and eaten away.

My father showed me how to end the misery. A swift, deep knife thrust to the jugular. Death within sixty seconds.

We started with my Great Uncle John. He was the oldest, his suffering the greatest. I remember, just before father struck, Uncle John smiled and said, 'Thank you, Lucas.'

"Since I was the healthiest," he paused for a long moment, "I was expected to do my duty. Obligation to family was everything to us, Moe. We started with the sickest, the ones who were most in pain. Finally there were only four of us left. Father, mother and my sister, Rebecca."

Nathan's eyes were dead grey pools, his voice dull like a machine.

"Rebecca nodded for me to do it. Father ended mother's misery. And then there were two."

Moe's pulse thundered in her ears but she had to hear this to the end.

"I loved and respect my father more than anyone. Even Caleb. He wept after mother died and fell to the ground, the last of his energy gone. He writhed in agony. 'Nathan, do your duty. Then survive, my son. You must survive to honor your obligation to your family. Do you understand?'

"Bloody knife in hand, I nodded. Father screamed as his insides contorted. 'Nathan, now is the time. End my pain.' "

"No," Moe whispered in horror. "No. Nathan, you killed your own father?"

Tears poured down his cheeks like a stream. He shuddered as the emotion ripped from his body.

"It's all right, Nate. You had no choice. If you didn't do it your father–"

"Moe," he screamed, "I couldn't do it. I tried, but I couldn't do it. Not to him. Because I'm weak. Always have been, always will be. I ran away, Moe. Ran and left him to die horribly. Ran until I could no longer hear his voice cursing me. 'You're weak, boy, weak and useless. Do your duty, you coward.'

"I know he was crazy with the pain and probably delusional but..."

He wept then, without reserve, wept as he had never done in her presence but had so badly needed to for so long. Wept till his friend's flight suit became soaked with his bitter tears. He had not shared his appalling shame with anyone. Instead it remained in his heart like a black poison infesting his soul. Moe wept with him. Holding him to her heart. Soothing him with meaningless platitudes. Helping him banish his demons.

Finally, with his mind and body spent, the agony of an exorcised soul tearing at him, he slept.

Now, like the lifting of a long-standing fog, it all made sense to Moe. She could not recall ever feeling sorry for her friend, regardless of his tragic history. Intensely curious, but never sorry for him. Nathan was too tough for sentiment. Tonight, all that changed and would do so for the rest of her life.

CHAPTER 68

Date: 20th August, 320 ASC.
Position: Monitor *Truculent,* running parallel to the Francorum border.
Status: Rendezvous with freighter *Rochelle.*

Nathan leaned back in his chair and rubbed his eyes. He had almost completed his admin duties. *Truculent* had expended significant stores during the patrol. The loss of twenty 'droids would undoubtedly raise a few eyebrows when the ANS Bureau of Ordnance received the requisition.

In the last four days he had immersed himself in work, using it as a cathartic patch over his most recent weaknesses. Was weakness the right word? Moe and he had spoken of his shame several times since that awful night. She repeatedly told him he had nothing to feel guilty about, reminding him he had been a child at the time. Talking had helped more than he expected. For the first time in his life he truly understood the wisdom in the old saying; confession *was* good for the soul. Although the ghosts of his past refused to leave him in peace, in the more practical ways he had never felt better. Moe's courageous support helped him to finally face his demons, if not totally redress his shame. Oh yes, the ghosts still lingered at the periphery of his thoughts, awaiting the night. Nevertheless, he sensed the first inklings of control over them. Work helped.

Since the battle, the worst of his wounds had healed, but the restlessness remained. Sergeant Redpath had paid him a visit the day before and laid his own brand of stress management at his door. For a ground pounder he showed remarkable compassion.

"It's normal to feel a bit itchy after a fight," he said. "Especially if it's your first." His hard features softened moderately. "That fight would have been a sickening initiation for anyone. Even a marine."

"How did we do?" Nathan kept his tone light.

"I've seen worse."

"Thank you. I'd be obliged if you would share your thoughts with the rest of the team."

"Already have."

"So, you saved the best for last?" He grinned sheepishly. Rusty shook his head and snorted.

"I've got work to do." Redpath turned to leave.

"Hold on."

Nathan removed the bayonet from a drawer. Holding it by the scabbard he offered it to Redpath hilt first.

"Thanks for the loan. It was a lifesaver and a life taker."

The marine removed the blade from its scabbard.

"I see you've given it a good clean. Good, I don't want headhunter blood on my weapons. Well, not for the long term at least." His hard, unfathomable eyes locked onto Nathan long enough to make him uneasy. Redpath handed the weapon back. "I've got a gut feeling you'll make good use of this in the future."

Redpath left Nathan too thunderstruck to reply. He cradled the weapon in his hands for a moment before returning it to the drawer. Nathan went back to work and had almost completed his latest requisition when his comm beeped.

"Telford."

"Mister Telford," Cmdr Demianski said, "your presence is requested in the boat bay."

"On my way, sir."

A minute later he swung from the drop shaft onto the longitudinal corridor outside the boat bay. His ribs still pinched a bit but were coming along.

The large landing boat from the Francorum freighter *Rochelle* sat ready to depart. Six men rested on gurneys awaiting their time to go aboard. The middies and some of the officers mingled with them. From the pack of milling humans a small girl darted out.

"Captain Nathan," she shouted.

He scooped her up, resting her on his hip. "Simone Garneau, how are you today?"

"I'm good, Captain Nathan," she said. "And how are you?"

"I'm fine, thank you." He surveyed the crowded bay. The children each stood by their father's gurney waving at him, some less shyly than others. Their mothers, who suffered such vile abuse on *Picaroon*, had been evacuated earlier. Their physical symptoms had been treated and from those they would make a full recovery. Their shattering psychological and spiritual trauma would take much longer to heal.

"Captain Nathan?"

"Yes, Simone."

"Thank you for saving us."

He smiled and bowed his head. "You're very welcome."

A Franc attendant pushed a gurney to where Nathan stood. On it a man of early middle age sat up.

"Daddy, this is Captain Nathan," Simone said.

Nathan placed the child next to her father.

"Nathan Telford," he said touching his right hand to his heart and bowing slightly in the Athenian manner. Even after fourteen years Nathan could not bear to shake hands with a Franc.

"I am Jules Garneau." The Franc's hand, which had been in the process of rising to shake his, fell back onto the gurney. "I wanted to thank you personally for saving my daughter from those vile creatures." His expression adopted mild surprise to find, upon meeting the man who had rescued his child, not a tall, lantern-jawed hero, but a twenty-year-old midshipman.

"My pleasure, Mister Garneau." For the sake of the child he kept his tone more or less affable.

The Franc was no fool and apparently sensed his loathing. "Simone darling, time to go now."

"Awe daddy," she whined.

"Go on now. I need to talk with, ah, Captain Nathan."

She waved to Nathan as she ran to join the rest of the children, who were being herded into the landing boat by attendants.

"Our two societies have not always seen eye to eye. But regardless of our differences, I have to thank you."

"I was doing my duty."

"I can see you are not as fond of adult Francs as our children. But no matter. You and your colleagues risked your lives to rescue us, for which I shall always be indebted. But you, *you* went back for our children and brought them safely home to us. I shall never forget what you did. I'm a wealthy man. If there is anything you desire, if it is within my power, it is yours."

Nathan did not trust himself to speak.

"Mister Telford? I meant you no offense but I have apparently done so. I only wished to express my gratitude."

"Very well, Franc, if you want to do something for me, here it is." Nathan fought to keep the emotion from his voice. "The next time you get the brilliant idea of wandering around the edge of the frontier in an unescorted freighter make sure you leave your family at home."

Garneau winced. "You are an extremely hard man for someone so young. However, you make a valid point." Garneau sighed and shook his head. "I don't know how else to express myself other than as I have. Again, thank you for my family."

Nathan nodded curtly and marched toward the waiting group.

***

Nathan followed Cmdr Demianski through the hatch with the Tackies following. They took their places around the briefing table. No white tablecloth and silverware adorned the table today. The captain wasted no time.

"Very well, Nathan," Waugh said, "you were the ranking officer on this little jaunt so let's hear it."

"The decision was mine alone, captain. The others followed my lead."

"We did so gladly, captain," Moe added.

"You disobeyed orders," the commander snapped.

"Not in the strictest terms, sir," Ozzie said.

"What?"

"We were ordered to wait for the landing boat," Ozzie continued. "We followed our orders. We were just a little late getting there."

"You could have gotten yourselves killed." The commander directed his irritation at Nathan.

Nathan sensed the blood rushing to his face. "You know what those animals would have done to the children. The opportunity to stop that from happening presented itself and I took it. And sir, given the same circumstances, I would do it again in a heartbeat."

"We couldn't leave the kids behind when there was a chance of rescuing them, sir," Moe said.

Commodore Waugh remained silent for a short time before speaking again. "I'm not entirely certain what I'm going to do about this. On the one hand you *did* disobey orders. On the other hand you rescued six civilians and aided in the destruction of a headhunter warship." She set her eyes on Nathan. He struggled to meet her appraising gaze. "What would you do in my position?"

Nathan cleared his throat. "To use the old expression, the buck stops with you, captain." He sighed deeply and stared into the captain's eyes. "Acting or not, I outranked everyone on the team."

"Hold on a minute – " Moe started to object but was stunned into silence by Nathan's glare.

"You don't speak for the others on this matter, Moe," he snapped. "It's not just you and me this time. They have great careers ahead of them. As do you." He turned to the captain. "They missed the rendezvous because they followed me. I made the first move. They would *not* have stayed if I hadn't. As you so correctly pointed out captain, I was the ranking officer."

Someone would have to hang for disobeying the captain's orders.

"Does anyone else have anything to say?" the captain asked.

"With all respect to the captain," Dearkov said, "I think these people deserve medals. I hope you're not going to be too harsh on them, ma'am. They, *we*, did our duty."

"I haven't decided what sort of action I will take." The captain glared at each of them individually and finally as a group. "But I assure you, it *will* be apt."

CHAPTER 69

Date: 23rd December, 320 ASC.
Position: Mount Kratos.
Status: Commissioning Day.

Not a single stone of the academy's main parade ground was visible through the great mass of bodies milling across it. The commissioning service having concluded, families and friends mingled with the newly commissioned officers, their tutors and a smattering of visiting brass.

Nathan took pictures in his mind's eye and stored them away. Moe's mother, father and three older brothers had made the journey from Kastoria and were talking with other parents. Caleb and Bernie chatted with Admiral Ponsford. The old warhorse and the two proud parent eagles.

Lucy, resplendent in her class A grays, held the rapt attention of several young men from her year. His kid sister had matured into quite the young lady.

Lewis of all people had taken a shine to Meta Kaspowitz. She caught Nathan staring at them and smiled as if she were responding to one of Lewis' remarks.

Nathan shook his head ever so slightly and took one glass of white Retsina and one of red from a passing steward. Plus a glass of water for Livvy.

Abner Lawrence could not attend but had sent a short note of congratulations and good wishes. Someone, he explained, had to stand guard over the abandoned Penkovsky and Okuma plantations.

Livy and her mother Finella stood in the mild sunshine wearing lightweight summer clothing in soft pastels, and matching broad-brimmed hats. They could easily be mistaken for a pair of heavenly sisters.

"It's a nice place you have here," Livy said, "but the service is dreadful." Her eyes begged a question.

"What?" he asked, as he passed glasses to mother and daughter.

"You don't see it, do you?" Livy cast her gaze to the surrounding crowd.

Middies passed by, their young faces glowing with awe. Even some of the senior instructors nodded respectfully.

"I'm trying to ignore it," he muttered.

"Might be difficult with that weighing you down," Livy said, pointing to the medal.

Nathan fingered the solid silver medallion hanging from his neck. His reward for killing without compunction.

"It's nothing, a piece of metal. Unlike this," he said, placing his hand gently on Livy's enlarged stomach. At six months she glowed.

Livy rested her forehead against his shoulder, sighing contentedly.

"Don't you two ever take a break?" Moe said, jostling through the throng. "I hope you're taking care of my Godchild?" Livy nodded wearily. "Good. For now I need to borrow your man for a while. Nathan, your presence is required."

Nathan excused himself and followed her into the great swarm of bodies. After battling through the sea of humanity they reached the edge of the square, where the crowd thinned. Moe leaned into to his ear.

"So ends the reign of Aletheia's Friend," she whispered.

Nathan held his finger to his lips. "Shhhh!" When he had chosen to tell her everything it meant *absolutely* everything. "And you said I didn't have a sense of humor."

"No," Moe retorted, "what I said was your humor is at times inappropriate."

Two ensigns wearing new, dark blue uniforms greeted them.

"Come on, Nathan," Ozzie said, "you're holding up the show."

The official vids of the platoons and squads had been taken yesterday after the Graduation Parade. A separate shot was made of the Kendo team. However, Moe wanted one more reminder of their time together on *Truculent*. Not to mention their rewards.

The newly commissioned ensigns were thrilled to receive such high recognition for their actions. The copper-coated Distinguished Service Medals were something officers spent years aspiring to. Not even Admiral Waugh had received such a high accolade whilst a lowly midshipwoman.

Nathan had garnered the higher award: the silver Achilles medal for conspicuous gallantry. In reality the medal he received back on *Truculent* meant a whole lot more to him. Hastily prepared by the senior officers, the WLE medal of excellence held a special place in his heart. The oversized, tasteless slab of material celebrated the Worst Landing Ever aboard a serving monitor. He would forever treasure the gaudy tribute to his good fortune.

They posed for the vid then shook hands and congratulated one another. They'd had little time to socialize since returning from *Truculent*. Intense study for final exams had filled most of their time.

Like the rest of his friends, Nathan was grateful to have had the opportunity to graduate.

Commodore Waugh never said another word about the Tackies 'missing the boat' and had apparently decided to disregard the entire incident. Except, of course, for her recommendation to cite them for gallantry. However, she did not tell them of her decision until they arrived back at base. This created a state of nervous expectation for nearly two weeks. In Waugh's mind the fortnight of sweat would undoubtedly work as a sufficiently unpleasant punishment. She had been right.

"Nathan." Moe jerked her head to his left. The new officers snapped to attention.

"At ease," Captain Jakovich said. Her left arm hung loosely at her side. The medicos had managed to save the badly damaged arm and three months convalescence had done the rest. "Thought I'd find you pirates congregating together."

"Good to see you again, captain," Nathan said, extending his hand. "Your recovery goes well I trust?"

"As well as can be expected."

"And I'm just fine," Sergeant Redpath said.

Nathan had a silver star on his epaulet and an Achilles medal hanging from his neck and it didn't faze the marine NCO in the slightest.

"I'm sure that nothing short of a direct torpedo hit would stop you, Sergeant Redpath."

Redpath shook Nathan's hand, the craggy lines on his face softening to a smile.

"I suppose you're all looking forward to your month's furlough before being posted," Jakovich said.

They all agreed.

"Of course," Moe said, "we have one last duty to perform before we head off." The marines' questioning expressions prompted her to add, "Ensign Telford is getting married tomorrow."

"Congratulations Nathan," the captain said, once again offering her hand.

"Thank you, ma'am. I would be pleased if you and the sergeant would attend. Naturally, if you have other plans I will understand."

"Will there be booze at the reception?" Redpath asked.

"Heaps."

"Thank you for your generous invitation, Nathan," Jakovich said. "I'm certain that I speak for the sergeant when I say we will be delighted to attend."

Nathan nodded. Sometimes, life works out for the best. And as for the future? *As long as the Pruessen Empire exists I will work toward its destruction. I have no other option.*

CPSIA information can be obtained
at www.ICGtesting.com
Printed in the USA
LVOW12s2311090916
504002LV00001B/18/P

9 780993 598456